The Oasis of Filth

My Chronicle of the RL2013 Outbreak

A Novel

The Complete Series

Part One: The Oasis of Filth

Part Two: The Hopeless Pastures

Part Three: From Blood Reborn

Keith Soares

Bufflegoat Books

Original publication date March 22, 2014

For *The Oasis of Filth - Part One*
Special thanks to my wife, Layla, for giving me the time and feedback to actually do this. Additional thanks to Jeff Yeatman for his copious notes on expanding this world, and to Susan Gd. G. Clutter for pointing out a rather indigestible error.

For *The Oasis of Filth - Part Two - The Hopeless Pastures*
Many thanks to Chris for his tremendous contributions while editing this book. Additional thanks to Layla, Jeff Yeatman, Bill Setzer, Scott Blum, and Jim Peterson. And a big thank you to Emily Savage for her medical insight.

For *The Oasis of Filth - Part Three - From Blood Reborn*
Special thanks to Layla, Chris, Clay Adams, Susan Gd. G. Clutter, Dennis Belmont, and Katie Mooers for their edits and contributions.

Edited by Christopher Durso.

Also from Keith Soares

The Oasis of Filth

Part 1: The Oasis of Filth

Part 2: The Hopeless Pastures

Part 3: From Blood Reborn

The Fingers of the Colossus *(Ten Short Stories)*
[Forthcoming]

PART ONE

THE OASIS OF FILTH

1

"Noah, you have leprosy," I said to the poor kid as he sat there, nervously sweating despite the coolness of the day. Noah Parker, just 14 years old. I wish I could have saved that poor kid. But more than that, I wish I had understood what I was looking at. He was the first one I ever saw. But obviously not the last.

Some people say, "How could you be so blind?" I tell them the truth. We weren't blind. We saw everything. We just didn't *understand.*

You know, as obvious as something might be, if you've never seen it before — never contemplated the possibility that something universally believed to be fiction might actually be true — then how can you possibly be prepared to accept it, even if it's sitting in your own office, chewing gum, wearing a green and white Wildcats high school football jersey? Or at least that's what I tell myself. After all this time, when you've seen the things that I have, if you don't tell yourself something to keep going, you'll just give up. I'm not quite ready for all that.

Not that I have much choice. Time is not on my side. Noah Parker got the bad news in my office almost 11 years ago. At the time, I was a 52-year-old family practice doctor in central Maryland. I made a good living, and most of the community looked up to me — the guy who made them feel better. Things change. Noah died 18 days later. It's amazing what the mind can recall and what it can forget. Whatever tragedies I went through yesterday — and I'm sure there were some — are all but forgotten in the blur of repetition and the daily effort to keep moving on. But this I remember clearly: In the fall of 2013, Noah Parker walked into my office with a few skin lesions. He told me it started as one, and he ignored it — he couldn't remember, but he thought it might have been from cutting himself while mowing the lawn. That specific lesion was tiny but looked ragged, like it had been torn or bitten. When the third lesion appeared, he was worried. He told his parents once he had six, and came to see me the next day.

I missed the forest, but I saw the trees. Leprosy. Before I went to medical school, I wanted to just go *somewhere* — get away. I knew the next several years of my life would be devoted to the singular cause of graduating and working toward my own practice. So before all that, I traveled to India for escape. My parents told me to be careful, watch out for this or that. For several years already, I'd been a solo backpacker, staying in tiny, rundown hostels every place I had visited, so I assured them that I could do it there, too. In India, with the seed of a medical education about to grow in my mind, I was confronted first hand with leprosy. Aimlessly backpacking, I stumbled across a leper colony, and curiosity took over. I talked to the one doctor I could find there. His English was excellent. He told me how they tickled the faces of young children to detect where they could no longer feel. He showed me what the skin lesions looked like. He told me the cycle of treatment; the isolation he said was required. I ended up looking into leprosy briefly during my freshman year. I learned, most importantly, that it had been cured. Nonetheless, some places like India kept alive the culture of the leper colony. I dug into it pretty deeply for a time. But like most random things, after a while the interest waned.

Then, here was this kid in my office. And it clicked: This looks *familiar.* I dug up information as fast as I could. But in the end, it was just instinct and experience. I know most doctors in the United States, even more experienced ones, would have totally missed it. But I knew: leprosy. When I told Noah, his eyes almost bugged out of his head. His parents were aghast. They blurted the obligatory comments. Was I *sure?* How was this *possible?* I told them that I could be wrong, but I'd seen it before, up close. And I told them that leprosy was completely curable. To me, the physician, that felt like a weight lifted off my shoulders; I could actually *do* something for this kid. Then I looked at his parents. They were shell-shocked. I might as well have told them their son was dying within the hour. The idea that their own flesh and blood had something so horrific as leprosy stunned them beyond words. Noah's mother, who looked like she was clinging to her youth with every fiber, wearing tight jeans and a fashionable yellow top, seemed to age 15 years as she crumbled into her husband's arms. Noah's father, for that matter, had lost his normal ruddy complexion and jovial nature. His eyes glassed over, shining empty above his dark navy sport jacket and white shirt worn with no tie. I stared. Could I be wrong? Did I just send an entire family into a downward spiral on a whim? No, I got it right, I thought to myself. Noah had leprosy.

In the end, it didn't really matter. Because what I missed were the other things. The flu-like symptoms, the anxiety. I was so proud of myself for being able to recognize leprosy that I completely missed it. The kid also had rabies.

2

Leprosy and rabies in one kid. What an unlucky bastard, right?
Well, of course, you must be familiar with the story. But maybe you
don't know the details. It wasn't just Noah. It was happening in lots
of places, all over the world in fact. Again, were we blind? No.
Nothing we believed prepared us for something to swoop in so
quickly from so many places. It was like a coordinated attack, but
there was no general, no army, no battlefield. Every soldier in this
attack operated independently. The only cohesion came from the fact
that it all happened at the same time. I was focused on the case of
Noah, who was getting rapidly worse, with other symptoms I didn't
understand. It wasn't until five days later, when Noah lashed out, that
I realized my hubris had made me miss the signs.

That fifth day, Noah bit my nurse, Terry Rawlins, on the arm.
Tore skin off in his madness. What the hell would make him do that?
That's when I realized this wasn't just leprosy. After I'd sedated
Noah, had him transferred to a hospital for round-the-clock care, and

was done patching up Terry, I started to analyze the other symptoms I was seeing. But give me no credit. That night, I turned on the news just to take a mental break. And there I saw it. Doctors in Georgia had identified three cases of people with leprosy *and* rabies, and were reporting that somehow these conditions had become *intertwined* within the patients — like they happened together. It was such a medical mystery that it appeared at the end of the newscast — not a top story of concern, but an afterthought, to make the audience scratch their heads and have something bizarre to talk about over dinner.

I sat upright in my chair. That explained the other symptoms! Noah definitely had rabies, too. I dialed into the office and looked up his records, then called his parents. After the briefest of pleasantries, I asked, "Was Noah bitten by an animal recently, like a raccoon? Has he been to Georgia recently?" But the answer to both questions was no. Regardless, I told the parents how I believed Noah's other symptoms may stem from rabies. They were incredulous. How could their son — their *own* son, living in America in the 21st century — have both leprosy *and* rabies? They must have thought I was a complete quack. But there was no time for that, rabies doesn't wait. I called the hospital and spoke to Noah's attending physician. He was skeptical. Even after I told him of the cases in Georgia, he found it hard to believe that there was any relation or truth to it.

It wasn't until the next morning that the attending physician started to believe. Noah — fitful from a night of almost no sleep — tore into a rage and tried to break free of his straps, simply from the sight of an orderly bringing in water. Treatment was ordered. It was too late. Terry Rawlins went mad, too. She lasted seven weeks in restraints, with researchers focused on her 24 hours a day.

Soon after, reports came out of Maine, Arizona, Utah. Then from overseas. Patients were cropping up all over with a combination of leprosy and rabies. Doctors tried — unsuccessfully — to treat one or the other, to remove at least part of the problem. Nothing took. Lesions, fever, increasing anxiety, lack of sensation in nerve endings, flattened nose, thickening skin, dementia, rage. All the classic symptoms of leprosy and rabies, combined. And patients got worse, all of them. Restrained and fed through tubes, they could last a really long time, although many died horribly. Or were killed. Sometimes it was quick, like Noah Parker, but sometimes it went on for many, many months before the end.

They called the disease RL2013, a not-terribly-clever nod to rabies, leprosy, and the year of discovery. We mostly called it *the disease*, or just *it*. We still do. "Stay away from him, he's got *it*," or "That baby has *the disease*." We called the infected by another name. Given the symptoms, the physical changes, the mental changes, the bloodlust. The fact that what they had was contagious as hell. These people — people you may have known, may have loved — became deformed, raging lunatics. They weren't some sort of undead monster, they had no magical powers, and you could kill one as easy as you could kill anybody else. But it spread like wildfire, and God help you if one bit you: There was no cure. So despite our best attempts to rationalize the hell around us, we had to admit it was true.

Zombies walked among us. And they were winning.

3

For more than 10 years, we lived in fear. But the funny thing was, it wasn't really fear of the zombies. It was fear of dirt, and what came with it. The government pulled in the walls of the cities — cities were the only things left with any infrastructure — and inside those walls was where we lived, in giant compounds. Well, we called it *pulling in the walls* as a cultural reference, but in truth they had to make the walls. The society that once was home to the freest, proudest people on Earth remade itself along quasi-feudal lines, with pockets of citizens huddled together, struggling through totalitarian rule. Because it kept them safe.

I made it to Washington, DC, and I got inside the walls. Others did the same in New York, Chicago, Houston, Los Angeles, and elsewhere. Some cities fell apart or were overrun. I heard an estimate that about 30 million Americans lived in the cities, which seemed like a lot — but just doing the math from where we started, that meant more than 300 million people were still outside. Even as contagious as the disease was and how fast it could kill, there must have been a lot of people struggling for their lives in what used to be the United States. As well as a lot of zombies. And a lot of dead. God only knew what the numbers looked like everywhere else in the world.

Inside the walls, everything had to be clean. Only by completely sterilizing our environment could we hope to one day overcome the epidemic. That's what the laws said. People were taken away simply for not keeping themselves and their homes and their streets clean. The government said this is why we still had outbreaks. If everyone could work together, keep every inch of the city free from grime or mildew or fungus, we could avoid additional infections. I understood their frustrations, to some degree — after more than 10 years, you'd think we could have solved this. But my experience as a doctor made me question this policy. I knew that some amount of cleanliness was useful to ward off infection, but I also knew that scrubbing a floor wouldn't save you from your neighbor coughing in your face. But always there were stories of some family, some person, some group home, where cleanliness was ignored, the filth built up, and then another outbreak occurred. The talk-show hosts shook their heads and reported on another self-induced tragedy. If only this family had kept to the law, kept their home clean, they wouldn't have become infected. Just the other night, there was a story about two parents and their young daughter. A neighbor went to check on them after not seeing anyone for about a week. When the neighbor entered the unlocked apartment, she found piles of detritus and blooms of mildew. In seconds, she was attacked by the father in a rabid rage and bitten repeatedly. When the authorities got there, they shot and killed the entire family. The neighbor died that evening.

"God has forsaken us!"

"It's the wrath of God, punishing our sins!"

"There is no God!"

"It is the End of Days!"

A lot of people had a lot of ideas about why it all happened. And a lot of those ideas involved God. I didn't know, and wasn't sure how much it mattered. Was there a God, and was that God allowing this to happen? Or maybe God was asleep at the wheel. Maybe it was a test. Or maybe mankind wasn't God's favorite after all.

On the odd occasion that I would tell my story, it didn't help. Many people who heard it compared my Noah — Noah Parker — to the Biblical Noah. But where that Noah rescued all creatures great and small from the flood, Noah Parker, people would tell me, started a flood to drown us all. It didn't matter to the zealots that Noah Parker wasn't the only case. This thing, this disease, appeared all at once in many places. Maybe that actually was a sign of divine intervention. Did the first single-cell organisms manifest in one and only one place? Or did they appear on Earth at a certain time, all over the globe, when the time was right? Could it be that the process of creating new life or new disease was simply following a schedule?

Everything was smaller, more compact. To allow a city to hold more people than it was ever intended for, everyone had to give something up. Houses and apartments were subdivided, methodically, mercilessly, to the smallest possible space that a person or family needed to live. At the same time, almost every sort of personal possession was taken away, so the boxes we lived in weren't just small but spartan. Families were given larger spaces to fit their size, but a single guy like me? I could cook on my stove and flush my toilet all while lying in my bed.

Clothes became a lot simpler. That was something I didn't mind too much. The whole idea of designer clothing became obsolete. There was some variation, but for the most part the government wasn't interested in a fashion show. They ran factories that produced workable, simple clothing. Solid colors, synthetic fabrics. Most people had four or five sets for warm weather, another four or five for cold. We cleaned them all the time, both so that we wouldn't run out and to maintain cleanliness. Even the idea of dressing up disappeared; there were no more suits, ties, ball gowns. In a way, with our flat-colored, synthetic clothing, we looked like we'd stepped out of a silly science-fiction movie, or that we were all on our way to the gym.

All our cell phones were confiscated at the very start. But there were communications between the cities, we knew that. The old wired and wireless methods still seemed to work, although only the government was allowed to use them. I assumed this meant that there were people who worked outside the walls, maintaining the connections and the infrastructure, but I never saw them myself or met anyone who did it. All the news we got came from the government, and that was very little. We had TV and radio, one channel each. The radio station played a lot of classical music, with occasional weather updates. TV wasn't much better. In between news reports on the latest zombie extermination — really thinly veiled threats about keeping clean — they played old movies and shows, mostly black and white, repeated often. It was bizarre to see dapper men in suits and ladies in fancy dresses, jet-setting around a world that no longer existed, or dancing in bright, hugely choreographed routines that parodied our gray, regimented lives. I guess they figured we needed some sort of entertainment. It was so alien, this stylized murk of black and white, that it could have been imported from another planet. Broadcasts would end each night at 11 p.m. with a reminder of the basic rules of cleanliness and stern statements about following government laws.

We always tried to stick to ourselves, stick to small groups. It was a lot safer. The more people you interacted with, the more likely one of them would end up infected. Even the hint of a rumor about infection brought the authorities in droves. Many people felt that turning in their neighbors might convey some extra benefit to them or their family. Backstabbing was commonplace. As for the government, its officers were covered head to toe in pristine white hazmat suits, and swooped in like anonymous destroyers, took what they wanted — who they wanted — and left without a word, without a trace. And always they found evidence of some lack of cleanliness to point to as the culprit. How could they not? Who could keep every speck of their lives spotless at all times?

So that was why we lived in fear. Life is naturally messy. But we did all we could to get rid of the mess. Any sudden discovery of mold in a dark corner was enough to give a person heart palpitations as they rushed to scrub every nook before word got out. In fear — fear of the zombies, fear of the dirt, fear of the government, fear of each other — people would do a lot of crazy things. A neighbor might turn you in if he noticed something he deemed unusual, like you wringing out a mop more than a few times. And sometimes, people would turn you in just because they didn't like you or they wanted something you had. When the government came to get you, there was no reasoning with them, no argument. You just went away.

In fear, we followed the rules. We tried to stay small. We took no risks.

"Stay clean. Stay alive." It was our mantra.

4

Given how small my social circle became, it's a wonder that I ever met anyone new at all. Prior to the outbreak, I spent my days as a happy and probably smug bachelor. I think my position of relative power as doctor in a small town gave me too much self-importance. Now that all that was gone, I would sometimes think about how many chances I'd had to make a life with someone else, maybe even gotten married. I was into my sixties, and knew that possibility was dead. I spent a lot of time with my own thoughts, which can make a person unfit for social interactions. Some of my younger neighbors thought of me as a grumpy old man. Then I met Rosalinda. It was random, like many things. As much as we tried to keep to ourselves, there were still the necessities of living. Most notably, you had to get your food somewhere. The city regulated all food production and kept registered production facilities along its borders. Were we eating fresh-grown food or something out of a laboratory? I suspected a combination. But we lived with it. I got mine from the Capitol Hill Community Food Dispersal Center, more commonly called the FDC.

The FDC was housed in the large, red-brick buildings that once made up Eastern Market, a popular indoor and outdoor marketplace where people would go to buy a range of fresh foods and other goods before the disease. Now we just lined up for our ration boxes. The Eastern Market buildings worked well for this purpose, because they were big and the government could contain people long enough to push them through the line efficiently.

The woman I would come to know as Rosalinda was a strange sight, rather young, pretty, perhaps a dozen people ahead of me in line. She wore a basic white synthetic t-shirt and matching skirt. In another time, she might have looked like she was dressed for a round of tennis at the country club. Here, her basic outfit was mirrored by several other women. Clothing options were fairly limited, but somehow she stood out. Having done the dance of the government ration line with the same neighbors for nearly 10 years, a new face was incredibly unexpected. Although rare, we still had cases of RL2013 inside the city, and they always involved elements of mystery, like new faces or unknown places. I have to admit, my first thoughts were fear and distrust, but they were mixed with a strange interest. How on Earth did someone new get here, and *why*? Did we need to be careful around her? Movement around the city was controlled. The government assigned jobs, housing, places to get food. But beyond that there was the self-imposed, self-regulating control of the people. No one wanted anything new, *anyone* new, because that was change, and change felt dangerous. We were a tremendously paranoid society. I noticed other eyes watching her. She was an outsider. She could be infected. Even 10 years after the outbreak, the disease spread. It was slower now, but it happened. And here she was, where we got our food. What was she doing taking it from us? If the government transferred her here, it said something about their stranglehold on information that they wouldn't even tell us why.

My rational mind tried to turn the tide. There could be any number of good reasons why she was here. It didn't happen often, but people did relocate. We all still had to do our jobs, to keep the small wheels of our confined society spinning and to earn a living. Producing food, making and distributing medicine, policing for outbreaks, maintaining the walls, keeping up the government's elaborate bureaucracy — it was all necessary. If for nothing else than to keep the people's minds off things like revolt. But sometimes those jobs disappeared.

As I shuffled along in line and got my ration box, I considered these options, but generally tried to retreat into myself, the way we all did so well. Then I heard the muffled sounds of trouble. Looking toward the commotion, I saw the strange young woman surrounded by several angry-looking men. They had their hands on her ration box and were saying something she didn't like. She hissed back that she just wanted to be left alone, trying to stay as quiet as possible. I could tell this was going to get very bad very quickly. I looked toward the government guards, clad in their pristine navy-blue uniforms, holding their shiny black firearms. *No one* ever wanted to attract the guards' interest. It wasn't good for your long-term health.

Immediately, I rushed over, cutting between the woman and one of the men. "What's the problem here?" I said.

"Keep out of it, or you'll regret it," one man said — a guy I had seen in the FDC probably once a month for many years. He was maybe 15 years my junior, stronger and taller, with a pointed nose and a close-cropped haircut. He squinted at me, recognizing me, but now distrusting my sudden interest in what he was doing.

"They're trying to take my ration," the woman interjected.

"Be quiet," another of the men said, this one a decade or more younger than me, with the same bullethead look as his partner. He closed ranks so that his black-shirted torso blocked some of the guards' view. I noticed he had a number of homemade tattoos. That told me a lot. A needle could be a very dangerous, dirty thing. There were no formal tattoo parlors anymore, but certain types of people kept up the practice in secret. It was a private little rebellion that made their usually very small minds feel superior. I had to be careful around these two.

But even 10 years into this new world, I guess I retained some sense of right and wrong. Some need for justice and propriety. "She's with me," I said.

"What're you talking about?" the first man scoffed. "She's never been in here with you before."

"I'm telling you, she's with me. Cousin of mine. Lost her job across town and got transferred. She's staying in my uncle's old apartment." In the back of my mind, I was amazed at how easy the lies came.

"Like hell," he frowned, making another tug at her rations. Behind him, I saw one of the guards tilting his head, looking in our direction. I leaned in to talk quietly.

"Listen. In about 30 seconds, that guard is going to decide he doesn't like the look of this, and all of us are going to end up nothing more than a bad memory. Either you let go of the box and she and I walk out without trouble, or I make sure we all go down together."

He leaned back, eyes widening. "Are you threatening me?" He was taken aback by my boldness. He balled his hands into fists. It looked like a common practice for him. That was another sure sign that he wasn't bright: The infected were violent. Most sane people avoided any semblance of violence, for fear of a one-way ticket to government confinement.

"You've got about 20 seconds to decide," I said. The guard was definitely staring in our direction. The man started to turn around to see if I was telling the truth. "Ah, ah — you turn around and he'll *know* we don't want him over here. That'll be the end."

He paused. His fingers loosened as the tiny wheels in his mind spun. "Fine. But get the hell out of here. Now." He shoved the box back into the young woman's hands and faded into the crowd coming out of the building. Out of the corner of my eye, I noticed the guard had turned his head away — someone else had done something that distracted him.

"Let's go, before this gets worse." The young woman just nodded and followed me.

* * *

"My name is Rosalinda," she said as we walked hurriedly away from the building. I grunted a response. She continued walking beside me, then after a pause said, "Thank you."

Rounding a corner and putting the FDC out of view, I turned to her. "What are you really doing here?"

"Huh?" She was surprised at the blunt question. "I... uh..."

I stopped. "Who are you? Why are you here? The trouble doesn't end just because I helped you out back there. People don't like strangers."

"Don't you think I know that?" she said. "Don't you think I feel the same? I *had* to come here. It's my mom."

"What about your mom? Is she someone from the neighborhood? What's her name?"

"Sonya Menendez. 12th and D."

"Don't know the name," I said. "What does she look like?"

"You wouldn't have seen her for a long time. She's been housebound, barely surviving on handouts from a couple of kind neighbors. But now she's dying."

I stepped back without thinking. "Oh *shit.*" What had I gotten myself into?

"It's not that!" Rosalinda looked panicked, and angry, too. "She doesn't have the disease. She's just old. I lived in Northwest ever since the walls closed. Seemed close enough to mom so that we could both live our own lives. I didn't know how bad off she was until a friend at work passed along the message from a coworker who lives here on the Hill. So I had to come. To help her. I applied for transfer and my office accepted. I do medical research."

I knew there was a small lab in the area, but I was skeptical. Rosalinda pleaded silently at me with her eyes. I looked her up and down, trying to assess her trustworthiness. That's when I noticed her bracelet. Little tiny bits of colored fabric woven together, red, yellow, blue, green. Just wisps. I assumed she did it by hand. I tried to think if other people wore similar things, and came up with nothing. It was simple, but unique. It made me think she was somehow more... *human.*

She saw me staring at it and cocked her head to the side, as she moved her arm and tried to shield the bracelet from my view. She seemed embarrassed that I'd noticed it. I'm sure she was trying to get a read on me, too.

"I'm here in this neighborhood now," she said. "And I really could use an actual friend, so the neighbors don't start thinking I'm some crazy loner, here to take all their food and infect them."

I looked at her. And she smirked. So that's how I, at the ripe age of 63, became friends with a beautiful 32-year-old woman. But it was really her mind I most admired.

KEITH SOARES

5

The Garden of Eden. Paradise. Utopia. Shangri-La. Ours was called "The Oasis."

Somewhere out beyond the city walls, The Oasis was a place where people were said to live freely, without fear of government, infection, dirt, attack. A community from the time before, where none of today's worries penetrated inside. Heaven.

In other words, a fantasy.

There were plenty of rumors about The Oasis, but of course, not one of the people talking about it had been outside the walls in 10 years. In office break rooms or playing chess in the park, they would say with utter certainty, "It's in Mexico." "No, Brazil." "No, it's in Kansas." I ignored the nonsense.

Rosalinda — who I had come to call just "Rosa" — and I spent a lot of time together, at least after work. There were too many doctors in DC for me to have continued my practice, according to the government hack that decided such things, so I was shifted to a large government pharmacy, filling prescriptions. It kept me alive, so I guess I didn't mind too much.

But Rosa was kind of important. She worked as a microbiologist with the National Institutes of Health, in a small lab they'd set up in Southeast. She was working with the government to find a cure. Once the initial wave of paranoia swept past, she made a few friends in the neighborhood. People constantly asked her what she knew — were we close? Any luck today? But in reality, she was told very little about the big picture, and just tasked to focus on the bacteria *Mycobacterium leprae* and *Mycobacterium lepromatosis*, which cause leprosy. She would tell me of minor triumphs, sometimes major failures, and the doldrums of working day after day on something that seemed to have little purpose or goal, and no discernable outcome.

We had dinner together often, and you might think that a romance was blooming. Maybe it was, but I was twice her age and never truly pushed it. We would talk for hours, and then I would head back to my apartment. With her mom's health in rapid decline, I was also useful to have around, simply to help out with day-to-day chores.

We just liked to talk. Our backgrounds in science and medicine gave us a similar mindset that made conversations feel comfortable. When we weren't discussing The Oasis, we'd wonder about the world outside the walls, or remember the time before the outbreak, or just chat about the latest news. Anything to keep our minds occupied. And sometimes it seemed like we'd keep a conversation going just to spend time together.

We did calculations on the disease outside the cities. Three hundred million left outside, 10 years ago. The disease seemed to be 100-percent infectious if a person was bitten or wounded by a zombie, resulting in a 100-percent mortality rate, eventually, from what we knew. But if you could avoid the zombies, maybe keep your own little space clear of the filth that stirred up the disease in the first place, you'd have a chance, or at least we thought so. Nonetheless, before the outbreak, around 3 million people per year died in the United States. Imaging a landscape without medical treatment, without any guaranteed food, we guessed that number might be much, much higher, maybe 25 million a year. Sure, there were likely births to offset some of that, but even putting the attrition rate at 20 million a year, the U.S. had lost 200 million people. That was our guess. More than half the country, gone. But that still left 100 million potential zombies to carry on the infection. And that wasn't counting the possibility that animals could carry it as well. Looking at the trajectory, we could see the outbreak couldn't last forever. The problem was, neither could the human race.

When the discussion would get overly serious and scary, we'd change the subject to something lighter. Dealing with an ill family member is a grueling affair, so there was comfort in just falling into a chair and talking about *anything else* with someone who understood the value of distraction. I asked about her bracelet. She laughed.

"Yep, I made it. I was just so *bored* of everything looking the same. When something wears out — a shirt, bed sheet, whatever — I like to take a little sliver of it before it goes to the recycling center. I keep it small, so it doesn't attract too much attention. And I make little things, bracelets."

"You have more than one?" I asked, raising my eyebrows.

She didn't reply. Instead, she stood up and walked to a small table, opening a drawer in the front. Inside, I saw dozens of little bracelets, in an array of colors.

* * *

Her mom died of natural causes a little more than five weeks later. There was a small, unassuming ceremony monitored by two bored-looking government agents who failed miserably in their attempt to blend in. This was common practice at funerals in the city — to ensure that the death wasn't related to the outbreak.

Rosa was devastated. Even in our world of hardship and fear, the loss of a parent was the permanent shutting of a door. At the same time, it opened another door to the realization that, after all, we were mortal; we all died.

Everyone says they know this, but losing a parent makes it hit like a hammer blow.

I kept going to Rosa's mother's apartment for dinners and other visits, and in short order just thought of it as Rosa's apartment. Sometimes Rosa would come to my place, since there was no one left at hers who needed attention, but we rarely tempted fate by having her walk home alone at night. Sometimes our conversations would turn to The Oasis.

One night at Rosa's apartment, after a light dinner, as she and I finished meticulously cleaning, drying and storing the dishes, she turned to me. "Wouldn't it be amazing? Just to stop all this. To go back to something normal?" I stopped, lowering the plate I'd been about to place back on its shelf. There was a twinkle in her brown eyes as she looked away, past me. I could see the dream meant something to her. It gave her hope. There was no way I was going to laugh and take that away from her.

After that, the topic came up more frequently. It seemed Rosa was organizing — in her head — a sort of compendium of thoughts about The Oasis. The most important detail she worked to figure out was simple: Where was it? Just answering that one question would be life-altering. For that alone would mean *it really existed.* The details of how people lived there, how many were there, all that would be far less important. Just *where was it?*

When people would say Kansas or Brazil or Mexico, it was clear they were generalizing. Brazil is a rather large place, and it was unlikely that the haven of all humanity set up shop in the deepest rainforest. Without any government backing, it seemed more likely that natural diseases like malaria would have a devastating effect there. That was one aspect of our situation that always amused me; in the midst of the most horrific outbreak in human history, we were still on the hook for such everyday maladies as the common cold, even athlete's foot or gingivitis. But these things were rare in the pristine society of the city — and if you did have anything unusual, you kept it quiet, for fear of disease rumors. Besides, you had to think fate was a twisted, cruel mess if you died from a zombie bite because you couldn't run away fast enough due to the discomfort of athlete's foot.

Because she worked as a government researcher, Rosa would sometimes get "Official Government Communications" — I've added the capitalization because somehow that's how she pronounced it every time. In her research, she had access to several computers, linked together with her colleagues and connected to some sort of repository of data — things the government had collected, other research that was useful as reference. She had extremely controlled access to email. She was allowed to send and receive messages from her colleagues related to work and office interests, but anything social or personal was forbidden. Breaking this rule could result in suspension or even termination. And you didn't want to be unemployed in the current world setting. The Internet seemed long dead, and even if it were still around, random browsing would have been forbidden as well. I imagine Rosa was tempted to search for The Oasis in her data systems, although I'm sure she could guess the outcome would be quite dangerous. In any event, Rosa did get messages from the government, usually in the form of email, but sometimes it required a real human being to deliver it to the lab where she worked. Because she was based on the Hill and not at NIH proper, the messengers often stayed for a while, whether to rest or just simply avoid their superiors for a while. On these occasions, when she could either hear something in their conversation or even ask a direct question without seeming like she was collecting information, Rosa would learn what she could about The Oasis. Actual news that wasn't from the know-nothing people in the neighborhood.

From these infrequent visits, a seed was planted. Rosa began to firmly believe that The Oasis, in some fashion, was real and existed in the western part of South Carolina, along the border with Georgia. Multiple hints and rumors talked about a vast emptiness outside the eastern walls of Atlanta, and a similar emptiness west of Columbia, South Carolina. In that sprawling expanse where someone should have been straggling, surviving, scraping by, the government wasn't seeing anyone. The occasional zombie, yes, but never any *people*. If our estimates were anywhere near correct — and I'm sure the government had much better numbers — there were still those 100 million people who should be around. But no one was ever sighted in that region. The area Rosa focused on had big lakes, some parkland, and plentiful forests. And it was just north of Augusta, a city that had been walled for about three-and-a-half years before falling apart. The government would admit to nothing, but the prevailing rumor was that Augusta fell because of some internal rebellion.

In Rosa's mind, the countryside was perfect, the rebellion in Augusta spoke of a starting point and possible resources for a new community, and the empty swathes told her something was different there. In only a few weeks, she became sure that The Oasis was real, and sat about 500 miles south of us down Interstate 95. Her growing certainty had two simultaneous effects on me: It was intoxicating, making me want to believe, and it terrified me. Had this person I'd come to care about so much lost touch with reality and pinned her hopes on a phantom?

As a man of science, I tried to offer alternate, more rational theories. It was possible that some other disease could have ravaged the area. Or there was radiation or some other contaminant that made it unfit for human habitation. Or maybe the reports were just wrong. Rosa would listen to my counterpoints, but she was headstrong. She'd parry every argument. Why wouldn't any of those other reasons bubble up from her information channels, she wondered, especially with a government that wanted to be in total control and typically left nothing to mystery? Shouldn't she have heard *something*?

There was more to be concerned about. Neighbors and coworkers slowly began to realize that she was plying them for any information. She would laugh it off and say she was just talking nonsense to pass the time, but when it happened repeatedly it was harder not to notice. At least one of the government messengers paused, gave her a long look, and then left her building without saying anything. Was her obsession putting her — perhaps even both of us — in jeopardy? It made me hesitate.

As I said, we spent *most* nights together, but not all. So it was not that unusual if I declined her invitation. I found myself turning her down sometimes for no good reason, although now I'm ashamed to admit that. I think her fascination with a fantasy made my older bones and older mind tired sometimes. And that's why on May 23rd, a date I'll always remember, I wasn't there when they took her.

6

You know how you could tell the government cars on the street from anyone else? Because only the government had cars anymore.

It was a picturesque spring evening, the weather cool but not cold, the bright sun beginning to set, making for long shadows and brilliantly illuminated west-facing walls. I was walking home, and a sense of guilt forced me to pass Rosa's street and pause to look in the direction of her apartment. I spotted a black vehicle just as its doors closed and engine revved, and watched it race northward. Immediately I knew what had happened. I ran to her apartment building as fast as I could and scaled the stairs more quickly than a person my age should. My heart, already pounding, stuttered when I found her front door open, no one inside. I ran to the window and craned my head to see where the car was going. But I knew. Everyone knew where they took you. Just as everyone knew you never came back.

Bolling Air Force Base, on the banks of the Potomac River. It was in Southeast, just over the bridge. They'd go north, turn east on Pennsylvania Avenue, cross the river, and then go south. I didn't hesitate.

Tucked behind her building, Rosa had a bike; it was an old, black, metal contraption. Since no one had cars, bikes with baskets were the preferred alternative when getting supplies. She liked to ride hers to work most days. With no sense in my head, I grabbed it, jumped on, and headed after them. Neighbors ran into the street to gape at me, the lunatic. I'm certain they believed they were seeing me for the last time. Rosa, too. So be it, I thought.

I could never catch up to the car, but knowing they were heading to Bolling was all that mattered. I kept going. I turned east onto Pennsylvania, pedaled as fast as my old ass could. The car was barely visible ahead.

Minutes later the black government sedan swerved left, then right. It went off the road just before the bridge and slammed into an abandoned fast-food joint. I wasn't close enough to see much detail. There were people spilling out. One ran for the river. My God, was that her?

It was. Rosa ran toward the river as shots were fired. One clipped a tree near her head, and my heart leapt into my throat. I stopped the bike. One of the men from the car ran after her, while another spoke into a handheld radio, probably calling for a slew of backup that would soon clog every road and pathway in the area.

But no one knew I was doing anything wrong. Sure, the local civilians gathering around the accident looked at me in that awful way reserved for strangers, but I could just ride home and be done. Go back to my life.

The hell with that. At that point, at that age, Rosa was my life. I would go with her or die trying. I turned the bike down a side street and raced for the river. In two blocks, I spied the government agent who was chasing her. I took the risk and biked up to him.

"You looking for a dark-haired woman?" I panted. "I think I saw her running up 11th."

He looked at me with a sneer of disgust and suspicion. "Why are you helping me?" he asked.

"Hey, I scratch your back, maybe you'll scratch mine," I said.

"You people, always the same," he said. He considered it for a second, then asked, "Where on 11th?" I mentioned a spot a block north. Enough to get him out of the way. The sun dropped behind the horizon as he thought about it.

"You realize what happens to you if you're lying to me." It wasn't a question. I nodded. He pulled out a device and pointed it at me, presumably taking my photograph. Then he walked off toward 11th Street.

I waited for him to get out of view, then jumped back on the bike. I figured I could outrun Rosa if she was just following the river south. I was right. I had to jockey the highway, but I caught up to her on Water Street, just off Maine. She was walking as nonchalantly as she could manage, only occasionally looking over her shoulder. I stopped the bike and she saw me.

"Go home. *Please*," she said, walking even faster.

"You know I'm not going to do that," I said.

"Don't waste the rest of your life on me!"

"The way I see it, you were pretty much the only enjoyable thing in my life this past year, so if you don't mind, I'm just going to stick with you. Where are we going?"

She stopped and looked at me. A combination of incredulousness, relief, love, fear. "I have no idea," she said.

"Okay, then I do. Come on."

7

We headed for the waterfront near the old, abandoned monuments. I had an idea that, while even dumber than racing after Rosa on the bike, might just work. We passed all of the boats docked on the Anacostia River, because while they would do the job, they were big, excessive solutions. But more than that, I had no idea how to start any of them. It was a long walk, but eventually we arrived near the Jefferson Memorial, neglected and forsaken by a country that had turned its back on its highest ideals.

I stared up at the rounded marble hulk, thinking about how far we had come from the days of Thomas Jefferson, author of the Declaration of Independence, founding father of a great country, now a sad, besieged city-state terrified of zombies and mold and its own citizens. If it weren't all so terribly true, it would have been funny. I remembered walking under the dome, many years before the outbreak, and I recalled the words inscribed there: "I have sworn upon the altar of God eternal hostility against every form of tyranny over the mind of man." If true, Jefferson, a founder of our government, would now be that same government's sworn enemy.

I made my way around the Tidal Basin to a tiny dock that once offered boats for tourists — small craft, easy to control, from what I remembered. The tourists were long gone, but a few of the boats still bobbed on the sick, oily water. I stared. Paddleboats. Really? Was this another cruel twist of fate? Couldn't we just escape in a canoe, or something a little more... *respectable?* No, we found only abandoned paddleboats. I was wondering if my so-called plan was turning out to be a joke after all. But we chose one, quite at random, and got aboard. Thankfully, despite 10 years of being ignored, its pitted fiberglass hull stayed afloat, and we started to pedal. But it was *dirty.* It terrified us to touch the thing. There were layers of filth, beyond anything we'd seen in years. I had visions of contracting the disease simply from touching the boat. But we went onward.

My God, the boat was loud! How would we escape the city without being detected? Water slapped with every movement of the pedals. Our hearts sank. We may as well have shouted, "We're escaping!" every 30 seconds to add to the sonic overload.

As it turned out, no one cared. DC had become a walled city to keep zombies out, but it seemed to bother very little with keeping anyone in. I suppose when you could avoid having one or two extra mouths to feed, you were fine with people disappearing. What a model of efficiency. Our government had created a society so organized that it knew that losing a citizen could actually make caring for everyone else easier. How shrewd! But we had yet to realize all of this, so we tried to paddle quietly, slowly, over to Northern Virginia. It must have made a comical scene, the most ridiculous escape in history, although I suppose no one ever saw it. Or if they did, they didn't care.

We reached Arlington in full dark. The only lights were behind us, in DC, since Arlington, Alexandria, and the other surrounding cities had largely been abandoned in the pullback. Stepping off the boat, onto land, with Arlington National Cemetery spreading up the hill to our right, overgrown but still recognizable, we felt like astronauts taking their first steps on another world. I'd been here before, many times. But 10 years of changes... well, it was a lot to take in.

We took one look back at DC.

"What now?" she asked.

"Good question." I scratched my head. "Jesus, there could be zombies anywhere. We can't just sit here all night." So we moved.

I remembered — and, like I said before, it's funny what you remember — that Interstate 395 was right there, just to our left. In the daylight, we could follow that to 95, our path south. But for now, shelter was the only concern. Too nervous and bewildered to go far, we walked straight ahead, to a marina in front of the Pentagon. It was dark and seemingly inactive, but filled us with an unbearable fear of the unknown. We found a boat that was still afloat and thankfully wasn't overrun with untold grime, and we climbed aboard. In minutes we were both asleep, lying above deck, close together in the cool evening air of spring.

* * *

Hours later, with the moon gone and darkness all around, with DC's light shimmering so near and impossibly far away, we awoke to a sound. It was a scraping, a scritch-scratching on the dock. It could have been a raccoon — it *should* have been a raccoon. But I felt it in my bones before I even saw anything. It was a zombie.

We propped ourselves up quietly. It hadn't noticed us yet. I got the feeling that scanning the dock might be part of its nightly routine, but who knew. I'd never sat so close to one of these creatures and just... *studied it.*

If it hadn't been for its rather feral motions, it would have been hard to declare it anything other than a human being. It — she —

was female. Maybe mid-40s, Caucasian. But she could have been in her 20s. Age was hard to tell. She looked ragged. Her clothes were too filthy to clearly recognize, but looked like a button-up shirt, possibly flannel, and jeans, torn and covered with layers of dirt. The skin on her face at this distance appeared... bumpy. Her hair was a tangled mess, and her shoes seemed to be long gone. She breathed with the labored rasp of an upper respiratory infection, and cocked her head to one side. She was agitated but not enraged. Her eyes had a milky appearance and she didn't seem to see very well; she spent a lot of time scavenging with her hands, which were clearly deformed. We watched, terrified and amazed, finally laying eyes on the monster we'd feared for so long.

And she stopped. With an almost casual manner, she turned toward us. Slowly, twitching, she shambled to the foot of the pier where our boat was tied. She took a step out onto the pier, wincing and licking her lips. She stopped, sniffed the air. I stiffened, willed myself not to breathe, felt Rosa next to me do the same. I stole a glance at her; she was frozen with fear. I thought *Please, Rosa, just stay still and be silent.* And my right hand, the one propping me up, slipped. I caught my slide with a dull *thump*, my elbow hitting the deck. The zombie flinched, looking right at us. For a split second, it seemed I got away with it. The zombie looked confused. Then that expression gave way to pure fury, her lips pulling back to expose rotted teeth. As Rosa and I scrambled to get out of the way, she lunged.

Her gnarled foot stepped off the pier, toward the boat. And she missed. Rage filled her face, just inches from us, as she fell into the water with a loud splash, followed by a solid thud — possibly her head hitting the hull of the boat. She splashed with even greater hatred, with increasing wildness. It was like she wasn't trying to get out of the water, but just trying to get all of it *off of her*. Again and again, she fell below the surface, then shot up with loud, liquid gasps and panicked splashing.

We scanned in every direction. Nothing we knew could have prepared us for this, sitting alone, outside the city walls, with a zombie making enough noise to wake the dead. Would the zombie's terrible bleating bring more like her? We stood on the boat, too terrified to get off, too afraid to turn our back on the drowning zombie, and too fascinated by this intense experience to do anything but watch.

It seemed like eternity. The zombie finally gasped, splashed, and sank for the last time. For a long while afterward, we felt like we could see her face underwater, staring up at us with icy hatred. We kept scanning the marina. No other zombies appeared. Maybe there were none close enough to hear. Maybe they simply didn't care, each locked in their own dementia. And yet part of me, the primal fear part, thought they were just waiting until we made a move.

We spent the rest of the night sitting back to back on the deck of the boat. We both dozed off momentarily here or there, but each time we awoke with a start, not only jolting ourselves but scaring the holy hell out the other. We never truly rested again that night. When I did sleep, I dreamed of deformed hands emerging from cold, black water.

KEITH SOARES

8

The next morning, our eyes were glued to the water as we stepped back onto the pier. The Potomac isn't terribly deep, but it's muddy as hell, and the water was usually greenish and murky. I may have seen something down there in the muck. I didn't want to dwell on it. After we passed over the gap, we kept walking to dry land and didn't look back.

We walked down the George Washington Parkway to the ramp for 395 and turned toward the right, away from DC. There was no wall on the south side of the city, facing us, because the river provided enough of a natural defensive barrier. I might have given the city one last look, but I don't recall, and actually would be surprised if I had. Funny, not knowing if I'd ever see it again, and not sparing it a memorable last look, not even up there on the highway, where you could take in the whole city. I guess survival and movement seemed more important at the time. We knew zombies weren't just creatures of the night, so we proceeded quietly and kept looking around. Walking in the middle of a wide highway gave us some solace, because we felt that at least we would see if something approached. There were cars abandoned here and there that blocked our view and made for potential zombie hideouts, but most of them were on the other side of the highway, heading toward the city. Either those poor saps made it in or they didn't, there was no way to know.

We made our way southwest. A short while later, as we walked in the middle of the three empty traffic lanes, we crossed under a pedestrian bridge. Two zombies appeared on the bridge, probably 20 feet above us. The bridge was walled by a chain-link fence they couldn't break through, or so I hoped. The one closest to the fence noticed us first. He looked to be a young black male. As we got closer, I could see he was missing one eye and bleeding from both hands and his face. Our presence enraged him, and he leaped at the fence to get to us, crashing into the woven metal again and again. It was pointless. A pedestrian bridge over a major highway is going to be designed to prevent suicide jumpers as its first priority. Flailing, the zombie bloodied himself even worse. We moved to avoid the splatter, which was disgusting and difficult.

From the other end of the bridge, the second zombie heard the commotion and ran in our direction. He also was male, but bigger, with dark, matted hair and a white t-shirt emblazoned with a day-glo logo I didn't recognize. As the first zombie railed against the fence trying to get to us, the second one launched into him, and they both collapsed to the deck of the bridge. We passed under as they carried on a brutal fight, tearing at each other. In minutes, the larger one had killed the other, standing up with blood now coating his t-shirt, hands, and face. He continued to circle the body, swatting and kicking, making guttural noises, shaking his head. We continued farther down the road and out of sight as quickly as possible.

Along with our experience the night before, the bridge incident made me aware that we needed some sort of weapon for protection. I found a solid dead branch downed on the side of the highway, tested it for weight and comfort, snapped off some errant parts, and began using it as a walking stick. I figured at least I'd have something in my hand if anything rushed at us. Rosa found another stick, a little smaller, for herself.

Around midday, we reached the Capital Beltway. The one-time world-famous border between the U.S. political establishment and everyone else. We passed through the complex cloverleaf — there must've been 12 lanes of pavement — threading around and through several huge pileups of cars. There was a tractor-trailer on its side that looked to have been carved out for shelter, now abandoned. Inside the trailer, we could see a small table with a bowl on it, set for a meal. The view immediately made me recognize how hungry I was. What an oversight. I had no idea what to do. Look for supplies nearby? Try to forage or hunt? Every possibility seemed absurd or dangerous as hell. Not having the first clue what native plants to eat, or how to hunt, we made our way toward some of the large buildings that lined the highway. It took most of the rest of the day to find anything edible, but finally, a couple hours before sundown, we stumbled into a bit of treasure trove.

In a parking garage, a beat-up old Nissan two-door sedan had crashed into one of the support beams. The driver, long dead and unidentifiable, clearly had been torn up by a zombie. On the passenger seat, there was a cardboard case of canned beans, wrapped in plastic. Rosa had the bright idea to pop the trunk. There we found other canned goods, bottled water, and even a can opener. The poor dope's emergency prep kit didn't help him, but we both silently gave him thanks.

We opened two cans of refried beans, each of which had a strange taste but were edible. They were similar to a bean paste we'd get in rations from time to time back in the city. We ended up scarfing down a can and a half each. We found a slightly ripped backpack and several fabric shopping bags, loaded up as much as we could carry, and scouted around the parking garage for a place to sleep. It looked like it would rain, so we ended up sleeping on the landing at the top level of the staircase because it was indoors, was the cleanest place we could find, and had working doors that hopefully would provide at least some barrier. Thankfully, other than the rain, the night was uneventful.

9

"Are you sure?" Rosa asked suddenly, during our second day of walking.

"About...?" I asked.

"This. Me. The Oasis."

I stopped walking, and looked around at the repetitive landscape of 95 South. Border trees and pavement. Cars and trucks huddled in clusters, sometimes abandoned, sometimes crumpled together in a wreck. "Yeah." I didn't need to think about it, but I did anyway. "Yeah, I am. Well, I'm sure about you. The Oasis? We'll see. To be honest, I think you're in for a disappointment, but I hope you're right. Even if there is an Oasis, it's a big world; it might not be where you think.

"But you and I both know we can't go back anymore anyway. You were already marked and grabbed by the government, so you show up and you're done. Me? At this point, I've gone missing from my job, my apartment, my neighborhood. It's enough to cause a lot of suspicion. Even if they didn't take me right away, it wouldn't take long. Besides, as easy as it was to get *out* of the city, I seriously doubt we could get back *in*. You saw that line of cars back there, piled up outside DC. They don't just throw open the doors for anyone who walks up. Particularly people that are wanted by the law in the first place."

She looked away. "You... you gave up your life for me and my crazy ideas, you know?" The weight of knowing this was evident on her face.

I shrugged, grinned. "Eh. I'm 63, I live alone in a walled city full of paranoid people, and I'm a pharmacist for the government. Mostly I just count little colored pills all day long. This is actually an improvement." She laughed. I don't think we ever talked about it again. It was settled.

"But I do need to ask." I gave her a sidelong glance. "How'd you crash that car?"

She stopped and smirked. The same smirk I saw outside the FDC that first day. "Men, even men who wield the power of the government, still don't understand women. We can just do crazy things, and you all... *believe it.*" She laughed. "I screamed that the handcuffs were burning my skin and they bought it. And I suppose their ego told them I was too small to cause trouble. But once the handcuffs were off, I just had to reach out and pull the wheel. That's it."

I chuckled. "Smart cookie," I said, admiringly. "You could've died in the crash, you know?"

"Wasn't I dead already?"

10

We walked all day. It was warm, and carrying our supplies made it a lot harder. We continued south, trudging along the wide swath of pavement formerly known as Interstate 95. I guessed the width of the road to be about 25 feet, three lanes for cars, shoulders on both sides, but still our forward progress could be slow. In addition to the abandoned or wrecked cars in various stages of decomposition, the road itself could be trouble; cracks, divots, and potholes made us careful with our steps, and in places where there were bridges, we saw several crumbling sections that we had no intention of testing with our body weight. Along the sides of the road, trees grew with what I could only assume was renewed vibrancy, no longer suffering through the toxins of human pollution. Bushes and tall grasses clogged the sides, from the forest to the edge of the road, and often sprouted up onto the pavement via cracks and holes. We had an overall sense of great vulnerability. Walking was slow, zombies could appear at any time, and places for them to hide in ambush were everywhere.

We saw some people, survivors and stragglers, but they were extremely guarded. The first one made himself known to us before we saw him, signaling that we wouldn't be sneaking up on him. As an exit ramp arced its way off to our right, we saw him standing on the rise beside the highway. Crossed in his arms was a long gun. Although he was some ways away, I could feel him stare at us, unmoving, until we continued out of sight. We kept turning back, keeping an eye on him the whole time until he was hidden from view; this was someone who had *made it*. Had lived. Outside the city. It warped my mind to consider it.

No one seemed to want to make contact with us, and we felt it was best to stay out of their way, too. My God, these people had survived on their own outside the wall for years. How the hell had they done it? The mortality rate must have been sky high. We didn't see any children, but almost every person we encountered stayed their distance, eyes locked on us, and most of them showed a gun. The meaning was clear. Stay away.

Rosa and I were incredulous at these first signs of human life. We had surmised there must be someone out here, but we'd of course grown accustomed to life in the city. Living out here? It was like another world. Like those TV specials I'd seen before the outbreak, where a "lost tribe" was found on some remote island, trapped in a life generations or centuries out of date. The people we saw on the road looked completely different from us. Rather than exhibiting the sleek look of synthetic clothes and rigorous attention to cleanliness, they wore what appeared to be hand-made garments of woven fabrics and animal hides. Where our clothes were bright white or bold primary colors, theirs were subdued earthen tones: browns, greys, greens. We saw at least one man, maybe 35 years old, with a missing arm. I imagined countless ways it might've been lost, as we walked on.

Finding a relatively safe shelter at night was our biggest issue. Apartment buildings, we learned, were no good. Too many people on top of one another, making them hotbeds for infection. In one high-rise apartment building we checked out for potential shelter, we didn't find anyone alive, but had a close encounter with a zombie. It came at me unexpectedly from behind the front desk. I had to club it with my stick. His head made a cracking noise and he fell, blood spraying everywhere on the marble floor. Rosa threw up. It was traumatic for me as well, but not because of the blood. As a doctor, my promise had always been to help people. Here I was putting one down like a sick dog. Needless to say, we didn't stick around.

Our food held for the time, but we scavenged for more whenever possible. So many people had hoarded so many provisions in the early days of the disease that it was still possible to find small stashes. Mostly we weren't too hungry and avoided trouble. But spending so much time looking for food, water, and shelter made the journey slow.

Two days out from the Beltway, as we were looking for shelter for the night, our luck changed. It started to rain, darkening the bright afternoon. Our visibility diminished significantly. We scanned the area for options, then discussed what might be worth checking out. The rain must've made us hasty. We set our sights on a high school, hoping we could lock ourselves into a classroom. As we approached the school, we saw small wind turbines spinning atop the building in the increasing wind. I felt a glimmer of hope that the place might even be making electricity.

"You don't think...?" Rosa asked.

"I seriously doubt it," I said, shaking my head. "But we could always find out." *Electricity*, I let myself think, *might mean hot water.*

A side door to the school was unlocked but closed. I told myself that was a good sign. If it had been sitting wide open, I might have been more wary.

Inside, we picked a hallway at random, stood quietly listening for any signs of trouble, then opened the door to the first classroom on the right. We got about two steps in.

Looking at them, you would have thought it was a normal day of school. Eight or maybe 10 teenagers — just kids — were sitting around the classroom. After that initial false sense of security passed, I realized they were all diseased. How had they lasted in here? How had they not torn each other to bits? In the seconds before all hell broke loose, I saw that one corner of the room was a bloody mess. I guess they had turned on each other, at least once or twice, and that was how they'd survived. Maybe this had been some sort of refuge or evacuation point for them before they'd changed.

One of them, a girl with dirt-caked, blondish hair, turned toward us with milky eyes. For a heartbeat, she seemed locked in a dream. Her head swayed, milky eyes gleamed. Rain tapped its irregular beat on the cracked, grimy windows. Then lightning struck somewhere nearby, and Rosa gasped. The spell was broken. With a shriek, the girl zombie leaped up, throwing herself toward us. The others saw the focus of her rage and joined the attack. Rosa backpedaled out of the doorway, back into the hallway. I don't know what she hit, but she tripped, falling backward. I stepped back directly onto her foot, twisted my ankle trying to avoid going down myself. The girl zombie was upon me and I swung my walking stick. Her face imploded, and she fell. Even in the rush of the moment, the guilt of killing this child hit me like a brick. I *killed* someone, *again*. In an instant, my mind dreamed up the life this girl never got to live. I hated myself, our world, our lives.

But there was no time. Another zombie, a boy, bounded over the girl, came at me. I couldn't swing in time. Just before he got to me, Rosa's stick came up and took him through the throat. He fell on top of the girl, partially blocking the doorway. The other zombies scrambled to get through. I had half a second to help Rosa up, and then we ran. I realized she was crying. Down the hallway, a random left turn, hoping to put distance and a closed door between us and the infected. Hoping we could escape the chase. My ankle hurt like a son of a bitch. Rosa seemed unhurt, but she sobbed as she ran. She helped me, dragging me by the hand as fast as possible. Thankfully, we still had our sticks and backpacks.

In seconds, the other zombie kids were out in the hallway, running after us. But now their rage actually helped us. They fought each other as they tried to follow us. It slowed them down. We took two more turns at random. In the back of my mind, I hoped we wouldn't just be running into the arms of another classroom of zombies. Rosa tried three doors — two were locked, the third opened. It looked like some kind of office. We skidded inside, closed the door.

Rosa turned and half screamed. Something hit me in the back of the head, hard, and I went down in a total blackout.

11

I wasn't out long, less than a minute. It was another kid who'd hit me, but human, not zombie. Maybe 16, messy, jet-black hair, wearing a pair of threadbare jeans and a faded red t-shirt that looked washed a few thousand times more than they'd been designed to withstand. He puffed himself up in front of us, maintaining a white-knuckled grip on the metal pipe that I assumed was responsible for the growing lump on my head. A lot of bravado, but why? Then it became clear. From behind a desk, a teenage girl appeared, light red hair, freckles, adjusting the shoulder strap of her black bra under her faded light-blue blouse. Shit. Even in the freaking apocalypse, kids would be kids.

Knowing the zombies were somewhere just outside, I quietly asked, "What's your name, son?"

"What the hell are you doing here?" he responded. Looking back and forth between us and his girlfriend, switching moment by moment between strong hero and sappy boyfriend.

"Listen," I said, "we ran into some kids with the disease and they were chasing us. We didn't mean to barge in on you..."

"You didn't *barge in* on anything," he said, too abruptly.

"I honestly don't care. The world is a mess. Make yourself happy any way you can. What's your name?"

"David. David Chen." Good-looking young kid. Chinese, I figured, based on his name and appearance. Not that it mattered. These days there were only two types of people: infected and not infected. I imagined racism was finally conquered.

The girl was cute, a little pimply. "I'm Siobhan McDermott," she said. They both still looked like rats in a trap.

"You're not supposed to be here either, are you?" I asked.

After a moment, David said, "Not really." Another moment. His eyes widened. "Wait. You ran into zombies? Here in the school?" David's look of concern made it clear that was unexpected.

I studied him, trying to gauge his reaction. "You thought this place was all clear?"

"Yeah, of course — I mean, it *should* be." It was obvious that someone had told him the school was safe. And here I was, a stranger, saying maybe it wasn't.

Outside, the zombies surged past the door, searching for us. The kid's eyes bugged out. As much as he might try to be brave and in charge with his girlfriend, he was still green as hell. I guess we all were, really.

"We need to get away from here," Rosa whispered. "It's not safe."

At the back of the office, another doorway led to some unknown place. "We need to go this way," Siobhan offered, opening the door.

We followed David and Siobhan as they led us through the administrative back ways of the school. It was raining harder outside, the drumming rain punctuated by snaps of thunder and flashes of lightning. After a few dark turns, we came to another door.

For reasons we didn't then understand, David and Siobhan seemed pensive looked at each other. After a sigh, they opened the door.

12

We stepped into an alien world. In a back room next to the gymnasium, supplies were stacked high. Everything was neat and tidy. Through a glass pane, we could see into the gym. It was arranged almost like a park, with tables and chairs spread around an open space. On the sides of the large room were makeshift enclosed areas that I assumed were for privacy or sleeping or both, their contents hidden behind plywood, fabrics swaths, whatever was available. Outside, the storm raged, but inside, the large gymnasium lights made everything bright and cheerful. *Damn*, I thought, *those turbines do work*. The sight of functioning electrical lights kept my attention for another minute before I continued to look around. There were even potted plants arranged to beautify some of the spaces. Dozens of people were there — people who lived *outside* city walls — talking, laughing, playing, carrying on like life was normal. Here we were, in the land that every living soul in the walled city feared, and not only were people not living in squalor, fighting for their lives, wrestling in the grip of the disease. They were reading books, playing chess, telling stories. They were just living. It took my breath away.

For a moment, I thought, *This is The Oasis. Or if it isn't, we don't need any other.* Then we met Hector.

He stormed up to us, in a matching dark-grey athletic t-shirt and shorts, with thick, close-cropped black hair, tanned muscles bulging in a show of strength. He blocked us from entering the gym. "Are you out of your mind, David?" he asked. "Have you forgotten the rules?" Looking around, I realized the other people were mostly teenagers. Maybe four or five of them were adults, but young, barely out of their teens themselves. Hector was the oldest person we saw, and he was maybe 30. I could tell right away that he used his age as an advantage with the group. And I could tell right away that he saw me as a threat to his authority.

"They were in trouble, Hector," David said.

"Aren't we all? Every day? Every minute?" Hector sounded like he was warming up for a sermon.

"They were being chased down."

"So what?" Hector snapped. "So it's okay to jeopardize the whole group because two *complete strangers* are in trouble?"

"It's not that —"

Hector interrupted. "Yeah, it is *that*. It is exactly *that*. Here's what's going to happen. You brought them in. You're taking them out. The back door. Now, before there's more trouble."

"But —" Siobhan started.

Hector turned to her with a scoff that closed her mouth immediately. It was clear that he wasn't used to being questioned.

"We only wanted a place to sleep out of the rain tonight," I said. "Can we at least get that? We'll leave in the morning and give you no trouble."

Hector stared. I think because I wasn't speaking like a raving lunatic, he didn't know what to say at first. It didn't last long.

"Oh, and we're just supposed to *trust* that you're not infected yourself? No way. Out. Now." Hector puffed himself up as big as possible.

"We're not infected!" Rosa said.

"And just how do you know that?" Hector chided.

"Fine. We'll leave," I said. "If you can help us with one thing."

"What?" Hector's surprise was obvious.

"You know this area, I assume. It's raining like hell out there. You must know some place close by where we can shelter for the night."

Hector thought about it. He seemed very reluctant to give up any information. Everyone was silent, looking back and forth at one another for a moment.

"The supply shed. Behind the bleachers." It was David who spoke up. "It stays dry, and we've been in there, so we know there aren't any zombies."

Hector put on a sour expression for effect and to maintain his air of control, but acquiesced. "One night," he said. "And you go there now."

In minutes we stood at the back door, gauging the rain and the best route to run to the shed. David pointed the way. "Sorry for, you know, knocking you in the head."

"Don't worry about it, kid. Thanks for trying to help us." I looked back at the gym, the warm beds and bright lights and plentiful supplies, and gave a regretful sigh. And we ran into the rain. The distance was maybe a few hundred yards, enough for us to get pretty soaked on the way. The shed was large and dry, but not built for comfort. As the storm intensified outside, we slept on the concrete slab floor. In the end, it may have saved our lives, despite the hours we spent shivering in our cold, damp clothes.

* * *

The next morning the rain had stopped. We awoke, ate some canned food from our provisions, and started back toward the highway. As we went past the gymnasium, a door flung open and Hector appeared. He ran toward us. He was holding a pistol.

"*You killed them!*" he shouted. Others piled out behind him, including David and Siobhan.

"It's not their fault!" David yelled, pushing past people to get to Hector.

Shocked by the scene, I stood in place as Hector approached. It was one part fear that running would mean a bullet in my back, one part good old-fashioned inaction in the face of danger. Hector charged right up to me and trained the pistol on my forehead.

"What the hell is going on?" I asked quietly. Beside me Rosa gasped and leapt forward. Hector slid the pistol over toward her and she stopped short. He pointed it back to me.

"Last night," Hector panted. "Because of you, we were attacked. Zombies *everywhere*. Goddammit. We were holed up all night. We ended up killing all the damn things — 23 of them. Eight of my people *died*. Just because you had to show up." He cocked the pistol. From what we saw the day before, there were only 30 or 40 people living there in the first place. The community had gotten a heck of a lot smaller in one night.

"Hector!" Siobhan shouted. "She's dead. This won't bring her back." Hector paused, and the pistol dipped a bit. Then he raised it in fury, back at my head.

"Please. Anna wouldn't want *this*." Siobhan extended her hand for the gun. I could only guess who Anna was. Hector's wife or girlfriend or mother or sister. The specifics didn't matter at the moment.

Wheeling around, Hector changed his focus. "Actually, I suppose it was *you two* who are really responsible." He looked toward David and Siobhan. "Pack up your things, you're out of here today."

Siobhan stepped back. "No! We'll die outside!"

I looked at Hector, into his eyes. He was on the edge, maybe on the edge of sanity. Anything could happen.

Quickly, he shifted the pistol's aim and fired, three fast shots, chest, shoulder, face. Siobhan dropped, dead. David leaped on top of Hector and they fell, rolling and fighting. Everyone scattered. The gun went off again, once, twice. If this was The Oasis, it was crumbling. There was nothing we could do to fix it. We ran.

13

Interstate 95 runs up and down the entire East Coast, connecting most of the big cities. In between long stretches of pavement sided by nothing but trees, there were clusters of strip malls and office developments sitting along the highway. If you couldn't find it along 95, you couldn't find it anywhere. We weren't really looking for anything in particular, except food and nightly shelter, but then we saw it: an RV dealership. The sign promised comfortable living and happy families traveling across the country. The appeal was instantly overwhelming: our own vehicle, to make the travel faster, to carry our gear, to keep us out of bad weather... and most importantly, to sleep in safely every night. Unfortunately, we weren't the only people to think that. The dealership was pretty much cleaned out. There were a couple of huge vehicles left, but peering through the window I could see I didn't have a clue how to drive them. There was a pickup truck with a camper trailer, but that would mean two separate, self-contained spaces to worry about — the truck cockpit and the camper interior. Around back, we got lucky, coming across a smallish integrated RV that might have been the owners' private ride. It was locked. Rosa went to the dealership office and tried the door. It, too, was locked, so she broke a small window, reached through, and let herself in. She had to step over a dead body, desiccated beyond recognition, with wisps of clothing and the last remnants of skin and hair clinging to its greyish form. She tried drawers and cabinets, and ended up with a ridiculous number of keys. Back at the RV, she tried nearly every one until finally the door opened, and she jumped into the driver's seat.

"Okay, now what?" she asked.

I checked the tires and found them in passable condition. "Do you know how to drive one of these things?" I asking, moving over to look at the range of dials and controls in front of her.

"I don't know how to drive. Period. I never got a license because I lived in the city." Rosa smirked.

"I used to drive a 'luxury sedan,'" I said. "That seems like another lifetime." Rosa hopped out and I got behind the wheel. I put the key in the ignition and turned it. Nothing.

"When I was a teenager, my parents made me learn a little bit about cars," I said as I reached under the dashboard, looking for the hood release. I pulled it, and the RV's hood popped free with a *kachunk*. I moved to the front of the RV. "I'm thinking it's the battery. I doubt it could sit here for 10 years, or even just a few years, depending on the last time it ran." I opened the hood and there was the dead battery, mottled with corrosion, mocking me.

"What do we do?" Rosa asked.

"Well, two ideas come to mind. First, we push this baby over to a downhill slope and hope that we can pop the clutch and get 'er started." I could tell that my sarcasm was lost on Rosa, the non-driver. "But given that this is an automatic transmission, that's out of the question."

She peered at me from the driver's side window. "Plan B?"

"I have a thin hope that our RV dealer friend was also into disaster preparation. Let's look around." We went back to the office and dug around, then wandered through a door and into a small workroom. Looking carefully, I found something I hadn't seen in several decades: a trickle battery charger. I put it on a countertop. I found some tools and was able to disconnect the battery from the RV and bring it back into the workshop, where I placed it next to the charger. I headed back outside with increased purpose, and followed the outer edge of the building. Tucked in a back corner where most people would never look, there was a thicket of overgrown bushes.

Underneath I saw the glint of metal and began pulling away the leaves and branches, revealing an old gas generator tied into the office building.

With a rush of excitement, I ran back to the workroom and rummaged about, eventually coming up with a small gas canister and a hose. Back at the RV, I prayed there was enough gas inside for us to steal some, then opened the tank, inserted the hose, and placed the canister on the ground. Pushing the hose inward, I heard a liquid *spoosh*. My heart raced. Rosa looked at me like I had gone mad. In my haste, I'd neglected to tell her anything about what I was doing. Now I put the loose end of the hose in my mouth and sucked. I jammed the hose into the canister and after a second watched as it filled with a clear brown liquid. Gasoline, thank God, pouring into the canister. I tried my best to estimate how much it would take to power up the generator and get some charge on the battery, while still leaving enough to drive the RV. In the end, as a total guess, I siphoned off maybe two-thirds of a gallon of gas.

Next I had to worry about the generator. I brushed it off and opened the screw top to the fuel tank. Delicately, I poured the gas into the opening, splashing a few times, cursing my jittery old hands. With the canister dry, I had a quiet, almost desperate moment of reckoning. I closed the screw top, reached for the pull chain to start the engine. "Wish me luck," I said, winking at Rosa.

"Luck," she said drably.

I pulled. Nothing.

I pulled again. Nothing but the slightest sluggish whir. I checked the choke, thanking my parents silently for insisting that I know something about this when I was young. Pulled it open. Tugged again. Nothing. Once more. A little rumble. Hope sprang. Again I pulled, feeling the strain already in my shoulder and arm. The motor sputtered, coughed, almost gave up... and then ran so high I thought it might blow. Rosa stepped back, surprised. Remembering something else about the choke, I rushed to push it in, almost too quickly. The engine slowed, came near to stall, but finally evened out. I looked at Rosa, unbelieving. A wide grin spread across my face, and she couldn't help but follow suit. Then I ran back inside. "Are you going to tell me what you're doing?" she yelled.

In the workroom, I flicked on the light switch, checking for power, but nothing came on. In the fading light of day, I saw the bulb was missing from the overhead fixture. I'd have to leave it to luck. I plugged in the battery charger, turned a switch. A tiny red light appeared, and I laughed out loud. "We're going to charge this battery!" I was giddy. "Or, well, I *hope* we are. If the gas holds out." I connected the battery to the charger, checked the gauges. It really did seem to be working.

"How long does it take?" Rosa asked, peering over my shoulder.

My smile faded. "That's the problem. This is a trickle charger. It's called that because it trickles the charge into the battery a little bit at a time. My guess is, as much as eight hours."

"Eight hours?" she asked. "You really think that little bit of gas will last that long? And what do we do in the meantime?"

"I guess we wait."

* * *

We holed up in the workroom, afraid that the noise from the generator might attract undue attention. It was a nervous night, but we finally dozed. It must have been around three or four o'clock in the morning when something suddenly woke us up. It was silence.

"What happened?" Rosa asked, groggy but wary.

"The generator died. Ran out of fuel."

"Now what?" Her eyes looked at me in confusion, hope, tiredness.

"In the morning, we try it out."

* * *

As the morning light filtered in, I unhooked the battery and grabbed a tool. From the office, I peered out the window to make sure the coast was clear. It was. Carefully, I walked to the RV and reconnected the battery. If this failed, the idea of trudging on foot another day made me feel so weary I couldn't move. I looked at Rosa, nodding for her to try the key. Though she didn't drive, she understood. She sat in the driver's seat and turned the ignition.

Somehow, the engine started. I rushed over and checked the fuel gauge: less than a quarter tank. A lot less. That was going to be a problem. We'd need to make finding fuel a priority, on top of finding food. We let the engine run, wasting gas but further charging the battery. Using the canister and hose, we checked all the other vehicles we could find on the lot and came up with another gallon and a half of gas, which we poured straight into the RV's tank. Then it was time to check out the rest of the RV's interior. What a lucky break. It was totally tricked out. Here we were in the ruins of civilization, and we would be driving an RV with leather seats, a refrigerator, stove, bed, even a bathroom. And it was clean. That was a relief after days of living in conditions that life behind the wall had taught us to fear. We didn't talk about it, but I'm sure Rosa was as afraid as I was that we might be exposing ourselves to the disease. The RV was tidy, and a place we could reasonably keep clean by ourselves.

* * *

Rosa was interested in learning how to drive. I found that I reacquainted myself with driving pretty quickly, and so I taught her. It was easy, since the car was an automatic. And it didn't hurt that there was a complete lack of other cars on the road. We had to navigate around potholes, frequent pileups, and abandoned cars, but that mostly just broke up the boredom of the drive. The freedom and exhilaration of driving was just about the most fun thing we had done in years.

All of the gas stations we checked were bone dry, so when we stopped to scavenge for food, we also looked for smaller stashes of gas. Given the state of the world, the desperate, aborted migrations that followed the disease, there were a lot of junked cars with spare gas cans in the trunk. We hoarded these and were able to fill up the tank. The small RV got decent gas mileage — about 24 miles per gallon — but even still, with 500 miles or so to go, we'd need more than 20 gallons. And that was assuming our destination was where we thought it was.

While scavenging, we also topped off the RV's water tank and loaded up the refrigerator and cabinets with anything remotely edible that we could find. We checked stores and houses near the RV dealership and off the next few exits along 95. With water and food, and a brand-new moving shelter loaded with a full tank of gas, we felt great.

Before we hit the road in earnest, I decided to try out the toilet, but wanted to be sure it worked first. The toilet fed into a tank labeled Black Water. I found out, much to my dismay, that it was already partially full. We decided the rest of the world wouldn't mind too much if we simply let the toilet drain out onto the road.

After all, we'd been doing our business outside since we began the trip. We doubted anyone would mind too much.

* * *

Having spent most of the day searching for supplies to fill the RV, we made little progress on the road, and the tension of the previous night made us tired early. As dusk settled in, we found a place to stop, on an overpass where we could see every approaching direction fairly well. We decided to get some sleep. Rosa went to the back while I locked up the RV and shut down the engine. I turned to go back to where the bed was located... and stopped. In the fading light, I saw Rosa slip out of her worn shirt and pants, standing in her underwear, her lean, olive-toned body reflecting the sun in warm curves. She looked up and paused, her eyes on mine.

I noticed I was holding my breath. "Uh... sorry," I said, turning and taking in air.

After a pause, I heard her say, "Don't worry." She got into the bed and turned toward me. "There's only one bed. We've slept side-by-side each night now. It's okay."

I looked at her, then looked around the RV.

"Come. Lie down. Here."

So I did.

14

We made great time all the way through to Richmond. But we had to be careful once we got there — last we heard, Richmond was a functional, walled city, like DC. We continued on 95, driving straight toward its heart. As we approached the Route 1 overpass, we saw that the space between the bridge and the street below had been filled in, walling off the entrance. Cars and trucks were heaped along the shoulders of the road, like they had been deliberately swept aside to clear the way. It was impossible to tell if the fortifications were guarded; if anyone still kept up the city's defenses. Rosa drove ahead. Slowly, carefully.

A blast tore open the ground just ahead, to the passenger side of the RV, with a sound loud enough to cancel out everything else and leave my ears ringing. My nose filled with an acrid smell. Tiny bits of pavement rained onto the RV. Rosa swerved left, more a flinching move than actual defensive driving, sending me flailing toward into the passenger door. The RV wasn't moving all that quickly, but it was tall and the turn was sudden. For a moment we skittered up on two wheels before thudding back down to the road, Rosa zigging to try to regain control. The RV slammed against a low concrete wall dividing the two sides of the highway and dragged to a stop, throwing sparks.

Rosa turned to look at me. "What the hell was — ?" Another shot missed overhead, cutting into an abandoned car in the opposite lane. There must have been some gas left in its tank; the car jumped into the air in a fireball explosion, making a low *whump*.

"Go!" I shouted. "Back the way we came! Turn us around!"

With a ripping of metal on concrete, Rosa drove forward. She had to get off the wall before she could turn around. "How far can they shoot?" she asked.

"I have no idea, just keep going!" Somehow she turned the RV around. Another blast, now behind us, lifted our back end. For a moment, it looked like the extra push of the explosion would send us crashing directly into a pickup truck that angled out from the side of the highway.

At the last minute, Rosa swerved. I was sure that I hadn't taught her anything like that. I think it was just her good instincts. Then she did something even smarter. She drove toward the shoulder, where a large tractor-trailer jutted diagonally into the road. She put it between us and the city wall, buying us the seconds we needed. As I looked back, I saw the barrel of the mounted gun — a huge thing, I have no idea what to even call it — turning to aim at us again. But as Rosa sped away, it didn't fire.

Maybe we were out of range, maybe we no longer appeared to be a threat, or maybe they just wanted to conserve ammunition. Either way, we lived.

15

We backtracked north for a few miles, passing several exits, before I finally asked Rosa to pull off at an interchange where it looked like we might be able to find supplies. After several wasted stops, we came across a convenience store a couple of turns off the main road that ended up being a great find — a storeroom held food, water, a small can of gas, and something we suddenly realized we really needed: a map. We vowed not to venture into the big cities again.

Using the map, we realized we could skirt around Richmond using 295 — we hoped it would swing wide enough to avoid any future confrontations. It did.

The RV was scuffed up on the driver's side and the mirror was broken off, but it didn't seem like we'd have to look behind us for too much other traffic, and we weren't terribly concerned about having the nicest car on the road. It still handled fine. Rosa had had enough driving for one day, and passed the job to me. Soon, she was napping in the passenger seat while I navigated around Richmond.

The rest of the drive through Virginia was uneventful, except for one moment in a remote, densely wooded section of the highway. Out of nowhere, a zombie ran directly into the road. Rosa startled awake as we clipped him with the passenger side of the RV, no doubt denting up that side of the vehicle, too. She screamed. I tried to defuse the tension. "The way we drive, they may take our license away," I said. She just stared at the blood that was dripping down the passenger window next to her.

* * *

Driving into North Carolina seemed like a huge accomplishment. First, we had been in Virginia since the moment we landed the paddleboats coming out of DC. And second, it just *felt* closer to South Carolina, our objective.

Just past the border, I had to pee, so we pulled over and I went to use the small bathroom in the RV. Rosa, seeming morbidly fascinated by the bloody mess on the passenger side of the car, got out to take a look. Afterward, I guessed that the combination of our vehicle approaching, doors opening and closing, and other sounds of human activity must have stirred up interest. A zombie we might otherwise have dismissed as a corpse on the side of the road stood, shook itself free of the underbrush, and made directly for Rosa. From inside the bathroom, I heard her shout. My heart raced, and I fumbled my way outside as fast as possible.

There, my racing heart almost stopped.

A frantic zombie was on top of Rosa, who'd fallen to the street, backpedaling desperately with her elbows and feet, trying for some purchase to get away. The zombie, formerly a dark-skinned woman, perhaps 50 years old, somewhat overweight, scrambled to keep Rosa down, to bite and tear at her.

I turned, flung open the tire compartment at the rear of the RV, and grabbed whatever I could. It was a small jack for replacing a flat tire. I didn't care. It was metal and heavy. I hefted it, and ran.

My only thought was: *Let her be okay.* Skidding up behind the zombie, I cocked my arm and hit the thing as hard as I could. The zombie woman didn't just fall, she was launched to the side of Rosa in a splatter of blood and gore. I stopped, looked at the zombie, ready to do it again. She didn't move. Given the state of her skull, I figured she'd never move again.

Rosa was up on her elbows, looking down at herself. She was incredulous, shocked. No, horrified. Following her eyes, I saw why.

Her shirt had a vertical tear, and under that it was clear that the zombie had slashed her across the belly.

As she slowly looked up at me, anguish in her eyes, the zombie's blood and her own continued to mix in the wound. It felt like the cut continued down into my core, my soul.

A tear opened between us, and the part of me that Rosa had become was ripped away.

16

She lived. We had no idea if it would be for long or for short, but damn it, she was alive. We would continue south, come what may. The journey took on even greater urgency. Where before, I had come along on this quest for The Oasis out of duty to Rosa, now it took on much more serious weight. I began to feel that I had to get her to The Oasis or she would turn into a zombie in front of my eyes. It was all I had to hold on to; they might shun us, they might have no way to help her, hell, they probably didn't even *exist*, but there was nothing else. No other option.

We had a good-sized first-aid kit in the RV, and I patched her up, wiping everything as clean as I could. But it was a pale comparison to what we'd known for the last 10 years. Life in DC was infinitely more sterile than the half-assed roadside clean up I was able to provide. Still, it would have to do.

Now I thundered down the highway, willing us to get to our destination as soon as we could. We tore through North Carolina — it was nothing but a blur to me. Rosa faded in and out of consciousness. The biggest concern I had was Fayetteville, which was the largest city near the highway, a potential bottleneck, possibly even a walled-off dead end. But we raced past the city like it was a ghost town. How many hundreds of thousands of people had lived in Fayetteville? I guess most of them were dead now. The futility of my every move felt like an anchor around my neck.

I'd reviewed the map we found, and knew that around Florence, South Carolina, I had to finally get off 95 and head west on Interstate 20. That would take us right past Columbia. I hoped not too close.

In the end, we covered hundreds of miles in a blink. We probably were the noisiest thing in the entire (former) state of South Carolina. From any other vantage point, I must have looked insane. Perhaps even diseased. I was driving as fast as possible down highways blasted with potholes, a never-ending boneyard of cars in various states of disrepair, rust, collision damage, fire damage. And our luxury RV was zipping in and out of lanes, trying to make time.

Interstate 20 was a blur. I guess we were wide enough of Columbia to avoid trouble, or maybe we came and went so fast they didn't have time to react. Rosa got a little better; at least she woke up. I could sense the pain and fear clearly etched across my face, knew she could see it, but she looked oddly calm. Like all was well, all was at peace... or perhaps, all was coming to an end.

Using the map, Rosa, her voice a whisper, guided me into an expanse of lakes and parks along the South Carolina–Georgia border. My heart dropped again, seeing the large swath of green on the paper map — it seemed impossibly huge to search. Even if The Oasis was there, could we find it in time for them to do something for Rosa? But studying the lakes, parks, and roads, she had a hunch, and directed me to Hickory Knob State Park, and damn if she wasn't right. We found them. Because they weren't hiding from anyone. The compound was right there, on the shore of Clarks Hill Lake. Makeshift but solid-looking walls blocked off the road. As we pulled near and stopped, dozens of people came out. They met us beside the golf course. Some people were even out playing golf. The idea was absurd, and knowing nothing of the game, I looked at them like they were from another planet. I saw that some of the people approaching us were carrying guns, but for the most part they all just looked curious. A small girl waved in welcome. They were alive. They were just people. And they were right where Rosa had said they would be. I turned and beamed at her, in awe of her brilliance. In the entire wide world, she had found The Oasis.

Rosa and I hugged, sobbing, for a long time.

17

They could tell right away that something bad had happened to Rosa. She was pale, her breathing shallow, and the large wrap of bandages on her stomach was seeping blood. Strangely, they didn't do what we expected; they didn't shut us out, shun us, run us away. Rosa had the disease and we all knew it, yet the people of The Oasis did... *nothing.*

A young woman stepped forward. "Where are you from?" she asked.

"DC," Rosa said, her voice weaker than I was used to hearing.

"Well, you're here now. We don't live that way, the way they do in the cities." No declaration of arrival to the hallowed Oasis. "I'm Caroline."

Rosa stretched to shake Caroline's hand, but winced in pain from the injury to her mid-section. Caroline turned to the older man next to her. "We need to see Harvey," she said.

"I hope you live," said a young voice. It was the little girl who had waved to us.

"Eva, shush," said Caroline. Turning to us, she added, "Kids overreact."

Behind them, the gate blocking the road rolled open. For a brief moment, I thought I had just traded one walled city for another, and wondered why. I felt a moment of fear. It wouldn't be the last.

"You'd be better off driving up," Caroline said, looking at Rosa's bandages. I nodded. Caroline and two others climbed into a pickup truck just inside the gate. It was the first time we'd seen another moving vehicle on our trip. The oddness of it struck me.

Back in the RV, it seemed almost like a victory lap — one last moment in our home on wheels. I hoped it wasn't a last moment for Rosa entirely.

At the end of a small spit of land jutting into the lake, the road blossomed into a wide, sweeping loop. Inside the loop a huge building loomed, austere brick with wide, white-paned windows opening on the lake. Additional smaller buildings, similar in style, with brick and large windows, stretched off to the side, and there were even tennis courts and a pool. I felt like I was in a dream, seeing the way they lived out here in the wild. Around the grounds, individual homes made neat rows; these had the appearance of being built more recently. Outside the looping drive, tents appeared scattered through the woods. I assumed we weren't the only stragglers to find our way here. There was a parking lot at the end of the road. Several well-maintained cars and trucks were parked there, but many spaces remained open. The pickup parked in one of them. Caroline guided us into another space, and she and her friends helped Rosa out of the RV. Together we all walked to the large main building.

It was called the Hickory Knob State Park Lodge, and we were told it offered 76 rooms and its own restaurant. The restaurant was bustling as we walked in, although people turned and stared at our unfamiliar faces. My first impression of the building being a huge home for one important family — heightened by the sense that we were being taken to their leader — was way off. This was more commune than palace.

Nevertheless, we *were* taken to their leader, Harvey. He was an older, rather disheveled man, with a comb-over hairstyle to hide his mostly bald head. Ten years into the disease, and small vanities still prevailed. His natural posture seemed to be a sort of half-stoop, accented by a heavy-set build and sloppy, rumpled clothes. He stood up from a tiny, plain desk in the small office behind the lobby counter, walked over to us, and put out his hand. "I'm Harvey," was all he said.

The place was... well, it was filthy. We had grown used to a certain amount of unclean on the road, but still held ourselves to the sterile standards of the city. *Stay clean, stay alive.* But not here. If this was The Oasis, it was The Oasis of Filth. I was stunned. Rosa seemed too ill to care, but I saw it. It was so different from our lives behind the wall, even from our lives in the RV, that it was shocking. Things were *not* pristine. Things were *not* scoured clean. Had we just traveled hundreds of miles, risked everything, only to expose ourselves to the disease here? But these people. They looked healthy, even happy. How did they do it? They must have some answer.

"We need your help," I said.

"Hold on, now. Where're you from?" Harvey cocked his head.

"She's been infected."

I swear he rolled his eyes. "I know. Where are you from?"

"DC. Come on! She's infected!"

"And you brought her here anyway?" Harvey asked.

What else could I say? "I thought The Oasis was her only hope."

"You were probably right. And stupid as hell." Harvey was crass, but seemed to be very smart. I stared at him. Was this wise, or the stupidest thing I'd ever do?

"Help her," I finally said, tilting my head down as a wave of exhaustion set in. His eyebrows raised.

"You think we *can* help her?" he asked, eyeing Rosa's condition, her bandages tinted pink.

"Yes."

"Why?"

"I... I have no idea. But there has to be some reason. A reason why I met her. A reason why she knew you were here. A reason we got here when we did."

Harvey scoffed. "I haven't found much of life works with reason."

"But you can help her?"

He paused. "Probably... but you have to do it our way."

"I don't know of any other way," I said.

One last sweeping look, to judge me, I guessed. To judge *us*. Then his expression changed. He became very businesslike. "Then we should move quickly. She won't last." Harvey turned to look at the people around him. A glance, a nod, then they were all set.

They took us back outside, led us to a private cottage. Its front porch was made of wood, knotty and comfortably worn, and held rocking chairs that begged to be used in the afternoon warmth. We stepped past all that. The front door was open.

We walked inside. Rosa coughed, stumbled. She ended up on her knees on the floor. I moved to help her, but was held back. The cottage's lobby looked like it was wrapped completely in plastic. Two people grabbed my arms from behind and dragged me away. I saw Rosa, seemingly unconscious, being carried in another direction.

"Rosa!" I shouted. She was taken into a room with bright lights. The door closed and she was gone. I figured I would never see her again.

18

They took me to a similar bright room, and just like the lobby, it was covered in plastic. "What the hell are you doing to us? Let me go!" I shouted, with no results. The two burly young men in light-blue medical garb who were holding my arms took me to a hospital gurney in the middle of the room. I struggled, but they easily strapped me down, then left the room. I was lined up next to another gurney, where another person lay strapped down. The whole trip, the whole idea of The Oasis, was a huge joke. They must be taking in stragglers off the streets for some perverse game.

Thinking that the person next to me — a man, I could see, maybe 25 or 30 — was someone who must have wandered into their grasp, too, I tried to make eye contact. And I realized he was really, really sick.

He looked feverish, nearly unconscious. I remembered Noah, sweating on that first cool day. These people had just strapped me down next to a soon-to-be-zombie. Was this their idea of fun? Maybe they'd watch as he turned, then tore at his straps until he was free to come rip me apart. All that plastic would make for easy clean up.

Why hadn't we been more cautious? Rosa, well, she just believed. And I was desperate to get her help. It was a pair of fatal mistakes.

The door opened again, and Harvey walked in.

"You son of a bitch!" I started. He just held up his two large hands in front of him, calmly.

"Hold on," he said. "I know how this looks."

"Really? Because to me, it looks like you're about to watch us die, for sport!" Harvey seemed confused. Then he turned to look at the other gurney, and my meaning dawned on him.

"Oh." His eyes got slightly wider. "Oh. You think — well." He stammered, but also seemed amused. If I could have ripped him limb from limb at that moment, I would have.

He leaned over me, eyes darting around, checking everything over. "This is going to be really unpleasant for you, I won't lie." Then he did crack a small smile. "But not in the way you think. The man next to you is named Todd. But he *doesn't* have the disease. He has the *flu*." Harvey turned and walked out, and a nurse came in, dressed all in white, a strange reminder of Terry Rawlins, my nurse before the disease.

She took my vital signs without a word. Then she prepped a small rolling cart carrying a tray stacked with instruments. To my surprise, she pushed it over next to the other man, Todd. After a brief check of his vitals and a few marks on a chart that hung off the end of his gurney, she raised a long, thin, wooden stick with a cotton swab on the end. Peeling Todd's lips apart, she twirled the cotton swab in his mouth, covering it with his saliva. Then she turned to me.

She reached for my mouth, and a combination of terror and revulsion went through me in a fast wave. "No! Stop that — leave me alone!" I turned my head away. Her latex-gloved hand reached out, grabbed my chin. She was strong and clearly used to these feeble attempts to ward her off. She leaned over me while tipping my head back, and managed to open my lips with her fingers. I was desperate. I tried to thrash my head back and forth. I may even have snapped my teeth at her fingers to make her back away. It was all pointless. She stuck the cotton swab into my mouth, and Todd's saliva mixed with mine. I had the urge to throw up. Instead, I spat at her, hitting her in the face. She flinched, but only slightly, then turned and methodically cleaned up herself, her tray and instruments. She tossed the cotton swab in a trash container in the corner of the room, and left without another glance in my direction.

19

Her name was Marian. She was 56, Caucasian, a mix of English and German in her family tree. She was about five-foot-10, and built solid — a battle-axe, someone my age might have called her. She'd been a nurse in Augusta before the outbreak, and remained one afterward until the city fell. She didn't know where to go once the walls came down, but in that part of the country the rumors about The Oasis were more persistent, and much more specific. She joined a caravan heading north. Harvey was impressed with her right away and, after her own processing, asked her to help with The Oasis' medical staff. She was pragmatic. She knew what had to be done and knew she could do it. Now here she was, processing Rosa and me.

Processing was the official welcoming procedure for anyone arriving at The Oasis. It was standard for them not to tell you what it was until they got you started. Marian told me that they used to try to be nice and explain it up front, but too many people refused to do it then still wanted to stay. So Harvey declared, and the residents of The Oasis agreed, that everyone who wanted to stay had to be processed. A couple of the ones who refused turned belligerent. There was some bloodshed. But processing continued, and The Oasis stayed safe.

I had a lot of time on my hands. Eventually, after three or four episodes with the cotton swab, two men rolled Todd out, and I stayed by myself. I started to feel sick, but in a more *normal* sense — sore throat, fever, aches and pains. It felt... old-fashioned. They'd obviously given me the flu by introducing Todd's germs into my system. Marian kept me hydrated and regularly checked my vitals, marking them down on my chart.

I learned that it all started as an accident. Before there was The Oasis, when the first dozen or so people came to Hickory Knob State Park Lodge, looking for refuge, two of them were in the very beginning stages of the flu. The two men had been chicken farmers, and the common theory later on was that they'd contracted a strain of avian flu. As the others began to notice their symptoms, the group fractured. The majority wanted to send the two men away, fearing they were becoming zombies and would infect everyone. One person objected: Harvey. He was just one of the group then, not a leader, but he was just as forceful, just as brash, and wouldn't let them condemn the others to die. He volunteered to take the sick men to a small building and take care of them. And that's how he became the first processing nurse of the community that grew into The Oasis. Under Harvey's care, the men got better in a few days. Then Harvey himself became ill, and the people who had railed against his plan said it was fate, that even if he had been able somehow to save the two men, now he himself would become a zombie. But he didn't. Harvey's wife, Anne, was one of the original members of the group and couldn't just let him die, and so she entered the building and served as his nurse, caring for him until he got better. In a just over a week, when they felt certain it was over, Harvey opened the doors of the small building where he'd first taken the two chicken farmers and walked out, with the two men behind him. All three were well. The rest of the group was forced to readmit them, but remained wary. Anne contracted the flu and remained in quarantine, with Harvey nursing her to return the favor.

A few days later, there was trouble. Back then, The Oasis didn't have any fortifications, just the lodge itself. And given its size, they hadn't been able to check out the entire complex. With the flu outbreak seeming to have passed, they finally went through every room, closet, office, basement, and workroom in the lodge and the surrounding buildings. After going through most of the spaces with no problem, they became a little careless. They stumbled onto a group of zombies locked into a lodge room, and were overrun. Hearing the melee, Harvey ran to help and was bitten. Three others also became infected by bites and cuts — including one of the men Harvey had nursed through the flu — before the zombies were dispatched. In time, the group watched as all four began to show signs of the disease, and began making plans to execute them. And that's when they saw that Harvey and the other man who'd just had the flu actually got *better*. As the two others continued to turn, Harvey got an idea.

He rushed the infected men to the small building and into the room with Anne. Others shouted that he was crazy, that he would kill his own wife. But he wiped mucus from Anne onto the two men, took them into another room, strapped them down, and waited.

They lived.

* * *

I asked Marian about Rosa all the time, and Marian told me she was having a rough time. The disease was already working its way through her by the time we got to The Oasis, and the processing was adding even more stress to her body. But Marian thought she would make it. During the time Rosa and I were being processed, during the deepest part of our illnesses, other new people were brought in and strapped to gurneys next to us, and they began their own processing, kicking and screaming. It was a cycle that couldn't be broken, strung out in a chain all the way back to those first two men and their avian flu.

In a week, I was released. Rosa came out four days after that. And she was fine, with no signs of the disease. Somehow the flu had saved her.

So that was why The Oasis seemed so filthy. They didn't care anymore about keeping every spot clean, of scouring every nook and corner. They just lived. A little dirt was okay when you knew you weren't risking zombie infection.

Rosa became obsessed. She'd spent years trying to find any clue that might help eradicate the disease to no avail, and now here was clear evidence of a cure, right in front of her. She asked for as many details as she could from The Oasis' processing team. Marian told her that they had to keep a live culture of the flu at all times or it wouldn't work. They tried preserving it but didn't really have any idea how to do that, which meant a constant cycle of people had to come into The Oasis and be processed. If there was any lull and no living person carried the flu to the next person, the chain would be broken and the cure would vanish forever. Rosa dove right into the middle of it, setting up a makeshift lab.

As far as I know, she only took one break that whole time, other than eating, going to the bathroom, and sleeping. She came and saw me. She looked nervous, which was uncharacteristic. "Hey, what's wrong?" I asked, trying to get her to look into my eyes.

She wouldn't make eye contact, and for a time I thought she might turn and hurry back the lab. Then she put her hand in her pocket. "I just..." she stammered.

"What?" I said, as compassionately as I could. "Look, we've been through just about everything together. Whatever you have to say, just *say it*." Finally she looked at me. When her hand came out of her pocket, it was holding something tightly.

"I just wanted to say *thank you*. And... I made you this." She opened her hand. Inside, there was a thin, multi-colored twist of strings. She reached out, lifted my hand, and began to tie them like a band about my wrist. I looked down at her hands as she did it, and saw she still wore her colorful bracelet from her days in D.C. Where hers was made of bright synthetic fabric, mine used organic strings, cottons of various colors. I could only guess she collected them from around The Oasis. When she was finished, she pulled back a few inches to look. And we stood there, each with a colorful thin bracelet, different but still matching.

"I don't know what to say... I —" She interrupted me by quickly leaning in and placing a short, delicate kiss on my lips. I felt nothing but an electric sensation of surprise. Just as quickly, she turned and rushed out, back to her lab.

* * *

Harvey was thrilled to have a true medical researcher in the group, and so he fully supported Rosa's work. She was given access to anything and anyone she wanted. She took samples from everyone being processed. Eventually, she needed more equipment. Marian thought Augusta would be the answer — there were several hospital labs back there. The Oasis had scouting groups that routinely went out for supplies, so Harvey had Rosa make a list. She did, and even drew pictures of certain items. The scouts — a wiry young brunette with a long, braided ponytail named Janine, and a tall, muscled Korean kid named Hank — pored over her requests. Their reply: "No."

"What do you mean, no?" Rosa asked.

"No offense, but, these drawings... they're terrible." Hank pointed down at Rosa's sketches. "I wouldn't trust us to get the right thing."

Janine held out one of the pictures. "This round thing. Is this a plate? Or a ball?"

"It's a Petri dish!" Rosa shouted, throwing up her hands. "I wrote *Petri* right next to it! As many as you can get."

"Can't read your writing," Janine said with a grimace. "Sorry."

Hank was holding one of the other sketches. "What is *agar*? And would any kind of microscope work?"

"It's a solution for growing cultures... and.... Look. Never mind. I'll go." We all turned to Rosa, wide-eyed.

Harvey objected. "Now look, I know you've been out there, but you haven't been a scout and you haven't been to Augusta. Besides..." He stared at her with a serious look tinged with what seemed like... fear. "You're our only hope to truly fix this. I can't risk sending you."

She thought about that. "No. You can't risk *not* sending me. These two," gesturing at Hank and Janine, "will try their best, but they might fail. They'll *probably* fail. Then what? I make some more sketches and send them again? That's time wasted that we don't have. If we miss this window, if the virus dies out now, we may never — the *world* may never — have this chance *ever* again." She let the idea hang in the air like the fetid smell of a rotting corpse.

"Fine." Harvey was a practical man, after all.

"Me, too," I added.

Now it was time for the scouts to object. "What? Come on, but aren't you a little..."

"Old? Yeah. But I go with Rosa."

"He does," she added.

In the end, they couldn't object and still get what we all needed. So Rosa and I joined Janine and Hank on a mission to Augusta.

* * *

The next morning, we set out. Hank and Janine had a jeep fully outfitted for their scouting runs, but we had to take out some items to make room for us in the back seats. As we drove off, I looked at the boxes piled on the ground, and hoped we weren't going to need anything we left behind.

"What's in there?" I asked, gesturing back at the discarded boxes.

"Mostly grenades," Janine shouted back as the car accelerated and wind whipped around us, muffling every other sound. Hank nodded to the two young men holding open the gate as we drove through, then raced along the twisty wooded roads, headed first east, then south, taking us through the coniferous woodlands down to US

378. From studying maps before we set out, we knew that our options here were to turn left toward McCormick or right to cross the bridge into Georgia. Hank turned left without a pause.

"After the outbreak, the bridges were pretty much the first thing the military took out, especially around the walled cities," Janine said, pointing at the map. "The bridge here over the lake is still intact, but farther south we'd have to cross the reservoir on 47, and that bridge is long gone."

We rolled into McCormick not long after that. Rosa and I were shocked by what we saw.

"Did a tornado go through here or something?" Rosa asked. "Why is this town... *flat?*"

As Hank steered into town, he pointed to an abandoned bulldozer. "Harvey's orders. See that bulldozer? We used that and a couple other ones to tear everything down. McCormick isn't much, but it's the closest town to camp and we saw zombies in the area. Harvey thought it would be safest to just run the place into the ground, so there was nowhere for them to hide." Hank turned right onto Mine Street, aiming south again. A few blocks along, I looked across a wide parking lot off to the left. It looked like it used to hold something big, like a supermarket or one of those big-box stores. The building was flat, like everything else. I turned back toward the road... and stopped, whipping my head back to the left.

"Something moved," I said.

Hank continued driving. "What? A deer? Got a lot of those out —"

"It's a person," I said. I could see a man standing just off the parking lot in the scrub brush. He wasn't moving, but something about him was off. "Looks infected."

"No *way*," Hank said, slowing the jeep and following my gaze. "We cleared this place out."

"Couldn't one of them just walk in from somewhere else?" Rosa asked.

Janine turned to look as well. "It's possible, but we come through here a lot. We took everything the least bit valuable out of that supermarket before we knocked it down." Hank turned the jeep back toward the parking lot. I had my eyes trained on the spot where I'd seen the zombie. Another one appeared. A woman, from what I could tell.

"There're two now."

"Shit." Hank pulled into the lot, jumped out of the idling jeep. He grabbed a metal baseball bat jammed into a tube on the jeep that was probably originally meant for a fishing rod. "Where?" I pointed. Hank looked, saw the two zombies, began walking toward them. "Wait here," he said without turning back to us.

We watched Hank approach them. As the zombies noticed him, first the man, then the woman, they became enraged. They rushed at him side by side. His first swing probably destroyed the left patella and lower femur of the woman, young and pale, with a rat's nest of black hair. She gave an inhuman shriek and fell. Hank looked to finish her, but the other zombie — an older, pudgy bald man with dark skin that might have once been brown but was now a sort of gray — was already upon him. With an upward swing, Hank shattered the zombie's jaw into his skull, killing him instantly. He fell in a lump. Beside Hank, the female zombie gnashed and flailed, reaching for him, pushing toward him with her good leg. Hank took a second to plan his attack. Deliberately, he swung hard into the left side of her head, and we heard a combination crack and pop. Her dead body dropped beside the other zombie.

As we continued to stare, Hank inspected the scene, then turned to walk back to the jeep. He made it three steps. "Behind you!" he yelled, pointing.

Rosa and I turned and ducked in a fear-induced reaction, looking toward the cemetery on the other side of the road. Janine was better trained. As she pivoted in the direction that Hank was pointing, she pulled out her handgun, saw a tall, skinny infected man rushing at us from between the grave markers, and fired. The first shot grazed his shoulder, and he kept at us like nothing happened. Janine fired again, hitting him in the throat, and he fell in a gurgling rage of blood, flipping his body left and right on the ground next to a pockmarked gravestone. Hank climbed into the jeep, got it moving. When we looked back, we saw another zombie shambling in our direction.

Hank turned to Janine. "Radio it in. I don't know what the hell's going on around here, but we need to re-sweep McCormick." Janine picked up the CB.

After hearing what happened, Harvey made his decision. "You all keep going," he said, his voice as sure as ever, even through the crackle of the radio. "We need that equipment. I'll get some others out to McCormick to clean it up. Good luck."

* * *

We took 221 south along the eastern side of the lake until finally, at the southern tip, we turned right and crossed over the dam. It was still in one piece, although from the dead quiet I'd say its hydroelectric generators must have ground to a halt years ago. We continued south and west through the woods until finally we connected with Interstate 20. That took us almost due east, into the western fringes of Augusta. Marian had told us to look around the hospital there, because there were several labs in the area. We found the first of them behind the hospital, off Wheeler Road, in a collection of small, evenly separated brick buildings with neat, long parking lots — the standard configuration for medical buildings before the outbreak.

"Which one?" Hank asked Rosa.

"How the hell should I know?" She shrugged. "Let's try this one." She pointed to a small, ornate, tan building with a sign out front that identified it as a medical lab.

Hank pulled up in front, turning the jeep back toward the road for the fastest getaway in case it was needed and we got out. The plan was for Janine to stick with the jeep. We each had a walkie-talkie that had been charged at The Oasis. They only had six total, so the four they handed out for this mission was a testament to the importance of what we were doing. We checked all four of them to be sure they were in working order. I grabbed a tire iron from the jeep, and Hank got his bat. At his side, he also had a pistol. Rosa refused to carry any sort of weapon, saying she wouldn't know what to do with it anyway. Then the three of us headed toward the door. The day was bright, and we could see into the building through a panorama of large broken windows. While the place was a complete mess, it seemed to be empty. I thought it must have been ransacked dozens of times, especially in the first year or two of the outbreak, and began to wonder how many labs we'd have to hit to get the supplies we needed. Hank peered in the open windows, then went to the front door. He tried the handle, and the door swung open easily. He looked back at us, maybe trying to reassure us, maybe gauging our mettle. Probably both. He must have been satisfied with what he saw; he went inside, and we followed, Rosa in the middle and me bringing up the rear.

We passed through the destroyed atrium of the front lobby. A large corporate logo was half on the wall, half strewn across the floor in pieces. A desk of some dark wood sat topped with marble where a receptionist would have sat. Wires remained, but the computer that must have been on the desk was long gone. For a moment, although the space was larger and much more corporate, it reminded me of the waiting room at the office of my practice, and another lifetime of memories sprang up. Giving an amoxicillin prescription to a worried mother whose son was wheezing with a sinus infection, setting a broken tibia for a man who fell from the loading dock at his job, recommending an oncologist for an old woman who came to see me thinking she'd eaten something rotten. I realized I'd paused in the lobby as the others moved ahead, so I shook the cobwebs out of my head and continued after them.

Hank led the way through a door and down a hallway, but without the swagger he'd shown earlier. I could tell this wasn't his bread and butter. He was unsure of himself, looking for things he didn't really understand in a place he'd never seen before. As he moved away from the lobby, the light grew dim, so he turned on his flashlight. We each had one, plus a backpack to carry things out. Hank looked back at us. "In here?" he said, gesturing to a doorway.

"Try it," Rosa said, nodding. Hank prepared himself, pushed open the door, holding his pistol forward and swinging his light through the space in an arc. The room was narrow, with counters on each side and rows of shelves above them. A small sink beset with some sort of mold was embedded into the countertop on one side. The room had been gone over, who knows how many times. There were supplies strewn everywhere, hanging from shelves, on the floor, many torn open. After a quick check, Hank let Rosa enter the small room. She looked around quickly with her own small flashlight, grabbing a few items, mostly for sanitation, and stuffed them into her backpack. In a couple of minutes, she turned back to us. "That's all in here."

Hank radioed Janine to tell her all was well, then pushed forward down the hall, passing an open bathroom and an office with a debris-covered desk. He rounded a corner, leading us farther into the back of the office. The light from the front windows all but vanished. On the left, a door read STORAGE. Hank waited for us to join him, then opened the door with the same sweep of light as before. The room had been tossed, but remained full of supplies. "This looks promising," Rosa announced with a smile, pushing past Hank. "Come in here!" We all entered the room, and Rosa grabbed boxes, test tubes, a tabletop centrifuge, plastic bottles, and an assortment of sealed paper packages, jamming them into any backpack where they would fit. "Wow. We lucked out here," she said. "This stuff must look useless to most people.... Well, I guess it actually is useless for most people. But we're lucky to find all of it intact."

"Did you find everything you need?" Hank asked, hopefully.

"Yes and no." She swirled a plastic bottle in her hand, peering closely at it with her flashlight. "This agar powder is the biggest question mark. Conditions in here may have turned it bad. I want to get as much as we can before we leave. Can we look for more here?" Hank and I looked at each other and shrugged. *Why not?* We zipped up our bags full of everything Rosa had found.

Hank led the way again, into the hall, deep into the back of the building. On the left, he saw another closed door and moved toward it.

As he opened the door, we were immediately blinded by light. How was that possible, here in the back of this dark building? Hank swung his pistol and flashlight in an arc, but for a moment we were all blinded by the piercing glare. After a moment our eyes adjusted, and we could see we'd reached the far side of the building and were standing outside a room full of medical equipment. The light came from a door on the far side of the room that stood open onto the back parking lot. Machines glinted in the sunlight. Hank squinted and turned back to us with a wry smirk. "Guess we could've just come in that door," he said. Then we all heard a low rumbling.

Not a rumble. A *growl*. Hank jerked to attention, whipped the flashlight back through the room. In the back, under a space in the countertop probably meant for a chair... there were *eyes* looking back at us. First two large ones, then additional pairs, smaller, all catching the light. Hank pointed the pistol and flashlight directly at the eyes, and we saw... dogs. Or *a* dog. A momma dog, I presumed, and several pups. The pups looked at us in surprise and fear. But the mother bared her teeth in a vicious snarl. The growl grew louder as she realized how close we were to her litter. Hackles pleated her back as she took a step toward us. She looked to be a mutt, but a bulky, powerful one. Maybe part Rottweiler, perhaps part Bull Terrier. Her coat was a mix of black and brown. We stepped back, jamming the space with our bodies. I positioned myself between Rosa and Hank, putting her at the back of our ranks. If anything happened to Hank or me, it was important that Rosa get back alive. That the supplies get back, too. As we moved, the mother dog leapt forward a foot or so, asserting her authority. Could we blame her? Three strangers had just invaded her home.

Suddenly a shadow fell across the back doorway as another dog stepped into view. The daddy, I presumed. He was huge, much larger than the momma, skin bursting with muscles, and now he too began to growl, teeth bared. We stepped farther away. And they came for us.

I had my own gun, but only Hank had any kind of shot through the doorway. The female broke to our left, while the male went to our right, forcing Hank to decide which was the eminent threat. He chose the male. Not really aiming, he fired two or three times toward the rushing dog, hitting it more than once and ending its attack in a high-pitched yelp of pain. Whether dead or just injured, we didn't know. There was no time. We turned and ran, Rosa leading me, with Hank following behind. The female caught him at the turn of the hallway, grabbing his ankle with her teeth. Hank fell to the floor, his gun and flashlight clattering out in front of him. Rosa and I turned as Hank kicked at the dog with his free foot. She twisted and shook his leg in a rage, seemingly trying to tear it off his body. Hank screamed in pain.

Without thought, I raised my pistol and fired, hitting the female in the hindquarters in a broad splash of blood that sprayed the white walls. Another pained yelp. The dog released Hank, and he pushed himself up and lurched toward us. "Go, get out of here!" he yelled. We turned and ran, Hank limping beside us. He still had the sense to radio Janine. "Look alive, we need to move!" he said into the walkie-talkie. We passed back through the lobby and made for the front door. Through the shattered front windows, we could see Janine had backed the jeep up directly to the door and was waiting for us. We pushed outside, jumped into the waiting jeep, with Hank last of all. Rosa and I helped pull him into his seat as Janine gunned the engine. At that moment, the wounded, bloody mother dog ran out of the slowly closing front door and leapt at the side of the jeep beside my leg. Janine thrust into another gear and the jeep accelerated, leaving the dog behind. As we burst onto the main road and pointed toward home, Hank looked back toward the building, where the dog stood still barking at us. "I wish I had brought the damned grenades," he said.

* * *

Hank took off his boots and inspected his ankle. It was red and swollen, but there were no puncture wounds. Luckily, he had taken to wearing very thick construction boots, and while the pressure from the strong jaws was intense, I could see there would be no lasting damage. Janine guided us back the way we came as Rosa inspected the backpacks in the daylight.

It turned out that we brought back everything Rosa had on her list. But then she needed eggs.

20

After using the new equipment to make cultures, Rosa put samples of the flu into fertilized chicken eggs and incubated them. Then came the risk she had to make someone else take. Since Rosa had already been cured, she couldn't test the solution on herself. But in two days time, a family of three came into The Oasis, with their little girl already in the process of turning. She had been bitten by an attacking zombie while the family slept in a tent two nights before they arrived. It was amazing they all made it to The Oasis on foot after that. Rosa talked it over with Marian, and took the girl to the lab. They decided to try the egg solution. Cracking an egg, Rosa carefully went through a series of steps to extract the part she wanted into a beaker, then used pipettes to transfer the results into several test tubes. Loading those into the centrifuge we had recovered in Augusta, she set it spinning. After a time, she unloaded the tubes, extracted another portion using another pipette, and put that into a clean new test tube. She turned around with a tube half full of a milky, yellow-tinged fluid, looking at me with a nod.

"You're the doctor," she said, holding out the test tube and a syringe. Wordlessly, I prepped the needle and jabbed it into the girl's deltoid. In her feverish state, she put up no fight.

"A very small number of people are deathly allergic to eggs," I said while working. "If she is, she dies either way." No one seemed to appreciate my honesty.

But the little girl wasn't allergic, and she didn't die. In two days, she was alert. In five, she was out playing with the other kids.

Rosa had found a way to deliver a cure for the zombie outbreak, and it even came in a convenient carrying case, inside its own shell. She made dozens of egg cures. In just weeks, the original processing of new people was ended — no more saliva swabs, no more gurneys and restraints, no more anxiety and terror. Everyone who came in was just given an egg.

Soon, Rosa felt compelled to share the answer with the outside world. She talked to Harvey. "I want to take this to Atlanta," she declared.

Harvey, as usual, was nonplussed. "To the CDC, I assume?"

"Yes. I can show them how easy it is to reproduce, to transport. They can verify my results. We can tear down the city walls and go back to living." She was passionate about it, and Harvey agreed we should try.

"But it won't be easy," he said. "They aren't going to just swing open the gates for you."

I thought about nearly having been blown up on the highway. "Richmond shot at us," I said.

"Yep. Cities tend to do that." Harvey thought for a moment. "I can send scouts. We can test out the range of their guns and find a way to deliver your message without being shot on sight." As anxious as Rosa was, she knew it had to be done. Within an hour, Harvey had recruited Hank and Janine for the new job. The next morning they were on the way. We had to wait three days for their return. It wasn't good news.

21

Hank and Janine looked shaken. Harvey had gathered his inner circle, eight of the oldest and I assumed wisest citizens of The Oasis. Next to Harvey's office in the lodge, there was a large event room offering some privacy, so we met there.

"Atlanta fell," Hank said, with no preamble. "There's no one at the wall, and several pieces of it look like they've been torn down. There was a lot of smoke, too."

Janine took over. "A *lot* of people are streaming out of the city. They're looking for somewhere to go."

"Do you think they know where we are?" Harvey asked.

Hank and Janine shared a sideways glance, embarrassed, guilty. "Maybe," Hank said, looking down.

"Oh, my God, did you *lead* them here?" It was one of the inner circle, a thin, nebbishy older man with glasses, named Gerald. The rest of the inner circle looked around at each other; some made whispered comments.

"No!" Hank looked shocked.

"Hold on, hold on," said Harvey, raising his big hands. He looked at Hank and Janine. "What happened?"

Hank hung his head. Janine started, "He didn't do anything wrong."

Eyes locking on Hank, Harvey said, "Son, no one here is going to blame you for doing a job I sent you out to do. Just tell us what happened." Harvey glanced at the others, willing them to be patient.

"Janine and I have scouted around Atlanta many times before...," Hank began.

"The very reason I sent you this time," said Harvey.

"Right," Hank said. "So, we knew the area. We knew generally where the defenses were strongest. We took our jeep in on Interstate 20. It shoots directly into Atlanta going west, so we can get pretty close. They don't hold that area behind their wall, they're in the downtown and northern areas." He took a breath. "As we got near Grant Park, we knew we'd have to be on our toes. Around when there's the split for 75/85 North, you can see the downtown, all the tall buildings. There's a fence there, but it's too far outside for anyone to guard. It's good for cover, if you want to sneak up and take a look at downtown. We'd done it before, but we'd never seen anything like this. A few of the skyscrapers were on fire, the golden-domed one and some taller ones farther north. So we decided to come up to the southern wall as close as we could to see what was going on.

"Closer to downtown, Interstate 75/85 is the south wall. There isn't a lot of great cover around there, so we did it slow and stayed hidden. By the time we went a few blocks, we could *hear* them. There were people — lots of people — outside the wall." He paused.

"From there, we started to see people all over, but farther away," Janine said. "Lots of big groups, making caravans, headed somewhere. It looked pretty disorganized — people going everywhere. But a lot were headed east. We went in closer. I think we were just... *curious*. We'd seen the outside of their walls so many times, no one around, nothing but the possibility of getting shot. And now there were people."

Hank took over the story again. "So we were trying to sneak around... and we stumbled right into a group of people standing in the parking lot of a small old building, some kind of old store." Hank dropped his head again, but kept talking. "They were loading guns, gear, food, water — all into some pickup trucks. We tried to go by without them seeing, but..."

"But you don't *look* like them," Harvey offered.

"Yeah. The city must have just fallen within a couple of days. They were all still trying to be really clean, really neat. They had on those synthetic clothes everyone wears in the cities, so when they looked at us, they just knew. They could smell it on us and see it in every fiber of our clothing — that we were different." Hank set his jaw, drumming his fingers on the table. "A couple of them, they had another look: *infected*. But I don't think the people with them had noticed it yet. One of them was even the driver of one of the pickups."

Gerald interrupted. "You saw a *zombie driving a truck?*" There were gasps.

"We saw him behind the wheel," Hank said. "And he came after us along with the others. So, yeah." Hank looked around the table, at all of us, like he was willing us to understand how seriously he meant this.

Harvey thought it over. Then Anya, the oldest-looking woman in the circle, spoke up. "I guess we shouldn't be surprised. Rabid animals experience a period of behavioral change, they don't just immediately become hyper-reactive. With RL2013, the disease acts even more erratically. Sometimes the various stages are longer or shorter. An infected person might have many days when they can still maintain normal functions — including driving — even though they're progressing downward into dementia. But an infected person behind the wheel of a car..." She trailed off.

"Would be like a lunatic guiding a missile." Harvey completed her thought. We all stared at one another until finally Harvey turned back and asked Hank and Janine to finish their report.

Janine took a breath. "We dodged them all we could. We thought we'd lost them by the time we made our way back to our jeep. We took side streets to stay unnoticed; they must've taken the highway the whole way." Harvey nodded, silently prompting her to continue.

"When we finally got back on to 20 East to make time, we saw them in the rearview behind us. But not just those couple of pickups. There were dozens of vehicles. They weren't too close to us then, but we stood out. We were the only moving thing on the road in front of them. It was too easy to follow us."

Hank had been nervously drumming his fingers the whole time Janine spoke, but now he stopped. "As soon as we saw them, we knew we had to try to send them in some other direction," he said, "so we got off 20 and went south toward Macon." Hank pulled out a worn paper map to show us. "We did a bunch of zigzagging to try to throw them off. We saw them follow us south, a whole huge bunch of them. But we really don't know how far they went that way, or how convinced they were."

"Especially since there are rumors," Harvey mused.

"Yeah." Hank shuddered.

Harvey addressed Rosa and me. "We know from people coming into The Oasis that they've heard rumors, at least throughout Georgia and South Carolina: *Go to the border lakes.* So if these people from Atlanta have heard the rumors, we could be in for a whole lot of company."

Janine nodded grimly. "That's what we're worried about."

Rosa and I exchanged a careful, noncommittal look. This didn't seem like the time to let them know that some rumors had made it at least as far north as DC.

Vincent, another member of the circle, snapped. "We're doomed! I mean, we're *done* here, folks." He had the frantic, smiling sarcasm of someone who thinks there's nothing left. "Kiss The Oasis *goodbye!*"

Harvey's stern voice stopped Vincent. "How many?"

Hank returned Harvey's frank gaze, dead serious. "Based on the number of people we saw, if half of them make it out here, we'll be overrun."

Harvey stared at the scouts for a minute, thinking. I knew he'd been through a lot as the leader of The Oasis, but this was a challenge to dwarf all others. Then he spoke. "We can't support an entire city of people, and we can't turn them back if they want to come in. So now what?"

Harvey's eyes traveled around his inner circle. No words passed. Where before they'd blurted out what they thought or felt, now we witnessed the full effect of Harvey's strength. Through force of will, he kept them from losing the self-control, the sanity and judgment, he knew he needed from each of them. He looked to each one in turn. In my mind, I assumed he was saying, "What would you do? If you have an idea, speak it now." No one said a word.

After a long while, Harvey said, "We're peaceful people. Here's what we're going to do. We're going to set up a new perimeter, as far outside the current walls as we reasonably can. Every able person will help in the effort. There are lodges all through the lake areas, not just here where we are. We'll stop them and tell them that we can save them, as long as they'll do it our way. We'll cure them of the disease if they come to us peacefully."

It was a brilliant plan that had no hope of ever working.

22

The first of them arrived that night, in vehicles of all sizes: cars, trucks, RVs, tractor-trailers. Regardless of our planning, they would have broken through, and did. The time we had to make a new perimeter wall was not enough. To my knowledge, Harvey was never even able to present his offer of a cure in exchange for mutual peace. By the time our scouts raced to tell us outsiders were coming, it was too late. The new perimeter — a wide arc of thick wooden posts from freshly cut trees, not even half-finished — crumbled like tissue paper. Then the real gate did, too. There were groups of men with guns, families, women caravanning together, kids scattered among them all. Too many, too enraged. Not infected, just too worked up with fear, adrenaline, and desperation to think straight. They plowed through our defenses just to get at what we had: safety, serenity. They paid no attention to the fact that their destruction was the antithesis of what they had come for.

People died. Their people, fighting their way in. Our people, holding the gates, or protecting their loved ones at every lodge door and campsite. Once the main gate was breached, their vehicles streamed in. But it was a small road, narrow, bordered by Hickory Knob's dense woodland. They all tried to get in at once and quickly jammed up. Cars and trucks were locked against each other, with new arrivals piling up behind them by the dozens or the hundreds, or maybe even the thousands. From somewhere far outside the gate, past the new perimeter, we heard a terrible noise that sounded like the end of all things. At least for The Oasis, it was.

The awful noise grew, a gnawing, grinding din that soon absorbed all other sound, turning more and more heads, until finally everyone, all of us, people of The Oasis and the people from Atlanta, seemed to be stopped, staring, waiting. And finally, there it was. Emerging from the back of the line, clawing through it, crashing into cars, trucks, people, came a tractor-trailer dragging a huge tanker of gasoline. In a perfect world, or just a better one, this would have been a blessing — fuel for countless uses. Here, it was the worst of all possible scenarios. The huge truck drove through the smaller vehicles like a bowling ball through pins: everything was crushed, shoved aside, flattened.

Rosa, hearing the commotion, raced to the lab and grabbed as many eggs as she could in an effort to protect her work. Then she and I were dodging through the chaos, racing for some kind of safety. Without thought, we made for the only shelter we'd known since we left DC: the RV. But the roar of the incoming semi stopped us. As the truck approached, lights from the lodge buildings clearly illuminated the driver. His face was snarling, eyes wild. He made manic gestures, blood streaked across his cheek. He had the disease, and somewhere on the road from Atlanta, he must have turned. Now, our worst fear was smashing through the gates of The Oasis.

The truck slammed into one of the buildings on the north side of the lodge, flipped, exploded. The tanker of gas disappeared in a fireball beyond belief. Rosa and I were blown backward by the blast, blinded for a time. The entire building and anyone near it were torn to shreds, then burned on top of that. The zombie driving was incinerated. If only he'd known he was steps away from a cure, would that have done anything to change his actions? At that stage of the disease, I doubted it.

Through the smoke and flames, I saw Harvey standing in front of the ruined lodge, shouting orders, but I couldn't hear what he said. My ears rang. A group of young men confronted him, and he tried to block their path. One of them impaled him on a long, sharpened stick, and left him on the lawn to die, gurgling blood. Rosa shouted Harvey's name. We both sobbed. It was pointless. He was dying or already dead. Only escape would matter now.

Ironically, the same semi that destroyed the lodge had plowed an open path through the crowded road out, pushing aside all the vehicles that had been clogging the way. Rosa and I saw our only chance. We got into the RV and started moving. Confusion was our advantage; before anyone else could fill in the gaps, we shot toward the gate, now a ragged, gaping maw.

About halfway there, a handful of cars and trucks started to move again, swerving back toward the road, right into our path. Rosa rolled down her window and shouted, trying to make people turn their attention in different directions, away from us. Whatever it was that she yelled, it made people move. Again, Rosa's mind saved us.

With new vehicles continuing to pour in from the south, the road was rapidly becoming jammed again. We cut off into the woods, where the RV took a terrible beating. We drove slowly, both to preserve the vehicle and to avoid detection. Eventually, we met up with a state road running north. It was eerily quiet. We stopped for a moment and listened. Back in the direction of the camp, there were muted explosions, screams, sounds of pandemonium. Rosa reached for me and hugged me, tight, still crying.

From out of the woods on our right, a figure lurched, illuminated by the moonlight. A zombie, spasming and angry, stepped onto the road. He was maybe 25, strongly built, filthy hair that might once have been blond. He looked brutal enough to tear the door off the RV and rip us apart. Rosa gasped, gripping me even more tightly, but the zombie walked right past the front of the RV and didn't look at us. He was clearly drawn toward the light and noise from The Oasis. Then we looked down the road. There were two more zombies, then four, following in the broken footsteps of the first. With new urgency, I hit the gas and we started back north, leaving heaven on Earth dying behind us.

23

The next morning dawned, and we were still driving. We had turned east, then back north, once again traveling on the big highway, Interstate 95. It was mostly a random decision. I was in a daze behind the wheel. Rosa sat motionless in the passenger seat, the carton of eggs in her lap.

After a long time, she said, "We have to try to tell them in DC."

I was silent. In Richmond, they'd shot at us. In Atlanta and even Augusta, things just fell apart. Two people and a carton of eggs were now supposed to drive into DC and save the world? I scoffed. "What?" Rosa asked.

"I think it's impossible," I said. "We'll be tossed out. Or killed before we ever get in."

She turned in her seat. "Look at me." While driving, I spared a sideways glance. "I've never said it, but I love you. You mean almost everything to me. But the one trump card there is, is *this*." She gestured to the egg carton. "This is what I — no, what *everyone* has been looking for, for 10 years. If we don't do everything we can to get this to the people that can use it, we're less human than the zombies." She paused. "If *I* don't do everything I can to get this in the right hands, I won't be able to live another second of this life." She waited for my answer. Rosa was like that. She made passionate arguments, then sat back and let you digest them.

I thought about what she'd said. But I already knew my answer. I gave her another glance, looking into her eyes as long as I could. "Anything in my power to do to help you, I'll do. And I love you, too."

We had to stop to scavenge gas four times, but still made it to DC in under 12 hours.

24

If Richmond had enough defenses to nearly blow us to bits, we knew DC would be risky beyond belief. We approached the outskirts slowly. Unlike Richmond, DC had a big river guarding its southern flank. That helped us. As we drove up 395, we curved into view of the Potomac and of the classic Washington, DC, landmarks — the Washington Monument, the Capitol in the distance, the Pentagon right next to us. We stopped. I had no idea what to do next. Rosa led us off the highway. She said she wasn't quite ready. We found a small hotel and chose a room. It was a mess, but we could rest and think there.

Rosa told me she needed a few specific items, and the next morning we started looking. In a boating store in Alexandria, we found a flare gun, and in an abandoned police car, we found a bullhorn. The boating store had enough flares that Rosa took a few, assuming at least one would be good. But finding a battery for the bullhorn was another story. We spent more than an hour rummaging through convenience stores and gas stations to gather a handful of batteries, all of which had an expiration date years in the past. Back in our hotel room, she tried each battery until she found a combination that offered enough power to bring the bullhorn to life. "It only has to work once," she said, winking at me. Then she sat and gathered her thoughts. We both assumed this was a one-chance deal. Finally, we returned to the highway overlooking DC.

Rosa held the bullhorn and flare gun. I had the egg carton. We both hoped we were out of range of any cannon or gun the people on the wall might have, but knowing the government's penchant for military expansion, that seemed unlikely. We took the chance anyway, because there didn't seem to be any other options. And it seemed unlikely the guards would waste a lot of ammunition on two people who weren't even approaching.

Rosa looked at me. She smirked. It was the same smirk from so long ago, back at Eastern Market, on the other side of the river we now stood beside. I nodded. She raised the flare gun and fired. The fact that it worked startled even us. There was a blast, then a slow, fizzling, reddish ember burned and descended through the sky. Across the river, we could see people — just everyday people — who had noticed it. Thankfully, the world outside the cities was a relatively silent place these days. When Rosa lifted the bullhorn to her lips and spoke, I was pretty sure the people on the other side of the river heard her words.

"Government of Washington, DC, and the United States," she began. "We have come bearing no ill will whatsoever. In fact, we bear a cure for the disease. This is not a joke. My name is Rosalinda Menendez, and I worked for the NIH branch lab on Capitol Hill until I escaped the city a few months ago. I worked for the government every day for nearly 10 years to find a cure. What I found, outside the city walls, was that we were looking in the wrong direction. We were trying to eradicate all disease, to cleanse the body, when really we needed to realize that the body is part of a complex ecosystem and *must* have some infections, some bacteria, some viruses, to remain an effective organism.

"My companion and I traveled to South Carolina and found The Oasis. It really did exist, but it's been destroyed now that Atlanta has fallen. I'm sure you can verify that via your own methods. At The Oasis, they learned that patients who were infected with a strain of influenza — possibly avian — became cured of the zombie disease, even if they were in the process of turning. I spent some time researching this, and discovered that the particular strain of flu The Oasis used is a virus with bacteria add-ons that are vital to the overall cure. RL2013, the disease that has come so close to wiping out humanity, is part rabies and part leprosy. Rabies is a viral disease. Leprosy is a bacterial infection. The similar tandem of virus and bacteria in this flu strain seems to eliminate the virus and bacteria in RL2013. It even gives what seems to be permanent resistance to future infection."

She paused, looked at me, smiled. We couldn't see the faces of the people on the opposite shore, but I imagined them staring, some looking incredulous. A single spark can start a fire. Rosa was igniting new sparks with every word.

"We have here a carton of simple chicken eggs. Any of my former coworkers at NIH can tell you that eggs are effective for carrying vaccines. Each egg contains the flu strain needed to cure the zombie disease. From these few eggs, we can make hundreds, thousands, even millions of additional copies, to send around the globe and *end this disease for all time and for all people!*" Her words echoed across the Potomac, crashing into DC like waves of hope. In that millisecond, I could not have been more proud, more in love.

Her temple exploded before I even heard the shot. She fell. I didn't even think, just dove for her. The eggs flew out of their carton and broke onto the unforgiving gray pavement of the highway. Rosa, blind in one eye, looked up at me with the other, pleading. She couldn't speak.

I clutched her with force enough to drive the life back into her. Held her in my arms, my multi-colored bracelet touching hers, and willed her to live, with every word of conviction I knew. She was the savior of the world, come back to the city, the place that tried to take her away once before, come back to rescue them from their deepest fears. My tears ran with her blood. She died there, on that strip of roadway, in minutes. No idyllic resting place, just the hard tarmac of the street below her. I looked at the splattered eggs, the last hope for humanity. I thought, momentarily, about salvaging some of the fluid. Then a shot tore through my pants leg and ripped a chunk out of my calf. I turned my head toward the city. As I did, another shot missed my cheek by millimeters. I ducked.

In what seemed like hours, I looked at Rosa and said goodbye. I pulled away my hands and eased her down onto the roadway. Another shot. I rolled away, behind the RV. There was a general commotion in the city now, and it didn't seem to be coming from the wall defenses alone. After a beat, I ran and tumbled over the guardrail. I stumbled back to the side streets and found the hotel.

25

I'm back at the hotel room. I came here in a complete daze, no idea what to do. Now I know. There's no point in saving the world if it doesn't want to be saved — or at least if the people with the power don't want to give up that power so that others may live free. All I care about right now is Rosa. She doesn't deserve to spend her last moments as a human — alive or dead — sprawled on a highway, outside the city that killed her. Through my tears, I have decided to retrieve her body, and to take her somewhere else and bury her properly. Maybe The Oasis is calm again. Maybe she could go there? I don't care, I just can't leave her *there*.

These people. These *civilized* people. She told you what she had. And you killed her.

What have you done? Damn you.

I'm going to get her body now.

PART TWO

THE HOPELESS PASTURES

1

I reeled. The shock of pain and of seeing my skin torn open. The frayed wound began to spout blood, crimson red shining in the warm yellow light. Tilting my head up, I squeezed my eyes against the blazing sun. Blood dripped down, touching the multicolored band at my wrist, and I thought of her, not bringing her name to mind for fear of making it... real. I looked away as I reached for the raw wound.

I thought of her.

Her face, smiling through tears the day we arrived at The Oasis, rose before my squinting eyes, a phantom in the sparkling sunshine.

I closed my eyes, blocking it out. But my other senses betrayed me. Her sound was gone, her touch was gone, her smell was gone.

She was gone.

The blood. My blood. Her blood, flowing. I squinted in the sunlight, embracing the pain. This little pain. This little blood. This comparative nothing.

I waved my injured hand and grimaced. "Sonofa—," I muttered, grasping my bleeding left thumb. The blue crab fell to the dock, skittered sideways, and plopped back into the safety of the water. I looked down at my early-summer harvest of crabs in the boxy wire trap; not bad. In fact, compared to before the outbreak, it was pretty damn good. The crab population must have thought that the lack of humans was about the best thing to ever happen to them.

I considered the trap, wriggling with crabs of various sizes, and figured I'd better wrap up my thumb before picking out any of the others. I had chosen the first because it was the biggest, and paid the price of a snipped-off thumb tip. The others weren't going anywhere, so I lowered the basket back into the water beside the dock and trudged up to the small, single-story waterfront home I had adopted. For a moment I thought of the crabs in the trap, how they walked themselves in but had no idea how to walk out. Like we all had, to our own deadly trap.

Stepping off the small dock and into the long, untended grass, I looked toward the house, seeing it illuminated in the afternoon's warm sunshine. Some of the dry wood siding hung crookedly, there were long rips in the mesh screens of the porch, the screen door had fallen onto the ground beside the steps, and the roof was littered with pine needles and other debris. The better to make it look empty, I figured.

It had taken a long time to find a spot that would avoid notice. For a while, I wasn't even looking, I didn't care. I just wandered. I'd sleep on the ground when I was tired, not concerned about passing zombies. To me, it no longer mattered if I lived or died. I walked on with no destination, nothing but numbness. For no reason at all, I headed south again, this time following the river, then crossed what was left of the old Wilson Bridge into Maryland. There, simply because it was the direction the bridge faced, I turned east. When the bridge ended, I didn't follow the curving Beltway but instead left the highway and broke out east. It was days meandering before I reached the Chesapeake. The idea came to me to just *stop* there. To give up. I turned my head left and spied the long metal arcs of the Bay Bridge. Like a zombie myself, my feet simply started going in that direction. Maybe it was because the western shore had too many memories.

In time, I reached the metal feet of the long, sweeping bridge, stepped over some unguarded barricades, and began to walk the length of the southernmost span. I considered the emptiness stretching before me, feeling it appropriate for the emptiness inside me. I vaguely considered that the military must have cleared away all the cars to keep the bridge open for their needs. The military. That thought alone made me stop walking. I stood there, alone in the middle of the huge span crossing the bay, and looked at my hands, clenching them into fists. Unclenching. Clenching. The only sounds were the wind, waves and a few lonely birds. There was no one to hear, and even if there were, I didn't care. I wailed incomprehensible noises out to the sky, my body shuddering.

Finally exhausted, I gasped to refill my lungs. I looked down toward the low rail along the side of the bridge, considered the great drop to the water below, and envisioned myself there, falling to freedom. But my feet started moving again, seemingly detached from my brain or my heart.

Reaching the Eastern Shore, I turned and looked back. Unlike when I left DC those months ago, this time I did think about this last moment. I thought I would never come this way again. In fact, I hoped that was true. I wanted nothing to do with DC, or *humanity*, ever again. Looking back toward the west, I saw thick undulating clouds rolling, all shades of grey. Winter was coming. I took a drink of water, what remained, and walked on. On the far side of the bridge, cars were strewn like flotsam on the ocean, turned every direction, crushed into one another. An attempt at a great mass exodus had occurred here. Not a soul remained now. I had to leave the highway at times to make any progress through the wreckage, continuing on for days. The sheer number of cars trying to head west, piled up together and yet *empty* was mind-boggling.

Some nights I stayed in houses. Breaking in wasn't hard; most had been left open and abandoned. I found out that anything remotely near the highway had been thoroughly picked over, with nothing left to use. So I went deeper, using the highway, Route 50, as a branching-off point. I stumbled onto homes filled with scared, threatening families… people who had somehow made a life out here hunting and growing for themselves and didn't want company. I hardly noticed their confused looks when their threats of guns barely registered with me, but knew they felt relief when I moved on, leaving them in their version of peace. For days I followed Route 50, as the temperature dropped and the weather threatened.

I holed up in Easton, Maryland, for most of the winter, sleeping in abandoned strip-mall stores and houses. It was a desolate place. I had found a backpack and kept it stocked as best I could with dry foods, some canned goods. The winter was cold and snow was frequent, so travel became more difficult, as did finding food. When the snow would let up, I'd move a bit farther south. One old supermarket looked promising, a place to find a couple of cans to replenish my stock, but inside was a shantytown of dirty, tired souls, huddled together in countless little makeshift rooms. The people there were shell-shocked, hollow. They seemed to be a transient bunch, everyone there for just a day or two before moving on, making my appearance nothing unusual. The kids were the worst; they wore a kind of blank expression, like life had boiled down to the simplicity of *What am I going to do now?* mixed with the apathy of having asked yourself that question far too many times. As I walked among the rows of empty shelves and crowded hovels, amid the smell of too many people on top of each other, a commotion broke out in the back of the store. Some people raced to see what was happening; others were beyond caring. I suppose I fell in the second category, and that's probably why my presence didn't raise any interest; my hollow eyes simply mirrored their own. At the end of one aisle, I could see what was happening. Someone, a young girl, was turning. I figured she probably wouldn't be the only one to do so that night, so I made my way out.

Just as the weather began improving, my food supply was gone. I collected snow to melt for water, but I went without eating for days. One night, I sat staring out the front window of the small appliance store where I was sleeping, and felt pain all over. It was a profound physical weakness, like my body had finally caught up to my mind and decided this was the end. I contemplated the uselessness of it all and faded into a last sleep.

In the morning I awoke, hungry but alive, continuing this life of nothingness. Fate wasn't done with me yet. I found a small stash of canned food tucked inside a cabinet in the store, and ate ravenously. Still with no goal, I plodded farther south that day.

Just after Cambridge, the main road turned west and I turned east. Here, the density changed. Fewer homes, more open land. Approaching one abandoned house, I heard a shot ring out, a *whoosh* of air whipping past me. I stopped and looked up to find a man pointing a long rifle from an upstairs window. I turned and walked off.

Spring was approaching finally. One day, as I was dragging myself over the brown pine-needle-covered floor of some woodland miles from any highway, I spied something just barely peeking over the treetops, turning slowly. Coming closer, I saw a well-concealed wind turbine, the kind for generating electricity. I was suspicious of another warning shot, but slipping out of the woods, I found a low nondescript house that seemed truly abandoned. To one side of the house, past what appeared to be the cap of a water well, stood a small clearing for growing crops; on the opposite was the riprapped edge of the Chesapeake Bay. A thin pier struck out into the choppy water, with no boat in sight. Perhaps these people had given up their home and set sail for the western shore and the promise of safety in DC. Maybe they heard the bridge was blocked and the water was their only escape. Who knew?

Figuring there was a good chance that something or someone was still in the house, I explored it gingerly, room to room, thinking every creaking board could be sealing my fate. Finally, when I realized it was completely empty, I stood in the kitchen. Thinking of the spinning turbine outside, I flicked the light switch; nothing. I went to the sink and tried the faucet; also nothing. But I was exhausted and figured the house would make as good a place to die as any other. I stayed.

The next day, I decided to check on the turbine, an exceptionally delicate and dangerous process because I had no way to stop the blades from spinning, but I had to climb up and inspect the head unit anyway. The wind was light, but the blades still turned. I assumed it would be hopeless given what little I knew about electrical systems, but as soon as I opened up the head I saw the issue. The main gear, spinning around and around slowly, belying the danger one wrong move meant, was disconnected from the gear on the generator. Otherwise nothing looked out of sorts, so I figured it might have been built to detach in high winds or out of some other safety consideration. Carefully reaching my hand in, I tried spinning the smaller generator gear manually. It barely moved.

With the promise of electricity so close, the last thing I wanted to do was force things together and break them, so I climbed down and looked for something to help. I found oil in a small shed, and after a while of working it in, the generator gear turned comfortably. As I stood on the ladder rungs, bored from the repetition of oiling the gear but always watching the large blades spinning just a foot away, I saw a lever. A red and yellow sticker had been attached to it long ago, but now only tatters of color remained. I tried it.

The main gear extended on its shaft and caught with the smaller gear on the generator, now turning together as a unit. Despite my precarious location, I clapped my hands in triumph.

Back inside the house, though, nothing worked. I noticed a small metal out-building that housed a bank of batteries and cleaned them of debris and corrosion. I figured I had done enough for one day, and ate some of my last food stocks while sitting on the pier.

The next morning, with the sun not yet up and the woods outside just beginning to lighten, I walked into the kitchen. Incomprehensibly, I heard a low *hum*. My eyes widened, looking toward the refrigerator. Was it… *on?* I went to the light switch by the door. Expecting failure, I reached for it. Flicking up, I was blinded by electric lights. In shock, I quickly flicked them off again, peering out the kitchen window to see if anyone had taken notice. I scurried through the house looking out every window as if an attack was imminent. But as the sun slowly rose, nothing returned my gaze but the bay on one side and the surrounding pines on the other.

That night, I conducted an experiment, one that I repeated many nights. I flicked on one of the lights, still amazed by the power generated from the wind turbine, and stealthily went outside. Ducking into the woods, I made a long, slow circle around the house, gauging how the light travelled. The densely growing pines worked like curtains, blocking the light from passing too far from the house. Over the next few nights, I increased the number of lights and used the house's own shades to diminish the amount of brightness pouring into the woods. After about a week, I felt confident that this place was unlikely to be found unless someone stumbled directly upon it.

The only gap in this shield was the dirt driveway, and that wouldn't do. I found a shovel and dug up saplings of various sizes from the woods, then transferred them in staggered bunches up and down the driveway. I moved loads of pine needles onto the barren dirt to hide the worn pathway leading up to the house. It wasn't perfect, but it would do. The driveway looked like something fading back into the forest through time.

The water well was probably deep and hit some large aquifer, but without a working pump it would be useless. With electrical power now flowing into the house from the repaired turbine, I checked the faucet in the kitchen. I was amazed when it sputtered, coughed and spat air. After a lot more air and noise, it suddenly burst out with splashes of rusty water, then started to flow. After I let it go for a while, it ran clean with cold, wonderful, fresh water. The same luck didn't hold for the hot water, however. The large heater tank had a huge rusty hole at its bottom. As for toilets, I didn't even bother to try them. They were bone dry, and I had no desire to risk filling my new home with my own waste; I could dig my own latrine. Even the stove was electric. Given the situation, the randomness of luck, I couldn't complain. I had electricity, water, privacy. Still, I needed more food.

I found and planted seeds that had been stored in the shed. Squash, corn, tomatoes, onions. But it would be many weeks before anything came of those. The rain helped germinate the seeds, but I needed food now. I found blackberries growing wild, not yet ripe but still edible, near the edge of the woods. During that time, I took up fishing and crabbing — things I'd done from time to time, especially as a kid, but couldn't exactly claim to be expert at. Pillaging the shed outside the house, I found two rods, various fishing tackle, and a faded yellow crab pot. I spent a lot of time, most of my day, fishing or crabbing. Sure, there was the need for food to survive, but also it just allowed me to *do* and not *think*. Even in depression, I realized the bay offered an incredible bounty. With very little for bait, I caught a few small fish. Using those, I caught larger ones, and baited the crab pot. It was a cycle. I could see how the old fishermen and crabbers of decades past could become entranced by its simplicity and ever-revolving truth.

Scouting the nearest other houses, I found a side-by-side double-barrel shotgun, but only seven shells. I went hunting, firing three times at different rabbits before I finally got one. Based on that ratio and thinking how much spray each shot made and still missed, I went back to fishing.

Rather than spruce up the house, I worked at keeping it sound but shabby. The house was small, just one bedroom and bathroom, plus a living room and kitchen, but more than enough for a man planning to be alone for the rest of his life. I kept it nice on the inside, apparently abandoned if anyone caught sight of the outside. Honestly, if anyone had walked up, saw the windmill turning and the crops growing in neat rows and thought the place *wasn't* inhabited, I would've been amazed. But just in case, I kept up disheveled appearances. Checking a mirror in the house one day, I realized I'd done the same with myself. My hair was long, shaggy, and grey, and I now had a scruffy beard to match. I peered into my own haunted eyes, barely recognizing the grey-haired monster in front of me.

It wasn't long before I had company anyway.

2

In the warming spring evenings, I took to rocking on a chair on the porch and watching the sunset, differing blobs of bright orange, red, pink, and yellow dwindling in the western sky. Sometimes the clouds obscured everything and there was just an overall diminishing of light, but even better were the nights that brought a healthy mix of sun and clouds. The warm hues of the sun would bounce off the cool, inverted terraces of the clouds and make for a spectacular light show.

On one such night, leaving late spring behind and moving into summer's real warmth, I rocked on the porch with the shotgun across my lap. A long day of fishing and crabbing in the sun, plus weeding the small crops, had worn me out. Once the sun went down there was pretty much nothing to do anyway. So I drifted off to sleep.

A sudden rustling noise, very close by, startled me awake. Hours must have passed; it was dark. The lights in the house illuminated the nearest surrounding area but cast hideously confusing shadows one layer back into the woods. The branches to my right swayed as if pushed, and I heard the snap of dry twigs being stepped upon. I raised the shotgun. The sounds grew closer, and I strained to see anything in the darkness beyond the lights. In my head, I cursed the fact that I hadn't worked on maintaining night vision, instead opting for the comfort of lights throughout the home. Now my blindness in the dark left me vulnerable.

A step. A second. Pine needles sliding off some unseen form. And then the creature stepped out of the woods only feet from me.

Flicking her ears, the doe looked at me, unsure if I was part of the porch or something alive. She hadn't smelled me yet, didn't know I was there. I slowly aimed the gun at her plump brown frame, thinking of the many days of venison steak dinners that had suddenly been presented to me. Then the deer stepped left and behind her two tiny fawns, maybe a few weeks old at best, appeared from the woods, moving into the clearing. The three walked timidly to the crops I'd planted and lowered their heads to eat the fresh vegetation. I shook my head, unable to force myself to take this mother from her children just to prolong my pointless life. I stood up. Still they didn't notice me.

Walking down from the porch I called out, "Hey! Shoo!" and their attention turned to me. I waved my hands as they approached my small rows of growing food, and the mother snorted. With a deft turn, she bolted, bounding back into the woods, gone in and instant. The fawns rushed to follow, and in seconds there was no trace of any of them, not even a sound. I paused to look in the direction they'd left, smiling despite myself. A tear welled to one eye — sorrow? joy? — and I pinched the arc of my nose to clear my vision. At that moment, I heard a hiss like a gas line broken open just behind me.

I wheeled about and the zombie was on me. Bringing up the shotgun, I had time only to get it between us, then the thing was pushing me backward. I used the barrel of the gun to try to repel the zombie. He — or what used to be a *he* — was huge, with a large round belly slamming into me. He outweighed me by 50 pounds or more. I could smell the filth of his tattered blue shirt and soiled jeans. The rot of his flesh from lesions all over his body. I tripped and he fell upon me, taking the wind out of me with another, louder hiss, his breath blowing into my face like the reek of sewage, his spittle dripping onto me. The zombie snapped at me, we rolled left and right. Angry teeth closed inches from my cheek, my wrist, anything in front of him. We rolled again, but his weight blocked my movement, and he had a clear advantage. As he dug his infected teeth deep into my shoulder, I yelled in pain and pushed harder into the roll.

Now slathering at the open wound on my shoulder, the heavy zombie rolled with me, bits of his leprous flesh falling to the ground. How long had this thing, this *person*, lived this way? We rolled to the edge of the riprap with me on top, and I pushed upward, using the shotgun as a lever. Breaking his hold, I scrambled and stood, hefting the solid gun. The zombie raged at my feet, gnashing his teeth and struggling to lift his heavy form as I slammed the butt of the shotgun into his face. I raised the gun and did it again. There was no need to do it a third time.

I stepped backward, snagging my pant leg on the first of the two steps leading to the small dock, and fell back onto the wood. Sitting there for a moment, I panted to regain my breath. I looked around warily at my torn and bleeding shoulder, the darkness, the woods, the lonely moon above. I thought of the infection seeping into my blood, the death sentence of our world. I thought of my mind slipping, my flesh rotting, my soul leaving me.

After a while, my heartbeat subsiding, I leaned the shotgun on the side of the dock and walked over to the corpse. Stepping behind him, I pulled his arms over his head, trying to avoid breathing the scent or thinking about the horrible texture of the flesh I was holding. I turned the lifeless form around in the grass and managed to pull him up onto the dock. God, he was heavy. After a breather, I continued dragging him until we reached the end of the pier. I considered saying something, some words, some empathy or sorrow for this life I'd ended. Then in a rush, I remembered the zombie that had lunged at me... at us... from another dock, a dream from the past, and I simply kicked the body into the water. It floated for a time, drifting south on the outbound tide. As he gained distance, he took on water and drooped lower into the bay. The wound on my shoulder pulsed, blood streaming out, and I became dizzy, almost falling. I had a vision of this rotund zombie, his face smashed in but still snapping and hungry, pulling himself out of the water and returning to me as I slept on the pier.

I grabbed the shotgun and raced up to the house, locking myself in tight and hoping I wasn't too late.

3

Thanks to Harvey and the people at The Oasis, I wasn't *infected*, I couldn't be infected. But bleeding to death was a different matter. I tore off my shirt. The bite was deep and my provisions were light, or at least lighter than I would have preferred, thinking back to my days as a doctor. I had a needle, thankfully curved, and some regular thread of various weights. In fact, having raided a sewing kit tucked away in a closet of the house, I had many designer colors to choose from. I opted for a good thickness of purple thread — I wanted to be reminded it was there, so I wouldn't forget to check on it and eventually remove it. I had found a bottle of whiskey at a nearby farmhouse on one of my scouting trips. I downed a big swallow of the burning brown liquid, then put my supplies in front of me under the bright lights of the bathroom.

For good measure, I splashed some of the whiskey on the wound, thinking that while I may not be able to become infected with RL2013, I certainly could be infected with something else just as deadly. The lightning shock of the alcohol on my open wound tore through me, threatening to make me lose consciousness. That would surely mean death, and although I no longer cared if I died, for some reason my hands took over, stitching my shoulder back together the way I'd done for countless kids who had fallen off their bikes many years prior. As each stitch went through, the pain of the needle digging through my flesh, the excruciating sensation of my torn flesh being pulled together, I steeled myself and continued. Finally, the gash, while still messy, was closed.

Satisfied with the work, I covered it with a bandage. It seeped blood but didn't gush; I figured it would hold. Staggering into the bedroom, I fell into bed immediately asleep, the full weight of the night's exertion like lead on my muscles and eyelids.

* * *

The next morning, light filtered into the bedroom in waves, and eventually one bright shaft of light landed on my closed left eye. I stirred, groaned, and struggled awake. My shoulder ached horribly, and looking down at the bandage, I saw that the seepage had stained the entire bandage an unpleasant color, like dark, wet autumn leaves, tinged yellow, orange, and deep red. I stood, dizzy and swaying, my mind still fuzzy, and thought of swapping the dressing in the bathroom. Then I heard something outside.

A voice.

"Is it?" a woman asked from some distance.

"I can't tell," a man replied, slightly closer.

Frantic, I leapt up, staggered, grabbed the shotgun, and checked that it was loaded. Had I shot the zombie last night? Yeah, I think I did. Wait, no, it wasn't last night. I was having trouble thinking straight. Shaking my head to clear it, I concentrated. There was a zombie last night, but I didn't fire at it. I broke open the action of the gun and checked. Two shells. Pulling them out, I saw they weren't spent. Okay, I thought, I didn't shoot anything last night. Holding on to that, I reloaded the weapon and closed the action, heading toward the front of the house slowly and quietly. What the hell was wrong with me? This must be fever from an infection, affecting my thinking. Distantly, this mattered to me. Again, I shook my head.

"Looks empty," the man said. I heard footsteps coming closer in the grass. Then a pause. "Hold on," he said. "These are *crops* growing here. This looks new." There was a slight gasp and rustling, I assumed from the woman.

I moved into the living room, peering carefully out the windows. I saw dozens of camo-covered soldiers filing out of the woods. I blinked and shook my head again. They were gone. In their place, I saw only a single man, young, disheveled, a dark mat of messy hair over his rough black beard and flannel shirt. He approached the house cautiously.

Bursting out of the house, I pointed the shotgun at him. He froze. "Hold it there," I commanded. Why was I sweating? Behind him, I saw the young woman, curls of dark hair framing her dirty but clearly pretty face, now showing a look of pure terror. I realized faintly that she was terrified of me. My focus returned to the young man. "You want to turn around and pretend you never saw this place," I said, my voice rough from not having spoken in so long. He stared, eyes wide and hands up, empty palms facing me.

There was a pause. Then... "Please," the woman said. Her eyes shimmered with tears. "Help us."

It was a conspiracy. They wanted to take over the house, they were the government, probably military. I raised the gun. "Get out of here. *Now*," I growled. They both shivered in fear. I could tell they were military spies. I steadied the barrels of the shotgun, aiming at the young man. From my temple, a drop of sweat fell, and I blinked. These were just kids.

"Please," said the man. "We just need a little food, maybe one night. Then we'll leave you alone."

He was trying to trick me. I raged. Stomping down the front steps, I trained the barrel of the gun on the man's forehead. "You need to decide to leave now, or you'll never decide another thing again in your life." More sweat blurred my vision, skewing his terrified face into a mask of deception. Did he think I was stupid enough not to see through his deceit? Blinking again, I saw only two scared young people. I wavered, then held the shotgun high and firm, aimed at his head. Behind him, the woman gasped, and I turned my head toward her just as a young boy, maybe six years old, appeared at her side, clinging to her leg. The boy's eyes bored into me with a haunted look. The joy and innocence of youth was gone; maybe it had never been there. I faltered.

The gun drifted in my hands; the barrel dropped and my mind spun. The man in front of me turned and broke into a run.

"Come on — go!" he shouted, pushing the woman and young boy to flee in front of him, blocking them from me with his body. I looked down at the shotgun as they raced away from me into the woods. I shook my head again. Who was this? This person who threatened children with guns? Was this really me? I blinked again.

"*Stop!*" I yelled. "Stop! Come back!" I meant it plaintively, but it came out gravelly and rough.

I raced after them, staggering. If it weren't for the boy, I never would have caught them. But he was young, with small legs and little stamina. I cornered them in a gap in the pines. "Stop! Hold on a minute!" For a moment we all stood there catching our breath.

The man and the woman looked at me in terror, shielding the boy behind them.

"We don't want any trouble! We'll leave. We just wanted a place for one night," said the man, nearly in tears. I realized my shotgun was trained on them; one simple pull could kill all of them.

Damn it, I needed to get a hold of myself. I lowered the gun.

"Wait, you don't understand," I muttered. The demons in my mind fluttered again so I shook my head, wiping sweat off my forehead. "Take the house," I said.

They looked at me, unbelieving, seeing me waver and shudder in pulses of fever.

"What are you saying?" the young woman said, her tears marring her beautiful young face.

"Take my house. I'm old, I don't matter," I slurred. "There's… there's nothing left for me, anyway." This was the right thing to do.

To give them a chance. I no longer needed a chance, or even cared to have one.

They looked at each other, to the boy, who I assumed was their son, and then back to me. The dawning joy, the elation in their eyes was evident. "Well, hey, mister. We don't need to take it from you. Maybe just share it, okay?" the man offered, stretching out his hand toward me. Why was he *lying to me*? Why was he trying to *steal from me*?

In a haze, I became jealous and enraged. As he stepped toward me, I raised the shotgun again. There was another gasp. The man stepped back toward the woman, shielding her and the boy.

"We need to go," the man said pointedly over his shoulder to his family. The woman nodded, holding the boy tightly. "I think he may be…" The man nodded toward me. I may be… *what?* I thought. Of course. The seeping shoulder wound, the fever, the behavior. He thought I was *infected*. I raised one hand to wipe sweat out of my eyes, clearing my vision. I stopped aiming the gun at them and just held out my hands in a gesture of peace.

"No, no, sorry, really…" Looking to the side, I saw blood dripping down my arm, the bandage badly in need of change. They pulled together and stepped backward, away from me.

I didn't know what to do or say. Suddenly a rush of fever came over me and I fell to one knee, catching myself with the gun as a crutch. They took the opportunity and ran, back into the woods, away from me.

The delirium held me momentarily and I couldn't move. "No!" I shouted. They just ran. I briefly envisioned this family raising their boy safely in my small, secluded house, but they ran away and so did the vision. "Wait!" I said, barely above a whisper. I heard nothing but fading footsteps, rustles on the forest floor.

I reached out, feverishly, toward the sounds growing more faint... and fell face first into a thick pile of pine needles and dirt.

4

Eyes closed, I laid still on the forest floor. Hours passed. The fever did its work. One moment, I felt a chill so deep in my bones that I curled up on the ground for warmth, grabbing my knees in a ball. The next moment, a heat so intense swept over me that I splayed out as if trying to make snow angels in the dirt. Was it four hours? Eight? More? I don't know.

I faded in and out, sometimes eyes open just an inch from the dry brown pine needles, sometimes looking up at the trees as the sun moved across the sky. I dreamt of the young family, huddled in a forest like this one. I watched them as a horde of zombies stumbled across them, tearing apart the parents, leaving the boy alive but infected. My mind fast-forwarded to the boy now a zombie, wandering the woods with mad, dead eyes, looking for me. The chill returned and I balled myself up again on the ground.

Finally, the fever broke and I woke up, filthy from sweating, seeping blood, and rolling in the dirt and pine needles. I looked up at the sky, colors dwindling to darkness as the sun set somewhere off to the west. With my mind finally clearing, I thought about what I should do, what I *should have done*. I vowed to give up the house to the next tired soul to pass my way. Maybe I'd stay a while, help them get settled, but it would be *their* place, not mine. A calm certainty came over me. I knew that once I left the house, I would reach my end. All avenues would have been played out and my story would be over. It was comforting. I'd already come to terms with the possibility of death, didn't fear it. Now I was embracing it, circling it on a calendar almost. Lying there, looking up at the darkened sky, I smiled. I let loose a harsh chuckle, laughing at the pointlessness of everything after all these years.

To my right, there was a sound in response. A low growl.

Turning my head slowing, squinting and blinking to adjust my vision, I saw a dog. When was the last time I saw a *dog?* Low and wide, he stared at me with teeth bare, his coat a mass of curly brown fur matted with dirt, wet in places. He stood his ground, maybe 10 feet away. Keeping my face turned toward him, I used only my eyes to look down at the shotgun. It sat maybe 18 inches from my right hand. I slid my hand toward it slowly. And the growl grew deeper, bubbled into a bark, then back to a growl. The dog's powerful body shuddered, front legs locked in an upside-down V, head low. He took a step toward me and instinctively I flinched. The motion made him stop, unsure, but increased the loudness and force behind his growling. Stretching out, I'd covered half the distance to the shotgun.

Snapping and barking, the dog took three quick steps, almost a leap, toward me. I pulled back, then he did the same. As he retreated, he circled to the left. I lunged for the gun and grabbed at it, then staggered backward and stood, pulling the barrel up in a sloppy aim toward the dog. He barked again as I trained in on his large, shaggy head. My finger settled on the trigger, and in an instant the dog would be dead or dying. Looking into the dog's eyes, I could see the fear, the desperation. A tired soul who had accidentally stumbled upon me and now faced the end of his short, probably miserable life. And I remembered my vow. To give up my house to the next tired soul passing by.

Why was I, once again, ready to inflict harm or even death to maintain my wretched life? A life too long, with no one left in it.

I lowered the gun and flopped down, settling on the ground with a dull thud. I looked at the dirt between my knees, the pine needles tossed in several directions. All of the fight left my body, I became calm. The dog growled, sliding farther left, unsure of what to make of this change.

And then I heard it. Silence.

The dog had stopped growling. Peering up through my shaggy grey hair, I saw him looking at me with his head tilted to one side, curious. Seeing me looking at him, he regained some of his fearful demeanor, a slight growl popping out. I looked down again.

After a moment, I heard him padding across the ground, getting closer, slowly. Without raising my eyes, I lifted one hand slowly. He balked. I froze. Another moment, another step closer. Then I felt his hot breath on my knuckles, sniffing me. He growled again, teeth bare, no more than an inch from my hand.

I just gave up, gave in, didn't move.

And the dog licked my hand.

5

The dog followed me back to the house and I gave him the scraps from my dinner. I grilled one of the rockfish I'd stored in the small fridge, augmenting that with some of the greens and berries I'd collected. Actually, I made too much for myself on purpose, giving the rest to the woeful-looking dog as we ate on the porch. His drooling reached epic proportions, pooling around his front paws as he stared at me. The intensity of his gaze, looking not at me but only at the *food*, was unbelievable. After we finished, I went inside and washed the few dishes, using a little of the water from the tap. I fully expected the dog to be gone by the time I returned to the porch, but there he was. Lying with his front paws dangling off the porch and on to the first step, he surveyed the yard like he belonged there. I took up my customary place in the rocker. When I eventually went to bed, the dog was lying on one side, breathing heavily, asleep.

* * *

In the morning, I got dressed and then stepped out onto an empty porch, feeling an unexpected pang of sadness that the dog was gone. I went back inside and ate a breakfast of dried strips of rabbit — nearly my last — and berries. Sitting at the kitchen table, I couldn't shake the wave of depression coming back over me. I decided to go check the crab pot to have something else to do. I left the house, the front door banging closed behind me, and trotted down the front steps, headed for the pier. About halfway across the distance, I froze. There was a splashing noise. Renewing and increasing my stride, I made it to the pier only to find the dog splashing about in the shallow water past the riprap. He was frolicking and drinking the bay water with glee. I couldn't help the sense of elation I felt. Looking at his curly brown fur, seeming to repel the waters of the bay off its oily surface, I remembered a similar dog owned by a cousin of mine many years before the outbreak. "Chesapeake Bay Retriever. That's what you are." The dog looked up momentarily, then went back to gulping the murky water.

I thought about what he was doing and realized I'd better stop him. "Whoa, whoa. Hold on there, dog." The bay water, though brackish and not as salty as ocean water, would certainly do a number on the dog's digestive tract. "Come here, come on up here!" I yelled, clapping my hands and whistling. He looked up and trotted over, climbing awkwardly across the rocks of the riprap. When he got to me, I looked him in the eye as if to reason with him. "Don't drink from the bay, it's not good for you." As if in response, he shook himself, spraying brown salty water all over the place, and all over me. Wiping flecks of mud from my face and arms, I turned toward the house.

Inside, I walked into the kitchen. Checking through the cabinets and the cupboard, I found an old metal bowl. I filled it with some fresh water and walked out to the porch, placing the bowl down for the dog. He lapped it up happily. "Bet you're hungry, too, eh?" I gave him the last strips of rabbit, but he refused the berries. Worse, he mouthed and slobbered on the fruit, but refused to eat it, leaving me with dripping, gooey berries to consider cleaning or throwing out.

I thought about other food options, knowing this wasn't enough for the dog. He had eaten fish, so that seemed like a good choice. I cooked him up some more, this time a croaker, and he ate it happily. But I thought about how much more food I'd have to catch and store to feed this second mouth. Then I remembered the crab pot.

Checking the pot, I found it full. I dumped all the big ones into a wooden bushel basket and carried them up to the house. I thought I would boil some crabs for dinner, for me and the dog. That day, I tended my rows and did some fishing. Later on, I began work on our crab dinner. After all the prep work and boiling time, and after pulling all the meat out to lay it in front of the dog, he turned up his nose, refusing what I thought was a feast. I ate what I could and stored the rest, making a mental note that fish were okay but crabs were not. This complicated our food situation.

Deer were plentiful in the area, often walking through in the morning and late afternoon. I considered using the shotgun to take one down, providing meat for the dog and me. After a moment's review, I laughed off the idea. First, I wasn't much of a hunter. Second, while my medical training gave me a pretty good idea how to do it, I'd never gutted and cleaned a deer, and the thought of it was daunting, especially at my age. But most importantly, where would I put it all? I had one small refrigerator, with a tiny freezer box on top. I could store 25 pounds, maybe, if I crowded it in with the fish and other stores I already had. I guessed a deer would yield about 50 pounds of meat. Any way you looked at it, I'd be wasting a hell of a lot of meat hunting deer. But rabbit... that might work.

After the dog had been with me for about a week, my supply of fish was dwindling. It was time to try something else. I grabbed the gun and we headed off into the woods toward a clearing where I knew rabbits liked to congregate. I found us a secluded spot on the west side of the open space and we waited. One by one, the little rabbits appeared, heads bobbing in the shaggy grass. I pulled up the shotgun, but none was close enough for me to feel comfortable firing. As I waited for them to get closer, I noticed the dog sit up in excitement. At first unaware of why we were here, now he had seen the rabbits.

Immediately turning predator, the dog slunk down and nosed forward. I dropped the gun barrel, watching him. Inching forward, he got closer and closer to the rabbits as they foraged through the small field, oblivious to what was happening. One rabbit strayed just close enough to the dog and in an instant the chase was on.

The dog turned left as the rabbit arced in fear. Right, then another left. The rabbit alternated swift turns, sometimes flattening its body, sometimes just outright running. The dog leapt after it, tearing up dirt and grass, and the rabbit appeared to be getting away.

I saw that the rabbit would be into the woods in seconds and figured the chase was done. But at the last minute, the foolish rabbit swerved left again and the dog cut off the angle. Suddenly, the frenzied chase was over. The dog closed his jaws on the helpless rabbit and shook his head, over and over, snapping the rabbit's neck. It hung limply out of both sides of the dog's mouth, pathetic and near death, gasping.

Dropping the rabbit to the ground, the dog put one front paw on the pitiful creature, then bit into it and pulled. With a splash of blood, the dog tore the still-living rabbit open and began to pull off bits of warm flesh to eat. I froze.

The sheer brutality of the dog ripping the rabbit apart, the sense of glee with which it happened, was shocking. The clamping teeth biting and tearing living flesh. It reminded me of the zombies themselves. Seeing the rabbit pinned down, being savagely pulled apart, I thought of Rosa lying on the highway, a zombie ripping at her torso, the same brutal intent. Rosa. It was her name that shocked me. Her name welled up in my mind, a name I'd put aside. A name that carried so much pain now. The vision was so clear, it was like I was there, coming around the RV to find them on the street together, and not standing in the clearing of the woods. I squinted and blinked, wishing the vision away.

I couldn't watch. As the sounds of the hideous death continued to play out, I turned and walked back to the house, leaving the dog behind.

* * *

Back at the house, I fell into the rocker on the porch.

Rosa.

I hadn't even thought her name, on purpose, in… how many weeks? Not to shun her memory, but because it was too painful.

Unbidden, I thought of her holding the bullhorn, her last smile. Absently rocking in the chair, I thought of the futility of my entire life. First a doctor, taking advantage of the perks of my position in the community and living off the largesse of the sick and old. Then, when I was needed most, failing to see the full scope of this disease until it was too late. Ten years spent like a rat in a trap. Then Rosa, and hope. But for what? The danger of our journey, yet the hidden joy of *her*, just being there with her. The Oasis. All of our efforts — all of *Rosa's* efforts — to turn a haphazard cure into something viable. And then destruction, everything lost again. She and I in one last mad dash, to a final hope that betrayed us, betrayed *her*.

I saw her head snap back, her blood fly. I watched in slow motion, over and over, the final second of her life. Rosa. Rosa. *Rosa*. I thought of her name, searing it into my mind, accepting it again, along with the pain it brought. I wept. She was gone, and so were my last shreds of hope. Looking down at the multicolored bracelet she'd made for me, I twirled one edge of it aimlessly. Peering closely, I saw a frayed end. Turning the bracelet around, there were more… two, three, four. How long would it last? She was gone. How much longer did this object of her memory have? The idea of it one day snagging on a branch, falling to the ground unseen, left to waste where no one would ever find it again, left me sobbing, remembering her.

The last time I spent with her came back to me, the time when the absolute devastation of her death hardened into thoughtless action. Walking onto the highway, oblivious to gunfire, hearing shouts and commotion from DC. Gathering her in my arms and carrying her to the door of the RV as another bullet tugged at a loose bit of my sleeve. I dragged her limp body inside and placed her gingerly on the bed, watched as her blood drained onto the pillows and sheets. For a moment, I stood over her, watching her in death. I got in the driver's seat and turned the RV around as shots from the DC wall shattered the windshield. Unconcerned with my own possible death, I drove. Heading back south on 395, the RV started to fail. Steam or smoke came out from the engine in short bursts. I knew I wouldn't be able to take it far. I got off the highway, but the next road was too big, too many buildings, too much pavement. I cut across an access road, made turns more by feel than by choice, then turned south again, now on a wooded road just beside the river. The billows of engine smoke became more frequent, then constant. I scanned the area for a place, a good place. Seeing an old, faded sign for a marina, I turned and followed a thin strip of road into a wooded piece of land that jutted into the river. The RV sputtered. I found a secluded bit of field surrounded by woods, and I stopped and turned the RV off for the last time. Billows kept coming from the hood. I stepped back and looked over Rosa's body. But this wasn't Rosa, this humorless, warmthless, lifeless form. I took a last long look, like a scene from a dream, and walked outside, deciding to put her name away in my mind like a time capsule.

Not wanting to simply leave, and having no way to bury her, I chose to make a funeral pyre. I took the small curtains from the RV's windows and tore them into strips, tying some together to make longer pieces. Opening the gas cap, I fed them into the gas tank as far as I could without losing a grip on them. One by one, I placed the soaked rags inside the vehicle. Outside, I found rocks, slamming them into one another until I found ones that seemed to be better at making sparks. I sat inside the RV, reeking of gas fumes, and tried to spark the gas alight over and over, until one finally one caught. I spread the flame around to the several rags, then left, gasping for clean air.

I watched as the RV burned. *As she burned.* She was being burned out of the world, into my soul. "Goodbye, my love," I whispered.

When a dull *whump* announced the first of the explosions, I turned, tears streaming. My feet had started walking, south.

* * *

I noticed that the dog had come back.

He sat next to me, patiently, nosing my arm to get my attention. Had he been there just seconds, or had it been hours? I looked down at him, his muzzle covered in dark blood. Contrasting this reminder of his brutal killing of the rabbit, his face was curved in what seemed to be a smile. His tongue lolled out, panting. Despite myself, I smirked, even chuckled slightly. He was, after all, just a dog.

"Come on," I muttered, gravel-voiced, "we need to clean you up." I led him down to the bay, and encouraged him to wade in. As he dropped into the water beside the dock, a duck leapt out from under the wooden structure, quacked noisily and was scared into flight. The dog was engaged and raced over to the dock. There was another sound under the wood. The dog closed in and I realized a second duck was under the dock, nearest to the shore. It was confined and confused, unable to get out as the dog cornered it. Quickly diving in, his predatory nature returning effortlessly, the dog attacked. I sighed. *Again?* I turned and looked back toward the house, putting my hand before my face.

And behind me, the dog grabbed and shook the duck. I didn't want to see it. There were splashes, footsteps, and an eerie silence.

I lowered my hand, and there the dog sat, directly in front of me. That same odd panting expression, like a smile, was on his face. He looked down, then back up at me. I looked down.

The dead but wholly intact duck lay at my feet. An offering, from the dog.

Again, despite myself, I smiled, thinking of roast duck for dinner.

"The faithful-servant routine, eh, dog?" I asked. He cocked his head to one side. Faithful servant. I reached down and picked up the duck by its limp neck. "You know what? If you're going to hang around, you need a name." I thought it over. "As my faithful servant, I think 'Adam' would be a wonderful name. *Wither wouldst thou have me go, Adam?* You know, *As You Like It?*" I chuckled at the ridiculousness of it. Then, as the midsummer sun waned in the western sky, the dog trotted into the grass, squatted down his hips and urinated. I'd never had a dog before, and had already seen this dog pee many times, but it finally dawned on me. I laughed out loud at how blind I had been.

"Wait a minute, Adam. You're not a boy at all. You're a girl." I paused, considering this. "How about *Addy* instead?"

She barked, as if to confirm the name.

6

Roast duck for dinner. My mouth watered thinking about it. Addy was way ahead of me, drooling throughout the cleaning and prep of the bird. For this special occasion, I decided we would cook outside by the water.

Using smaller rocks from along the riprap, I made a fire circle by the pier, dragging dry wood in from the forest. I'd scrounged some matches from a nearby house, and carefully used them to light some paper under the kindling. The stove in the house was electric and easy, but I clearly needed more practice with starting campfires because it took me five matches to get the thing going. I only had 14 more after that.

The sun was setting across the bay as I gathered my gear for the roast. It was quite the feast. I used some bigger rocks to form an opening where I could rest an iron skillet from the kitchen and tossed in some new potatoes I discovered growing near the garden. For the duck, I made an impromptu spit out of sticks, allowing me to turn it over the fire. I wasn't at all sure how long to cook it, so after a while I started prodding and testing the meat every five or 10 minutes — probably because I was hungry and had nothing else to do. As it got closer to done and the potatoes were softened, I added some peas to the skillet as well. Finally, unable to take the wait any longer, I pulled the duck off the spit and cut it into steaming pieces on a plate right there beside the fire. I tossed a big handful to Addy, and they were gone before they hit the ground, her focus intense on my every move. Grease dripped down my chin as I enjoyed every warm chewy bite of the bird, then sampled the potatoes and peas, savoring the most delightful set of tastes I'd experienced in a long time. The smell alone was divine.

The smell.

I noticed a low pair of eyes watching us from a short distance off in the darkness. Thankfully, I had 50-plus years of exposure to the world prior to the outbreak, so I presumed that the little would-be thief was a fox. I was right. As he circled, taking in the smell, I could occasionally see glimpses of his dirty reddish fur in the firelight. Addy saw him, too, but clearly didn't consider him to be a threat, as she failed to even get up or stop chewing her bits of duck; her only concession to the fox was to turn and follow him with her eyes as he moved. She had no plans to let him steal any of our food.

Suddenly, the fox's eyes darted right and he looked back toward the house. In an instant he was gone, scampering off in the other direction. Moments later, the hackles on Addy's neck went up and she froze. Approaching slowly, eyes reflecting the flames, was a much larger beast, a coyote. A coyote on the Eastern Shore? That wasn't something I was familiar with, but given that the natural world had more than 10 years to rebound from humanity's effects, I supposed anything was possible. It came close enough for us to see its size, around the same as Addy. It sniffed the air and licked its lips. Clearly the roasting duck was broadcasting our presence for untold distances. Addy finished her piece of meat in a gulp and got to her feet, keeping low in that upside-down-V pose, like when I first met her. A low growl began to come out of her throat, and was met by a raspy echo from the coyote. The thing just looked sketchy, like it was built for trouble. It traced a slow arc around the fire while keeping its eyes on Addy, sizing her up. The dog stood her ground, keeping the coyote in front of her as it moved. I looked down and realized the shotgun lay only feet from me. Dropping a bit of duck meat and spilling some potatoes, I set down the plate and reached for the gun.

I knew there were only a few more shells, and the noise of the gun would only add to the attraction of the smell we'd been sending into the forest. I scanned the ground as the coyote took steps closer, gauging. Grabbing a rock about the size of my fist, I threw it, hard, at the mangy beast. It sidestepped and was only barely clipped on one leg. It barked a bit at the affront, still staring at Addy. Finding a second, slightly larger rock, I threw again. This time I scored; with an *oof*, the rock thudded into the ribcage of the coyote. It turned its head my way for once, finally considering me as a threat, too. It let out several deep barks toward me. Addy echoed them, regaining the coyote's attention.

I reached for more rocks, grabbed two, and quickly launched both. One flew just over the coyote's neck, causing it to duck. By chance, the next throw was low, smacking the coyote dead in the forehead with a *crunk*. The coyote leapt backward, uttering a combination yelp and bark. I put out a hand for Addy, trying to keep her from lunging as I grabbed another rock and let fly, hitting a rear paw this time. The coyote, now seeing two adversaries where it had assumed there was only one, turned and retreated into the woods.

* * *

We cautiously resumed our feast, all the while scanning the darkness for sound or movement. Just as we were finishing up we saw them. Walking with a feral mien, two zombies stepped out of the woods and approached. Tall, thin, scraggly ones, both of them. One male in the front, a female farther behind. Their greyish skin mimicked the grey tone of their dirty clothes and hair, giving them a sort of monotone appearance. I immediately grabbed my gun and stood, taking aim but hoping not to use the loud weapon after all this interest in our dinner.

The first zombie, the male, reacted to the firelight, becoming enraged. Loping toward us, he snarled and yapped, himself a human-shaped coyote.

Addy leaped.

In two quick bounds, she covered the distance, flinging herself at him, her teeth biting into his upper leg. The zombie flailed and grabbed at her, diving his teeth into her back as he doubled over on to her. I heard her squeal, saw her release his leg for a moment, then tear into his chest with another fierce bite. The zombie tumbled onto Addy and they flipped, her ending up on top. But the thing had a grip on her now. She made savage rips in his clothing, skin, trying to get free. I couldn't do anything but watch the flailing, spinning fury of it all. Addy bit again, the zombie sunk his teeth into her ear.

Finally, the zombie extended upward and Addy dove down, taking his throat in her jaws. Like a much larger version of the rabbit she'd shaken to death in the field, she held and shook the zombie as he fought to free himself. The vulnerable tissues in his neck ripped apart, blood spraying, and his spine snapped. Like with the rabbit, she shook him again after he was dead, just for good measure.

I sighed with relief, a split second before realizing that I'd lost track of the female zombie. As I turned to scan for her, she fell on me from behind. But that one instant of recognition was enough. I slid down and she overshot me, grasping at thin air.

As she stopped her momentum, I adjusted my grip on the shotgun, grabbing the barrel like a baseball bat. She turned around in a rage and I swung, a *swooshing* sound mocking me as I missed. She dove, pushing me backward, and I staggered, falling down into the nearest of the riprap. A sharp pain struck like lightning in my head, another bolt ripped along my lower back, and I arched with a howl. The zombie kept coming at me, and, in pain, I fell to one side. Pushing up on the gun, I stood and she grabbed me, snapping at me with her jaws, her greasy, stringy hair whipping about. This time, adrenaline took hold of me and I shoved her, feeling a sharp sting of pain in my back. She slid backward in the dirt. I cranked the shotgun in a huge backswing, then let loose, the heavy stock of the gun cracking hard into her forehead, dropping her into a lump. Racing over, I delivered a second blow, straight down, then a third, fourth. She twitched and shook, then came to rest.

I looked for Addy, but didn't see her at first. I needed to get rid of the bodies and smelly duck carcass as soon as possible. I tossed the remains of our dinner as far into the bay as I could. Turning to the corpses, I dragged them along the dock as I had the last zombie, kicking them both into the water and watching them float off.

My heart was racing, but just minutes after the fight and the exertion of cleaning up, I could feel the tightness in my lower back. I touched the back of my head, where the other pain was, and pulled back my hand, wet with blood. Where was the dog? Turning back to find Addy, I saw her lying off to the side in long grass, licking at her wounds. I walked over to her and she stopped licking, looking off into the distance with a glassy-eyed appearance.

"Addy, you with me, girl?"

Eyes flickering in the reflected firelight, she just stared straight ahead, panting hard.

7

I groaned awake. The *light*. Damn, it was bright. Where the hell did all this light come from? I squinted in pain, shielding my eyes with my hands. I rubbed the back of my head, feeling crusted dry blood. My back seized as I sat up, and I winced, dropping one hand to rub the aching spot. With one hand up and one down, I stepped out of bed. I was a mess. I peeked through the hand shielding my eyes to look for the dog, but she wasn't in the bedroom.

I shuffled through the small house, like a zombie myself, looking for Addy. She wasn't in the living room. I went into the kitchen, not seeing her. Then I peered past the kitchen table and found her, lying still on her side on the kitchen floor. As I approached, I could see the matted blood on her fur. A shadow fell beside her.

No, not a shadow.

A smear of blood spread across the kitchen floor. My heart leapt into my throat. "Addy!" I exhaled loudly. She didn't stir. The details of the previous night flooded back to me.

I stepped closer, saw her tongue hanging out of one side of her mouth, motionless. A wave of nausea came over me and I grabbed at the edge of the sink. I vomited loudly for several minutes off and on before the feeling subsided. Surely the commotion woke the dog. Looking over, I saw Addy still motionless. Lifeless.

Noisily, I pulled out a chair from the small kitchen table, a collection of old metal posts with thin padding held together by a flowery plastic cover, and collapsed into it.

Must *everyone die*? Everyone I encounter? Having just started to care again about anything, here was Addy, dead on the floor. I thought of Rosa, lying dead in the RV, of Harvey dead at The Oasis, the other people lost there. Marian, Hank, Janine. Did they all have to die? I put my head in my hands, crumpling out of the cheap chair and onto the floor. I had lived in a shell, as a shell, for so long, then that shell cracked for this dog. This poor sweet dog who died saving me.

"Addy..." I sighed, looking down, feeling the guilt of her death on me.

I crawled over to the dog, slowly, lost in a fog, placing one hand on her body, over her heart.

And she blinked, opened her eyes, and looked at me.

I startled, gasped. Then, in just a second, I laughed. As Addy slowly woke up, I gave her a huge hug, tears dripping into her fur. Tears of joy for a life returned. And tears of sorrow for the lives that could not.

Addy squirmed to get up, and I released the hug. "Come on, girl," I said, rubbing the top of her head. Though she struggled to move, we went outside to relieve ourselves, each in our own place.

Smiling, I couldn't stop the tears from streaming.

8

The next days were rough. The simple acts of moving around, making food, doing the daily chores to ensure food would be there tomorrow… it was everything I could do to get through the day. I must have had a concussion, since my head continued to ache and I found bright lights hard to bear. I made sure to rest more and the symptoms improved over about a week. But my back. That was a different story. I knew that I would heal more slowly at my age, but my lower back felt just about as bad on day seven as it had on day one. Meanwhile, in couple of days you would never had known the dog had been hurt at all. For me, a few weeks slid by in a haze of aches, itchy healing scabs, repetition, but the pain remained.

* * *

One day a steady, soaking rain came. It stayed from late morning well into the night. Eventually tired of being cooped up for most of the day, Addy and I went to sleep early, her on the floor beside my bed. In minutes, we were out.

Clump shhhhh clump…

We both startled awake to near-complete darkness, the rain still pouring down. But that sound wasn't the rain. We knew that sound. Steps on the porch. A zombie? Wandering in the rain?

Addy started to growl, very low, and I grabbed at her, soothing her. "Shhh, girl," I whispered. "Let's just let it move on."

Clump… clump shhhhh clump… clump…

We waited.

Creeeeeaaak… thud.

The door? The zombie had gotten through the front door? Had I forgotten the latch, left it easy to push open? What a mistake, on this of all nights. My heart raced.

I reached for the shotgun beside the bed, still holding Addy quiet. We listened. Through the living room, we heard it move.

Shhhhhhh clump… shhhhhhh clump… shhhhhhh clump…

Addy growled through my hand. "*Shush*, girl," I hissed. We were closed off in the bedroom. Safe, I thought. I tried to hear how many of them there were.

Shhhhhh clump... shhhhhh clump...

A sloppy, shuffling sound, now moving into the kitchen. It sounded like just one of them. The sound only came from one place, a uniform pattern. Now, from the kitchen, there were other noises.

Clack clack shikka... thud... shhhhh clack... thud...

What was that thing *doing* out there?

"Stay here, girl," I said, and got up and tiptoed to the door. I cracked the bedroom door and put an eye to the slit opening. I saw nothing but the dark living room; the kitchen was around the corner, out of view. Slowly, I snuck out of the bedroom, slid over to the corner, and tilted my head slightly to look into the kitchen.

There I saw a form. A human form, nondescript, dripping wet from the endless rainfall. Shuffling slightly, it stepped toward the refrigerator.

Shhhhhh clump...

It wore grey baggy clothes, matching its grey mat of soaked hair. There was a zombie in our home. Luckily, the only light was the muted moonlight coming from the rain-soaked window past the zombie; my shadow, if I even made one, would be cast behind me as I approached. I stepped into the room and slid silently next to the kitchen table. The zombie fumbled for the handle to the refrigerator, tugging, opening the door.

With the butt of the gun held before me like a bayonet, I leapt ahead, aiming the hard wooden end directly at the back of the zombie's head.

It heard me.

The zombie moved quickly, sliding to its left, dodging my attack as the butt of the shotgun slammed into the freezer door. As I fell forward, I looked over just as the zombie reached up, one hand grabbing the barrel of the gun, the other adding to my momentum and pushing me hard into the refrigerator, rattling the old door and the things inside. The force of hitting the fridge stunned me, sending shockwaves of pain through my head and back. I gasped and grimaced, while the zombie took hold of the shotgun and wrenched it from my hands.

It stepped back and turned the gun around, aiming it at my head. I stared, not understanding how this *thing* could do that. Then it reached up and pushed off its thick mane of wet, grey hair in the dim light.

It was a man.

What I thought was hair was actually a wet grey hood, part of the soaked grey sweatshirt the man wore. He was a thin, light-skinned black male, close-cropped hair, very young, maybe mid-twenties, with angry, distant eyes that now were staring at me down the barrel of the gun. My gun. The man was panting, flush from the shock of my appearance, eyes huge.

His sudden surprise and fear turned instantly to anger. After all, without warning I'd tried to kill him. With a rush of fury and adrenalin, he clenched the gun, then steadied it, ready to pull the trigger. Then Addy rushed in.

Swinging the gun as the dog ran forward, I saw in slow motion what was going to happen — he was going to shoot my dog dead in our kitchen. I pounced across the room. Not at him, not to get the gun. But to get her, to get between her and the gun.

Grabbing Addy, sliding with her across the floor until I pinned her against the cabinets, I held her tight. I crouched before the stranger, putting my body between him and the dog. The man stepped forward, shuddering with anger. The barrel of the gun shivered from the way he held it, his grip so tight, white-knuckled, like he was trying to bore his fingers into the thing. But it remained trained on me. Pulling his arms in tight, he steadied the gun and its point-blank aim on my head, breathing hard from the rush of emotions and events.

I looked down at the floor, eyes drooping knowing the certainty of this fate, this death I had somehow avoided so long. Then I simply looked up at him, with a steely stare directly into his eyes.

"If you're going to shoot, shoot me," I said in a voice like liquid gravel.

"But leave my dog alone."

9

I waited for my life to end suddenly, for the light to go out. Or, at least, for the click. The bang.

Nothing happened.

I continued staring into the stranger's eyes, with a cold, hard look. *What the hell are you waiting for, kid?* I thought.

Looking back at me, I saw his resolve disintegrate. He lowered the shotgun.

Voice still full of rough, I said, "Look, kid. You just want some food or a place to stay, I can give that to you." I thought of even giving him the house, but I was conflicted. What would become of Addy? "What's your name, so—?"

"It's... Alain," the kid replied abruptly, looking nervously to one side. "My name is Alain, and don't call me *son*. It just sounds weird. And you're not my dad." He took a deep breath. "Oh, and it isn't 'Alan' — it's *Alain*. Uh-LAIN. Got it?" I nodded.

So now what? I thought. The kid wasn't going to give me his name just so he could shoot me, right? I hoped not. "So… are we all good here?" I asked tentatively.

"What the hell does that mean?" Alain asked, waving the barrel of the shotgun around. "I broke into your house, you tried to kill me, and now I could shoot you dead. 'Are we all good?'" he repeated, mockingly. "Yeah, sure, we're fine."

"Look, son," I started.

"Don't call me son!"

"Fine, fine, sorry. Look. I thought you were, you know, *one of them*, and you can understand why I wouldn't want you in my house, right?"

He considered it. "I guess, yeah."

"So…" I considered the situation. "There's a couch in the living room. Pretty comfortable. You wanna sleep on it, it's yours. Deal?" I held out my hands, palms up, gesturing toward the living room.

He looked at me, so much suspicion. But why? He broke into *my* house. What was his angle?

"How do I know that you won't just have the dog attack if I put down the gun?" he asked.

I wrinkled my forehead with a pondering smirk. "That's a pretty good question, but the dog does what the dog wants." I paused and looked over at her. "Right, Addy?" She looked at me. "Watch this." I gave Addy a stern look. "Sit!" I commanded.

She stood staring at me. Panting with that silly grin.

"SIT!" I tried again.

We waited. Addy ignored the command. "She just showed up here a few weeks ago. I am pretty sure she only answers to herself," I said.

Alain considered that.

"Sit," he said in a firm but low voice. Addy turned toward him and sat, looking up at him with that same goofy grin.

"Of course," I said, rolling my eyes. "Listen, son—" He started to protest, but I put up one hand, stopping him. "I mean, Alain... I'm much older than you and I'm tired. Do you think we can take this up in the morning? The couch is over there. The dog — Addy — and I will be in the bedroom. Okay?"

The stranger Alain waited. Then, as if breaking from a flood of weariness, he nodded. "Okay. But I keep the gun."

10

Another sore, aching morning. My lower back continued to be the worst of my pains, with the added misery of a dull throb in my right cheek where I had hit the refrigerator the night before. I got slowly out of bed and noticed the door to the bedroom was slightly ajar. Addy was nowhere to be found. I went out to the living room.

There, I found them both; the dog, asleep on the floor beside the couch, and above her, this new stranger, Alain. I moved the shotgun into the coat closet, just to keep it out of sight for now, then I coughed lightly and they both stirred. Alain gave a brief start, glancing around quickly before the realization of where he was set back in. The dog just looked at me. I peered out the window to ensure nothing was amiss. The rain had gone, leaving everything soaked. We all went outside to relieve ourselves, each in our own private spot.

Walking back up the porch steps, I called out. "I'm making breakfast if you're hungry." I'd barely entered the kitchen before they both came in.

* * *

"Three mouths to feed," I noted, dividing one of my last cans of beans among three plates. "We'll have to be careful with food, and we'll have to get more."

Alain might have pondered this, or perhaps he thought he wouldn't be around long enough for it to matter. He devoured everything put in front of him. I imagined it had been some time since he'd had a full meal. It was difficult to say who ate faster, Alain or the dog.

As we all sat back, plates clean, I looked at Alain. "Mind if I ask how you got here?"

"I just walked up. It was raining, so I tried the door. You left it unlocked." He eyed me, clearly with disapproval. I sighed. "When I got inside, I thought I'd scrounge for food. Couldn't believe it when I realized your fridge was *on*."

I waved that off. "What I mean is, what's your story? What're you doing out here, in the middle of nowhere, wandering?"

Alain considered the question. He was a cautious person, not timid, but wary. I didn't think he'd say a word, but I guess he must have wanted to tell someone.

"I'm from Norfolk. You heard of it?"

I nodded.

"Well, then you know the whole place is locked *down*. It's not just a walled city, it's a *military* city. There wasn't any way zombies were gonna get in. Too tight." Alain paused, looking at me. "But they did."

"You mean, *en masse*, like an assault?" I asked, incredulous.

"Not exactly. Anyway, listen, I don't know how old you are, mister, but I'm only 20. This zombie shit is all I've really ever known, since I was like 9 years old. In that way, Norfolk was great. You know, we appreciated that it was locked down. Sure, it got old, feeling like you're in a trap all the time, but if you thought of the alternative, well, it was all right. 'Course, now I sit here and wonder if we had it all wrong." He looked around at the house, maybe thinking I had it good here, too.

"Doesn't matter. We had it better than most." He stopped and drank some water, like he was getting ready to share something big. 'The port stayed open. Not as busy as I heard it used to be, *before*, but still ships came and went. Big naval ships on patrol, gas tankers, even cargo ships loaded with metal crates. The Navy would escort the gas and the cargo ships, too, since no one trusted anyone anymore. The world was too messed up."

I leaned in. "The rest of the world…" I pondered. "Still out there." I rubbed the scraggly beard on my chin. Of course they were, but it seemed like a dream, to think there were still people walking the Champs-Elysees, drinking vodka in Red Square, maybe sunning themselves on some Caribbean island. I think Alain saw my wistful stare, my slight smile.

"Don't get your hopes up. The rest of the world is just as messed up as us." I sighed. Of course. "I don't know exactly how many other ports were open, something like two dozen from the lists, I think. I heard stories that before the outbreak cargo ships would bring in things like fancy cars and clothes. What they called *luxury items*. Well, I imagine those ships were still bringing in luxury items, but the concept of luxury got changed. Now, they brought in things like bananas and gasoline. We traded out things we had that no one else had. The biggest was tobacco. People at those other ports would give us a lot of stuff to get some tobacco."

I interrupted. "Where the heck are they growing tobacco?"

"Don't ask me," he shrugged. "Outside the walls, obviously, but you wouldn't catch me there." Then he looked around, at where he was. "Well, you know what I mean." He paused, perhaps not sure where to go next.

"A lot of places really fell apart," Alain said, starting up again. "Japan. Too many people, not enough resources. We haven't heard from them in a *long* time. Anyway, the things that came in on those ships were mostly for the brass — the top dogs in the military. You can rest assured I never had one of those bananas in my life. Not even sure I know what one is. And I'm pretty sure they shipped stuff to other walled cities, DC, maybe Richmond. We certainly brought in more than just our brass could use. Point is, the rich got richer, while all the rest of us lined up for food rations like prisoners."

"So that's what happened," I said. "People got fed up."

"Well, yes and no. We grumbled about it all the time, mocked them and their fancy clothes, fancy food. But like I said, we knew it could be worse outside. That's not the way it started in Norfolk."

"Then what?" I asked, intensely curious now, leaning in. In contrast, Addy ignored us, twitching in her sleep on the floor, probably chasing some rabbit in a dream.

Alain rubbed his nearly bald scalp, scratched at the thin layer of dark hair. I noticed healing cuts in places on his head. "Greed. Too many cargo ships, too many crates. It really had to happen, don't know why they didn't see it coming. They tried real hard to quarantine the sailors when they came in, and they were really thorough, but after a while even a million-to-one shot comes in. Somebody missed something.

"We first heard there was a big brawl in the barracks, some of the younger men, maybe a little drunk on homemade hooch, started something with another group. It got out of hand, all kinds of people fighting. Turns out the ones who started it had just come back from Italy, and they were infected. They got put in the brig to settle themselves down, but by that time you had a bunch of other infected sailors patching themselves up back in the barracks. Within a week, all hell broke loose. Lots of little fighting, meaning lots more infected.

"The military tried really hard to cover up and clean up the mess. There was a big crackdown. They tore through the barracks and gathered up anyone the least bit suspicious. Then they did the same all over the city; seems like they were everywhere, all the time. They found other zombies in the civilian areas, and that just made it worse. So yeah, I guess eventually the contrast between the guys in power and the rest of us is what made the real mess."

"Is the city still standing?" I asked. "Or a total wash out?"

"No idea," Alain said, shrugging. "Someone blew up one of the bridges over the James. The military went even more nuts cracking down on everything. You couldn't move, couldn't even look at them sideways without them getting in your face. And then finally people fought back — there was an uprising. But I wasn't part of it.

"A lot of people pushed to get out. At first I wanted nothing to do with it, but then it became clear that the civilians — all of us — were at risk. People said it was possible the military was going to wipe out all *non-essentials*. We all started to think twice about staying. Finally, when a huge mob pressed toward the tunnel — the Chesapeake Bay Bridge Tunnel — I went with them.

"The first group in was annihilated. Gunned down as soon as they hit the gates. I don't think anybody survived. The second group took huge losses but breached the barricades, made gaps. I was just after that group, which put me in with one of the first groups to make it past the border. We took losses at the gate, too. But most of us survived." He hesitated. "Then we had to get through the tunnel. That was hell. It was dark, pitch black. There were things, living things, down there, I have no idea what. Things moved, some of them running away from us, some toward. Things attacked the group on the sides. We lost a couple of people, some others got torn up a bit. Walking through that darkness was hell on Earth. I have no idea how long it was, but it seemed like about a thousand miles. We held on to each other and pushed through until finally we reached the other side." He paused, looking down, eyes wide remembering. It was clear that what he said didn't do justice to what he went through down in the tunnel.

"How many made it out?" I asked.

"In my group? Oh, I'd say 30 or so. But there were a whole lot more coming up behind us. Once we got back into the light, I decided to leave the group. I thought it would be better to fend for myself." Alain looked up for a moment, studying my expression, before continuing. "I peeled off west toward the bay, scavenged here and there, slept in empty houses. I wanted to keep moving fast, running mostly north, but I had no idea where I was headed, just looking for something with some security." He paused again. "And... and I guess that's it. I ended up here."

I looked the kid over. I was no expert at recognizing lies or half-truths, but I felt Alain was leaving something out, maybe a lot of things. No matter. I wasn't going to push it. While having him around meant another mouth to feed, it also meant having a pair of 20-year-old arms and 20-year-old legs to do some of the hard work around the place. It was settled, at least in my mind. "You know, this place isn't much, but it works for me. If you can stand the couch, you're welcome to it as long as you like," I said. As if in agreement,

Addy finally got up, stretched and walked over to Alain, placing her head on his leg. At first, he looked pleased by the show of warmth, but in a moment his expression changed, becoming harder. He gave me a sideways glance.

"Yeah, thanks." He looked around, almost nervously. "But I think I'll be moving on in a couple of days." Then he got up without another word and walked outside, the front door smacking against its frame as he left.

.

11

Uneventful days passed but Alain remained. We settled into a routine of household chores, tending the rows, taking turns fishing, baiting and unloading the crab pot. I noticed that Alain was even less familiar with how to do these things than I was. One day, in the mid-afternoon heat, with the sky threatening a thunderstorm, I noticed he seemed particularly flustered. I was weeding the rows and he was supposed to be fishing, but the line had become tangled up with the crab pot and some other debris underwater, making a mess of the thin translucent strands in odd loops and knots.

"How long has it been?" I asked.

He stopped fiddling with the line and looked up at me, still wearing that grey hooded sweatshirt, although it had to have been 90 degrees and humid. "Since what?" he said, sweat dripping.

"Since you left Norfolk."

He stopped. Looked at the sky, thoughtful. "Don't know exactly. But I'd guess two weeks. At least."

"You ever fish back where you come from?" I asked.

He dropped the rod on the dock with a thud. "You wanna do this?" he said, full of annoyance and swagger.

"No, no, no," I waved my arms. "You're doing fine. I just wondered if this stuff" — I gestured toward the house, the crops, the dock — "was familiar to you."

Alain thought about it, looking down at his blistered hands. "Not really," he said after a pause. I just looked at him, face unreadable. "Okay, not at all. I've never done any of this outside-the-wall stuff. How could I?" He threw his hands up in frustration.

"It's all good, son." He started to protest. I held up a hand. "Sorry. Didn't mean to call you 'son' again. But I understand. For most of your life you lived in a controlled city. I'd be more surprised if you actually knew how to fish."

He looked a little relieved.

"What about fight?" I asked.

"Don't worry about that. I can *fight*." His tone was angry, venomous.

"I'm not trying to say you *can't*. I'm just asking if you *have*."

He puffed up. "Oh, I have."

"Zombies?" I asked. He shrunk a bit.

"Well, not really. I've seen 'em. Avoided 'em. But fight them directly, no. No, I haven't. You?"

"Yeah, I have. You see me rubbing my back?"

"All the time," Alain said.

"That's from a zombie — actually two — that walked right into this yard."

"What happened?" he asked. So I told him about the night with the roast-duck dinner. He laughed.

"It isn't exactly funny," I said.

"Come on. You roasted a duck on an open fire and you were *surprised* when company showed up? Maybe just post a sign on the highway, too." He laughed again. I held my face still. After a moment, I cracked a smile.

"Yeah, all right. It was pretty dumb. But, damn, it tasted good." I laughed along with him. "But, back to fighting. I think it would be best if we talked about strategy."

"Okay," he said, "what did you have in mind?"

"They're not immortal, they're not super-human. But if you break one of their arms or legs, they may just keep coming at you, even more pissed off than before. If you're using a bat or something like that, aim for the head or throat. You cave in a skull, the threat is gone. If you have a gun and you're willing to shoot, aim for the middle of the body. Not necessarily because that'll stop them in one shot, but because you don't want to miss. Ammo is in short supply everywhere I've looked."

"Not in Norfolk," Alain joked. I nodded, with a wry smile. "What if you don't have anything?" he asked.

"Run."

"Or if you're trapped?"

"Go for the eyes," I suggested. Alain shot me a look. Did that horrify him? "We should practice a bit. I'll set up something, like a scarecrow. A dummy." He nodded.

We went back to our chores, Alain bent over the tangled fishing line while I plucked more weeds from our garden. A drop fell on my back, then a second. I looked up at the darkening clouds above.

"If you haven't fought zombies, who have you fought?" I asked.

Alain stopped, turned toward me. "Sometimes the zombies aren't the worst enemy out there. Sometimes it's the *people*." In the distance, a peal of thunder cracked across the sky.

12

Summer rolled onward, hot and humid, with regular thunderstorms. During one of the fast, intense storms, a pine fell, striking the side of the house. We found a rusty old axe in the back of the shed and set to work on it when the rains stopped. Alain cut off the branches first, so we could get a clear view of the damage to the house. As he dragged several branches off into the woods, I saw the hole. One branch had connected at a sharp angle with the side of the house, poking a hole into the living room. We could probably live with it, and in fact hadn't even noticed it from inside, but Alain wanted nothing of that.

He was working up a tremendous sweat, chopping and dragging the branches, starting in on the trunk of the tree. "I'd rather not have a hole like that leading into the place where I sleep. Who knows what'll get in there?" He wiped his forehead, covered with perspiration.

"Why don't you take the sweatshirt off? It's hot as hell out here. You'll give yourself a heat stroke."

"I'm fine," he said, clearly flushed from the heat and exertion.

Alain, I was learning, tended to be a tough guy almost all the time. I wasn't really sure why, since I was just an old, scraggly-grey-haired fellow with a bad back. I was no expert at any of this survivalist stuff, just making it up as I went along. And that was obvious. But Alain put on a show like he knew everything, even though you could see him struggle. To his credit, he succeeded. He'd persevere until the job was done, pretending he'd planned it that way all along.

For hours, he meticulously chopped the pine, stacking anything of reasonable size alongside the house. We'd decided that we would need something to help warm the house in the winter. Luckily, there was a small wood stove in the living room. A small stack of logs had stood against the house from before my arrival. With Alain's work, it tripled in size. All the while, he was wiping sweat, cursing, but getting the job done.

Once the pine was completely cleared, we set about filling the hole and boarding it up. We didn't bother making it pretty, just added to the overall shabbiness of the house on the outside. But the hole was closed up, and Alain was happier about that. I supposed I didn't really want a house full of field mice, either.

That night, sitting together at the small kitchen table, dining on fish and vegetables, I looked over at Alain's hands, his long thin fingers, as he reached for a plate. Continuing to chew, and trying not to make a big deal about it, I said, "Hands look pretty roughed up."

Alain reflexively rubbed them together, staring at the blisters that grew large and enraged from his hard work with the axe. "I'm fine," he said.

"Not saying you're not, but those blisters look like they hurt. I know *I'd* be hurting if that was me. Was that your first work with an axe?"

I wondered what he'd reply. Would he keep up the tough act, or actually tell the truth? Thankfully, he went with truth. I guess we'd been spending enough time together that I was growing on him. "Yep. First time."

"What exactly did you do in the city?" I inquired, mouth full of food.

He paused a second, then must have figured that answering wouldn't change anything. "I worked a desk job. OFM. Office of

Food Management. I basically kept track of where the food came from and where it went."

"Explains why you knew about the bananas," I offered.

"Yeah. What about you?"

I stopped, thinking about my past life. From so long ago. Was that even really me? "What did I do in the city?"

"What did you do... *before?*" Alain asked, putting his fork down to look at me as I thought over the answer.

"*Before,*" I echoed. "Ah, then." I took another bite. "I was a doctor." Alain's eyes widened, like this was important information he was just finding out. "But don't get too excited. First, I was a small-town doc. General practitioner. Doesn't mean I'm a dummy, mind you, but I wasn't some world-class brain surgeon. Plus, for 10 years I just pushed pills around in a government pharmacy. That's the job they gave me in DC. So, I'm a little rusty."

"Still," he said. "Doctor seems pretty useful, out in the woods like this."

"You know what would be really useful, out in the woods like this? Medicine. I could sure go for some painkillers. I'd love an

Oxycodone tonight, but I'd settle for plain ol' acetaminophen. Without medicines, my options are rather limited. Sure, I can set your arm if you break it, but a lot of choices are out the window now."

Alain listened. Then, as we sat in the glow of the electric lights, he asked more quietly, "Did you have family?"

How long had it been since I thought of my family? "Uh, well… My parents died a long time before the outbreak. Both of my parents were government engineers, a long time ago. They made enough money working up the government pay scale to afford to send me to medical school. Probably wouldn't have happened if I wasn't an only child, though, so there's that. My father died from lung cancer, and my mother went two years later, probably from a broken heart."

"What about someone else? A wife?" Rosa's face appeared before my eyes. Alain must have seen the change in my expression.

"Not a wife. Not ever. I… I don't even know what to call her. But she was definitely someone special."

"What was her name? What happened?" he asked cautiously.

"Rosa. Her name is — was — Rosa." I couldn't help the tears, tried my best to wipe them away nonchalantly, like there was just something in my eye. I doubt Alain was fooled. "We were outside

DC, and they shot her. Just like that." I snapped my fingers, my anger flicking on. I stopped myself, shut my mouth.

"For deserting or something?" Alain asked.

I looked up. There was so much to say, Rosa's life to reveal. "Something like that," I muttered. Wanting to change the subject, I asked, "What about you?"

"I didn't grow up with my parents around. I was nine when Norfolk was closed off. My mother got me and my brother inside before the gates were shut for good, but they wouldn't let my dad in. We were headed to live with my aunt and uncle — my mom's sister and her husband — so we were in good hands. Mom told us she loved us, then she demanded to be let out of the city to be with her husband. I never saw either of my parents again. Growing up with my aunt was fine, she treated us well, but it just wasn't the same. My brother and I missed our parents every day. We knew they died together, outside the walls, separated from their kids." Now it was Alain's turn to wipe his tears. "And my brother was killed on the way out of the city. I guess I forgot to mention that before."

We sat, a couple of grown men, silently crying over what was lost.

"So that's why I just can't *care* about anything anymore. Everything dies. Nothing lasts." Alain spit the words out, like venom, like something he'd been holding in for too long. He was echoing my sentiments, the hollowness of being unable to care.

Then I looked at his hands again. The hands that spent all day being worn to blisters chopping wood to keep us all warm this winter. Alain, me, the dog. I looked around at the walls. The house was feeling oddly like a home.

I couldn't make myself believe Alain didn't care. And then I realized that the same thing had happened to me. I cared again, too.

13

A few days later, we were again sitting at the kitchen table, eating dinner while the electric lights hummed around us and darkness crept over the outdoors, when we heard a strange noise. A splashing sound, mixed with odd grunts.

We flicked off the light instantly, as Addy started a low growl, wary of whatever was out there. I peered out the front window and could just see something down by the pier, splashing in the water. Grabbing the gun, I went to the front door.

"Stay here with the dog," I said.

"I'm coming out, too," Alain said.

I stopped and looked back at him. "Listen, this may be nothing. I go out, see what it is, come back. If possible, I just let it go past, whatever is out there. But if you come with me, we double the chances of being noticed." I looked down at the dog. "Actually, we triple it. She barks, and we're found." I waited for him to agree, not willing to accept another argument. He nodded.

I slipped out of the house as Alain held Addy back and kept her quiet. Tiptoeing into the garden, I used the plants as cover — the corn was growing shoulder height now, so I only had to crouch to stay out of sight.

The sound continued. *Splash splash… errr urk. Splash.*

I finally crept close enough to see, raising the barrel of the gun to put the thing in my sights. It was incredible. A zombie — male, bald, pasty skin, wet and dirty in jean overalls — was splashing through the shallow waters by the dock. What the hell was he *doing*? I watched as he looked around, left, right, furtively, with his milky eyes. Then he thrust his hands into the water with a loud splash.

Was he… *fishing?*

I couldn't believe it. What was this? Was it an indication that, somewhere below the surface, these creatures could still *think?* Or just some sort of natural instinct to eat, to stay alive? I watched the zombie from the end of my gun as he grunted and dove for fish in the dark waters. He staggered closer and closer to the end of the dock. I wondered if he might drown himself simply from lack of understanding, but he stayed back when the water got too deep. There was definitely something going on inside that head.

At the edge of the dock, the zombie staggered in the water. Almost fell. I tightened my grip on the gun. The thing looked into the water, reaching down and pulling at something. Up came our crab pot, full of live crabs. The zombie seemed both jubilant and perplexed. Did it understand what the mesh box was? Did it remember that this was a way to get food? It reached in, but couldn't figure out how to get the crabs out of the wire basket. Blue crabs shuffled side to side, avoiding the zombie's fingers. Finally, it got a grip on a crab and pulled, able to tug it closer but stopped by the mesh of the crab pot. The crab snipped at the zombie, finally pinching a finger in its front pincers. The zombie felt nothing, a symptom of the leprosy, and continued to try to extract the crab.

Another snap from the crab. I saw flesh tear, blood spill. Finally, the zombie felt something, reacted. He smashed at the cage of the crab pot, flinging it back into the water, then raged at the water itself, all around him. He pummeled the dock, tearing apart his hands, before finally calming some. After a while, he moved around the pier, headed south and wandered off. I watched for perhaps half an hour before I could no longer distinguish the zombie from the distant waves.

As I walked back to the house, I thought over what I'd seen. Inside, beneath the raging, irrational surface, were they still *human?*

14

Alain sat with rapt attention, listening to me tell about the zombie in the water.

"Do you think… they could come *back*?" he asked.

I didn't have to think about my answer. "You mean, do I think that a person who has been fully transformed by this disease could return to being a normal human? Be *cured*? No. Not at all."

"Why?" Alain seemed disappointed.

"There are simply too many physiological changes, too much damage done once the body has fully turned, to make a cure reasonable. Even if it were possible to remove the disease, you'd be left with a shell of a person. Their skin would be hardened and damaged, rotted away in places. They'd have limbs torn or broken.

Their vision would be severely affected. Lesions could be treated, but the scars would remain. More importantly, their brain simply undergoes too much internal trauma. Swelling, fever. Even if you remove those symptoms, the *damage* from the symptoms remains. The person would *never* return to what they were before. It's impossible. Speaking as a former doctor, that's my firm opinion."

"But that's just it — it's just your *opinion*," Alain said. "You said yourself that you weren't some big-deal brain surgeon. Maybe someone else knows better than you?"

It was hard not to be offended by the remark, as silly as that was. I was ticked off. "You're right, Alain. I wasn't the most important doctor in the world, no. But you know what I do have that you do not? *Medical training*. That means I know what I'm talking about. Look, I don't want to write off the majority of the human race, either, but facts are facts. Anyone who has fully turned is *gone. Permanently*. There's no hope for them. The only time a person can be cured is before they fully turn."

Alain tilted his head to the side, like a dog hearing a high-pitched sound. "Wait. What?"

I looked at him, confused. "Huh?" I asked.

"You just said, 'The only time a person can be *cured...*' Are you saying there's a cure?" Alain stood up, intensely focusing on me.

I'd said too much. I'd never talked to Alain about The Oasis. About the cure. I kept quiet, looking away.

Alain came right over, in my face. "Hold on, no. You're not going to just clam up now. *What do you mean a person can be cured?*" There was no use in denying it or making up a story.

"Yes, that's correct. A person can be cured." His eyes popped. "But *only before* they're completely turned." Alain backed away. Unbridled joy welled out of him. He spun, looking around, laughing.

"That's *incredible!*" Then he stopped, coming back close to my face. "But *how* do you know that?"

"I've seen it. First-hand." I could see he wanted more detail. "There was this place, called The Oasis—"

"I know about it!" he interrupted. "That's where we were all heading when we left Norfolk!"

"Well, you went the wrong way. And it's gone." He deflated.

"No," he said, shaking his head.

"Yes. It's gone. It was in South Carolina, a place called Hickory Knob State Park. But it was attacked and destroyed. I was there. They had a cure, a real honest-to-goodness cure."

I waited, unsure if I should say it, but nevertheless, I told him. "In fact, I've been cured."

Alain stopped so quickly, the dog startled from her napping on the floor. "No way!" he said, incredulously. "You're lying."

I pulled my shirt down and away, exposing the scars on my shoulder, the definitive shape of a bite wound, healed. "This was a zombie bite, from a few months ago. Before you even got here." He stared at it, unbelieving, mouth agape. He looked into my eyes, back at the wound, then back into my eyes. I pulled my shirt up. "But it really doesn't matter. The cure is gone. Lost. And so is The Oasis."

"This is a miracle," he said, sitting back down in his chair and staring at me. He sat that way for a long time.

15

After that conversation, we kept going about our business, but I could see Alain was always thinking now. Wondering. My news had changed something in him, given him some new form of hope. But I knew that hope was dead and gone. I tried once or twice to reiterate that point, but Alain ignored me.

A couple days later, Alain seemed antsy. "I'm going to head out for a bit, check out other houses nearby, see what I can find."

I just nodded. "Okay." I got the feeling I wouldn't be seeing Alain again, ever. That he was really going off to find The Oasis. The place that was no more. I'd told him just where to look. I figured the temptation was too great.

* * *

About three hours later, he returned. Not a casual reappearance from a routine supply run, but a dead sprint. Alain ran through the woods as fast as he could, racing up to me on the dock. Addy barked and loped beside him as he came up next to me. "What's the big hurry?" I asked, not bothering to even put down the fishing rod.

He stopped, leaned over with his hands on his knees and panted. "There's... a whole bunch... of *people* out there."

I dropped the rod. "Where? How close?"

"To the east, and south. Travelling the highway, but groups were branching off, searching for something."

"Do you think they're heading this way?" My mind raced, wondering what to do.

He considered it. "Yeah. Yeah, I do. I saw them from that red house on the hill south of here. I could watch them as they came up the road. They were using the highway as their main path, but breaking off in both directions. They're looking for something."

I thought about it. "Well, I don't know what they're looking for. But I do know what I don't want them to find." I stepped past Alain and walked quickly toward the house.

* * *

Under an hour. That's how fast we did it. Turned our home into a ghost, a shell.

We'd left the outside of the house shabby on purpose, thankfully, so there wasn't much to do there. The trees I'd planted in the driveway were adding much-needed privacy screens from that direction. But anyone stumbling into the clearing would notice the organization of the place. The neat rows of vegetables in the garden, the tidy dock, the hum of electricity.

We flipped all the breakers, cutting off everything. The house went silent. We dragged rotting branches from the woods and scattered them about in what seemed like a realistic, natural way. We found a little driftwood and littered the dock. But saddest of all was the garden.

In the distance, we started to hear them coming, and Addy perked up, listening.

"Take her in the house, okay?" I said to Alain. "Keep her quiet." He nodded and went.

We had quickly harvested everything we could from the garden. The only thing left was to destroy it.

I walked down the neat rows swinging a rake, lopping off the tops of plants, smashing others. Then I dragged more branches from the woods and dropped them haphazardly over my carefully tended crops. I threw handfuls of pine needles and leaves over the neatly weeded ground. I thought to myself that we might have just sealed our fate anyway; we might have made it impossible to survive the winter. But I continued until the garden looked as shabby as the rest of the yard and house. Then I turned to rush inside.

We could hear people talking, walking, coming closer, not concerned about the sheer amount of *noise* they made. In our clearing, the only sounds were the slow spinning of the wind turbine and the breaking of the waves on the riprap. We huddled in the shadows of the house and waited.

The crowd came closer. Alain and I alternated holding the dog to keep her quiet and looking between the drawn curtains in the kitchen, out the window facing east, toward the sound. Keeping low, we wished for nothing to happen, one big stroke of luck. The talking and the sound of footsteps got closer and closer, no single voice decipherable in the overall din of the group. "How many do you think there are?" I whispered to Alain.

"Gotta be more than a hundred people," he replied. My heart sank. A hundred people, steps from our door. The possibility that they'd just pass us by seemed remote.

I reached out two fingers and slid the curtain to the side, the barest move.

In the woods, I saw a person, red shirt glaring against the natural browns and greens of the trees. He was walking north. Then I noticed another person, a third. They were *here*. I held my breath.

Addy started to growl.

My eyes darted to Alain, and he leapt toward the dog, landing as silently as possible. We'd both gotten caught up in looking out the window and left Addy by herself. As Alain grabbed her to quiet her down, she let out a small bark.

We froze.

Alain held the dog's muzzle and she looked wide-eyed up at him. After a moment, I turned and looked outside, terrified of what I'd find.

More and more people streamed by, some distance off, weaving through the pine trees.

But no one came closer.

We waited. In time, maybe 20 minutes, we could tell the mass of the crowd had moved north. Stragglers continued through for a while. We didn't move, almost didn't breathe at all.

Finally, we realized we hadn't heard any noise in some time. But we waited some more. Over an hour later, Alain spoke. "I think they're gone."

I didn't want to move, or acknowledge it, for fear of being wrong. I looked out the small slice between the curtains again. But I had to admit, there hadn't been anything for a long time. "Yeah, seems that way. Where the hell did that many people come from?"

Alain looked at me. "Norfolk. That'd be my guess."

He let go of Addy and she jumped up, shaking her whole body like she was ridding herself — ridding *us* — of the weight holding us all down.

* * *

Another hour passed and there was nothing. We breathed a sigh of relief, even laughed at the whole thing. "I'm going to make dinner," I said.

A short while later, I plated up croaker and corn for myself and Alain, after deboning another croaker and tossing it to the dog.

"You wanna sit outside?" Alain asked.

"Sure," I said, holding out his plate for him. He took it and walked toward the living room.

As I turned to grab my plate and follow him, I heard a crash. Addy and I ran to the front door, where we saw Alain standing, blocking the open doorway, hands empty. Below him, shattered on the threshold, lay the broken plate, food spilled all over. Alain stared out the door.

I approached and tilted my head to see past him.

There in the yard, just steps from the porch, stood a man.

He was large, imposing, in jeans and a flannel shirt, with rough, dark beard and shaggy hair. Most notably, he had only one eye. The other was an empty socket. Then I noticed a second man behind him, blond, skinny, tattered t-shirt, dirty jeans. They both looked at us. The bearded one — the one-eyed one — smiled, showing a mouth of yellowed, rotten teeth.

"Well, hello again, Celia," he said.

16

"Celia?" I echoed.

Alain, as if waking from a dream, turned past me and went back into the house. I just stood there looking at these strangers, here in *our home*.

"Who's Celia?" I said, distractedly, slowly turning.

Addy took notice of the men, felt something amiss. She growled. The one-eyed man hefted a large, heavy stick, holding it like a bat. "You're gonna wanna hold yer dog," he said, nodding toward Addy. I reached toward her, but she jumped, flying down the porch steps. She leapt to attack the one-eyed man.

He swung.

Addy let out a high-pitched yelp and crumpled to the ground, broken. The second man rushed up, also brandishing a heavy stick.

"Stop!" I yelled, rushing down the steps toward Addy's motionless body. Behind me I heard footsteps on the porch.

I turned and saw Alain, lifting the shotgun.

"Hold up! Wait!" shouted the one-eyed man. His partner pulled up quickly, maybe 20 feet back.

Like a clap of thunder in my ears, Alain fired the gun. The one-eyed man was propelled backward, riddled with pellets. I heard him exhale a giant *oof!* as blood splattered the clearing. He fell, forever silenced.

The other man paused for a second, looking down at his fallen friend. Alain swung the gun past me, past the dog, to face this second stranger. The man looked up, eyes bugging, and Alain fired again.

The shot was wide, grazing the man with a few pellets. He turned and ran back into the woods, bounding left and right through the trees.

Alain broke the action of the gun, popped out the used shells and reached in his pocket for new ones. He fumbled, too unfamiliar with the process. It was too late. The man was gone. I rushed to Addy.

The dog winced at my touch, but she was alive. Alain walked over with the shotgun, barrel dangling down.

I felt Addy's body. Broken ribs. I hoped none had punctured a lung, but there was nothing I could do. I looked at Alain.

"Celia? Who's that?" I asked, reeling from the rapid-fire events.

"Me," he said. I looked at him sideways.

"You're a woman?" I asked.

"Is that a problem?" he — no, *she* said.

Raising my hands, I replied, "No, no. I just... *had no idea.*"

"That was kind of the point, genius. But now, we have to leave."

The realization hit me like a punch to the gut. There was a man running free, probably an offshoot of the large group that had passed us. He knew we were here. He'd want to avenge his friend. And they'd all figure we must have some supplies they'd want, too.

"The guy you shot. How did he know you?"

Alain — I mean, Celia — looked into the woods with a face made of stone. "There's no time now. There will be others. We need to leave." She looked down at the dog. "Is Addy going to make it?"

I nodded. "I think so. Unless she's popped a lung, but for now, I think she just has a couple of broken ribs."

"Then come on." Suddenly Celia was all business. "We gotta pack up."

We grabbed bags and filled them with extra clothes, food, lots of water, other supplies. We were weighed down, carrying everything we could. Addy stood up, wobbly, but she could move about. We gave her some water, and she drank it.

Celia. How did I never see it? She'd covered herself in that grey sweatshirt, her hair gone, her face grimy and harsh. What before seemed to me to be a thin young man was suddenly revealed to be a young woman. I stopped for a moment, thinking of all the things we'd been through, the chores, the hard work, the downtime, the conversation. And yet, this.

"Is the rest true?" I asked.

"The rest of what?" Celia responded.

"Your story. Norfolk. Your brother. The uprising. The group that left in the tunnel."

"Yeah. It's all true. Alain was my brother's name."

"But why the secrecy? You've been here for weeks."

She looked at me, cold. "We need to go. Now." She picked up her bags and pushed past me out the door.

We left the house, a sanctuary for so long, and never saw it again.

17

Woods. Hills. Fields. They all went by in a blur. My back ached, I was carrying so much. But we plodded on. Addy limped beside us, willing to endure whatever she must.

Celia led the way. I followed, blindly, trusting her to choose a path. My mind wandered.

How? How could this happen again? Just when things had become *good*.

This world we lived in was too much to bear. I found myself falling into a depression, unable to even contemplate the thought of starting over, yet again, somewhere else. For what? How long would that peace last?

Celia. What did I really *know* about this person, anyway? If she'd kept such simple things as her gender, her name, from me, could I really trust her? She felt like a stranger to me, albeit one who looked just like someone I knew.

And the dog. Poor Addy, struggling to keep up with us. Maybe she should stop, maybe we should leave her to fend for herself. She'd done it before. Or would that be a death sentence, leaving her behind, injured? There were times when she drifted back, even out of view, and I thought that would be it for her. But she always managed to catch up.

I could feel the weather changing, the approach of fall. The approach of our downfall. Living through one winter outside the city had almost killed me. I felt certain a second winter would finish the job. So why try? Where were we going, why did anything matter?

It was a long day on the road, heading nowhere, from what I could tell, but as it came near dark, Celia approached a house. She carried the gun, waving at us to wait as she went to investigate by herself. Addy and I were more than happy to stop.

Celia silently padded up to the house, then circled it. She went to the front door and tried the handle, but it was locked. We saw her circle around to the back again. Then, nothing. For several long minutes.

Finally, Celia opened the front door, gesturing to us. "Come on," she said.

It was a hovel compared to the house we'd left behind. This one was bigger, two stories, but empty except for debris. No furniture. We checked, but there was nothing in the way of food or water. It would just be a roof. We ate a bit from our packs, in silence, then each found an open spot of floor and went to sleep.

In the morning, I went to Addy, wanting to see how her ribs were doing. She eyed me carefully. I reached out and touched her side, where the stick had caught her. Addy flipped quickly onto her feet and snapped at me, canines chomping inches from my hand. I moved backward quickly. There was a strange look in her eyes, one I didn't like. But she'd been hurt. I remembered that animals would often lash out when injured. I let it go.

The next day was much the same, with another empty house that night. They blurred together, meaninglessly passing us by, meaninglessly marking our progress toward an unknown destination, for an unknown reason.

18

Another night, another abandoned house, less food, less time.

We spoke during dinner, really, for the first time since we had started this journey to nowhere.

"Those men. The one you shot, and the other," I said wearily. "How did you know them?"

Celia the woman put up the same hard exterior as Alain the man. She looked at me, as if she were gauging whether to speak. But I could see she was tired, too.

"They were part of the group I came out of Norfolk with. They were in the tunnel." She went back to eating.

"Well, then, I guess I can see why you left that group."

"The big one. The one with only one eye?" she asked, keeping her head down, eating.

"Yeah?"

"He raped me. The other one helped. Just over a week after we got out of the tunnel." I opened my mouth to reply and stopped. Now it made sense. The shaved head, heavy sweatshirt, pretending to be a man. Celia had been through something no one should ever endure, and clearly she had no intention of letting it happen again. No doubt she looked at me with suspicion as well. What man could she trust after that?

"I'm… sorry," I said, trying, failing, to say something of use. "I thought you shot him because of what he did to Addy. But now I see…"

"I *did* shoot him because of what he did to Addy. And also for what he did to me." We sat in silence for a while.

"I know you're not asking me for more of the story, but I don't want to keep it to myself anymore."

I just nodded, letting her find her own path there.

"The big guy with the beard was a loudmouth. A trouble maker. Named Burt. The other one was your typical sidekick. Weak. Mean. I don't even know what his name was. He only had any power at all because he would do whatever Burt wanted. They knew that together they were more intimidating.

"We had a group of around 30, like I told you. But most of those people were scared, tired. In Norfolk, they had worked desk jobs, like me. None of us ever planned to be outside the walls, no one was ready to take charge. That meant survival of the dumbest, or at least the biggest oaf. Burt was a pretty big oaf. He shot his mouth off about where we should go, everything we should do. When people would dissent, he'd have the other guy back him up, act like it was a group decision."

Celia's voice picked up a little, became stronger, like she was leaning into the story. "It didn't take long before he was becoming a true tyrant, having his way in every way. And then he wanted something else. Me. He approached me several times, first trying his ugly attempts at charm, his witless version of coming on to me. It was hideous. I considered the possibility he might attack me, but dismissed it. We hadn't fallen *that far, that fast* already, right?"

She stopped, looked at me. I didn't say anything. She nodded, then started to talk in a lower, emotion-filled voice. "We had. One night, as I was about to go to sleep, Burt approached me from behind and grabbed me, and he and the skinny little bastard dragged me into the woods. Burt raped me. I only wish that I'd fought back sooner. But I did fight back, eventually. When I finally snapped, I screamed and shoved my thumb into his eye. Burt's eye. You saw the results of that. He yelled and yelled, acted like he was dying. Screamed curses and threats at me. I just wish the sonofabitch *had* died then."

I shook my head, unable to truly fathom her pain.

"I took off, running. And I just kept running. As long as I could, for days. I tried to sleep here and there in houses, but I kept hearing Burt coming up behind me again. Thought I could even smell his foul breath on me. His rough hands. When I did sleep at all, I dreamed of him. In some of my dreams, I killed him. In others, he kept raping me, endlessly, until I think I died. When I finally got to your place and you snuck up behind me, well…" She turned her palms facing upward, like, *what did you expect?* I just looked at her, having no words.

She looked dead straight at me with a cold expression. "But now Burt is dead, and I'm determined to make sure that *no man — nobody* — will ever take advantage of me again."

19

When Celia thought we'd gone far enough east, she turned us north. I followed without question, allowing myself to be freely directed for the first time in a long while. I vaguely considered that north was the direction the mob had gone, but figured we'd traveled far enough inland to avoid them.

As we plodded northward, Addy wandered off, agitated, acting strange. I wondered if she'd come back. This life of constant walking must have seemed so unusual to her. I considered how little *I* knew about where we were headed, then compared that to Addy. She truly had no idea what was going on.

Addy was gone for more than a day. It seemed like she would follow us on the fringes, able to return when she wanted, but otherwise she remained out of sight. Celia and I assumed she was hunting, finding something with more sustenance than we could provide. Our bags dwindled, even though we ate and drank as little as we could. Eventually we only needed one bag.

When Addy finally returned, her eyes seemed lighter, stranger.

One day, we approached Route 50 from the east, and carefully scanned the highway from the shadows of the trees. I vaguely remembered taking this road before. We saw nothing in any direction, so we followed along the road to speed our progress north, staying to the edge.

Celia eyed the many abandoned cars and trucks longingly. "We should get a car," she said.

"I did that once, on the way to The Oasis. I seriously doubt that lightning will strike twice." As usual, Celia didn't take my word for it, stopping to check car after car. In cases where she could find the keys, every battery was dead. I told her about the RV and having to charge the battery overnight with a generator. I thought that would dissuade her, but instead she started to look for battery chargers, generators. It was fruitless.

My back was a terrible hindrance, forcing us to move more slowly than Celia wanted. With the dog often wandering off alone, and me limiting her progress, it was a wonder Celia stuck with us. I have to wonder how things would have turned out if she'd simply decided to *go*.

As one day turned into evening, the chill of fall in the air, we came upon a farm along the side of the road. A large barn stood off to one side. Celia investigated the house first, but came back with bad news. "Full of mice, maybe thousands of them; smells like mouse turds," she reported. We checked out the barn instead, just as Addy came into view.

The barn was empty, except for some old straw on the floor and more in the loft above us, perhaps 12 feet off the ground. We spotted a ladder. After talking it over, we thought we'd have a more peaceful rest up above. "What about the dog?" I asked.

Celia shrugged, not an offhand, *who cares?* kind of shrug, but the deflated kind. No good answer came to her mind or mine. *What else can we do?* In the end, we ate our light supper on the floor of the barn, then as the moon rose, we closed the barn doors and were left in darkness. Celia and I went up to the loft, me struggling to pull myself along the ladder as my lower back spasmed. Addy stayed below. I felt awkward about it, like I might be betraying my good friend, my faithful servant, this dog who had been nothing but good to me for so long.

In the middle of the night, there were strange noises. Celia peered down into the barn's main interior, but said she didn't see the source of the sound. But she did see Addy sleeping motionless throughout the noise, on the rotting straw floor, as a single line of moonlight fell across her from the crack between the barn doors.

20

I awoke in a world of pain. My lower back had seized during another night of harsh sleeping, causing me to pull myself into a ball, trying to stretch in some way to provide relief. It was useless. I was useless. I told Celia to leave without me, that I wouldn't be able to move at all that day. She looked at me, looked aside. I could tell she was considering it, hard. In the end, though, she stayed.

Addy slept very late, hardly moving. Finally, in the late morning, she stirred and we gave her some food and water. She seemed jittery. It was unlike her. I was deeply concerned, having an idea of the problem but not wanting to voice it. Was this rabies? Or, was it... something more? The very thought made me shiver.

I remained in the loft all day. Celia went out, perhaps to scout ahead or check nearby for supplies. She came back late. I don't know if Addy was around or not, considering that I spent most of the day huddled in a ball or asleep. My age felt like it had crept upon me, latched on, and wouldn't let go. I had troubled dreams of Addy, wondering what she was going through, imaging horrors too great to describe.

* * *

We had a small meal late in the afternoon. The day of rest had helped me out, but now I was trying to work out the kinks of sitting idle for too long. I had insisted on climbing down the ladder and eating with Addy. As I heaved myself down beside the dog, my back let out several loud cracks in succession. Celia looked at me with a raised eyebrow, and I shrugged. Addy sat with us as we ate, absently taking small morsels from my hand.

After the meal, I felt surprisingly tired. I tried to play it off for a while, but there was no use. Addy was already asleep again in a corner of the barn. Celia closed the barn doors as I went to the ladder and climbed back up.

In the night, we again heard a strange series of sounds. Hisses, yaps, snarls and growls. Celia once more scanned the barn for the source. I joined her, having improved the condition of my back with a day of rest. We sat, side by side, looking for something, anything, in the darkened hulk of the barn.

To our left, the sound continued. To our right, something took form and moved below, walking out into the center of the floor. It was Addy.

The sound grew and came in closer, from the left. Addy looked in that direction, almost in a fog. Then, two large, puffy raccoons skittered in. The smaller one had half an ear, the rest clearly missing from a bite. The two creatures seemed very confident, familiar with their territory. We could almost see their distaste for Addy, as well as their lack of fear. They approached her, clearly in the process of preparing an attack. They stepped forward, slid sideways, circled. Several times they bumped into each other and started up that *sound* again, raging at each other. A front paw, claws out, slashing. The same, mirrored. The raccoons were angry, feral, ready to fight anything, and they approached Addy without fear. Addy looked weary, perhaps unconcerned, perhaps unaware.

As we looked down from above, the raccoons circled Addy in the middle of the barn floor.

Addy, easily heavier than the two raccoons put together, tracked their circles but couldn't escape the movement of both of them at the same time. As one circled away from her, the other moved in. A slash. Addy bled. She let out a yelp of pain, coming to her senses enough to begin defending herself.

We just *watched*.

Addy stood her ground. The two raccoons took up places opposite each other, with Addy in the middle. She would face one, be attacked by the other. The three circled together, like fates intertwined.

The half-eared one lunged from behind, striking Addy in the meat of her back leg. Her flesh was torn open, bleeding.

I'd had enough.

I looked at Celia. "She's *ours*," I said. She nodded.

Without another word, we rushed to the ladder and slid down. As my feet hit the ground, a jolt of pain flashed up my back. I ignored it and grabbed a pitchfork that had been discarded nearby. Celia raised the shotgun. The light was dim, so I stepped over and threw open the barn doors, letting a wide bath of moonlight flood the interior.

The light fell across Addy, and she *changed*.

She turned toward us, as if the light was burning her, causing her pain. It was only the pale glow of the moon, but compared to the darkness inside the barn, it seemed bright. Addy suddenly raged, turning her head left and right, shaking her body.

The smaller raccoon with the half ear chose to lunge at her at just that moment, nipping at her hind leg. Addy wheeled, leapt on the raccoon, and savagely bit into its neck, behind its ears. The thing uttered a horrific, snarling wail as Addy tore the life from it. Like she'd done while hunting that poor rabbit, she clasped the raccoon's neck in her powerful jaws and shook, snapping its spine. The raccoon fell dead at her feet. Then Addy turned toward the other, still shaking her head with rage, like she was trying to get the madness out of her by sheer force.

The second raccoon, perhaps the smarter of the two, turned to flee. It raced across the floor of the barn, but Addy wouldn't let it go. She pounced and bit, severing its tail from its body. The raccoon yelped but still tried to escape. Addy grabbed it by a hind leg. The raccoon railed against her, full of terror and fury. Addy dropped it, and it spun on her in self-defense, snarling with teeth bare, spittle flying. Addy ignored the show of strength, as well as her own safety. She stepped forward and, as the raccoon bit her repeatedly on the face and neck, she dove for its underside. The smaller animal flipped over unwillingly.

The dog, now seemingly alien to us, a wild beast, went for the kill. She chewed at the raccoon repeatedly, without mercy. As she turned away, it lay gutted and writhing on the dirty floor, its blood seeping into the matted straw.

Then Addy looked at us.

The cold steel of fear penetrated my body like a weapon, as I saw Addy's eyes. Not the warm brown eyes of the dog to whom I'd thrown food scraps for many months, but greyish eyes glowing in the moonlight.

She walked slowly toward us. We could see countless bite marks, bleeding dark blood into her disheveled fur. She shook her head again, but just slightly.

Addy walked past us both as we stood dumbfounded by the barn door, and padded back to her bed, leaving bloody wet paw prints all along the way.

21

We climbed back up the ladder wordlessly. In the loft, I turned to Celia with a pained expression.

She thought for a moment, then slowly whispered, "Do you think...?"

"What? That Addy is sick? That maybe it's rabies?"

"No. Well, not exactly. Do you think she has... *the disease?*" Celia asked, wrinkling her brow as she leaned in to emphasize the question.

"Rabies is capable of being spread between different mammals, like a person infected from being bitten by a rabid animal," I said. "But I don't think leprosy spreads between different species, even though there are leproid diseases for cats and dogs." I sat and mulled it over. "It would be fairly rare for something like RL2013 to jump species. But... I suppose it's possible." The idea left me reeling.

"If she is… how?" Celia asked, shocked.

I thought about it. The raccoons Addy fought couldn't have infected her so quickly, and they actually didn't seem infected themselves. So then what?

I thought of the night we had roast duck.

"You've seen my shoulder, where I was bitten. That night, there were two zombies. Addy killed the other one, but not before she'd been bitten several times." It was the only thing that made sense. How long had it been festering, latent? Was that possible?

And if this was true, what did it mean for the rest of the world? If the disease could spread to other species, what effects would that have? I imagined a chain of preposterous entirely imaginable events, like an infected wild dog attacking livestock used to feed the cities, spreading the disease back into the last bastions of safety left in the world. If that were to happen, only the loners would be left, pinpricks on the Earth's surface, barely noticeable. And as I well knew, survival in the wild was hard. I hadn't even made it through two winters yet. If the disease spread as I began to fear, it could well mean the final death knell for the human race, and many other species, too. Like Earth was being rebooted.

I stared down at my hands. My empty, useless hands, unable to do anything for even the dog below me, much less for the entire world.

Celia considered things for a moment. "If dogs can catch the disease, too, where does it end?" She looked at me, knowing I had no answer, but pleading with her eyes anyway.

"I don't know. Maybe it doesn't end," I sighed. "Maybe we do."

Below us, something stirred.

Addy.

She scratched at the floor in her sleep as we peered down at her. Slowly at first, then with growing strength, we heard a woeful sound. A long, low, rising howl came out of her, even as she slept. As the pitch rose, her eyes opened and she stirred awake, seemingly unable to stop herself from making the sound. She stood on jittery legs, head down, as the pathetic noise grew louder.

I looked at this poor dog. A dog I had become responsible for. My friend.

"I have to do something," I said in a low voice.

Celia turned to me. Even in the thin light of the barn, I could see her eyes fill with tears. The barn doors remained open, forgotten after the events of the evening. The entire place had a haunted, dim blue glow. "What can you do?" she said with a hollow voice.

"I don't know. Anything. Sit with her. Comfort her."

"She's not Addy anymore," Celia said. "She might..." I knew what she might do.

Below us, her pained wail increased.

I crumpled, shoulders falling. I knew it was true, that I could do nothing. But she was my friend. Why was this happening? Why this dog, this poor damn dog that just wanted to splash in the water? I squeezed my eyes closed and imagined us back at the house, playing in the shallows of the bay, Addy endlessly retrieving sticks as I threw them from the dock.

"Then I'll have to kill her. To put her down," I said, hating the words coming out of my mouth. Celia gasped, but didn't reject the idea. We spent a moment staring at each other. Did either of us have the strength to kill our companion, even if it was out of mercy? We wavered.

And then, finally, I decided it had to be done. If Addy was truly gone, then the monster trying to replace her had no right to live in her body, to take her form. I turned and picked up the gun.

As I stepped toward the ladder, Addy's horrible wailing stopped. Celia and I looked quickly downward, just as Addy began to shake and twist.

She turned in half-circles, she bumped the walls. I lifted the gun and put my foot on the ladder, determined to end this misery.

Whether Addy sensed some danger or just fell into a madness, I couldn't tell. Turning toward the open doors, she fled.

A short while later, we heard her moaning howl again, from the east, fading.

22

I held my hand out toward the barn door, as if that alone would return Addy not just to the barn, but to her old self. But she was gone.

I dropped the gun onto a rotted bale of straw in the loft and collapsed.

Celia came to my side, putting a hand on my shoulder. "Addy was a really, really great dog. But that isn't Addy anymore."

"We don't know anything for sure," I said, angry and irrational. Knowing that we really *did* know all we needed to know.

Celia grabbed both of my shoulders with her hands and turned me to face her. She was crying, tears streaming freely down her face. "Listen. I love Addy. When I ran into you two, after that first night, she took to me right away. You know what I went through with those bastards, that man Burt and his friend. I trusted the dog more than I trusted you. You were just another man. Another somebody to keep my eye on. But the dog, I could just love."

"You're afraid I might do something to you?" I asked, stunned.

She shook her head. "No, not now. Not for a long time. You're a good man. You really care about people."

"Me?" I scoffed. "Care?" I couldn't stifle a sarcastic laugh. "I holed myself up, alone, in the woods, scared, hiding. What people did I care about?" I shook my head.

"Her. I know you cared about her. *Rosa*," Celia said. It was the first time I heard Celia ever say the name. "And then she died and you needed to be alone, so you were. For a time." She looked right at me, her brown eyes glinting in the filtered moonlight. Near bald and mostly dirty, Celia held herself like a queen. Proud. Then I realized she *was* proud, of *me*. "But then a dog came along, and that dog would've died on its own. You saved her. Addy. And later a person came along, and you could've just shot me. I don't mean just the first night, but any time. Or smothered me in my sleep, or whatever. But you didn't. Instead, you gave me food, water, a place to stay dry, warm. Not since my aunt and uncle back in Norfolk has anyone *taken care* of me." Her lips quivered. The tears kept flowing. I wiped my eyes, noticing that I'd joined her. I looked down, embarrassed and ashamed to hear so much praise.

"Why is life *like this*?" I asked. "Why?" I balled my fists into my eyes, then turned and looked at the rafters of the barn. "We fight and fight, and sometimes we meet someone we care about... and then..."

"And that's the *reason* we fight. We fight because we *have to* have those moments. Those people we care about. Otherwise, it's all shit." Celia waved her hand at the barn, the world.

"Why Addy? Why that poor dog?" I asked no one. Then the idea came to me, strong. "I have to go find her. To do the right thing. The thing I was about to do here."

Celia shook her head. "How? You'll never find her out there, not unless she wants to be found."

"Well, I have to try."

* * *

The next morning, I gathered my gear. The gun. Some of our supplies in a knapsack. Celia did the same.

"Which way are you headed?" I asked her, just making conversation as I put things in order.

She pulled up. "With you," she said, matter of factly. I turned and looked at her, frowned.

"No. Come on. This is my responsibility."

"Stop," she said. "I love Addy, too. I'm coming with you."

"But—"

"But what?" she asked. "It isn't like I knew where I was going anyway."

I couldn't help but laugh.

* * *

We were ready to go before the morning got late, stepping out into the yard beside the barn. We took only one bag, our supplies were so light. We pointed east, away from the barn, the farm, the highway behind it. Ahead were woods and unknown.

As we crossed the small clearing and stepped into a thicket of trees, we heard an unusual and unwanted sound: *people.*

I knew instantly it was the big group that had passed us at the house. Moving faster because it was just the two of us, we circled them, east, then north, coming up the highway ahead of them. Now, after our days in the barn, they'd caught up. More and more we heard them. People ranging to our south, east, west.

We ran north, away from the sound, and into the dry fields of corn.

23

Yellow. Everything around me. The drying stalks of corn, withering unpicked. The clouds, looming in the late morning. In the distance, the yellow leaves on the trees signifying that fall was here in earnest.

The wind blew across the fields as we made our way north to avoid the refugees from Norfolk, tramping along somewhere behind us.

Ripples chased across the dry stalks, making waves of movement and a hollow rattling sound like the clacking of skeleton bones.

Celia ranged out in front of me, her grey hood up over her head and carrying the gun while I toted the last of our supplies on my back. As she crested a hill in the cornfield, she turned to look back at me. I gave her a half smile, to tell her that my sorry old bones were keeping up with her, able to carry the load. She smiled back, then turned away. In that moment, she reminded me of Rosa, standing and overlooking DC.

The wind picked up and so did the rustling noises. From our right, a particularly strong gust bent the wildly growing corn in a line heading toward our path, a line of dry stalks aimed directly at Celia.

From between the shifting yellow plants, I saw a brown blur. I froze.

"No!" I shouted, disbelieving.

Celia turned to see what was the matter.

Like a specter of death, Addy shot out of the corn and launched herself at Celia, who had turned just enough to spot the movement in her peripheral vision. The dog leapt with all the force of her weight behind her, slamming into Celia's midsection. The gun flew away as both dog and woman were propelled into the corn on the left of the path, out of view from where I stood. I raced up, noisily jangling the pack of supplies on my back as I ran.

I saw Addy, the dog we both loved, standing over Celia. Celia screamed as Addy bit into the flesh of her upper leg, making a terrible gaping wound. The dog was vicious and wild, its brown fur matted, wet-looking.

I stood stunned. My world spun. My friend. My *friends*. This couldn't be happening.

Celia screamed again, rolling away from the dog. Addy shook violently, spittle and blood flying, speckling the dry yellow corn stalks. Then the dog turned toward me.

For what seemed like forever, she simply stared. Then, emitting a low, gurgling growl, she approached.

"No, Addy, no," I pleaded, hands up before me. "Please. Stop. Please." Still she crept forward, looking at me with milky, seeping eyes.

I stepped backward and nearly tripped on something. The shotgun.

"Addy, please," I said, knowing it was pointless. Addy, my dog, was gone, replaced by this monster. A portion of my heart froze solid as I decided to act.

I wheeled and grabbed the gun. Addy took two steps and sprang at me, but even as she did, I spun the barrel toward her and fired.

My friend, my innocent, lovable friend, fell dead in a gasping lump, riddled with pellets from the gun. I sat gaping as she took her last breath. She looked up at me, not for an apology, not for pity, not with anger or mindless rage. In those last seconds, her eyes seemed to regain some of the warmth of life, just as that life was leaving her.

* * *

Hands shaking, I dropped the gun. I imagine it stayed right there until some other lost soul stumbled across it, who knows when later. All I knew was that I never wanted to touch it again.

I crawled over and put a hand on Addy. She didn't move. I wept as I stroked the bloody fur of her shoulder.

Off to the side among the corn, I heard a moan. Celia.

I jumped up, grabbed my pack, ran to her.

She was on her side, laying among the broken corn stalks with blood splashed and splattered all around her. I could see right away that she was in very bad shape. Her breathing was shallow and weak. I had to struggle to find a pulse. She barely opened her eyes to look up at me, then drifted back into unconsciousness. She was pale. Very pale.

Looking at the blood loss, I knew this was hypovolemic shock, and she would die, *soon*. Maybe in a hospital or even in my old office, I could save her, but we were in a damn cornfield. My will gave out and I flopped down, sitting beside Celia as her lifeblood escaped. I pounded the dirt with a balled fist. The wound on her leg was infused with dark blood and saliva. The metallic smell of blood filled my lungs.

I was sure that Addy had been infected by a zombie. And that meant...

Celia was now infected, too. Even if she didn't die here and now, she was dead. Rosa's cures, those eggs, weren't around to save her. I had nothing.

I sat with my arms wrapped around my knees, my head hanging low, as Celia's whispering breath went in and out.

Damn it. I felt so useless, doing nothing as my one friend lay dying, my other friend dead by my own hand just feet away. What a twisted triangle we'd become. Celia moaned slightly, her one hand shivering.

I lifted my head. I was *not* going to let Celia just die. I had to try something.

I rummaged through the supply pack until I found just what I wanted: the curved needle and some of the stronger thread. I pulled those out, along with a t-shirt and a tall plastic bottle containing our remaining water. I scurried over next to Celia.

First, I pulled off my belt and wrapped it around her upper thigh, tightening it to at least slow down the flow of blood. Then I used the water to rinse the wound. It was ragged, and any patch job I attempted would be difficult and heal poorly. That didn't matter, as long as it did heal. Even with the makeshift tourniquet, blood would seep again from the wound as soon as I rinsed it, so I pressed hard into the opening with the t-shirt. Then, to free my hands, I intertwined my legs around Celia's wounded leg, to hold the t-shirt in place and apply pressure. I pulled out the needle and thread.

Fumbling, hands shaking, I tried to thread the needle. I missed, over and over, eyes squinting at the tiny hole. Then, success. The thread went through. I held it and reached for the t-shirt, moving my body around for a better angle. That movement pulled the thread out, dropping it to the ground. I cursed at myself and twisted back. Again, I stabbed the thread at the needle, willing it to just *get the hell in the damn hole*. Finally, I got it.

This time, I held the threaded needle with a death grip, determined not to let it slip out again. I shifted my body and grabbed the t-shirt in one hand. It was getting soaked with Celia's blood, and her color was draining. How long did she have? I just acted on instinct, my training from younger days.

Jabbing the needle into her flesh, I made a series of haphazard stitches, a gross effort, just to pull the wound closed. Then, a quarter inch at a time, I made more precise stitches to pull her skin back together, down the length of the long gash. The end product was messy, like an intentionally grotesque scar for a Halloween costume. But the main bleeding seemed contained. The wound, however, still seeped blood. I had nothing left in the supply pack, so I simply improvised. I covered the sewn wound with the bloody t-shirt, wrapping leaves from the dried corn plants around the leg to tie it in place. I undid my belt tourniquet and moved it down to where it could hold the wound closed, tightening it enough to provide pressure but not cut off the blood flow. I took out a jacket and then stuffed the knapsack under her legs to prop them up. The jacket went on top of her as a blanket. Stepping back, I saw a ghost of Celia, a pale, deathly ill woman, lying in blood-soaked dirt, with the most laughably makeshift bandage ever made around her upper leg. But it would have to do.

To the south, in the far distance, the sound of people came again. The last sound I needed to hear.

I jumped up, ran to the top of the hill, scanned the surrounding land. To my left, not far off, a small barn with rotting, red-painted wood was standing. I charged over to it, into its shaded interior, looking wildly left and right. I found an old wheelbarrow covered in dirty cobwebs in one corner. Grabbing its handles, I pulled it down, turned back toward the door, and raced back to Celia.

Thankfully, Celia weighed much less than I did, but still I struggled. I tried to move her without tearing open the work I'd done on her leg, or even dislodging the ties of corn leaves holding things in place. I eventually got her into the wheelbarrow, head down in the metal body of the thing, legs angled upward toward the handles. I wanted to keep what little blood she had pooling near her head, in her brain. Sliding the pack onto my back again, I lifted the handles and began pushing north. The sounds of the approaching crowd increased to my south. I didn't dare turn around to look.

Stumbling down the path and over the hill, I pushed through the cornfield.

What was I doing? What was the point of all this? I didn't even know where I was going, just trying to get away. I'd left Addy, dead, behind me, and wheeled Celia, soon to be dead, in front of me. She was infected. This was pointless. Why was I doing it, still?

The whole world was a living hell. This whole world that kept tricking me into *trying*. Into *caring*. In the distance, maybe a mile to the north, I saw a small town. I headed there for no reason other than it was there and it was away from the mob to the south. Here I was, once again, trying to save someone, when I *knew* that saving people was impossible. Look at The Oasis. How many people had it saved, really, in the end? None. They all died. Look at Rosa. How many people had she saved? None. Not even herself.

Rosa: dead. Addy: dead. Harvey, Marian, Hank, Janine, the others: dead. And Celia. Even if I'd delayed her last breath for now, the disease had her. She was dead, too. Even I was dead, just a ragged old man shambling through fields, beyond salvation, the walking dead.

I let myself cry for all the lost ones, and for no reason at all, as I pushed the wheelbarrow toward a small road. Passing through the farmland, through the fields, I looked with wet, blurred vision at these hopeless pastures. There was no point to doing it, but I walked on.

Falling more than walking down the side of the small road toward the town, I nearly spilled Celia out of the wheelbarrow and into the rain-filled ditch that shadowed the road. My strength was leaving me rapidly.

I turned down one of the small streets lined with old shops that indicated the center of this little town. I vaguely scanned the front windows of the shops, thinking of finding shelter from the approaching mass of people.

I stopped.

There in front of me was an unexpected sight: a small medical clinic.

Its front door stood open, shadows hiding what was inside. I pulled the wheelbarrow up beside the door and left Celia there as I went in.

Everything was ransacked. I'd hoped to find medicine but there was nothing but smashed and empty bottles. I felt another wave of despair. Then I noticed that many of the clinic's other supplies remained. In addition to basic things like gauze and tape, there were blood-collection needles, drip tubes, clamps. Stuff that most people wouldn't know how to use. But I did.

In the back, I found several patient rooms. I chose the one that was the least cluttered, cleared off the exam table, and tried to make sure things looked as free from dirt as I could make them. It gave me visions of living in DC, keeping everything clean, holding off the tide of filth. But here, although I knew that I didn't want to risk additional infection, my ability to truly sterilize the room was nonexistent. I gathered supplies, organizing them on a wheeled U-base table and putting that next to the exam bed.

I went out to where Celia still lay upended in the wheelbarrow, feet up, head down. I tilted so that she was moved into a sort of standing position, then slid myself under and in front of her so she fell across my left shoulder. Hefting her up, I struggled into the clinic and managed to get her on the bed. She flopped down hard, but didn't budge, didn't make a sound. She was beyond pale, worse than even before, when I thought she might be dead. The t-shirt and corn leaves were soaked with blood. I had to work fast, but very carefully, doing something intricate that I'd never done before but only studied in basic theory, decades ago.

Bringing the rolling table along side, I reached for the water bottle and some gauze. I wet the gauze and cleaned her arm as best I could. There was nothing to truly sterilize her with, so this would have to do. I did the same to myself.

I gathered up two blood-collection sets and looked at them closely. They weren't meant to connect to each other, but I had to do it. On one, I uncapped the spike at the end of the drip tube. On the other, I removed the drip tube completely, carefully fitting the flexible PVC tubing over the spike of the other unit, making one long system, needle end connected to needle end. I was worried that it would become detached or that the spike would puncture the PVC, so I took the spike's cap and taped it to the connection point, like a splint for a broken bone, so it couldn't twist at that point. With more tape, I wrapped the connection, firm and complete, but not so thick and rigid that I wouldn't be able to get to a problem if one arose. Each kit had a rolling clamp on the PVC tubing; I closed both.

I knew my blood type was O negative, so a transfusion of red cells would be okay. But this would be a *whole*-blood transfusion, and anything could happen. Staring down at Celia's pale complexion and recognizing it as at least a Class III hemorrhage, possible Class IV, I had to do it. If she died, it was no different from what was already happening. And if for some reason I died... well, I think I'd seen enough for one lifetime.

My plan was to connect the flow of two bloodstreams together: anastomosis, it's called. Being right-handed, I put a rubber tourniquet on my left upper arm, and chose the most promising-looking vein near my left elbow. I shook my head in frustration, knowing that the simple act of inserting the line was something I could have offhandedly left to an assistant in my past life. I had to focus. I chose the median antebrachial and inserted the large bore needle delicately, remembering anatomy classes from so long ago, books and charts from my doctor days. I poked myself once, twice, three times, four. Sweat beaded on my brow. Looking over, I could barely see Celia's breathing, barely detect color in her skin. I tried to hit the vein again and failed. I was concerned that I'd have to try my right arm, complicating everything else I had to do, when the needle suddenly found the mark and blood flowed into the PVC tube, up to the rolling clamp. I taped the needle down, more than usual since I would be moving around, and sighed in relief. But I was hardly done.

Moving to Celia, I took the other side of my homemade transfusion kit and uncapped the needle. I took the tourniquet off me and put it on her upper arm, then I tapped her arm at the elbow to find the best vein. The median cubital seemed to be my best option, so I went for it. As I inserted the needle, her side of the PVC tubing also filled with blood up to the clamp. I'd have to remain standing, my arm higher than hers, to let gravity help the process. I returned the tourniquet to my arm, above the needle, so I could increase the pressure a bit more.

I rolled open the clamps, first on my side, then on hers, and watched the blood flow between us. I scanned her carefully for allergic reactions, but given her state, I probably could have been pouring arsenic into her veins with no visible effect.

I made my best guess on how to regulate the flow from me to her, trying not to overdo it but still working fast because of her condition. And then I was done. After the attack, the gunshot, triage in the field, the frantic flight that got us here, there was nothing to do but sit and wait.

Time passed.

A fatigue began to slowly, relentlessly seep into my bones. My eyelids slid down. I forced them back up. I tried to gauge the time, the flow, the amount of blood transferred, Celia's color. I had to stay on my feet.

Why was I doing this? She was still dead. The disease had her. I thought again about all the hard things, the horrific things, I had seen and done, all stemming from this one disease.

I closed my eyes and saw myself gun down Addy.

Time passed.

They say that time heals all wounds. I didn't believe that. Time *inflicted* wounds, one after the other, some small, some big, until finally you could no longer endure. You died. Time was not the healer of all. It was the destroyer.

Time passed.

I could barely stay awake. My knees trembled, buckled. I stumbled beside the bed, dangerously yanking the connected tubing between us.

One last thing…

I have…

To do…

I rolled the clamps closed and fell to the floor unconscious.

24

White.

Everything was blindingly white.

Was this death?

The barest of shadows passed in front of me, a form. A human form. A woman.

Rosa.

And then she was gone. Again.

* * *

Singing. I heard singing.

I tried to open my eyes, but the blinding whiteness outside was even greater than the blinding whiteness inside.

The singing stopped. "You awake?" a voice asked softly.

Celia.

Squinting, I raised my hand to shield my eyes. Why was my hand so heavy? Where was I?

Looking around, I saw the bottom of the exam bed, the legs of the U-base table. I was still in the clinic, on the floor. But I could feel a wad of clothes behind my head, a thermal blanket over me. In a raspy, dry voice, I asked, "How long?"

Celia knelt down beside me. "All told, I don't know. Because I don't know how long I was out. But it's been over a day since I woke up."

Over a day. Based on what I remembered of her condition, she would've been out for a while. It could have been as much as three days, total.

"I woke up *dying* of thirst," she said. "I drank what I could find, then got some of the last food from our bag over there." She pointed to it. "I figured you'd be really thirsty, too, so I put tiny capfuls of water in your mouth now and then. You sputtered them out pretty good a couple of times."

I suddenly realized how thirsty I was. Looking around, I saw Celia had a partial plastic bottle of water. I motioned toward it and she brought it to me. Drinking was hard, my throat uncooperative. But it was heaven.

She looked me in the eyes. "You saved my life. Thank you."

Returning the look, I had a moment of joy. Yes. She was *alive*.

But wait. What about...?

"How do you feel?" I asked, looking at her sideways.

Celia shrugged. "Fine, all things considered. My leg is a wreck, really hurts, and the stitches *itch*, I've got a headache, still weak, some other minor stuff, but you know... I'm okay."

"Fever?" I asked.

"I don't think so."

"What about any other symptoms? Lesions, lack of feeling on your hands or face, any delusions or fits of anger?" As I sat up, she pushed back, understanding my point.

"Wait, you think I'm...?" She couldn't say it. *Infected.*

I paused, trying to break it to her gently. "The dog. Addy was sick. Infected. The disease — RL2013 — I'm sure she had it."

"But I don't feel infected, not with... *it*... Not like I've heard about it."

I thought about it. Three days, as an estimate. And she didn't look infected. I reached out and touched her cheek, her fingertips. "Feel normal?"

"Yeah."

"Well, I agree. Normal skin." I sat and thought some more.

The blood. The *whole* blood. The red cells. The platelets. And the white blood cells.

Unlike during a normal blood transfusion, I hadn't separated my blood out, filtered it, radiated it. I hadn't done anything but put my blood — my whole, *cured* blood — into her body. My eyebrows raised.

She noticed. "What is it?" She was nervous about what I was saying.

"Maybe — just *maybe*," I held up one finger in a cautioning pose, "my blood passed something along to you during the transfusion. Antibodies. A resistance."

"You mean… the *cure*?" She said it quietly, like she was afraid the idea would run away from her if she was too loud.

"Yeah." I grinned. "That's what I mean."

A dawning smile broke across her face. "You're not kidding with me, are you?" She was beginning to bubble up, excitedly.

"I wouldn't kid about that," I said.

She flung herself at me, hugging me. She laughed, and I had to join her.

There we sat, on the floor of an abandoned clinic, in some small, desolate town on the Eastern Shore of Maryland, laughing like hyenas, hugging, rocking back and forth. We must have made a hell of an unexpected racket.

I started to cry. The first tears of joy I could recall in who knows how long. The blood. *My* blood. I truly believed it had cured Celia. And if that was the case, things had changed. They had changed beyond my wildest imagination. There was a new cure, and it was me.

After plodding along for so long, finding something then watching it stripped away, thinking there was nothing at all left for me to live for, now I suddenly had this: *I needed to live, so that others could, too.*

Then suddenly from outside the room, there was a voice.

"Hello…?" a woman said, tentatively.

We froze, holding our breath.

"Hello? Is someone back there?" the woman asked.

I looked at Celia, and our eyes met. Looking around the tiny, enclosed exam room, it was clear. There was no hiding this time. No escape. I nodded to her, and she pushed away and up. I stood, gingerly. She followed me to the door of the exam room.

I turned toward the front of the clinic, toward the waiting room, and there stood a middle-aged woman with brown disheveled hair, her white blouse and jeans splotched with dirt, a pistol strapped to her side. Behind her, people crowded all around the waiting room. Men — old, young, some of them also carrying guns — women, even a child or two. Their numbers led back out the open door to the street, where I could see dozens more standing in the sunlight, all looking toward us. A few of them looked concerned, or surprised, but mostly they were tired, spent.

Celia and I stepped into the hall and the woman in front pulled her hand up to the pistol at her side. I raised one hand, palm outward facing her.

"Hi," I said.

PART THREE

FROM BLOOD REBORN

1

I stood on shaking legs, one hand raised toward the woman in front of me. She lifted an eyebrow. *"Hi?"* She was confused by my greeting. And she was backed by dozens of people lined up out of the room, out of the building, into the street, piling up even as Celia and I were still dragging ourselves back to life in the small clinic, somewhere on Maryland's Eastern Shore. The woman's hand rested on a pistol strapped to one hip. I knew I had to be careful, but damn I was tired. And thirsty.

Celia stepped around me, toward the stranger. "Kate?" She looked incredulous.

"Celia? Is that you?" The woman, Kate, looked even more confused. "Wow. I only barely recognize you without... *hair.*", Kate seemed a little embarrassed for bringing that up. Celia self-consciously scraped one hand over her nearly bald head with a *scritch*, gliding across a tiny stubble of black hairs growing back slowly from her brown skin.

"Yeah, I cut it." Celia shrugged.

Kate squinted at her for a moment, then seemed to move on. We were all refugees in a world of disarray. There wasn't much point in dwelling on someone else's choice of hairstyle. "It's... good to see you again. Honestly, I'm *surprised* to see you. On your own for so long, I thought you were dead." Then she looked back to me. "But I guess you haven't been completely on your own." She eyed me up and down, unable to get a read on the scraggly, pale, bloodstained old man standing in front of her. I couldn't help but laugh. Again, Kate raised an eyebrow.

Celia gave a brief — and heavily edited — description of how and why she came to be traveling with me. She left out the real reason she had separated from the refugee group that had left Norfolk. But she did mention Addy. She paused, conflicted between feelings of love, anger, and betrayal. The dog had nearly killed her.

"We saw all the blood back in the fields," Kate said with a solemn look. She pointed at me. "You're saying he brought you back from *that?*" Now she was beyond confused.

"I used to be a doctor," I said. "In another life. Time immemorial. But I guess I remember some things." I scratched at my scruffy face absently.

Kate stared at me in an all-too-familiar, almost greedy way. Back when I lived within the walls of DC, I used to see that same look on the people in line with me at the old Capitol Hill Community Food Dispersal Center. A desire to have what someone else had. Then, it was food. For Kate, it seemed it was me. A doctor. It gave me pause. I didn't like Kate thinking of me as a commodity, especially one she coveted. I grimaced and turned away.

"Seems like everybody thinks *doctor* is a magic word," I said. I raised my voice and scanned the eyes of everyone crowded into the room, then looked back to Kate. "It isn't. These days, with no medicine or fancy equipment, I can do something when there are broken arms to set, or wounds to clean and stitch. But infection and disease? I'm as lost as you. I might be able to tell you *what* you have, but without medicines, all I can tell you is how soon you'll die."

Kate lowered her chin, her hand finally moving off her pistol. In her stained green shirt and jeans, she looked weathered, imposing. I realized then that she wasn't just the person who happened upon us, she was this group's leader. She scratched behind one ear, then spoke.

"We have two nurses with us. They're good. But your training…
it may give us more options."

May? Well, I guess these days that was about right. At least that
look of near-lust was off her face.

"What're you saying?" Celia asked.

Kate turned to her. "Join us." Celia hesitated, even taking a half
step backward. Kate continued. "I assume you're thinking about
Burt. I don't know what he did to you, Celia, but I know what you
did to him, and I know what he was like. Whatever that bastard did, it
had to have been something bad to make you take his eye." Celia's
face was stone, but Kate didn't flinch. "And to make you kill him."
Celia opened her mouth, closed it. Kate wore the look of someone
who was used to knowing more than everyone else. "Aaron told us
you shot Burt. At that house by the bay, where you two must've
lived." Aaron must be the skinny sidekick, the one who got away.

I frowned at Kate. It had been a long time since anyone knew
much of anything about me, and I didn't like hearing her tell a story
that I knew firsthand and she knew third. I started to say so when
Aaron himself burst into the clinic.

Tall and gangly, with the same stringy, unkempt blond hair he'd
worn when he and Burt arrived at the cabin, Aaron looked at us with

something like shock. Then he saw Kate standing across the room. "Oh my God. Celia. Well, isn't this nice?" Aaron's tone was mocking. He puffed himself up, seeming to expect the group to support him. "Kate knows about you, Celia. She knows all about what you did, and you're gonna pay for it."

"I'll pay?" Celia frothed. "*I'll pay*? What crime did *I* commit, Aaron? The crime of being raped by Burt, with your help? Or maybe you mean that I killed Burt. The man who *raped* a member of the group, just because he was in charge." Kate and the others pressed closer, hands on their weapons, and I reached out for Celia, trying to calm her. She brushed me aside.

Aaron looked at Celia with disdain. "Rape?" he asked. "Is that what you're calling it now?"

Celia seethed, fisted clenched. I knew her too well. *Don't*, I thought. *Don't*. She did. Spying the medical supplies on a nearby counter, Celia snatched up a pair of scissors and raged toward Aaron.

He raised his pistol from its holster, and she stopped, frozen.

Aaron was smug. "You see, Kate, dontcha? She's not right. She's violent. Just like I told you. Maybe she's *infected*, you know?" He smiled, then went straight-faced, an awful attempt to hide his true feelings. "You best drop that, Celia," he said, and she complied, tossing the scissors back on to the counter with a *clang*. Everyone's eyes went to Kate.

I saw that she had quietly trained her pistol on Aaron, holding it low, at her waist. After a pause, he noticed it, too, and Kate spoke. "Aaron, your true intentions are no mystery. And Burt wasn't what I'd call an innocent victim. Put the gun *down*."

Aaron withered. His gun slid sideways and ended up pointing at Kate, perhaps inadvertently, but she didn't miss the gesture.

Several others saw what was happening and turned their guns on Aaron, too. Even he could see that he was hopelessly outmatched. He might have killed Kate with a quick shot, but his victory would be short-lived. He nervously looked around at the weapons facing him.

"Hey, now," he said, licking his lips. "What's this?" His eyes roamed the room, but his pistol remained on Kate.

Her voice was brutally serious. "You will point your weapon somewhere else if you know what's good for you, Aaron." Her tone was unmistakable. One false move and he would die. Suddenly, I liked the idea of Kate as group leader.

A moment passed and no one gave in. I steeled myself for the ensuing gunfire, stepping instinctively to block Celia from harm.

After just bringing her back from the dead, I'd be damned if was going to let someone gun her down.

Then Aaron dropped his gun, returned it to its holster. "Kate. Seriously?" He was indignant now, trying to hide his sheepishness. "You're not turning this back on *me*, are you? This woman *killed* one of *us*."

Kate paused. But her resolve didn't swerve. "She killed a man that probably deserved every inch of killing he got." Aaron knew he had lost not only the battle but the war, and gears seemed to be turning in his head, trying to figure out what to do next. Kate lowered her pistol, but no one else in her group did. Apparently they took any threat to their leader very seriously. Celia and I remained frozen, unwilling to enter into this internal struggle.

Kate turned away from Aaron, now ignoring him. "I apologize for the interruption," she said, calmly returning her gaze to Celia and me. Behind her, Aaron fumed. Even more than her words or her gun, Kate's *dismissal* clearly stung him. He turned and stormed out of the room, pushing past people angrily, and several gun barrels followed him until he was gone. Kate looked at each of us. "We could use a doctor. Will you join us?"

She was all business. I wondered if Celia took offense that Kate's offer didn't really mention her at all, or what she might bring to the table. And I loathed that a tiny part of me was relishing the attention of once again being important. I scowled. "Yeah, we'll join you. For a while."

"*What?*" Celia wheeled to face me, incredulous. I met her gaze, trying to calm her without words.

"But no commitments," I quickly added, addressing Kate, but looking into Celia's eyes, hoping she'd understand. "No expectations. I'm not a miracle machine."

Kate looked skeptical. She glanced down at Celia's patched leg, and I could tell she thought otherwise. Her eyes met mine. "Deal." She held out a hand. "Can you travel?"

"I think so." I took her hand and we shook on it, as if that meant anything anymore. But it felt appropriate.

Celia stayed quiet, brow furrowed, her eyes boring holes through me.

2

"Are you *crazy*?" Celia asked in a hushed tone after most of the group had left the clinic.

I stopped packing our meager gear. "Maybe. But what good is it going alone now? There's strength in numbers." What a hackneyed phrase. Celia's grimace told me she wasn't buying it.

"And danger, too," she hissed back. "What about *Aaron...*?" I knew that Aaron wouldn't be the only bad seed in such a large group. I just hoped that with a leader like Kate, most everyone else would be good people. Or at least stay in line. My recent experience with human nature told me I'd be very lucky for that to be the case.

I pulled a bottle of water from one of our packs and took a huge drink, and thought for a moment. "You recognized her," I said. "What do you know about Kate?"

"She was with us. After we got out of Norfolk. After the tunnel." Celia shuddered at the memory of her long, dark flight from a known enemy and into an unknown world. "Burt — the guy I killed back at the house — was pretty much in charge, and Aaron was with him, but mostly because no one else stepped up."

"They were in charge, but you told me you didn't know Aaron's name. How's that?"

She chuckled, but there was no humor in her voice. "We called him *Ernie*, because he and Burt were inseparable. But I knew that wasn't his real name. Anyway, I think a lot of people could see Kate would be better for the group, me included. So at least I can say that I think the group's better now, with Kate in charge."

Okay, that was a good start. Celia confirmed some of my impression of Kate. Maybe we could work it out.

I still felt obligated. Now that I knew it was *possible*, I had to figure out a way to help them, help someone, overcome the disease. "Do you know where they're headed?" I asked. "Are they looking for The Oasis?"

"Probably," Celia said. "There were a lot of different rumors when we were traveling."

"Why north?"

"Baltimore was one possibility. So was Syracuse, up in New York. But they may be headed somewhere else."

I considered the long, cold march to upstate New York, and knew I had to stop this mad rush to nowhere.

My blood had saved Celia. But I couldn't start giving out transfusions to everyone in the whole group. Not without dying. And, for the first time in a long time, I felt like there was a *reason* not to die. I felt like there was something I had to do.

But *how?*

Damn it, I wished Rosa was there. I was a general practitioner, a family doctor, meaning I knew enough to be dangerous. She was the medical research specialist. I *needed* her. The thought made me wince. And Celia noticed.

"What?" she asked. She was frozen, studying me.

I felt like I'd been caught. "Nothing," I said, turning away.

Celia rolled her eyes. "Listen. I get it. You lost someone really, really special to you. I lost my brother, my parents, friends, and... Addy, too." The memory was bittersweet for both of us. "Everyone's lost someone special. Someone that *should* have been with them to the end. But you've got to get it together. We need to be smart."

I scoffed. Really? Celia, basically a child, was going to lecture me on what I needed to do. That I needed to get it together? It made me angry. I considered a really ugly remark or two, but instead I waited. I was too old for that sort of nonsense. I took a breath.

"Celia. You're right. And you're wrong. It's true, I was thinking of Rosa. But not just in some wistful way. Hell, that's a disservice to her memory anyway. She was better than that. You know, she didn't *find* the cure to the disease, but she was the one who found the way to spread it. Now it looks like *I'm* the damn cure. And I don't know how to spread it. The only thing I can figure is that we need to connect with people — maybe a *lot* more people — until we see who can help us figure this out. If Rosa was here, I bet she'd know. But she's not. So we need to find others. And that's why we need this group." Celia seemed to thaw a little. I pressed on. "And besides, I'm tired. I don't know if I can keep trying on my own. Or even just the two of us. I'm a lot older than you, remember?"

She lowered her chin and gave me a wry look. "Did you think I could forget *that*?"

"Okay, smart aleck. Are we agreed? We join the group?" I lifted our near-empty bag of provisions.

The gesture wasn't lost on her. We had nothing else. "Yeah, come on," Celia said, and walked past me and out of the room.

* * *

Outside, we noticed the chill in the air as we caught up with Kate, but the late fall scent of decaying leaves decay conjured up pleasant memories, not bad ones. Sunday-afternoon football and trick-or-treating and a thousand other things we might never do again. Kate sat on a bench outside the caved-in remains of a bike shop, examining some items that members of the group had found in the small town — cans of food, a couple bottles of water, and several winter coats. Seeing the coats made me feel the cold wind even more. If we didn't find a more permanent home, we were all going to need a lot more than those few coats very soon.

"Where're you headed?" I asked Kate bluntly as we stopped in front of her.

She paused, looked up. From her eyes, I sensed that she was silently asking herself and me why she needed to justify her actions to a new person, an outsider, a no one. But she waved away the others who were gathered loosely around her, so that only she, Celia, and I stood together.

"Baltimore, most likely. At least, that's the current plan."

I frowned. *"Baltimore?* Why?"

Kate blinked. She wasn't used to being second-guessed. She paused, gauging her answer. I knew right then what the truth was. No matter what she said, I'd made up my mind. She was hoping The Oasis was in Baltimore.

But she wasn't going to admit that to us. "We discussed this as a group," she said. "Baltimore seems like a good place to find a pocket we can fortify and make our home —"

"Are you kidding?" I said. Celia shot me a warning look. *Take it easy.*

Kate was aggravated, but simply raised her eyebrows and said, "I take it you disagree."

I flailed my hands. "Baltimore fell right at the beginning. What do you think you'll find there?"

Kate didn't flinch. "Walls. Safety. Security. A place to start again."

"Walls that *fell*. Safety that was a *lie*. Security for *no one*." I stopped myself, took a breath. Changing my tone, I asked, "Have you heard something about Baltimore, something that makes you want to go there?"

Ever so slightly, Kate blushed, and she turned away. My hunch was right.

"The Oasis, *right?*" It wasn't a question so much as an accusation.

Kate froze. She wasn't used to people guessing her mind. She looked like she was fumbling for a response. "All right," she said, nodding. "I can see I'm not dealing with someone who blindly plays 'follow the leader.' The Oasis. That's it. That's what we're hoping to find." She spoke like she was daring me to argue with her. But knowing what I knew, what choice did I have? Just to follow along?

"The *Oasis?*" I didn't mean to sound derisive, but I'd been in her shoes before. I'd blindly plodded down this path, hoping The Oasis was at the end. By chance, the *true* Oasis was at the end of that one path, but I knew it wasn't at *the end of all of them*. I twisted my eyes back to meet Kate's. "Well. Just stop." I wasn't sure what to say, or how to say it. But the words came out anyway. "It's not there."

"And you know this *how?*" Kate's cold eyes studied me.

Before I fully thought about the consequences, I said, "Because it was in South Carolina. I was there." I could see she didn't quite believe me, and so, like I fool, I forged on. "They even had the cure, and they fell. There's nothing left there now."

Kate gasped.

Immediately, I realized my folly. I'd just met this woman, these people. And now, I was telling them everything. *Who cares? Shouldn't they know?* My mind was as tired of this aimlessness as my weary muscles and bones.

Kate held her tongue, like someone who was used to sizing up other people, trying to figure out whether to believe them. "You're… *serious*, aren't you?" she asked.

I grimaced. "Yeah, I am." Kate's expression didn't change, but something in her eyes collapsed, and guilt hit me. I had just taken away the one thing that gave her hope.

"Wait…" I started, then stopped, not knowing the right thing to do or say.

Kate looked into my eyes. "Tell me the whole story, everything about The Oasis, or I have no reason to believe you, and we'll head to Baltimore as planned." She was shrewd and to the point. I owed her the truth. But I had no intention of telling her anything about Rosa. No one got those memories for free. So she heard a shorter version, one that I hoped left out all the questions I didn't want her asking. I told her about leaving DC, the search, finding the camp, then the cure. And then I told her about the fall.

Kate was quiet. Seconds seemed like hours, as if I could count the span of time between her eyes blinking. Finally, she looked at me again. "You're *cured?*" she asked in a low voice.

I hesitated, suddenly aware of what my next response might mean. Still, her eyes never wavered. And, for better or worse, I relented. With a sigh, I said, "Yes."

Celia fidgeted next to me, and Kate's attention was drawn to her. "And you? Were you at The Oasis, too? Are you cured?"

"No — well, um." Celia hesitated.

Kate turned back to me. "Which is it?" she asked. coyly, regaining her normal demeanor as the head of the group.

Celia was flummoxed, not used to the scrutiny. "It's both," she said. "And neither…"

"Both yes and no," I said. "Celia wasn't *at* The Oasis. But she *is* cured. I just cured her, back where you found us."

Kate almost couldn't comprehend what I was saying. *"You cured her? Here? Now?"*

Where moments ago I had taken away Kate's hope, now I gave her something even more. She beamed a broad smile.

3

If you were living in hell, and there was news of free ice water, that news would travel fast. Not surprisingly, so did the news of the cure.

By the time our conversation with Kate was over, a knot of wide-eyed people had formed around us. They looked at Celia and me like we were saviors. Or mythic creatures. Or freaks.

It wasn't long before the murmuring began. Among the low tones, I could hear bits of questions, demands… *Give it to us … Why are they keeping it to themselves? … Can we take it from them?*

Kate heard these, too, and showing herself to be a true leader, she stepped up onto the bench she'd been sitting on when Celia and I had first walked up. A cool breeze brought the early, foreboding scents of winter, pushing aside the more complex aromas of fall.

Turning left and right, Kate waved her hands and shouted, commanding everyone's silence and attention. "Enough! Listen. I understand. Like you, I just found out that our new companions *may* be cured of the infection. Hell, right now, no one knows if that is even *true*, but I don't know what good it'd do to lie about it. And I'm excited. And scared. And thrilled. And thinking about a better tomorrow. But we don't know enough yet." She gestured to me to come closer. When I did, she crouched down and whispered in my ear, *"Tell us all how we can be cured."* The mix of hope and desperation in her voice was painful to hear, especially when I knew what my answer had to be.

I looked down at the cracked sidewalk, another memento from a vanished age, from a time when lovers and families strolled safely and aimlessly down the street, and I gathered my thoughts. As the wind blew colder, I turned to the group, and saw all eyes on me, nearly 200 in all. I decided to rip the bandage off first. "I can *not* cure you all!" I shouted. A collective moan emanated from the group. "At least, not immediately. Not today." In the back, where the bravest cowards always hide, there were jeers of *Why not?* and *He's lying!* Kate moved to intervene, but I waved her off. "Hold on, hold on," I said. "I understand you all want this with every fiber of your being. To be cured. To make this long nightmare end. But I can't do that for you *now*." More murmurs from the back.

"I've been to The Oasis. I've been cured of the disease. But I have to tell you that The Oasis is gone." Gasps and wails, but I pushed onward. "My friend Celia here, she was a member of your group when you left Norfolk. She and I met by chance, and later she was bitten and infected. I didn't know what to do, but I didn't want her to die, so I gave her a blood transfusion." People looked at me skeptically. "Not only did she live, she lost all signs of the disease. She was *cured.*"

A renewed fervor of cries, people demanding the cure for themselves. "I used to be a doctor," I said, my voice fraying with the effort, "back before the outbreak, but that doesn't mean much anymore. But I think my blood knows how to fight the infection, and through the transfusion, Celia's blood does, too. That's the good news."

People alternately cheered and demanded more, some demanded their cure immediately. It was time to drop the hammer. "This is the bad news. Even if I wanted to cure every single one of you, right now that would mean giving you each a transfusion of my blood. Not only is that generally risky, it's not something I can physically do. Back before the outbreak, the general rule of thumb was only to give blood every eight weeks. And that was just for giving a pint of blood — I gave a lot more to Celia. It may take a lot more to make this work, I don't know. But if I have to wait eight weeks between every transfusion, and there are, what, a hundred of you all? That's a long time. And I might die doing it. Or one of you might die, from some complication."

Shouts again in the back. *Make the woman do it, too!* I couldn't blame them for wanting to be cured, but I needed to defuse a potential mob scene. In a low voice, I asked Celia, "Do you know your blood type?"

"AB, I think," she replied, unsure. I grimaced. My O type was the "universal donor," while hers was far from it. If we needed plasma, she'd be great, but in most cases my blood was the only one that was going to help.

I called back to the crowd. "Celia's blood type isn't right. If some of you remember anything about blood types — A, B, AB, O — and about donating blood, you'll know what I mean. My blood is type O, and I can give it to any of you. Celia thinks hers is AB. And that won't work."

Grumblings told me they weren't all convinced. I kept at it. "But I want you all to know this. I want to help you. I want you to have the cure. I just need your help. We need to find a way to make it possible for me to give it to you all, and to replicate what I have. That's why we want to join you, and that's why I *don't* want you all to go to Baltimore!"

Kate flinched, clearly upset at me for going to the group when our discussion hadn't been concluded. She stabbed a look of anger in my direction, then jumped up. "Okay, folks," she said, arms stretched out to her sides, hands gesturing for folks to calm down. "I know many of you want more answers, but now you know everything we know. We're here in this town, the sun won't stay out forever, and it's already getting pretty cold. We'll stay here until morning. Everyone, find shelter. Eat at daybreak, pack and out one hour after that. That's it, go about your needs." She clapped her hands, and it was clear she was dismissing the group. Some grumbling remained, but everyone listened and went about their duties.

In the back, I saw Aaron. As the others separated and moved to their various chores, he stood still, staring at me.

4

"DC," I said the next morning as Kate and her inner circle packed gear and readied to go.

"What?" she asked, annoyed.

"We need to go to DC," I said, crossing my arms, unflinching. "That's the best place to find the people and the labs where we can figure out how to spread this cure. Baltimore is just chasing ghosts."

"Well, I appreciate your unsolicited input, but we're going to Baltimore," Kate said. "This has been decided. You don't just tag along and get to call the shots." Her offhanded dismissal told me I'd better be careful. If I wanted to have a say in what the group did, where we went, I needed to start earning her trust.

"Take the Bay Bridge," I said.

Kate stopped working items into her backpack and turned to me, curious, concerned. "We thought about it," she said, "but we're concerned about being exposed, and about the condition of the bridge."

"I walked it a few months back. It was fine then, I bet it still is now." I knew the bridge was the fastest way to Baltimore, a desirable choice if that was her goal. Plus, it was the most direct route toward DC.

Kate thought about it, then seemed to come to a decision. "We'll take a look at it. I'd rather not go all the way around if we don't have to." Then she leaned in close. "But listen. You need to understand a few things. I don't make arbitrary decisions. You standing up and making me look bad doesn't help *anyone*. If people stop responding to my leadership, fine, but I don't see anyone else stepping up. Most of these people just need some sort of structure or else they'll give up. Before I took over, Burt was in charge." She paused to let that sink in. "You met Burt, albeit briefly. I'm sure you got a good sense for what kind of leader he was. People needed something more, someone better, someone they could trust. I didn't want the job, but folks wanted someone who'd help them, not bully them. I was basically drafted, and by enough people that Burt couldn't argue. Aaron has no love for me, and there are others who dissent. It happens. So when you stand up and disrespect me, rally people against me, you're helping Aaron and his kind. Is that really what you want?"

My respect for Kate grew in bounds as she spoke. Still, I had to ask. "You think every decision you make is the *right* one for the group, then?"

Kate shook her head. "Wouldn't that be nice? No, I don't. But at least I do *think*."

"Then why not listen to reason about Baltimore?"

Kate seemed ready for that. "People need hope. They believe The Oasis is in Baltimore. We *need* to go there, even if we don't find anything. Otherwise, they'll always be wondering, trying to get away to see for themselves, rather than help us here. Now."

I could hardly argue with her. Hadn't Rosa and I been drawn to The Oasis not so long ago? "Listen," I said. "I want what you want — good for the group. And more than that, I want good for *humanity*. I'm bringing you a new hope." I knew I sounded ridiculous, but kept looking at her, silently pleading, no more words to offer.

After a moment, she nodded. "If it's clear, we take the bridge. After that, we'll talk." She pointed a finger at me. "But *don't* go lobbying the group with speeches again."

I bowed my head in agreement.

* * *

It took two days to march the group to the eastern edge of the Bay Bridge, with men, women, and children hauling everything they owned on their backs, in push carts, or in wheelbarrows. The bridge was actually two different spans, one next to the other. Out of habit, we followed the backed-up line of abandoned cars until we reached the northernmost stretch, a three-lane slab of road pockmarked with ragged holes.

As the morning dragged on, the weather began deteriorating, with a slow, cold rain falling. At the foot of the bridge, Kate stopped to assess what she saw. One of her closest advisers, a tall, muscular blond kid named Jacob, handed her a pair of binoculars. She studied the bridge, or at least the part she could see in the rain. After a while, she announced her decision. "It's got plenty of defects, but it looks solid if we're careful. But I don't like this weather." As if in response, the wind kicked up. She turned to Jacob and another adviser, a sturdy, short-haired brunette named Vera. "What do you think? Bridge, or north and around?" Her gaze swept to the right, northward. The bay stretched as far as our eyes could see. I could smell the damp sweetness of rotting leaves, and tried to concentrate on nothing beyond the steady drum of the rain.

It was clear that no one wanted to take the long road. Finally, with a curt nod, Vera said, "We should take the bridge."

Kate returned the nod and it was done. We prepared to move out. "We'll take the front," Kate said. "Tell Marcos, Yolanda, and…" She considered her options. "And Aaron to take the back. Let's get going." Kate's lieutenants passed down her orders, and we began crossing the bridge, hoping the weather would hold.

It didn't.

5

The Chesapeake Bay Bridge is more than four miles long. An average human walks at about three miles per hour, but our speed was reduced significantly by the size and makeup of our group. Adding to the problem, the bridge had countless little gaps and breaks, and, as we made our way along its convex surface, we noticed the grasses and other small plants that had been sprouting in pockets and corners where dirt had accumulated since the outbreak. It was a surreal reclamation by nature of something inherently unnatural.

As we progressed along the bridge, getting higher, I sensed a collective feeling of unease. People pulled their coats more tightly against themselves, and clustered toward the center of the road, as far from the edges as they could get. The water fell to more than a hundred feet below us, an icy grave for anyone who was careless enough to fall. It was more than two hours before we reached the halfway mark, and for most of that time we were looking back constantly to ensure the group and its provisions were still with us.

Then the weather got worse. The wind increased dramatically as the rain intensified. Our visibility was cut to 250 feet, maybe less. Kate soldiered on, trying to lead the group over the midway point, so we could start on the faster downhill side.

It was as good an idea as any. But without warning, three infected attacked the rear of the group. My guess is they'd been holed up in one of the many wrecked cars on the bridge, or maybe in several of them, and we drew them out as we passed. They launched themselves at our rearguard. Seeing them, Aaron lost what little spine he had and came running forward through the group, leaving his point unguarded. As the zombies attacked, I later learned, Marcos and Yolanda tried to repel them. But without Aaron, there was an opening.

Near Yolanda, a mother was trying to coax her tired and unwilling young son to follow the group. The boy, with a mop of dirty blond hair and an untucked plaid shirt, resisted in the way only exhausted children can, not understanding his own plight. They'd been making their way slowly across the bridge, barely keeping up. Without Aaron to stop it, one of the zombies hit the mother and son like a freight train, knocking her down and sending the boy tumbling on the wet pavement. After an initial scream of surprise, the mother saw what was happening and shrieked. The zombie mercilessly leaped onto the young boy.

From the front, we heard a gunshot rip through the air, for a moment stilling even the sound of the storm, and we all stopped. Then came the mother's horrific wail. I looked to Kate, saw her breath puff like clouds in the frosty air, the pitiless rain continuing to fall all around us. Her hair was wet, matted to her forehead, and her expression was one of determination and resignation. Without a wasted moment, she rushed through the group toward the source of the noise. Celia and I followed. Along the way, we passed Aaron, who was scrambling in the opposite direction. Kate shouted something at him that was lost in the rising sounds of the storm and the commotion.

A mother. Howling over her lost child. As if in answer, the wind began to rage and the cold rain pounded even harder, almost blinding us.

Nearing the scene, we saw mayhem and slowed to get our bearings, just for a moment. Something was happening to our right, hard to see in the rain. In the center of the bridge, Yolanda stood over a dead zombie, her gun drawn. Then we saw the mother, a petite brunette in soaked jeans and a soiled red coat, as she madly dove at the zombie that was on her son. In an instant, it turned on her. We ran to help.

Just before we reached them, Kate vanished.

Panting, I swiveled my head to look for her. I was disoriented, saw nothing in the pouring rain. My attention was drawn back to the horrible scene in front of me. I was weak from the transfusion, slower from age. I could do little but stare. The boy seemed to already be dead. The mother wasn't far behind. The zombie had knocked her down, and although she fought, it was stronger than she was. Celia ran toward them, delivering a kick to the gut of the zombie that sent it rolling off the woman. But the effort was hard on Celia and her newly repaired leg. She crumpled, landing on the road just feet from the infected monster.

Screams seemed to come from every direction around us. The rain, wind, people running everywhere, fighting. It was impossible to take it all in.

The zombie rolled, began to get up. Celia tested her leg, and, although she grunted from the pain, she stood and began backing away. The soaking wet zombie, what remained of a large man in a tattered jacket and ragged slacks, maybe a businessman or lawyer in his former life, rose up and took a step toward her. And another shot rang out. The zombie's forehead exploded, and he fell backward.

For a moment, Yolanda just stood there, shaking, her pistol held out in front of her, like her arm was frozen. A sound came from the right — a man's desperate cry. Yolanda snapped out of it, whipped around. Through the rain, we could barely make out Marcos, fighting another one of the infected.

Near the crumbling outer wall of the bridge, Marcos staggered. One zombie lay beheaded near his feet, but another had grabbed him from behind, and Marcos flailed to get it off. His weapon, a rusty but formidable-looking scythe he'd probably pillaged from some Eastern Shore barn, was useless with the zombie so close.

"*Marcos!*" Yolanda shouted. She waved her gun, but it was clear she didn't have a shot. Marcos and the zombie continued to struggle. Marcos pushed upward into the zombie's face, trying to get it off his back. The thing bit down onto his left hand, tearing through flesh, and Marcos screamed. In pain, he twisted and shoved, desperate to get free.

We saw what was happening just a moment before it was too late.

Whether Marcos intended it or not, I couldn't tell, but with a lurch they both tumbled over the edge of the bridge and were gone. Even the sound of their fall, their crash into the frigid waters below, was lost in the howling wind.

I gazed around at the others, stunned. Celia stood with her mouth agape. Yolanda slowly lowered her pistol. Some others in the group who had witnessed the fight remained cowering where they were, unbelieving. We all shivered in the cold, whimpered, traded hollow stares.

At that moment, a voice echoed in my head from a distant past. I had been in residency at a small hospital in rural Virginia, shadowing a codger named Dr. Hawthorne, when three people were rushed in. They'd been in a bad car accident. One of the three was nearly cut in half, and all I could do was stare at his lifeless form. Hawthorne leaned toward me, and in a whisper, harsh, not unkind, said, "There's nothing to be done for the dead. Save all you do for the living." Then he rushed to help the other two victims, and I followed.

Leaving my daydream, I thought of the young mother on the bridge in the cold rain, and ran to her side. Her breath was rapid, ragged, and she was soaked in icy rainwater and blood. I checked her pulse and felt nothing, not knowing how much of the problem was my fingers, numb from the cold. Nonetheless, I figured she didn't have long. I turned toward the boy and could see that the life had already left him. *There's nothing to be done for the dead.* At least neither of them would have the indignity of becoming zombies themselves. It was very small solace.

Standing, I looked toward Celia and Yolanda, and I could see the question in their eyes. I shook my head. *"Both?"* Yolanda asked, desperately. I nodded, and her shoulders fell.

That's when we heard a new sound. It was barely audible. A low, plaintive cry, coming from somewhere nearby. *"Help —"*

"Is that…?" Celia turned her head.

"Kate!" Yolanda shouted, completing Celia's thought. Instantly, we spread out, frantically looking for Kate. We swept around abandoned cars and debris, searching the width of the bridge. Others who had been huddled in fear now turned their heads, rose to their feet, tried to help us locate her.

Near the northernmost edge of the bridge, down low, I saw her hair.

Kate hung below the bridge, in a ragged crack that cut deep into the surface, her feet dangling freely some 150 feet above the cold waters of the Chesapeake. It seemed impossible. What kept her from falling? Surely she couldn't be hanging on by her own strength, not for this long. I reached down, looking for a way to help her back up without sending myself off the edge. And I discovered what had saved her. Or perhaps what had damned her.

As I reached down to help lift her back to the bridge deck, my hand scraped against a thin shaft of rusted metal — *rebar.* I saw several of the twisted bars poking out of the crumbled edge of the bridge. Three or four of them had dug into Kate's clothes, acting like an industrial-strength coat hanger. But one stabbed directly into Kate's right armpit. Blood streamed down the rebar, obscenely bright against the dull metal, and her right shoulder was hunched up at a strange angle. Kate appeared to be in shock, but still had the strength to shout in pain when I started to move her.

"Is she okay?" Celia asked, appearing next to me, Yolanda right behind her. "Is she gonna make it?"

"Only if she's lucky. But first, we have to get her out of this crack." I stood, gave Celia and Yolanda a serious look. They seemed overwhelmed by the yawning gap that opened below Kate. I needed to focus them. "It's going to hurt her," I said. "*A lot.* But if we fail, she either bleeds to death here or she falls. So when we move her, it has to be all the way up, all at once. No second chance, understand?" They nodded, gravely. "We need help, too." I looked around at the other members of the group who had joined us, pointed at a strong-looking young guy with a thick, dark beard. "*You!* We need your help here, right now!" I didn't leave room for rebuttal. He looked around, sheepishly, hoping I was pointing at someone else, but joined us.

As quickly as possible, we prepared a wheelbarrow as a makeshift gurney. Then it was one big tug, wrenching Kate up, screaming in pain, out of the crack. Slumped in the wheelbarrow, she reminded me of Celia only days before. We started to move and I did my best to plug up the wound, but I needed someplace dry to work. *Fast.*

So we rushed to the western shore ahead of the group, maneuvering around cars, dodging holes. Bumping over rubble as Kate screamed until she passed out.

The rest followed as quickly as a hundred souls —now 97 souls — could manage, hoping the bridge held no more surprises.

6

The rain had slowed to a drizzle by the time we made it to the far side of the bridge. Celia, Yolanda, and I trotted alongside of Kate in her wheelbarrow gurney. The young man with the beard — his name was Evan — pushed.

As we came off of the bridge, we saw two structures. To our left were the destroyed remains of the eastbound tollbooth. At some point, probably during the massive evacuations that accompanied the first outbreak 10 years ago, cars had taken out most of the supports, and the roof had caved in. But on our right, a red-brick building stood whole. It was marked with a faded four-color Maryland crest above its door, and just in front of the building stood a small bell. I couldn't tell for sure, but it seemed like a replica of the famous Liberty Bell from Philadelphia. The reminder of time gone by momentarily shook me. Old phrases and notions popped into my head, vestiges of an education that now felt useless. *Give me liberty or give me death!* Hell, just give me a minute to breathe. I wouldn't know what to do with liberty, and I'd had enough of death.

We entered the building, with Evan now backwards-hauling Kate up a few stairs. Thankfully, she remained unconscious, and we were glad to be out of the spitting rain. It even felt nominally warmer, since the walls cut the wind. I grabbed for my pack. As the others slid debris off a table and moved Kate onto it, she awoke, briefly. In a low, strained voice, she said, "We have supplies. Get Renee. She's a nurse. She has what you need." Then she faded out again.

I nodded at Yolanda, and she left to pass word to Renee, who was still part way up the bridge. We had to wait for her arrival.

Even unconscious, Kate seemed to moan as I pressed on her wound, desperate to slow the bleeding. Finally, Renee arrived. She wore a backpack, a dour expression shadowing her face. "You have medical supplies?" I asked. She nodded, then she looked down at Kate, lying on the table, with a sense of disdain that I didn't understand. Shaking it off, I asked for the supplies I needed, and Renee took them from her pack.

Without anesthesia, we simply plowed forward. "Do you have sutures, ski needles?"

Renee glared at me. "I know how to do my job," she said, pushing me out of the way. Still, I peered over Renee's shoulder to inspect the wound. Kate was lucky. The rebar that had gathered in her clothing was what stopped her fall. She had scratches and cuts here and there, but they were minimal, and the major injury to her right armpit was manageable. Some cleanup and a few sutures, stuff Renee could ably handle, although I watched her work carefully. Barring infection, Kate would live. Renee finished the work silently, and left.

As if on cue, Aaron stormed in. Behind him, a small group of supporters streamed through the door. "There you are!" he spat.

Yolanda reacted first, lifting her pistol. "Shut your mouth, you son of a bitch. You abandoned your post!"

Aaron pulled up, hands raised in innocence. "The hell I did! I was *attacked!* I went for help, to *save* everyone. If I hadn't brought in the others, a lot more people might have died."

Celia roared at him, fists balled tight. "We saw you running away, you *coward!* Because of you, a mother and her kid are dead, and Kate is lying here!"

Aaron's hand dropped to his holstered pistol. "Hold on now…" he started, ominously. I realized then that I truly hated Aaron.

The others behind him pressed in closer, but Yolanda already had her gun drawn, and she was seething. "Go ahead, Aaron, make a move." Her pistol vibrated in her white-knuckled hands, tense, energized. It was clear she didn't need any encouragement to kill Aaron, and with Kate subdued, no one was trying to stop her.

Behind Aaron, the others spread out, maybe to avoid the line of fire, or maybe to make it impossible for Yolanda to defend against them all at once.

I had to do something. I jumped in the middle.

"Stop it, all of you!" I said. "We've been through something awful. We've lost people, a child. Let's not make it any worse by fighting each other."

"Yeah, listen to him, everyone," Aaron said, once again feigning compassion. A hack actor on a pretend stage. "Our new doctor here is the one who said we should take the bridge — let's be sure to listen to *him* again!" He pulled out his gun.

And I wheeled on him. Sometimes, combinations of factors work in your favor. This time, the fact that Aaron was at heart a coward, and that I had very little to live for, made it easy for me to swat his gun away in a single gesture. The heavy pistol clattered to the floor, and Aaron looked at me wide-eyed with alarm and dismay. In a low voice, I said, "Get out of here now, Aaron. And don't try me again."

He turned and fled, and his cadre of supporters gradually followed.

7

We stayed the night in the building near the tollbooth, and continued west early the next morning. The day dawned clear but very cold.

Kate recovered surprisingly well. She had scrapes all over, and you could tell she was clenching her jaw to keep from wincing with every step, but she was able to keep moving. Vera and Jacob stayed close to her, often carefully holding her up as she walked. Although the frigid rain had stopped, the air actually felt colder. We kept walking away from the bay, heading west on Route 50. After a while, as the road curved to the left, we saw another bridge, much smaller. Compared to the Bay Bridge, this was nothing but a small arch. A rusting sign nearby said it passed over the Severn River.

Inexplicably, my blood ran cold, freezing my heart for just a moment. I had no reason to dread this place, but I did.

Then, scanning along the bridge, I saw them, toward the middle of the span. First one, then another. Zombies, breathing steam out into the cold air like dragons. They'd come out to forage now that the rain had stopped. They were some distance from us, but we were a big group, with so many people it was nearly impossible to be truly quiet or go unseen. The zombies heard something of interest and with their clouded vision began looking in our direction. They probably couldn't actually see us, but, following their instincts, they began to slowly walk down the bridge, toward us.

"What do you want to do?" I asked Kate. Breathing hard, swaying on her feet, she tried to project an air of strength. It failed. She ended up looking to her advisers with an unexpectedly lost stare. Jacob seemed confused by this new Kate he didn't recognize.

Vera was more pragmatic. She turned to me. "What would you do?" she asked, part plea, part dare.

I put my hand on my shaggy chin. On my wrist was the multicolored bracelet Rosa had made for me, frayed more all the time, but still there. I touched it, as if it would help me decide. Rosa had always seemed so confident in her decisions. I wasn't sure what to do, but I could almost hear her saying, *Help these people. Keep them safe.*

Looking south, I saw three tall, metal towers. Radio towers. Ghosts from a past where communicating with someone on the other side of the world was as common as talking to them face-to-face. Nevertheless, they gave me a direction.

"Kate could use some rest," I said. "Everyone is freezing, and our path is blocked by two zombies —"

"There're three now," Jacob said, jerking his head toward the bridge.

"Okay, three zombies, even worse. We're a big group, but if we cross that bridge now, we'll have to fight them. And the last time we fought zombies, we lost good people." I let that sink in. There were silent nods all around me.

I tilted my head toward the three towers in the distance. "I say we get off this highway for now, go south. Toward those towers. Find some shelter and get some rest, out of the cold."

"Why the towers?" Celia asked, wrinkling her forehead.

"I don't care about the towers per se. It's just a direction to go. There's an exit going south, just behind us, and I can see houses down the river. We can take one of those for a night." I checked to see if anyone disagreed, even Kate, but no one did. "And I want us all in the same building, so we don't have to worry about defending more than one place. Understood?" I realized these last words came out of my mouth like a command.

"Let's do it," Jacob said. I didn't know the kid well, but he was one of Kate's advisers, and a big, strong guy. I was glad to have his support within the group. Vera and Kate both nodded, and we began the process of turning around.

Within a half-hour, we were headed south down the exit ramp. Walking through the woods, I soon felt that I'd made a mistake. Houses weren't plentiful, and the ones we did see were too small, in shambles, no better than sleeping under a tree.

As we emerged from the woods, I could see that we needed a change of direction. In front of us, the highway turned toward the heart of Annapolis via another bridge, but a wide section of its middle was gone, presumably collapsed into the cold waters below. The damage seemed precise, specific, like the bridge was destroyed on purpose. Either way, it meant we turned aside again.

I did it without speaking, knowing that people would object if they realized I was just changing direction at random. So I led the way with an air of purpose, following the road along the side of the river, then turning inland and back among the looming trees. The road narrowed, and grumbling began. Somewhere behind me, I imagined Aaron and his cronies were talking. I knew I had to make good on my plan somehow, and as soon as possible. I continued walking like I knew the way, and thankfully the frequency of houses increased. I was just looking for the right one. But Kate was shuffling, in pain. We needed to rest, and soon.

All of a sudden, the trees cleared and we were standing on the edge of… a *golf course.*

My vision flashed to that little girl, waving to Rosa and me as we drove past the golf course and into The Oasis. The little girl's name was Eva, if I remembered correctly. I wondered where she was now, if she'd made it someplace, to safety.

Then another thought occurred to me. Golf courses have *clubhouses* — usually a good-sized building. A building that could *fit* a hundred people inside. I knew there was a good chance that I was wrong or that the building might be damaged, but I smiled in spite of it all. "Come on!" I said, grinning, a little too enthusiastic. The others looked at me with raised eyebrows, but followed.

The road ran straight through the middle of the golf course, with wide green fairways on either side, now overgrown with long grasses and scattered bushes and trees. With no caretaker, it was returning to the wild, but still it was wide open compared to the forest road we'd left. Up ahead, we spied something unexpected. A double set of chain-link fences stood across our path as far as we could see, from one side to the other. The fences were intact but patched in places with sheets of plywood and other scraps. Along the top of each fence were curls of rusted razor wire. Clearly this was a barrier, something meant to keep things out. Across the path, each fence had a large, rolling gate.

And just beyond, off to the left, there was a long, low brick building with a grey shingle roof. That could only have been the clubhouse.

I led the group toward the fences. As we approached, I kept expecting someone to shout *Halt!* To send us on our way, chased by a hail of gunfire. But nothing happened. There was no movement, and no sound except the accumulated noise of our feet and rolling carts and the cold wind whistling through the surrounding pines.

At the first gate, Jacob reached for the latch. He worked at the mechanism for a moment, then was able to lift it and force the gate to the left by an inch or two, the metal scraping and creaking. "It's open," he said with a shrug. As the gate protested with squeals and shivers, Jacob rolled it farther open and passed through. He repeated the process with the second gate, and we led the group toward the clubhouse. We walked up a driveway that ended in a circle, and I heard something I hadn't heard in a long time.

Faintly, through the faded green double doors of the clubhouse, the sound came. I turned and held up my hands, imploring the group to be quiet. The sentiment was passed around, and at first, the numerous calls of *shhhhh* simply made even more noise, blocking every other sound. But finally, the group fell silent, every eye looking toward the doors.

And we all heard it, distinctly: *music.*

Classical music, wafting lightly through the air. Strains of violins, cellos, clarinets, instruments of a forgotten time, now dead to the world, flittered about, leaving me dumbstruck. How was this possible?

I approached the door, one hand out, slowly, unsure, like I was about to open a doorway in time. My hand trembled as I pulled on the big brass handle, and the heavy door slowly opened outward, hardly making a sound.

The music immediately grew louder. Inside I saw *light.* Electric lights, shaped like the flames of a candle, were blazing in several brass chandeliers hanging from the ceiling of the large, open room. A few tables were scattered about, some surrounded by plush, high-backed chairs in faded light-blue upholstery. And it was *warm.* Blessed heat filled the room and reached out to greet us.

At the same time, the frigid air of the outside gusted into the heated room. From one of the high-backed chairs facing away from us, I saw movement. Leaning over the arm of the tall chair, a little man, late fifties, pudgy, balding with wisps of grey hair, looked at us. Thin metal glasses were perched on his nose, and an open book dangled from his pinkish left hand.

"Oh my," he whispered, then let his mouth hang open as he took in the mass of people suddenly on his doorstep.

8

His name was Oliver. Oliver Rowland. Maybe five-and-a-half-feet tall, chubby in a worn red sweater vest, he stared at us. I felt from the very start that if he could have, he would have cast us out. But there were too many of us. Our need too great, his power too little. Grudgingly, he welcomed us to his home, even offered us some food.

When we'd settled in, every last one of us inside and warming up, I talked to him. Kate sat nearby, but soon faded into sleep. Celia, Jacob, and Vera paid rapt attention, and together we learned his story.

Oliver had been an English professor at the Naval Academy before the outbreak, living along the waterfront beside the road we had just left. When the disease began to spread, the Navy started putting up fences to protect various assets, and this was one of them. Not for the golf course. For the *towers*.

Those three tall spires standing off in the distance were radio towers, known collectively as NSS Annapolis, a naval communications station dating back to the first World War. Oliver told us the station had been rendered useless by satellite technology in the 1990s, but with the world going to hell, the Navy wasn't taking any chances. They set up the fences to protect the station, stocked the place with supplies, and made sure the towers were fully operational.

Oliver said we were on a strip of land protected on three sides by water and on the fourth side by that double line of chain link. The fences ran from one body of water to the other, and he'd patched them up whenever they needed it.

I sat back for a moment, thinking about what that meant for our group. The *options* it gave us. Including one option most likely not available anywhere else. Safety.

Oliver continued his story. As the epidemic got worse, the Navy must have realized that, working or not, some old radio towers weren't a top priority. Something bad happened across the river at the Naval Academy — Oliver didn't know exactly what, faculty had been told to stop reporting not long after the outbreak — and all military personnel were pulled back to better defend the campus. Whoever was out on the peninsula was called back so quickly, they simply left everything behind. As they retreated into the city, they blasted the bridge to avoid having to defend another flank. Eventually, Annapolis, and the Academy itself, fell. Whether it was zombies, infighting, or something else, Oliver didn't know. Soon, he found himself alone in his house by the river.

Oliver, a lifelong bachelor, avid reader, and music aficionado, didn't actually mind. He sort of liked it, even. But he knew the small stash of supplies at his house wouldn't hold, so he approached the double fences, found his way in, and took up residence in the clubhouse.

Much to my dismay, Vera told him about the cure lying dormant in my blood. Oliver's eyes gleamed, but he said nothing. He absorbed it almost as if he'd been expecting the news, with a nod.

He asked us if we'd seen the sports complex building across the way. None of us had. Oliver explained it was several times larger than the clubhouse, and for that reason he didn't try to live there or keep it heated. But the Navy had used it for storage, and it was packed with fuel, food, and water. My mind reeled. Now it was time for our eyes to gleam.

The clubhouse had been Oliver's, and Oliver's alone, for well over six years. In the early days of living there, he told us, he'd had to be diligent. People would come, trying to take what he had. He would run them off, firing blasts from one of several shotguns he kept, always staying safe behind the fences. But he hadn't seen another non-infected human in over a year. He'd tried to maintain discipline, patrolling the fences every hour or two, climbing to the roof of the clubhouse each afternoon to scan the surrounding area, but eventually it became tedious. Finally he just took to reading and listening to music most days. His guard had been let down by complacency.

Hearing him talk, I had a thought. "The radio towers. Do they still work?" I tilted my head, considering what he might answer.

Oliver puffed out his cheeks and took his glasses from his nose. Wiping the lenses on the button-up plaid shirt he wore under his sweater vest, he said, "I don't know. I never tried them. I never had a reason to. And I'm not sure I'd know how to work them even if I wanted to." He put his glasses back on. They gleamed dully. "Why do you ask? Who would you call, anyway?"

I shrugged. I didn't have an answer.

* * *

The place was something magical. I can see why Oliver stayed, even alone. It was *comfortable*, in a way that none of us had expected. The first day turned into two. Then four. Then a week and more. With the fence keeping us safe, we were free to explore the peninsula. We took supplies from the sports complex, and used them to set up living quarters.

Because of the clubhouse's layout, we ended up with two areas where people slept, one at the north end, another at the south. Oliver's own small room was in the north section, and maybe because of that, Kate chose a place nearby. Whether that was out of respect or a desire to keep an eye on him, I didn't know. But Celia, Jacob, Vera, and I did the same, making little homey areas in the north wing. Human nature being what it is, Aaron and his counterparts took up residence on the south side.

The vast majority of our group maintained no special allegiance and simply filled in wherever there was space. What did they care about Kate or Aaron, or me for that matter, when for the first time since Norfolk they were safe and warm and well-fed. But one thing was clear. The people in power were on one side of the clubhouse. The people who wanted power were on the other side.

* * *

The sports complex building was huge, many times the size of the clubhouse. Its roof and walls were intact, and although it wasn't heated, it was a hell of a lot more comfortable than being outside in the cold. I remembered the school Rosa and I had found as we trekked along the interstate, a tiny reflection of an oasis. I imagined the sports complex could be that one day. I began to feel obligated to give the gift I carried in my veins to more people. We had so much — I had so much — and now there was the chance to share a cure. Rosa's memory tugged at my mind, urging me to spread the word. But how?

The answer literally towered over me each day as I walked the roads of the peninsula. The radio towers.

I gathered Kate, Celia, Oliver, and the others. "What would it take to get those towers running?" I asked.

Oliver rolled his eyes. "This again?" he asked. "How would —"

Kate cut him off. "Why?"

"I want to send a message to DC," I said. "Tell them to come here. Let us help them."

"*What?*" Oliver looked panicked. "Bring all those people here? Are you crazy? We don't have space or resources for an entire city to come *here*."

"Why not?" I asked. "We have the sports complex. It's, what, fifty or sixty thousand square feet. I mean, depending on how many people come here, they might be stacked up like cord wood, but there's space. There's two other houses farther down the peninsula. And we could build."

Oliver scoffed, but Kate, a bead of sweat on her upper lip, considered it. "We could also push out the walls," she said. "There are houses nearby, outside the fence. But we'd have to be self-sufficient. How do we do that?"

A silence came over the group. Then Celia chimed in, eyeing me. "Well, we were growing crops on the Eastern Shore. We'd have to find seed, which could be pretty hard. But those big lawns out there, the fairways, might make good fields for planting." I grinned, proud of her, thinking it was a pretty good idea. The city kid who'd blistered her hands working her first field a few months back was now teaching these other folks a thing or two about surviving in the outside world.

"This is *preposterous!*" Oliver said, chubby cheeks reddening. "You can't possibly think that bringing thousands of people here is a good idea. We'd starve in weeks!"

"There's more," I said, stopping Oliver's complaint. "We *need* them to come. The only way we can take the cure in my veins and give it to everyone else is by finding someone who knows how to *do* that. I don't. And unless you're keeping something from me, neither do any of you. We need people from DC. Specifically, from NIH — the researchers who have been working on a cure for the last 10 years. Now we have one we can drop in their laps. We just need them to figure out how to share it." Even Oliver, who clearly missed his days of solitude, didn't have anything to say to that. The idea of being cured was something none of us could discount.

Celia spoke again. "About the towers. We may have people here already who can help with them. People who worked for the Navy in Norfolk. Engineers."

A dawn of understanding broke over Kate. "That's true. Reginald is one. And... the tall guy, with the dark hair that's starting grey — what's his name?"

"Dennis?" Vera offered.

"That's him," Kate said. "He's always tinkering with something. He might know how to get those towers back up and running." She looked around, grinning.

"So," I said, "we're agreed to try?"

"No!" Oliver crossed his arms, a spoiled child who wasn't getting his way. "No, we are *not* agreed!"

"Well, we'll vote then. All in favor?"

Every hand was raised. Except Oliver's.

9

Reginald and Dennis, the engineers, were joined by two former Navy communications specialists, Blake and Emily. Together, they worked nonstop to get the towers back online. The idea that their work might directly help cure the infection had them fired up. We didn't need to do anything more to coax them.

There was a building at the base of the northernmost tower, and inside was a generator, an insurance policy left by the Navy. The four of them were able to clean it up, fuel it, and get it running. It gave them a communications headquarters and also powered the tower above it. They started calling their building Comm Center. With it up and running, they were ready to try broadcasting.

For our first test, Kate, Oliver, Celia and I joined Dennis, Reginald, Blake, and Emily at Comm Center. I'd found an old battery-powered radio and the batteries to run it. Turning it on, I scanned the airwaves. All across the radio dial, I found nothing but static. Then Dennis tried the first transmission.

We had to use Morse code. It was the only option, given the situation. In a way, my heart sank. We were asking a lot. Whoever was out there had to be able to pick up our transmission, know what they were hearing, find a way to translate it, then have the guts to pack up and come to us. But it was better than nothing.

As Dennis tapped out the message, I held my hand on the tuner of the radio, expecting to have to search the dial for the transmission. But I didn't need to bother. The second Dennis made his first tap, the sound came out of my radio like a gunshot. I jumped up and yelled in surprise. Joy overcame us, and we began hugging each other. But Oliver stood off to one side alone, and Reginald and Dennis were reserved. "Don't get too excited," Reginald said. "It's loud because we're right underneath the tower. Who knows if they'll hear it in DC?"

Our enthusiasm faded, and we got down to business. Blake and Emily took over the desk. They set up a schedule. They would trade shifts, tapping out our message, hoping someone would hear it.

Near Annapolis. Three towers by river. Need medical researchers to spread cure from blood. Come to us.

* * *

Outside, the dark early winter was upon us as we made the frigid walk through the woods back to the clubhouse. The air smelled of coming snowfall, and the moon made a fuzzy white glow behind ominous clouds.

Dennis and Reginald, finally allowing themselves to bubble at their success, walked briskly in front. Celia and I trailed them, with Kate walking stiffly behind. Oliver sulked at the back.

Through the woods we walked, Dennis dismissing the silence of the trees with his exuberant, excited talk. Reginald laughed and followed suit.

Suddenly I heard Kate gasp. Celia and I wheeled about, only to see Oliver rushing toward Kate with a pistol drawn.

Time froze.

Kate flinched, backed away. Celia and I only had time to turn and watch. Why hadn't I anticipated this? We had taken away Oliver's privacy, his home. We were threatening to bring untold masses of people down upon him. Everything he'd held dear for six years was turned upside-down. He thrust the pistol out — a gun we didn't even know he carried, given the protected nature of our location — with Kate's life in his hands.

And he fired.

Still stiff from her injuries, Kate flailed wildly, fell to the ground. A hideous shriek. The sounds of pain and death. The burnt smell of gunpowder. Oliver ran up, gun pointed down at the ground.

Not at Kate. *Beside* her.

There, next to Kate, a milky-eyed raccoon convulsed in the grass, dying. Kate rolled away from it, bumping over the root she had tripped on, dumbfounded, incredulous at what had happened. Reginald and Dennis could only stare.

Oliver stood over the raccoon with no mercy. Another explosion tore through the silent, dark night, and reflexively we all covered our ears. Then the raccoon was still. A tiny twist of smoke floated up and away from Oliver's pistol, into the cold moonlight. He looked at us slowly. "I think it was rabid," he said, panting. "It was coming for Kate."

I looked at the raccoon. There was no way to be sure, but the thick look of its skin, especially around the face, made me believe it was true. "Not just rabies, I think. RL2013."

Oliver's eyes grew wide with alarm. "That... is that *possible?*" he asked.

I just nodded, reaching out a hand to help Kate up.

10

"Oliver," Kate said in a quiet voice, almost timid. "Thank you. You might've saved my life." She reached out a hand.

Oliver waved it off. "I just saw it was... you know... it was going to *bite* you, and I, well, I thought I shouldn't let it *do* that." He fumbled his hands awkwardly as he spoke, then turned away shyly.

"Well, thank you, again," Kate said.

"Are you all right?" I asked her.

She nodded, seeming unsure. "Yeah, yeah. Just startled me. But..."

"But what?" I asked, frowning. It wasn't like Kate to be unsure or confused. I didn't like where this seemed to be headed.

"Well, my mouth. It feels strange. Tight." She rubbed at her jaw with her hand.

"Let's get back," I said. "It's cold out." We continued toward the clubhouse, this time in a tighter group.

As we walked, I thought of what Kate said. My natural instinct as a doctor was to figure out what it meant, why it was happening. It didn't take me long to reach a likely conclusion: tetanus. The rebar that had jabbed into Kate's side, sheared and rusty, could easily have exposed her to tetanus. And that was bad. Very, very bad.

Tetanus is fatal if untreated, and I had no way to treat the infection. If I had the right *medicines*, maybe, but I didn't. I would need to keep a close watch on her. If it got worse, I'd have to consider going into Annapolis, looking for drugs.

We stepped into the clubhouse. Within moments, an eruption of happiness swept over the group, sparked by the tale of the first radio transmission, and even by Oliver's unexpected rescue of Kate. Only one thing dampened the group's spirit. If there was an infected raccoon inside our gates, what else could appear? We'd have to be more careful.

Still, people laughed and enjoyed themselves, sounds of happiness that this part of the world probably hadn't heard in a long time. The revelry continued into the night.

Kate sat off to one side. Listening and sometimes smiling, but never really joining in.

* * *

The next day, Kate could barely open her mouth. She sat at one of the tables, seemingly asleep. I knew what I had to do.

I took Celia, Jacob, and Vera aside. "We have to go into Annapolis," I said. "I need to see if I can find some medicine to help Kate."

"What's wrong with her?" Vera asked.

"I can hear you, you know," Kate said, opening her eyes but not raising her head from the table.

I turned to face her. "Kate. I think you have tetanus." I could tell from her expression that she regarded this as a trivial concern. "It's serious." She looked surprised. I kept at it. "Back before the outbreak, tetanus was *nothing*. A little medicine, and *boom*, everything was okay. But *now*. We don't have the medicine. Tetanus can kill you." Everyone suddenly got my point. The air ran out of the room.

Celia spoke first. "Okay, let's go then. Get some medicine." I looked toward her and gave her a smile. She was fearless, like always.

"We have to try," I said. "I have no idea if we'll find anything, but we'll go."

"Then it's me and you," Celia said, considering it a done deal.

"No, Celia. I want you here for Kate, for the group," I said. She started to object, but I held up my hand and turned. "Jacob and Vera. Will you take me into Annapolis? Watch my back? Help me help Kate?" As Kate's closest, most trusted advisers, I knew they couldn't refuse. They both simply nodded.

Celia looked at me angrily, but I wouldn't meet her eyes. There was no point arguing. I wanted someone I could trust holding down the fort.

* * *

Before we set out for Annapolis, Oliver gave us some advice. He suggested we try buildings just north of the highway, right after we crossed the bridge. There were a number of medical buildings there, he said. We'd have more options.

The trip itself was uneventful. We went back to the main highway and turned west, crossing the bridge. The zombies, the ones who had thwarted us before, seemed to have left the area, at least temporarily.

We spent a whole day searching through anything that looked remotely like it might hide a stash of medicine. We saw a good number of zombies here and there as we traveled around, but we were few and silent. We avoided them.

We searched from building to building, collecting small medical supplies and a number of different drugs, intent on bringing anything we could find back to the group. Finally, we found a small supply of Valium. It was a depressant but also a muscle relaxant. It would help with Kate's symptoms. But it wasn't a cure. My worry increased.

By early evening, I suspected we'd found everything we were going to find. We headed back over the bridge and home.

* * *

I walked into the clubhouse's main room to find it spilling over with life. Families played card games together. Other people sat and talked. The sense of normalcy was as apparent as it was odd. To the side, Kate sat asleep, pretty much where she'd been when we left. I went to her and touched her shoulder, and she opened her eyes.

"Hi," she said, still fogged with sleep. "What's the good news?" She forced a smile.

"Here, take one of these," I said, holding out a pill. Vera offered water to help rinse it down.

"What is it?" Kate asked.

"Valium."

"How long do I have to take it, you know... to get better?" She still wore a slight smile, but her eyes betrayed her deeper concern.

I squeezed her shoulder, summoning my old bedside manner. "We'll see. Take this now, and we'll see how it helps you." I smiled, hoping she couldn't see through me.

Suddenly Dennis skidded up in front of us. "Celia," he said, panting.

"What is it?" I asked.

"I don't want to alarm you if it's nothing, but… she's gone."

* * *

"Split up, look everywhere," I said, marching through the building. "Where was she last?" I asked Dennis over my shoulder.

He jogged to keep up with me. "Emily was on shift at Comm Center, and Celia said she wanted to check on her. After a couple of hours, we were surprised she didn't come back, so I went over there. Emily says she never saw her."

"Is anyone else missing?" I said. "I mean, is there anyone else conspicuously out of sight today?"

Dennis thought. "Yeah, now that you mention it. I haven't seen that nurse, Renee. Or…" He set his jaw. "Aaron."

I started to run.

* * *

The clubhouse was big enough for our group, but it wasn't endless. It wasn't long before we'd checked it thoroughly and found nothing. The sports complex was a lot bigger, but most of that was one big, open room. Within an hour, we had that cleared, too.

What else was there?

"You said you went to Comm Center?" I asked Dennis.

"Yeah, she's definitely not there," he said.

That left someplace outside the fence.

Or those two empty houses by the other towers.

* * *

Dennis and I hurried to the houses, joined by Jacob and Vera, each of whom carried a pistol. The other three were younger than me by decades and had to slow down, waiting for me. As we made our way down the path, the dark woods closed in on both sides. If we didn't find them in one of the houses... if we had to check the *woods*.... Eventually, the four of us stood in front of the two seemingly abandoned buildings, as scattered flakes of snow started to drift down around us.

"We're going inside," I said, puffing bursts of white breath into the frosty air. "Two in each building. One through the front and one through the back. Dennis, Jacob, take that one." I pointed to the house on the left, a nondescript brick structure with patches of aluminum siding. "Vera and I will take the other one."

Dennis and Jacob immediately went their way, and we went ours. I silently motioned to Vera that I would take the front. She nodded, crept around to the back. I stepped up to the front door.

It was unlocked and opened easily. That bothered me more than if it had been locked up tight. Directly inside the door, there was a short hallway. I began to walk down the hallway, toward a point about halfway along, where doors opened on the left and right. A sound that I couldn't quite place came from somewhere down the hall, and I stepped quietly to find its source. A sound like plastic, slightly crinkling?

It wasn't dark inside the house, but dim. Dim enough to obscure my sight. As I reached the juncture with the doors, I peered first into the one on the left. Just an old, empty room. An overturned chair, stuffing pulled out of it. A small end table coated with a thick layer of dust. I turned to the right and again saw nothing. Another old room littered with artifacts from time gone by. A broken lamp, shade crumpled and off kilter, lying on the floor.

Then I heard another sound.

A shuffling sound. Feet. Sliding across the gritty floor, scraping like fine sandpaper. It came from in front of me, from behind a door at the end of the hall. The door stood ajar by an inch or two. I moved up, placed my hand on the scarred wood surface, gently pushed it open.

Inside, I saw two bodies splayed out, one on a table, the other beside it on a couch. Another person stood at the far side of the room, back turned toward me.

The one on the table, lying still, as if in a dream, was Celia.

Lower, on the couch, Aaron mirrored her position, eyes closed.

And turned away from me, the nurse, Renee, worked at something on a counter up against the back wall. Idly, she shifted her weight, and her foot slid a few inches across the floor, making that gritty sound. *Shhhhk.*

I saw tubes connecting Celia and Aaron, and a dark flow of blood was passing from her to him.

The bastard, the *coward*, Aaron, was taking Celia's blood.

"What the hell do you think you're doing?" I thundered. Renee wheeled around, Aaron's eyes flew open.

Renee moved toward me, and I immediately tensed for an attack, fists raised. But she darted past me, eyes huge and bulging in fear. She ran into the hallway and was gone, out of the house.

Celia was unconscious, but I could see she was breathing. She appeared to be drugged.

Aaron looked at me, unsure of what to do.

"This ends *now*," I said, and, reaching down, pulled the needle out of Celia's arm. That's when Aaron launched himself at me.

We fell, him on top, and slammed to the floor, sliding through the dust and dirt, piling up against the wall. He reached for my throat and I pushed and punched at him, trying anything to keep him from gaining hold. Above us, I saw Celia's arm dripping red. I knew I had to stop the flow, apply pressure, so she wouldn't lose more blood. Who knew how long the transfusion had already been going on? Every drop was her life, falling away.

Aaron and I rolled, and out of simple desperation, I managed to slip free and stagger to my feet. Aaron scrambled up, slapped at a counter nearby, finding an old letter opener. He raised the rusty metal blade and pointed it toward me. I had nothing. He approached, a smile on his face.

There was a sound like thunder in the small room, and Aaron died with that smile still on his face, his body knocked to the far wall. Vera stood in the doorway, the smoking gun held steadily in her hand. She looked around quickly for any other threats, then stepped into the room.

I rushed to Celia's side, applying pressure to the site where the needle had been ripped out. Then I scanned the room, zeroing in on the counter, where Renee had been organizing medical supplies when I walked in. I saw a bandage. "Get me that!" I pointed, and Vera grabbed the package. After a few minutes, Celia was safe, bandaged, but still unconscious from whatever drugs they'd given her.

Dennis and Jacob soon joined us, and together we carried Celia back to the clubhouse. We left Aaron behind, food for whatever vermin found him later, assuming they could stand the taste.

* * *

We walked slowly, partially from exhaustion and partially to keep Celia as comfortable as possible. Jacob did most of the carrying, but the rest of us helped.

As we approached the clubhouse, we heard a commotion by the gates of the outer fence. The weather was bitter cold, so I was surprised to see so many of our group outside. Some of them were even in t-shirts and shorts, like they had no idea they were going to be outside.

I asked Jacob to take Celia inside and find her a comfortable place, and to keep his eyes open for Renee. He nodded, headed for the clubhouse. Then I walked into the crowd by the gates.

Pushing my way through, I got closer to the inner fence. And I saw something glinting in the muted twilight.

A car.

There, outside our fence, sat a dull blue car, pockmarked with brown rust, but with chrome parts seeming to glow in the shadows. Its engine was off, but from the sweet smell of its exhaust, familiar and unexpected, I could tell it had been running recently. Both doors stood open, and beside the car on my right stood a young man, early twenties, with a shock of dark hair and thick glasses. On the other side of the car was a pretty, young woman, reddish hair, wearing a thick green coat. But under that coat... her *clothes*. And his. They looked like those quasi uniforms we had in the city.

I was stunned. The hesitant flurries of snow left flecks of white in their hair, on their shoulders.

"What's going on here?" I asked.

Someone near me, a young boy in faded jean shorts and a ripped grey t-shirt with the letters USNA written in deep blue, said, "They just drove up! They're from DC!"

I moved to the front, to the inner gates. I started to open my mouth, but, exhausted, realized I couldn't figure out what to say.

Then the young man by the car spoke. "Is this The Oasis?" he asked with a hesitant smile, eyes so full of hope and joy that I thought he might burst from the effort to keep them contained.

And I thought of The Oasis, the *real* Oasis. Of those people in South Carolina, offering a cure. Of Harvey, and Marian. Of Hank and Janine. And of Rosa.

A cure. Offering a cure. Wasn't that what we were doing? Wasn't that what our radio message promised? I looked at my feet for a second, then looked back up at the young man, maybe a third of my age. Who was I to shatter his dreams? And weren't we exactly what he was looking for, anyway?

"Yeah, I guess it is, now," I said.

"Welcome to Oasis, Maryland."

11

Life at the new Oasis fell into the repetition of habit. The winter dragged on, but we didn't mind. Our supplies held. In fact, they seemed almost endless. But Kate and I didn't trust them to last forever. We asked for volunteers to serve as scouts, and they went into Annapolis regularly, and to some places even farther out, to gather anything they could find. Food, water, medicine, and fuel were our top priorities. And the scouts found stores of seed that we held on to, readying for spring, hoping to plant in the fields that surrounded us.

Celia recovered within a day. Luckily, the transfusion hadn't been underway for long when I found her. She told us about her ordeal. Aaron snuck up on her as she walked the path to Comm Center alone, drugging her with something provided by Renee. The look in her eye when she described him grabbing her from behind told me it was a terrifying reminder of her previous encounter with

Aaron and Burt — the reason she set off alone in the first place. I'd heard enough and didn't want her to have to relive any more of her nightmare. "It doesn't matter," I said. "You're here now, and Aaron is dead."

Renee was another story. It was the first time any of us had to decide such a thing. What did we do with someone who couldn't be trusted to remain with the group? Kill her? Improvise some sort of jail? Or even send her out, banish her? We considered everything, and in the end did nothing. We still needed a nurse, and in the world of the infection, survival trumped justice. We knew we had to keep our eyes on her, but that was it.

Then there was Kate. Tetanus had a hold of her, and she was suffering. The Valium helped ease the symptoms, but it wasn't making her any better. She spent her time either rigid and in pain, or doped and asleep. Eating and drinking became torturous. Vera was a saint, sticking by Kate, helping her in any way she could. Keeping her fed, giving her water. Keeping her alive.

Several more cars arrived from DC, those black, nondescript government sedans, but filled with refugees, not federal agents. A big white van came in, loaded with two families. The people told us that DC was in turmoil. The government had fallen, or at least retreated to somewhere none of them knew anything about. What remained were pockets of people banded together inside the city walls, trying to live. The power was out. Only folks with battery-powered radios had a chance to hear us, if they even bothered to listen.

Oliver heard all this and argued it was time to stop wasting fuel running the towers. I ignored him. And, without anyone asking, Blake and Emily changed the message.

Near Annapolis. Three towers by river. Need medical researchers to spread cure from blood. Come to The Oasis.

I asked every one of the newcomers about NIH — if they knew of any researchers left in DC, or if there was anyone still working for a cure. No one had any idea.

Days went by, and weeks. Our numbers grew slowly, with refugees continuing to trickle in, mostly from DC. By midwinter, we had doubled the size of our group. The hardier arrivals, more adventurous, set up their living quarters in the sports complex. It remained unheated, but they were able to make it work. They called it indoor camping. During the day, the main room of the clubhouse was typically overrun with people. Talking, idly playing games, just staying warm.

The scouts brought in a small but steady stream of additional supplies, but their excursions weren't without risk.

One afternoon, there was shouting at the gates. A pair of scouts had returned, and were rushed inside. People called for me, for a nurse. At the fence I found one of the scouts, a man so young he looked to me like a child, holding the side of his face, blood all over him, red and black in blotches.

Instinct took over. "Carry him inside and tell me what happened." It had been a zombie, of course. They didn't see it coming until it had a hold on the kid and was biting into his ear. The second scout, slightly older and bulkier, killed it. But the kid was bitten. Everyone knew what that meant. My nostrils filled with the metallic smell of blood mixed with the musty sweat and sour breath of the kid as I leaned in close.

"You…" the kid started, hesitantly looking up at me as I cleaned the wound. "You can… *save* me, right?" He offered a weak, hopeful smile that turned into a wincing grimace as I used alcohol to disinfect his ragged ear.

I stood up straight. It had been weeks — a couple of months? — since I'd saved Celia, but was that enough time? I had given her an awful lot of blood, more than a standard transfusion. But the kid was going to turn. All I could do was try.

* * *

We set up a clean space. Other than myself, Renee seemed to be our resident expert on how to get it done, so I made her help, under careful supervision from Celia, Jacob, and Vera. We didn't say it out loud, but I think we all considered this to be Renee's chance for at least partial redemption.

I was one table in the clubhouse, the young scout next to me on another. Renee swabbed our arms with alcohol wipes, sank needles into them, her touch surprisingly gentle, and that's all I really remember before I passed out. I wasn't ready, my *body* wasn't ready yet. Jacob told me later that Renee tried to keep going, but Celia made her stop.

A couple of days later, the kid turned and Jacob took him into the woods. Around the clubhouse, almost 200 people sat silent and staring as the distant gunshot ripped through the air and echoed across the river.

12

A day went by. No one said much of anything, each of us just going about our own routine. A somber mood filled the clubhouse, a poisonous gas that choked out everything else. In corners of the room, you could hear sobs. I felt like a failure. I had let the kid down. Let him die. I never even learned his name.

The following afternoon, I was sitting by a window in the clubhouse, fingering the ragged knots on my bracelet, when I heard a gasp from the other side of the room. Looking over, I could see people standing around a figure lying on the floor. Peering between their shuffling legs, I saw Kate, her back arched horribly. Tired and weak, I ambled over, but there was nothing to be done. I went to her anyway, crouched down, felt for a pulse on her neck. It was thready, almost gone. *This is it*, I thought. With one last, awful seizing clench of her muscles, her body twisted and stretched, then gave way. Her last breath tumbled out of her like a balloon deflating, and she didn't move again,

The group, already in shock, collapsed in dismay. Old fears, tamped down during the long march from Norfolk, now sprang free. Some people broke down, some lashed out. Arguments started. There was even a fistfight somewhere toward the south wing.

I began to speak, but my throat was dry, rough. Gravelly and low, I said, "That's *enough*." A couple of people near me turned, but the group was too big. Most didn't hear me. So I tried again, louder, stronger. "That's enough!" More heads turned toward me, and over the course of several awkward moments, everyone stopped and fell silent, looking to me.

"Enough tears. Enough fighting. Stop it! If you want something to fight, let's fight for our lives!" I didn't know what I was going to say. The words were coming out on their own. I had everyone's attention. So I made a decision, right then and there. I took a blanket from a sofa nearby and gently spread it over Kate, taking care to cover her face. I bowed my head for a short, solitary moment, then stood up and turned back toward the group. "We need to act," I said. "We need to stop sitting back here, in relative comfort, *hoping* something is going to happen. That someone is going to show up and save us. It's not going to happen. We need to save ourselves. Kate died because we don't have the right medicines. That kid died because we don't know how to spread the cure, even though it's sitting right here. In my own veins. I want to cure all of you, but I don't know how."

I paused to let that sink in. People blinked, or folded their arms, or held on to one another, but I had no idea if I was getting through to anyone. "It's time for us to go to DC and find what we need," I said. "The right people and the right machines to take my blood and turn it into something that can cure everyone. We can't stop every disease, every infection, every accident or tragedy, but we can stop this one." I took a breath, thinking. *God, am I ready for this?* But what else was there to do? "I'm going into DC. I used to live there, and I know my way around, at least parts of it. I'm going to find what we need to spread the cure and bring it back here."

A murmur ran through the crowd. Finally, a reaction. Then someone spoke up, a man's voice, from the back where I couldn't see his face. "You can't go. You're *in charge now.*"

Now it was my turn to blink. What the hell was this? In charge? Then others joined in, calling out, "We need you!" "With Kate gone, you've *got* to be our leader."

My eyes scanned the room, seeing imploring faces looking back at me. Then I saw Oliver, off to one side, simply staring at me, his eyes squinting slighting through his round glasses. I shouted to stop the noise. "You don't need me to lead you *here*," I said, "doing nothing, doing the same thing every day until we die. I need to go to DC. I need to get this done. If no one will come with me, I'll go alone."

"I'll go with you." Celia stepped out of the group to stand next to me, and I offered her a small smile of thanks, nodding my head like a little bow. The two of us would be back on the road again, like old times.

Then another voice spoke up. "I'll go, too."

It was Oliver.

* * *

The various newcomers from DC gave us all the news they could. They knew where to find some people, the ones who wouldn't join them when they left, but they didn't know any researchers. They warned us about the dangers. There were now infected roaming the city, inside the walls. It wasn't safe to wander.

I thought about how things had changed. Rosa and I, we had left a city that, while stifling and strict, at least *functioned*. Then we went back and stood outside the walls and Rosa made an announcement that apparently broke the spell, woke everyone up, and ended 10 years of totalitarian rule. How many people had died in the ensuing months?

The irony that Rosa delivered a message of hope and salvation, only to have untold numbers of people perish rather than be saved, was heart-wrenching. I knew she wouldn't have wanted it that way. But it wasn't her fault. All she did was try to help.

I wondered if I was about to make a similar mistake, to somehow damn these people to a fate I couldn't predict.

I didn't know what the future held, whether I would have any luck. Like Rosa, all I could do was try.

13

We decided on the big white van. It had enough gas to get us to DC and back, and room enough to carry me, Celia, and Oliver, a few other people, and some gear, assuming we found anything worth bringing back. Two men joined us — a thin, olive-skinned guy with a haze of black stubble across his chin named Ray, and a taller, round-faced one named Zachary. They brought long rifles that they kept slung over their shoulders like they were going on safari. I drove, with Celia next to me in the front passenger seat. Oliver, Ray, and Zachary sat on the floor in the open back of the van, leaning against the walls. We all carried a small supply pack with water, some food, a few spare items of clothing, and whatever else each of us felt was important. Plus, Celia and I each carried a loaded pistol. We offered Oliver a gun, but he waved it off.

The entire group, 200 or so strong, came out to see us off in the morning, waving as we drove out through the double gates. I could see a mix of emotions, as some people smiled and cheered, while others couldn't hold back their tears. I felt both emotions myself: excitement over the chance to try to change things, but a looming fear of the unknown dangers ahead.

We drove north, through the woods, then up the ramp and onto the main highway, where we turned west toward DC.

As we drove, the noises of the road drowned out the sounds of Ray and Zachary talking in the back. Oliver seemed to be sitting quietly, or might have been asleep.

After a while, Celia cleared her throat. I noticed she had kept her head shaven, more neatly than before, without the cuts and scrapes. She must have decided to keep this new style, this reborn person she had become. Reborn like magic, from my blood. I couldn't help but think of her like a daughter, with a mixture of pride and love. As well as a deep concern for her safety. Maybe I shouldn't have let her come along.

"Do you ever wonder if there's any point at all?" she asked, looking off through the windshield at the passing landscape.

I uttered a single, surprised laugh. "*Ever?* Do I ever wonder that? Heck, that's all I think about." I gave another small chuckle.

Celia turned to look at me. "Really? You're kidding." She actually seemed surprised. "But you're the one who's always moving forward, getting things done. You don't get bogged down by what's happened, you move on to what's next." She said it like she was trying to convince me.

I shrugged, keeping both hands on the wheel as I slowed to navigate around several abandoned cars. My bracelet, Rosa's weave of many colors, still clung like a promise around my wrist, but frayed and stretched. "I can't explain that," I said. "Sometimes my body keeps moving, and I'm just a passenger along for the ride."

"Well, you had me fooled." Celia sighed. After a moment, she added, "What do you think of this business of you being in charge?"

I drove in silence for a minute or two, watching the passing pines along the side of the road. "You know," I said, "I think *that's* what fuels my body to keep moving, even if I don't consciously think about it." I rubbed my forehead, thinking back. "Before I met Rosa, I just looped the same day, endlessly. Ten years of repetition, doing what I was told, when I was told to do it. Then *she* was there, and things changed. I moved forward. And before you arrived, before Addy arrived, at that house, I was pretty much done. I'd stopped caring and stopped moving. But with you and the dog, I regained some purpose. Internally, something took over, and I got back to work. Now, with all these people back at our new Oasis, I don't know if I'm smart enough to be their leader or not, but it gives me something to do. Keeps me moving."

"Don't you ever want to stop?" she said. "Just to relax?"

"No. Not really." I moved my hands higher up on the wheel, stared down at the bracelet. "Not anymore."

14

We fell into silence as we drove along, weaving among the remains of a dead civilization. Celia seemed lost in her thoughts; I retreated to my own.

In the back, Ray and Zachary finally went quiet, staring out at the never-ending landscape of buildings, stores, cars. I had the feeling that for them, it was less about the regret of seeing objects from days gone by and more about the sheer anomaly of it all.

And Oliver slept.

Driving only my second vehicle in the past 10 years, I couldn't help but be reminded of the RV, and of Rosa. Those thoughts increased my mental isolation from the group, my self-imposed quiet. I realized I had a new regret, and it was almost bottomless. While I had told Rosa my feelings for her, I'd never been proactive. All that time at The Oasis, I let her spend her days on research. The work she did was important for us all — hell, for everyone in the world — but ultimately it was short-lived. I never stopped her and asked for at least a little time for us just to be together. I thought farther back, to those days in her mother's apartment in DC. The times we shared then were possibly the happiest of my life. And I remembered how I'd started to avoid those moments, avoid her, fearing her growing fascination with The Oasis.

I pounded the steering wheel of the van with one fist, lightly, a hollow echo of my mental mood. Celia snapped out of her daze. "What?" she asked. "What is it?" Her eyes studied me.

I gave her a quick look, then tried to shrug off my distress. "Uh, nothing. Nothing," I said. "I just... hope this works." My half-hearted grin and inability to meet her eyes told the real story. But she knew me. She stayed quiet.

* * *

A short while later, I eased the van to a stop. The congestion of abandoned and destroyed cars had increased steadily as we reached DC, but, approaching what must have been the city's easternmost wall, I saw that they jammed every available space. We weren't within sight of DC, but still we had to abandon the van and walk.

I felt like we hiked for miles, past hundreds and hundreds of cars, and who knew how many twisted, desiccated corpses. Dozens of cats, dogs, and rats skittered off as we passed by. I was surprised none of them seemed infected, and wondered how long that would last.

Then we saw it. The wall.

Built into an old overpass, the wall was sheer metal from the ground up, towering several stories over our heads. The government had been thorough. The walls of the original Oasis, or even the formidable structure I remembered glimpsing outside Richmond, before they started shooting at us, were like a child's fort next to this massive bulwark. I looked left and right, and saw the wall's smoothly armored flank curve away from us in both directions, fading into the distance through the leafless trees.

For a moment, I held my breath, expecting the worst. Images arose in my mind of Rosa frantically wheeling the RV around after someone on the walls of Richmond fired on us. And of Rosa falling to the ground maybe a few miles from here, gunned down in Virginia, just outside DC's western border. But there was no one here, not a soul.

I thought back to when I first entered the newly fortified city, at the beginning of the epidemic. A sudden memory came to me. *This is just for a little while*, I had told myself, standing in the long line of people streaming into DC. *Until things calm down.* How wrong I was. After 10 years, millions upon millions dead, an entire civilization in shambles, things had not calmed down yet. And they didn't look to be calming down any time soon.

When I came to DC, I'd arrived from this same direction, on this very same road. But it was before the wall was anything like the metal beast it had become. Back then, it was a chain-link fence, with a couple of gates. It looked more like the camp we'd just left outside Annapolis, but swarming with military. Now the wall was huge and solid, but devoid of life.

Puffing out white clouds in the cold air, we made our way forward. Ray and Zachary guarded our flanks, guns drawn. Celia stayed close to me, while Oliver seemed to drift in his own cocoon.

Unable to go through or over the wall, all we could do was pick a direction and follow it, hoping for a break. In places, the government had been frugal, using existing buildings to complete parts of the structure rather than creating everything from scratch. Luckily for us, those old, decaying, red-brick buildings were a weak point. It wasn't long before we found one where the doors and windows had been knocked out, and we passed through the wall's perimeter with ease.

We stepped into a dark maze of abandoned rooms heavy with the damp smell of concrete, dust and age thick in the air. Celia drew her pistol, but I kept mine tucked away in my waistband. My eyes slowly adjusted to the dim light as we slipped from one room into a hallway, down through another room, and onward. Trying to find a way through to the other side, into DC.

As we entered a third room, Oliver tripped on a pile of debris — crumbled brick from the walls, bits of plaster from the ceiling — and fell. In the empty building, it sounded like thunder. He immediately jumped up and wiped himself off, fumbling and apologetic.

As we regrouped, I thought I heard something from back in the hallway. I held up a hand. "*Shhh*, wait a second. *Quiet.*" Ray and Zachary held their guns ready, looking in every direction for a target, but finding nothing. We all froze, but heard nothing else.

On the far side of the room was a small office set off by a wooden door. Beside the door was a large window, streaked and dirty now, but I imagined some supervisor, in the time before the infection, sitting on the other side of the glass, watching workers in the main room go about whatever their tasks had been. The window was caked with grime, but a distinct light was filtering through. I opened the door and the light grew stronger. Through another filthy window, we could see the warm glow of sunlight. There was a door on the far side of the room that looked to open to the outside.

Anxious to get out of the building and into the city, I went quickly to the door.

The old metal knob turned with a gritty sound, most of the way around, but not enough to clear the latch and open. I tried a second time as the others piled into the small office behind me.

Celia stood by the window, trying to peer through the filmy surface.

On my second try, the knob turned farther, *scritch scritch scritch*, and some of the grit seemed to loosen. I shouldered into the door with a *thud*, hoping to jar it loose. I turned and pulled at the knob with all my strength, willing it to open.

Beside me, Celia's face was just an inch from the dirty glass pane as she squinted and said, "Hold on. There's something mov—"

The glass shattered inward as a large infected man with milky white eyes and a bloody gash across his left cheek burst through, tumbling into the room and nearly toppling onto Celia. She screamed, her pistol clattering away across the dusty floor as she fell back.

The knob clicked in my hand and the door swung open, revealing a small courtyard. Outside, I saw four more zombies scrabbling toward us in their feral way. Before I could close the door, their hands were clawing at the frame. I stepped away.

"Get back!" I shouted as Ray pulled up his gun, trying to get a clear shot. In the small room, with so many of us jostling for space, humans and zombies, any gunshot likely would do more harm than good. Zachary seemed to realize this, and flipped his rifle around to wield it like a club. But the size of the room prevented that, too. Pushing back out of the office and into the main room, we staggered away from our attackers.

And into an ambush.

From the hallway came another two zombies, flailing at each other with fury, pushing to get into the room.

Zachary moved forward, swinging his gun and smashing the skull of the nearest zombie. The second one fell upon him before he could swing again. Zachary's head hit the cement floor with a hideous wet *crunch* while the enraged zombie ripped out his throat. I hoped the fall killed him, so he didn't feel the slow death of the zombie's bite. Either way, Zachary was gone. We'd been inside the walls of DC for maybe 10 minutes, and we'd already lost a man.

Zachary's death splintered our group instantly. It seemed like everyone was running in different directions, with zombies collapsing upon us from all sides. I had no time to get my bearings. Suddenly I realized Oliver was pulling me out a side door. "Wait! Celia!" I shouted, as we fell into another dim room and Oliver slammed the door shut. "Celia!"

From the other side of the door, I heard her muffled reply. "We'll find each other! Just be safe for now!" Then there was the loud *crack* of Ray's rifle and an inhuman shriek, then something thudded frantically against the door, shivering it in its frame. Oliver held it shut, shoulder against the wood, right hand clutching the knob, refusing to allow it to turn as he muttered something under his breath.

A second shot, slightly less loud. More feral sounds, and a door slamming. Some muffled yelling, one voice clearly Ray, the other Celia. Then the noise diminished, and for a long while Oliver sat with one ear pressed against the door, but neither of us could hear anything outside. The turmoil was replaced with eerie silence. And we waited.

After a time, Oliver turned the knob and opened the door a sliver. One of the zombies was lying dead against the other side, and as Oliver opened the door farther, its gore-covered remains fell into the room, spilling blood across the floor. The thing stank of rot and blood, and the uneasy smell of infection.

Oliver stepped over the body, peered into the room. Two more zombies were dead on the floor — the one Zachary brained, another presumably shot by Ray. In the middle of the room, Zachary himself lay dead, open eyes staring at the ceiling, like a man waiting for an angel from Heaven to come to his rescue. Uneasily, Oliver and I tiptoed past the bodies and into the hall.

"Where'd they go?" Oliver asked. He seemed on the verge of panic.

I tried to remain calm, but my worry for Celia was growing. "Let's just try to find them as quickly as possible, okay?" I said. Oliver nodded.

Without another word, he hurried off down the hall. "Hold on!" I called to his back. "We should look together!" But it was too late. Oliver turned a corner, moving quickly in his squat, waddling way, and was gone.

I stood alone in the hall, wondering what the hell to do. Wondering what the hell just happened. I chased after Oliver, but after a few turns, I had no idea if I was getting closer or farther away.

After some time, maybe eight or nine minutes, I heard Oliver cry out from down a long hallway. "This way! They're here!" I hurried to catch up to him, desperate to be sure that Celia was safe, barely thinking about Ray.

In the shrouded darkness of the building's interior, I found Oliver standing at the bottom of a stairwell that rose in stages toward an opening that shone bright with sunlight. He pointed to it, giving a strange little smile. "There." His eyes darted left and right, but that smile stayed. "They're up there! Through the door at the top of the stairs. They went up to get away from the zombies." He even made a little giggle, then caught himself and took the first step, turning back to gesture for me to follow.

We advanced up the stairs side by side, in silence. As we started the third and final flight before the top, I could feel Oliver looking over at me, and not for the first time I found myself wondering about this bizarre little man. This hermit whose home we'd invaded and whose life we'd turned upside-down. I wish I'd known him better. Maybe I would have seen it coming.

At the top of the stairs, I shielded my eyes against the blinding sunlight streaming through the open door. "Celia?" I asked excitedly, hoping for our group, what was left of it, to be reunited so we could keep going, do what we came for, and be gone. But mostly I just wanted to be sure she was all right. I stepped to the edge of the open door and, through squinted eyes, blinked and looked out. I didn't see Celia or Ray, or much of anything at all, for that matter.

And that's when Oliver pushed me from behind, and I fell, tumbling out into the bright, empty world.

15

I burst into the blinding light and fell like I'd been dropped from the sky, twisting toward my left side. I crashed to the pavement, *hard*, a snap and crack jolting through my left arm, air driven out of me. My small backpack absorbed some of the impact and probably saved me from even worse injuries, but it also forced me into an awkward lurch as I gasped and rolled, trying to find some angle where it didn't *hurt*. None existed. I knew right away that my left forearm was... *wrong*. Radius or ulna — maybe both — broken, possibly shattered beyond repair. My medical training leaped into my mind, but I tried not to think about the struggles of setting a complex fracture by myself, or the long, dubious recovery for someone my age.

I found myself on my back, looking up at the doorway. Outside its frame, tiny spurs of rusted orange metal were the only remnant of the landing and staircase that used to be there. The entire structure looked to have fallen in a heap of debris on the ground, where I'd missed landing on it by only a few feet. I suppose I could thank Oliver for at least pushing me out past the jutting metal that would have skewered me alive.

In the doorway, I saw him looking down at me through his round glasses. He pulled out a pistol I hadn't even realized he was carrying, and I steeled myself. Through gritted teeth, I said, "So now I meet the real Oliver." My left arm was propped close to my chest, like the broken wing of a bird.

For a long moment, Oliver didn't say anything. Finally, he snapped, "Why'd you have to show up, anyway? The clubhouse, that whole place, was mine, and everything was *fine*." He seemed like he had more to say, but it was lost in the voiceless rage that had bubbled to the surface. He sputtered and tried to speak, but eventually waved a hand, dismissing me in frustration. Then he raised his gun, sighting carefully, almost comically, down the barrel, until his eyes suddenly slid past me, saw something, then darted back. With a smirk, he slammed the metal gun against the rusty, open door three times, making a harsh, gong-like sound that echoed over the courtyard.

Behind me, I heard a grunt. Then another.

I was still spread out flat on the ground. Gingerly, I tilted my head up, giving myself an upside-down view of the space around me.

The courtyard was actually a dead-end alleyway, surrounded on three sides by the crumbling red-brick husks of connected buildings. Given the ruin of the exterior stairs, there was no escape except directly behind me, where the alleyway led out to an unknown street. And in that direction, something was moving.

Like a weasel returning to its den, Oliver slipped back into the doorway and was gone.

I rolled toward my right and struggled up onto my knees, trying to keep my left arm from touching the ground. But the arm slipped down with a flat, dead *thump*, accompanied by tiny crackling sounds that I felt deep inside, and I half-gasped, half-screamed at the pain. How many times in my previous life had I internally mocked some kid screaming and carrying on as I set his broken arm? I mentally apologized to any and all of those patients as I heaved myself to my feet and looked toward the alley entrance and whatever was out there.

My eyes focused on the movement, and my fears were confirmed. Two male zombies were skittering in my direction, investigating the sound Oliver had made. They didn't seem to have seen me yet — one benefit of the milky white eyes of the disease. But they were approaching and it wouldn't be long, especially given the fact that they were blocking my only way out. I looked from side to side, hoping for a miracle. I didn't see anything promising. In fact, I saw something less than promising.

Drawn by the sound, an infected dog, a German shepherd, I think, came into the alley and followed behind the two zombies shambling my way. The dog picked up its pace, thick, white froth falling from its pale tongue. Even from that distance — 50 yards or more — I began to make out the smell of the infected: fetid, rotting, filth, and disease. The humid mixture of sweat, blood, puss, urine, and feces, the worst combination of smells a living creature can produce.

I eased to my left, seeking the wall of the alley, maneuvering to protect my wounded side as I tried to find a place to hide or even mount a defense. There were a few steel trashcans overturned against the wall, and I slowly made my way to them, trying not to make quick movements or do anything else that might render me visible.

That was a mistake. In my haste, I'd forgotten about the dog's acute hearing, even given the ravages of the disease. It turned toward me as if I'd set off a flare gun. Padding more quickly, the dog passed the two zombies, moving straight toward me. I frantically scanned the alleyway for any sign of hope.

And I spotted my pistol on the pavement, just a few feet to my right. It must have slipped out of my waistband when I hit the ground.

The dog's sense of smell was another oversight. It now had a lock on me, and paused momentarily to prepare its attack. Its front legs formed a tense, inverted V as it let out a beastly, slathering growl. On either side of the dog, the two zombies continued forward, creating a three-pronged assault.

I thought to myself, *This is it.*

And I sprang for the gun.

Oh! The pain stabbed into my upper body, the jolt of another hard landing on the harsh pavement traveling through my cracked forearm. With my other arm, I reached out for the pistol, grabbed it, turned back toward my three attackers, fired.

The zombie on the left — dirty, green shirt, soiled khakis, thick work boots — took a hit to his left shoulder; the sound was like dropping a stone into thick mud. He spun backward, let out a garbled moan as he fell.

I knew I had to do better. I'd been aiming at the damn dog.

Who, even more incensed by the loud *bang* of the gun, leaped forward. I had only one more chance. At point-blank range, I fired again.

In a spray of blood and black-and-gray matted fur, a hole appeared in the dog's forehead, and he fell.

With no time to spare, I turned the gun toward the other approaching zombie, this one with the close-cropped haircut I remembered from the guards and military around DC. Based on the fact that his hair was still so short, I wondered if this was a relatively new one, recently turned. I pulled the trigger, and his left knee cap exploded. It was a debilitating injury, but *damn*, two bad shots. Like I had trained Celia, I'd been aiming for the gut, center of mass. He staggered and fell, tracing a long, slow arc toward my right. I tracked him on the way down, fired again, taking him through the center of his chest. He was dead when he hit the ground.

And suddenly I was facedown beside him, pain shooting up my arm. I yelled out, then bit down hard, clenching my teeth in an involuntary wince. The gun nearly flew from my grasp, but I held onto it like it was my last hope.

Which, I suppose, it was.

The other zombie had recovered from my first shot and was now on top of me, on my back, all snapping jaws, scratching, ragged fingernails, and violent thrashing. He tore into my backpack, but luckily not into me. I felt the grinding of bone on bone in my left arm as I jabbed backward with my right, launching my elbow into his side. The blow pushed him far enough to allow me to get the bulk of his weight off me. I turned over halfway. Furious, the zombie reared back on his knees, preparing for a final strike at my gut, one that would leave me flayed and dead in this unknown alleyway in DC. I rolled the rest of the way over onto my backpack, leaving my unprotected belly pointing toward the sky and the zombie.

As he lurched forward, I lifted the pistol to his forehead and squeezed the trigger.

The only sound was a dry *click*. Empty.

Now it was the zombie's turn. He ignored my useless gun, tore into my chest with his teeth and fingernails. And I *screamed*. I *screamed*. I *screamed*. No words, no language, just the incomprehensible sounds of unbridled pain. Every muscle tensed. Every nerve ending alive. By reflex more than anything else, I used my good hand, the one still holding the gun, to punch at his head. In my frenzy, the butt of the pistol became a hammer, and I turned into the embodiment of fury, slam, *slam, SLAM, SLAM, SLAM, SLAM.* Then there was a new sound. A wet, gooey *SPLAT.* The zombie rolled off me, dead.

All I wanted to do was catch my breath. Catch my breath. I couldn't. It was too hard. I tried, I tried, but it was too hard. I dropped the pistol, touched my chest, found torn skin and blood, too much blood. My breathing wouldn't slow down. There wasn't enough air in the alleyway, not enough air in the world, how was I supposed to breathe? I panted, gasped. A vague thought in the back of my mind said to fight it, to calm down, but I couldn't. I tore my shirt open, trying to get more air, even though the winter day was so cold.

And the world fell away, nothing left, no sky, no sun, no light, no cold, no alleyway, no zombie, no blood. No air. *No air.*

16

Black.

Everything was black.

Through a thick, sleepy fog, I turned my head, opened my eyes, but the blackness was complete. I couldn't see a thing, not in any direction. *Where the hell am I?* It was my only coherent thought.

In time, I faded out again. To black.

* * *

Then the world was grey. Differing shades, from light to dark. A sense that it was morning.

I opened my eyes again.

I was in a room, a large room, institutional ceiling tile overhead, moldy and water-stained, in repeating rectangles. There were light fixtures up there, too, but none were on. And, almost directly above me, a small circle of light-colored plastic.

Was that a smoke alarm? My God. Had the whole thing been a dream? A decade of disease and death, just a figment of my imagination? A smoke alarm. Such a mundane thing, so commonplace, and yet it'd had no place in the universe I'd dreamed up, the world of RL2013.

I raised my head as much as I could, until my chin nearly touched my chest, and looked around. I was in a hospital, lying on a bed, with white sheets covering my body. Maybe I'd had some sort of episode, maybe I'd been in a coma. That might explain how my mind had turned in on itself, and fabricated all of it. Ten years of an imaginary plague. I grinned, a stupid grin, a sheepish grin. I felt like a fool, and like the luckiest man in the world. The dream was over, and everything was back to normal.

My chest *itched*.

I went to scratch it, but my hand, the left one, felt like it weighed a ton. How strange. Straining with extra effort, I tried to raise my left arm. And I couldn't. I tried my right arm. Nothing.

Not because my arms were too heavy. But because they were strapped down.

Okay, I thought. *Maybe they didn't want me flailing or rolling out of bed. That's understandable.*

I heard a creak, and a thin shaft of light broke across the room. Footsteps.

Tilting my head, I saw a low, squat woman in a dark grey dress amble into the room, toward a table in the far corner. She walked quietly, not talking to me or even looking in my direction.

"Hey —" I tried to speak, but my voice was dry and cracking, barely audible. I licked my lips and swallowed, trying again. "Hey. You there."

The woman stopped in her tracks and turned in my direction. After a brief look through squinting, calculating eyes, she turned back toward the door. "James, I'm going to need you in here," she said. Her voice was craggy with a lilting uptick, some sort of brogue, but if she'd ever had a true accent, it had mostly faded. She was short and thick, with curls of grey hair that only hinted at their former brown.

From outside, a deep voice replied. "Yes, ma'am." The sliver of light grew and a shadow stepped through it. A large, dark-skinned man in green fatigues, walking toward her in long, purposeful strides. The room remained dim, but the light from the open door was enough to see clearly. The man, James, made no effort to hide the pistol on his right hip, or the hand that rested on its handle, ready. When he reached the old woman, he turned toward me and stopped.

The woman came closer.

"What's going on here?" I started in a slow, tired voice. "How long have I — ", She grabbed at my chin, opening my mouth and looking inside. Then she turned my head from side to side, peering at me in a curious way. I figured she was my nurse, though I was far from impressed by her bedside manner. Her hand left my chin, and she pulled down the white sheets, revealing large wraps of bandages across my chest. *I must have had some kind of accident*, I thought, still in a fog. The woman reached across to prod my left arm, checking it. With the sheet pulled down, I saw a cast — a sloppy, makeshift job, in my opinion — covering my forearm. *Was I in a car accident or something?* And I saw the straps, holding me tight.

I looked up at the woman, studying her for a second or two, blinking my eyes to try to clear my head. I noticed smudges of grease on her forehead. Her fingernails were ragged, dirty. In my daze, I asked the first thing that came to mind. "Shouldn't you wash up before seeing a patient?"

She pulled up, eyes wide, forehead wrinkled in surprise. She mocked me with a tiny bow, her hint of brogue blooming into a full-on Irish accent. "So sorry, your highness," she sneered. "Please accept me deepest apologies. I'll submit me resignation and be gone in the morning. In the meantime, can I get you a pair of fluffy slippers, or perhaps a cup o' tea?" She huffed and walked toward the door.

"Wait!" I pleaded, but she didn't turn.

To James, she said, back in her normal voice, "Well, I guess it's true then. Hell, I guess it's *all* true."

"Isn't that a *good* thing?" James asked.

She stood, head down, then turned to look back at me. "It is. And thank the good Lord, if He's still paying attention." She stepped quickly out of the room, followed by James, and the door closed behind them, punctuated with a loud click.

* * *

Hours passed, and I drifted off to sleep again. I'd tried shouting after them, but to no avail. No one came.

Finally, I awoke to the creak of the door. The old woman and James stepped into the room and just stared at me.

I turned my head toward them, unable to do anything else. "Can't you at least tell me what's going on?" I slowly shook my head, trying to chase away the butterflies clouding my thoughts.

She shook her head. "I can't."

"Who are you, at least?"

She shrugged. "My name's Hilde, not that I matter a whit. But there is someone who wants to see you." She regarded me skeptically. "Do you think you can walk? I don't have a wheelchair, your majesty."

I winced and shook my head. "Look, I'm sorry about earlier. I just don't know where I am. Or how I got here. Was I in a coma? I had this terrible dream."

She considered what I said with a wry look. "Terrible dream, indeed. You've been out a few days, mostly because I kept you knocked out. Better for you. It took a lot of my drugs, and I hope they weren't wasted on you." She tilted her head, set her mouth. I couldn't tell what she was thinking about me, only that it was… *complicated.* My mind still foggy, I couldn't understand everything. *Why was this nurse skeptical of me? Why was I under armed guard?* And more than anything, looking up at the dim ceiling, *why were the lights still off?*

Turning to the man next to her, Hilde said, "Come on, James, let's try to get him up."

17

We stepped out into the hallway. And there, any sense of my past 10 years being a dream shattered. RL2013 was real, not a fantasy. Not a coma-induced hallucination. On either side of the hall, filthy children and adults huddled, watching me stagger past, half-carried by James and Hilde. This wasn't a hospital from days gone by, with pristine walls and gleaming floors, and guidelines on everything from sanitary procedures to visiting hours. This was *now*. And *here*. A time and a world where simply having a place like this to recuperate was a luxury. Although I was thankful for what these people had given me — a place, a way to recover — I'm sure I couldn't hide the disappointment in my eyes.

My legs were unsteady, untrustworthy from days of disuse. James and Hilde continued to help me along as we made our way down unknown corridors and halls.

I was uncovered and untethered. My pants and shoes had been left alone, thankfully, but my shirt was gone, exposing my bandaged chest and my left arm, now encased in a makeshift cast. The people in the halls ogled. Men, women, children, they all stared. I suppose I would have, too, seeing this old grey beast walk by, held together by spit and glue.

A young boy, maybe 12, stepped in front of me suddenly, reached out a hand, touched my good arm. "Now there are three," he said in a wistful sort of voice, before James pushed him gently but firmly out of the way. As the kid ran off down a connecting hall, he said it again, louder. "Now there are three!" More faces turned to look at me.

Three? Three what?

"What does that mean?" I asked Hilde.

The three of us paused, and Hilde stared at me with knowledge behind her eyes. But it was knowledge she wasn't willing to share. "I already told you, I don't matter a whit," she said. "And I like it that way. Keeping to myself, doing my job, it keeps me out of trouble, and it keeps trouble away from me. Far as I am concerned, you're someone else's problem now. I want to go back to my simple routine. If you have questions, you're going to need to ask someone more important than me."

Hilde nodded to James, and they started up again, directing me down one hall, turning, down another, through a doorway. I became tired, feet beginning to drag.

"Come on, old-timer. It's not far now," James said, more kindly than I would have expected. Helping me walk, he guided me through another door and into a room crowded with people, all of them standing. We pushed our way into the middle of the room, where I was relieved to find a chair, blocky and cushioned, with squat legs, probably borrowed from a waiting room, assuming the building used to be a hospital. I sat down heavily.

The crowd parted and settled, finding places to stand along each wall, or sitting on the floor. It seemed clear from the way people were inspecting their fingernails or idly running their hands through their hair that they were waiting for something.

Finally, when I was nearly ready to doze off in the chair, I heard someone enter from a door behind me. Footsteps crossed the room, and the murmur of the crowd died off.

The chair was too big to slide around, and I was too tired to get up. I waited for whoever had entered to come to me.

"Good, you're awake."

That voice. *That voice.* It was…

"Hank?" I asked, craning my neck to see the person behind me.

"And me," a woman's voice said, and she stepped into view, her braided hair falling across one side of her denim shirt. The man joined her in front of me, like the reveal at the end of an incredible magic trick.

Hank and Janine. From The Oasis.

"I don't believe it," was all I could manage. I sagged back into the chair and squinted up at them, amazed, my jaw hanging open like I was trying to catch flies.

18

I'd only just come to terms with the fact that I hadn't created the whole outbreak in a dream. And now, here were Hank and Janine, ghosts from my past, threatening to once more upend my reality.

Hank and Janine, the very same scouts from The Oasis who first guided Rosa and me to the supplies she needed to mass-produce the cure. And who later accidentally led the hordes from Atlanta back to the camp, resulting in its downfall and destruction.

"What're you *doing here*?" I finally asked.

Hank chuckled and shrugged. "We have some shortwave radios around that still work, and I hear there's a new Oasis. In Maryland. You have anything to do with that?" Now it was my turn to shrug. *Perhaps*. I wasn't ready to tell everything just yet. It was all too confusing.

So they told me their story. Part of it, I already knew, because I'd lived it, too. The attack on The Oasis. The mayhem, the rush and struggle to break free.

After that, Janine said, they just *guessed*. They knew that Rosa and I were from DC, and they'd seen our RV's mad-dash escape. With Atlanta gone, they correctly guessed that we might try to take the cure to DC. After all, it was nominally in charge of what was left of the country.

They couldn't escape from the besieged, burning Oasis by car, but were able to run though the surrounding dark woods to freedom. They made it out with their ready-packs, loaded with supplies they always had available for scouting runs, and one gun each. For weeks, they hiked on side roads, avoiding highways in case anyone from Atlanta continued north from The Oasis. They scrounged any food, water, and supplies they could find. The fact that they were traveling as a pair saved them. Countless times, one of them found water where the other had seen nothing, or fended off a random zombie attack the other had stepped into. As they told their tale, finishing one another's sentences, sharing private looks, it dawned on me that Hank and Janine were more than just business partners.

Somewhere in Virginia, they chanced upon two bicycles with flat tires. After only a day, the struggle of pedaling with the floppy, deflated tires was too much, and they abandoned the bikes by the side of the road. They walked the rest of the way to DC.

By the time they reached the city's walls, Rosa's message had done its tragic work. The government had been overthrown. People rebelled, not only against their totalitarian rulers, but against each other. Fighting had broken out all over the city. Thousands had died. The chaos lasted for months. Those who were left clung together in pockets. After a time staying across the river in Virginia, Hank and Janine slipped easily into the unguarded city. And then, living in the city, they joined forces with some of the survivors.

As they related the story, I could barely hold back my anguish. Janine put a hand on my shoulder. "We heard about what Rosa said, and what happened to her," she said softly. "It's pretty much a legend among the people who are left here. You couldn't have known what was going to happen, how everyone would react. But those of us that remained... since then, people like us have been looking everywhere. We've been looking for *you*."

"You said *thousands* died!" I could feel the tears, and didn't try to stop them. "*That's* our legacy. We came here to offer hope and a new chance. But what we really offered was *death*." I buried my head in my hands. Through my palms, I choked out the words: "These people would have been better off keeping the damn government, and never knowing about the cure."

There was silence. Neither Janine nor Hank had a rebuttal for that. They just looked at me, with sympathy that burned like scorn.

An earnest young man stepped forward, maybe 18 or 19, with a shock of dirty blond hair drooping down over a face that was just showing signs of beard stubble. "No," he said. He stopped himself, looked at Janine and Hank like he was weighing the political consequences of interrupting them, but decided he wanted to talk anyway. "No, we wouldn't be better off. Look, people decided to fight each other, no one can change that. But what you told us was that *there's a chance*. There's a reason to have hope. That means more to us than the walls and the security and everything else. We lived like prisoners. Every choice was made for us. Now, we're *free*." He swept his hands around at all the others sitting on the floor and lining the walls, and I saw nods of agreement. "Sure, we struggle, but it's *our struggle*. It's our choice to make, not just some assignment to keep us placated. And now that you're here, there's *three* of you. That alone is incredible." He looked from me to Hank to Janine. *There are three.* Of course. That's what the kid in the hall had meant. *Now there are three people with the cure.* "Plus, it's *you*," he said. "From across the river, from the day we learned the truth. And you...." He trailed off, suddenly unsure of himself, and Hank stepped forward.

"Everyone here knows about us," Hank said, gesturing to himself and Janine. "And they all know about you. Only a few people heard Rosa in person, but the story spread like wildfire. I daresay some of the folks here could recite what she said that day word for word." A low murmur spread through the crowd. "They know we're unique — Janine, you, and me, the only people left who were cured by the fabled Oasis." The murmur grew with anticipation, a sound almost like reverence. Hank's face was a tangled knot of hope, concern, excitement, utter fear. "Do you still have *it*? Do you have the eggs? *The cure?*"

The crowd didn't move, didn't whisper. Every breath was held waiting for my answer.

How long ago had Rosa and I stood overlooking this city? How long had it been since she spoke the words that ended her life, and ripped these people's world apart? Months? More than a year. How much more? Now, I was about to shatter every one of their remaining hopes.

"No," I said.

Hank's face dropped. Janine turned away. The crowd erupted in shouts and wails. People either argued with each other or consoled one another, or both.

In one corner, I saw her.

A little girl, 4 or 5 by my estimation, sitting cross-legged by herself. All she did was look at me. Her eyes were like those of a dead animal, staring, seeing nothing. A girl who should have embodied the innocence of her youth, the joy of simply being a child, instead looked shell-shocked and hollow. Those empty eyes glistened for a moment, then tears began to stream down her cheeks. Her hands clutched at a dirty, fuzzy shape in her lap, a beloved toy or blanket, something to give her comfort. Still, her gaze remained locked on me.

I felt like I was suffocating. It was too much to bear, the hopes and dreams of every other living soul. But I'd come here for a reason, and seeing the dead-faced little girl in front of me, that reason came slamming back into my mind like a door closing, shutting out my own despair, blasting away all the cobwebs of indecision and fear.

I pushed myself up out of the chair, held up my right hand. "But," I said.

The crowd was too loud, too absorbed in their own anger and misery. I cleared my throat and spoke again, much louder, with all the force I could muster. "But —"

People in the crowd turned in surprise. Janine heard me and began waving her hands to quiet people down. "Let him talk!" she yelled.

As the group slowly grew silent, I waited until everyone's eyes were on me again. "But there is still hope." People looked confused, overwhelmed, accusatory. I kept talking. "I don't have the eggs, and I can't just give you the cure. But I *have* given it to someone else. A woman, a friend. Her name is Celia, and I've cured her, too. With my blood. And I know there's a way to get it out, for the rest of you. I came here to look for the right people — people Rosa would've worked with before the government collapsed. People who can take what's inside me — inside Hank, and Janine, too — and get it out. Replicate it. Give it to all of you."

Scanning the room again, I could see a strange look on people's faces. *I had cured someone else.* They seemed dumbstruck, like they didn't know what to believe anymore. I couldn't blame them. "You tell me that you struggled, and that the struggle was worth it," I said. "And maybe a lot of that struggle was to find me. Well, I'm here now. But I'm not the *end* of the struggle. It's time for all of us to struggle together. To find the people I need, to end this damned disease forever." As I spoke, my voice gained momentum, volume. My last words rang out as a shout in the crowded room.

Everyone stayed quiet. Then the young man, the one who'd interrupted us just moments before, came over and embraced me. A few other people did, too, and finally, the little girl with the lifeless eyes got up off the floor and held out her arms to me.

My God, I thought. *What have I done?*

19

"That's across the divide," Hank said, sounding concerned.

"The divide?" I raised an eyebrow. The room had been cleared, leaving only Janine, Hank, and me. I told them my plan, what little there was. My first thought was to go to the NIH branch nearby — the lab, the place Rosa used to work — hoping it was still there, with people who could run the machines we'd need to manufacture the cure. It was a pretty ambitious hope.

Then, as Janine unconsciously twirled her long, braided hair, she told me how I'd come to be in this room, whatever and wherever it was. After the organized fighting in the city had died down, gunshots were relatively rare, so when one of their scouts heard shots fired, he naturally went to see what was going on. Luckily for me, that scout stumbled across the dead-end alley where I was lying unconscious, surrounded by two dead zombie humans and a dead zombie dog. He

had no idea who I was, but Hank had also been scouting nearby —
never one to pass his duties along to someone else, even though he
was in charge now. Although he had to look past my longer hair and
scraggly beard, Hank recognized me, and with the other scout,
dragged me to get help.

They'd taken me to this old hospital, formerly called Providence
Hospital, in the northeast quadrant of the city. It served as their
headquarters — part home, part sick bay, part operations control. It
probably hadn't been all that new when the outbreak happened, and
the ensuing decade had only added mold, dust, and the crumbling
detritus of decay to its already bland, boxy appearance. The damp
scent of mildew filled every breath, and I felt my old, ingrained fear
of dirt and filth crop up, illogical as it was.

They asked me how in the hell I ended up half-dead in that alley.
I told them about my mission to spread the cure, and with something
very close to hatred, I spoke about Oliver. I paused, trying to regain
my composure.

I told them I was I wanted to go to the NIH branch lab on
Capitol Hill, the facility near my old home where Rosa had worked.
But they dissuaded me, telling me that their scouts had been all
through that area. The only people left were a few pockets of
survivors that shunned their attempts to connect. And, of course, the

zombies. So I changed the plan, and decided that we needed go to the main NIH campus instead.

"The divide," Janine said, digging out an old stubby pencil. "It cuts the city in half, basically. North-south. Do you remember the layout of the city?"

I nodded. "I think so. Maybe even better than you, given that I lived around here... *before*."

"Well, fine, but a lot of what you remember has changed." She began to draw, right on the surface of the table in front of us. "DC is shaped like a diamond — half of one, really — but the walls weren't built around the whole thing. Mostly, they protect the government buildings — here, from the river, through the middle of the city, and up to the north a bit." She drew an irregular shape outlining where the walls stood. "Anywhere the density of the buildings and population dropped off, it must not have been worth it to make walls. Or maybe someone was just playing favorites. Anyway, a lot of this up here —" she pointed to the northeast section "— isn't inside the walls, and they stop on the west around here, too." Her pencil tip hovered over an area just west of the city center. "Then, they made another pocket over here, so there's a whole different set of walls that enclose this area." She drew a crude oval over the western portion of the diamond. "There used to be a connector between the two walled sections, before the fighting, but it didn't take long for the government to destroy that. Now the two parts are completely separate."

"That middle portion, in between the two walled areas — what you're calling 'the divide' — it's... Rock Creek Park?" My mind forced up these ancient memories.

"Yeah, that's it," Janine said. "Well, it used to be a park. Over time, the woods have become much more dense, but it's probably the best source of fresh water around. So, like you might expect, it draws a lot of *animals*. Animals of all kinds. Including zombies. *Lots* of zombies." Janine tapped her pencil on the open space in the drawing to make her point.

Hank jumped in. "So, what's she's saying is, if you want to go to NIH, you gotta go through there."

"We couldn't, you know, go around or something?" I asked.

Shaking his head, Hank said, "Nah, not really. To the south, it connects to the Potomac. And it runs pretty far north. You could go around it that way, to the north, but that'd be much more dangerous than just going through it. The shortest path is near the middle, where the two walls are closest together." He paused, letting me think about it. "And one more problem. Once the government pulled out of the city, that's the direction they went. And they blew up the bridges on the way out. The only way across the divide is literally to cross the river. We'll need to get our feet wet."

I sighed deeply. *Can nothing be easy?* Then I thought about the Bay Bridge, and those zombies on the other bridge that forced us south. "Okay, fine," I said. "Maybe I'm sick of bridges, anyway. When can we go?"

* * *

To say they babied me would be overstating things, but not by much. More than six weeks passed before Hank would agree to let me go. In that time, I saw how they lived, holed up in this old hospital, sleeping on floors, using anything they could find to make a "normal" life. Old privacy curtains became walls. The undersides of desks became bedrooms.

I thought of Celia a lot. I asked Hank to send people out to look for her, and he did, but they didn't find her. Or Ray. Or even Oliver. I hoped against hope that she had made it to safety, back the The Oasis. I wanted to go back, to make sure she was okay. But I also needed to push on, to seek the cure. Then I could go back, bringing something they really needed. If Oliver was there, I'd deal with him. Of that I was sure.

But first, I had to suffer through the tedious weeks of recovery. I spent a lot of time learning how they lived, if only to take up the time.

Keeping on top of the food and water supply was hard, but manageable. DC had been stocked for a larger population, and now that the numbers were much smaller, it was possible to make do. Even my old FDC on Capitol Hill was found to be rather well-supplied with food, tucked into secure rooms in the basement, and every bit of it was brought back to the hospital.

Janine and Hank's group was even rather ingenious about their method of managing the other half of the food-consumption process: waste removal. A large section of the third floor on the east end of the building was converted into a series of stalls that opened to the outdoors via holes. People could go in, do their business, and have it drop to the ground stories below. No one had to risk disease by fouling their living space, or risk attack by going outside. A crew of people had the unsavory job of shoveling, tilling, and burying the waste at intervals, but it worked. Hank told me the idea came from medieval castles, from a history buff in the group. Up on the third floor, on days when there was a breeze, you could hardly smell it. Well, that's a lie. But you could smell it a lot *less*.

I talked to as many people as possible, asking a lot of questions. On one occasion, I sat with James, the same man who had guarded over me when I first arrived. We talked about life in this DC. I asked where the other people were. Pointing out a window, across the city, he replied. "They're out there, all over. We've asked people to join up, but everyone seems happy to stay where they are for now. Over there," he said, gesturing north and east, "there's a pretty big group. They've got a lot of firepower, so we keep an eye on 'em. Their leader, a guy named Duke, seems like a decent fellow. But he doesn't trust us enough to join up."

When six weeks were up, I was so ready, I could taste it. My chest was still heavily scabbed from where the zombie had gouged it, and my left forearm, while free from its cast, felt weak, tentative. But I didn't care. My life during recovery was relatively comfortable, but had been reduced to a boring repetition of mundane daily tasks. And on top of that, I'd felt their eyes. Every day, wherever I went, they were on me. Eyes of expectation, and hope. Eyes that, as days passed, started to *demand* something from me. To implore me to do something.

When it finally came time to make preparations for the trip to NIH, we had to decide on a team. The journey involved significant risk of zombie attack, so it made sense that Hank, Janine, and I would go — a bite to us wasn't a death sentence. Many of the others opposed this, saying it was too risky to have all the leaders gone at once, but Hank and Janine brushed aside their concern. As for me, I didn't see how I could be even considered one of their leaders, so I didn't say anything.

* * *

We set out on a cool, overcast morning, as winter was giving way but spring still felt remote. Each of us had a supply pack and a pistol. As we headed west toward the divide, Janine carried a folding map of DC, so old that not even RL2013 could be blamed for its demise. Having been almost completely replaced by GPS years before the outbreak, we were fortunate to have the old paper dinosaur as a reference. A sudden gust of wind kicked up, so Janine carefully folded the map's vertical rectangles to show only the section of the city we needed. One long flap in the back caught the wind and tore loose with only the faintest rustle. "Damn," Janine muttered, pulling the pieces back together.

The route west took several zigs and zags, each of which Janine confirmed with her map. As we walked, I couldn't help but stare. DC had been my home for 10 years, but this part of the city was as alien to me as another world. For reasons I couldn't explain, a larger road marked as Georgia Avenue was divided down the middle by a row of parked cars and trucks — from the smallest coupes to minivans and even box trucks — that stretched as far as I could see in either direction. Some of the vehicles were burnt and hollow, blackened husks left to decay on the crumbling pavement. Others looked like you could start them up and drive away. Was this some sort of defense? If so, from what? And yet, beyond this makeshift barricade, some things were familiar, or cut from the same cloth as my old life. We passed this neighborhood's Food Dispersal Center, and the very name reminded me of the day I met Rosa. But unlike the large brick building I was familiar with on Capitol Hill, this FDC was split into two parts — small markets across the street from each other, with signs denoting them as Petworth FDC 1 and 2.

A short section of fence stood in front of Petworth FDC 2, and from somewhere behind it, we heard a noise. The sound of someone or something rummaging though trash. We all froze. Hank made the completely unnecessary universal gesture to be quiet, holding his right index finger up to his lips. Then he pointed the same finger down the road, in the direction we'd been traveling. *Let's just keep going, quietly.* That was the most obvious solution, so we did.

But it wasn't going to be that easy for us. The wind blew hard, and again Janine's paper map caught it, snapping with loud *fwap*, just for a second, then tearing apart. As Janine reached for the section that was about to blow away, she let out an involuntary gasping sound. *Hmph!*

From the fence, a ragged woman stood up straight and looked right at us, long, blonde hair clumped and greasy with neglect. Instantly, a rage took over her face, and she snapped her jaws at us, making a slathering sound. She lunged at the fence, but it stopped her, and for a brief moment she didn't know how get to us. Then, shaking her head, with what little consciousness remained, she shoved herself away from the fence, staggered to the side.

Hank took advantage of the zombie's momentary confusion, stepped up to the fence, and deftly planted a tool that looked like a combination hammer and ax into her right temple. She let out a hideous shriek as the blunt metal weapon ended her life with a sickening wet crunch.

"Hank — " Janine started. He didn't look up, wiping the mess off his hammer. "Hank!" she said, more urgently, and he snapped his head around. Janine was pointing to an alley that joined the street ahead of our path. There, three more zombies stumbled out from behind a low brick wall. Drawn by the commotion, they stepped toward us.

"Ah, damn," Hank sighed. "We haven't even reached the divide yet. I didn't expect all this trouble so soon."

"What do we do?" I asked.

"Fight or run," he replied.

"Run? How far is it?"

Hank looked to Janine, who glanced at her map. The zombies ambled closer, the one in front desperately trying to see through milky eyes, to find out what these strange noises were.

"To the divide?" Janine said. "Six or seven blocks — *long* blocks."

"You two have any idea how old I am?" I wasn't liking the sound of either option.

Hank nodded to Janine. "Then we fight. Kill these three, quiet as possible." The two of them set to work. The zombies, as they approached, became enraged, sensing prey or danger. I pulled out my pistol, aiming it at the closest one, thinking to myself, *I'm going to shoot someone by mistake.* Hank brained the lead zombie as it leaped toward him, filthy hands raised like claws. Then he looked back, waved a hand at me. "Put that away!" he hissed. "Too much noise!" Janine, her map tucked away, had produced a hammer tool like Hank's and shattered a zombie's kneecap with a quick, hard strike. As the thing fell and started to wail and snap, she hit it a second time, a fatal blow to the head. The third zombie rushed in and got a hand on Janine before she could pull back her hammer, but Hank was there, and it died from a single, brutal shot that smashed in its face. It fell away from Janine in a lump.

Moving with surgical economy, Janine and Hank scanned the surrounding area as they wiped down their tools and tucked them away. Janine pulled the map out again, pointed down the street, whispered, "This way. Come on." We walked as quickly and quietly as we could, toward the divide.

20

The wall followed the north-south line of 16th Street, but was far from secure. It had been battered and broken, with whole sections fallen into the street in ruins. In this part of DC, the wall was metal and brick and block — anything they could cobble together to make a run so many miles long, it seemed. Whether the broken sections marked places where people tried to get out or where something tried to get in, it was impossible to tell.

We stepped over piles of brick and through a large rift, and suddenly we were standing in the place they called the divide.

At first, the city looked much the same — rowhouses fanned out down side streets. But the houses were long abandoned, roofs collapsed, windows gone, porches caved in. The natural world was slowly reclaiming its land, with weeds and long grasses growing everywhere. Bushes, saplings, and trees sprouted all around, filling huge cracks in the pavement, and pushing up through the center of some homes that were no longer enclosed by four walls. What used to be a tree-lined street was now much less of a street and more like a forest.

I realized with surprise that it smelled different. It smelled *better*. Where the city had always carried the lingering scent of decay, trash, even death, the divide smelled like *nature*. Like life. I took a deep breath.

Within a few more blocks, the empty rowhouses gave way to empty single-family homes, some of them large and stately. *I wonder what that place must have sold for*, I thought to myself as we passed a huge Victorian with a wraparound porch, chuckling a bit until I considered how long it had been since the idea of *money* had even crossed my mind, then guffawing out loud. Janine looked at me with a sidelong glance, but didn't ask what was so amusing.

As the day wore on and our journey continued, the trees grew denser. The sun was muted behind thick clouds. We walked a long, slow, downward route, knowing there was a river somewhere in front of us. Finally, we approached a bend in the road and saw it. To our right, the remains of a bridge had fallen in crumbles of concrete and rebar into the river, neatly severed on both sides by what I guessed was some sort of explosion. Just like the Navy had done in Annapolis.

We stepped over a rusted guard rail and shuffled down to the water's edge. The river looked chilly and swollen, probably from an early spring thaw upstream. Hank was the first one to the bank, and he turned and looked back at me. "It's going to be really cold," he said, "but I don't think it's too deep here. Besides, we can use a lot of this debris like stepping stones." He gestured to the fallen bits of the bridge. "Be careful and be quiet. We haven't seen anything here yet, but that doesn't mean it's safe."

As if on cue, a raccoon emerged from the woods on the other side of the river. Although it was some distance away, I thought from the look of it that it was infected. It drank some water from the river, then hobbled off along the bank and disappeared. Hank stepped down into the water, and we followed.

Within a few steps, Hank gingerly toed himself onto a slab of concrete, leaving wet footprints. With a delicate leap, he jumped to the next slab. Janine followed his lead.

Damn, it's cold, I thought as my feet touched the water. I quickly hopped onto the first concrete steppingstone, now wet with dripping footprints. Hank was maybe a dozen feet ahead, pulling himself up onto another block of concrete, and Janine was dropping down into the water just behind him. I positioned myself to make the little jump to the second block — and saw something move out of the corner of my eye.

In mid jump, I turned my head to the left and saw them. More than a dozen zombies wading through the shallow waters. Like the one I'd seen so long ago by my dock on the Eastern Shore, I thought, *Are they fishing?*

And I fell.

My foot hit the second concrete slab and slipped on its slick surface. The hard slab rushed upward, slamming into my hip, scraping against my ribs. The air was knocked out of me in a loud *whoosh* as my legs splashed loudly into the water. For a moment, I felt dizzy, like I might faint. Then the cold rushing waters surrounded me and I thought that I might even drown. But violent hands grabbed me, and when I snapped out of it Hank and Janine were lifting me to my feet. "Move!" Hank shouted, inches from my face. "Come on! Now!" Hoisting my arms over their shoulders, he and Janine mostly carried me through the frigid waters.

My head lolled, my eyes blinked, trying to find focus. When I had regained my breath, the world around me wasn't quite so fuzzy, and I saw them. All of them. Streaming toward us on both sides, sloshing through the river. Dozens of zombies. A sound like the buzzing of bees filled my ears, but louder. An inhuman collection of grunts, snarls, growls, as the swarm approached us, from left and right.

Hank and Janine ran through the water, flat out dragging me with them, no longer making any attempt to be quiet, only trying to get away. I wanted to help, but my legs felt like they belonged to someone else. I paddled my feet in the water like an infant learning to swim, without power or purpose. "Up here!" Hank said, guiding us up the tiny incline on the far side of the river. We slipped in the mud, almost fell. The closest zombies were so near I began to smell their fetid reek. Then my mind exploded with a sound too sudden to bear. My ears rang, my vision flashed. Janine had fired her pistol toward the left, dropping a zombie dead into the water. Two more leaped on top of it, snapping and tearing, aimlessly raging.

Hank pulled me up the slope. "You've gotta help us, or you're dead." His eyes were wide, serious.

I shook my head once, twice. " Okay," was all I could say. I put weight on my legs, they held. I took a step, with Janine still supporting me. "Okay." I nodded. It was the most sincere gesture I could manage.

Another blast, and another, as both Hank and Janine shot at the approaching zombies. Panning my head in a slow circle, I saw them in tattered groups off into the distance. The gunfire was drawing more of them. More than I'd ever seen in one place before. The reality of it sapped my will, my ability to think straight, to even hope we had a chance.

Janine grabbed my arm and Hank pushed me forward. We tumbled along a two-lane street and into the woods, with a line of zombies trailing behind, tracking us in their animal way. Hank took us in among the trees, hoping for cover. We found an iron fence and followed it, until we discovered a missing section and stepped through to the other side. Hank used several fallen branches to block the gap in the fence, and we kept moving.

Just behind us, the zombies hit the fence, lashed at it, lacking the simple logic to aim for the open section. But there were so many. *So many.* Several of them found the gap by sheer accident, falling over the branches and through. Others followed, and they continued to chase us, as Hank dragged us farther and farther into the deep woods.

Then, all at once, decaying houses stood before us, first single-family homes, then rowhouses, the reverse of what we'd encountered on the other side. We were through the divide. Janine pulled out her map, tried to study it as we pushed west on crumbling streets, a pack of zombies still tracking us. My focus returned, or at least a sense of self-preservation, and I forced myself to press on. But I was tired, and sore. And old. I felt so very old. Hank guided us in arbitrary circles, looping around houses, trying to lose any of the zombies still hunting us.

"Rest," I gasped, falling backward into the brick wall of one of the houses. Hank nodded, held a finger to his lips. *Shhh.* He peered around the side of the wall.

After a time, I caught my breath, although breathing remained difficult. I suspected a broken rib or two. Maybe cracked my hip up, too. Janine was absorbed in the map, looking for nearby street signs. When Hank finally gestured that all was clear, we gathered around Janine.

"We're *here*," she said, tapping on the west side of the green swath labeled Rock Creek Park. Then she dragged her finger up and to the left, to a grey blob beside one of the larger roads. "And this is where we need to go."

"Then let's go," I said, trying to use a businesslike demeanor to hide the pain I was in. Hank just nodded, and we set off.

Quietly, cautiously, we made our way north and west. At last, we stepped onto a wide, six-lane boulevard marked as Wisconsin Avenue. Janine pointed north. "NIH is just up the road here," she said.

* * *

It took hours of laborious, deliberate walking for me to make the journey. Hank and Janine were equal parts patient and restless, wanting to push ahead faster, but knowing I couldn't.

At last, we found what we were looking for. A large metal wall blocked the road, encircling a wide campus of buildings on our left and right. From Janine's map, we knew that the National Institutes of Health were here, just ahead of where we were standing. A solid, closed gate barred the way.

Hank approached the gate. Remembering other encounters at other walls, I was certain that at any moment he would be gunned down. But nothing happened.

Hank disappeared, following the wall around a bend and out of view, trying to find a way in. A few minutes later, the gate in front of us slid open, and we saw Hank looking out at us from inside. Gesturing for us to follow, he strolled into the compound. I closed the gate behind us as we continued north.

After a time, we spotted a series of large, uniform signs telling us we were in the right place, and we approached a glass and brick building. With a sinking feeling, I saw that several windows had been broken in. We climbed in one and made our way down a darkened hallway.

Then Janine stopped. "Do you hear that?" she asked.

We paused, listened. There was a very low hum coming from somewhere up ahead. We crept forward, tracking the sound, trying to bring it closer. Slowly, slowly, it got louder.

As we turned a corner, we heard something else: voices. A hurried conversation. My heart raced. We were here. *They* were here. Could it be? Just ahead, the hallway ended in a set of closed double doors, and from between them, a tiny sliver of light escaped. In an instant, that light vanished, accompanied by scraping noises and a loud click. In the sudden darkness, I noticed a red light high on the wall, and guessed it was a surveillance camera. They'd seen us coming, at least once we entered the hallway. Behind the doors, it sounded like someone was making a shushing sound, telling someone else to be quiet.

We approached the door, and Hank tried to push it open. On the other side, a chain rattled. Locked, maybe reinforced. We heard a low gasp, another *shush*. Janine raised an eyebrow.

So I spoke.

"Hello." There was no response.

"Hello? We… we come in peace." I sighed. What a stupid thing to say, like I was an emissary visiting another planet. Whoever was on the other side of the wall remained quiet. Hank and Janine also tried to get them to speak — "Anyone there?" "We don't mean you any harm" — then relented. Still no response.

I took a deep breath. Then my mouth opened and words came out on their own, without thought. "I know you don't know me, don't know any of us," I said. "And I know you have a good reason not to trust us. But I'm *tired*, I'm *really tired*, and we need your help. So, since I know you're in there, I'm just going to sit down here and tell you my story. The whole thing. Then you can decide what to do."

I plopped down on the floor and rested my back against the locked doors. And for the better part of an hour, I just talked.

* * *

After I was done, we sat there in silence, the three of us, matching the silence we heard on the other side of the doors.

A moment passed and nothing. Then, quietly, a man spoke. "You carry the cure in your blood?" he asked, skepticism mixed with a barely detectable note of greed in his voice.

"Yes," I said, smiling at the sound of this new voice. Janine and Hank were wide-eyed with surprise. I guess none of us actually expected a response of any kind.

There was another long pause. Some muffled words, a debate we couldn't hear.

"You're going to have to prove that," the man finally said.

I sighed. "And just how do you propose I do that?"

The doors moved, just a little, and I jumped up, allowing them to swing free. But they didn't open very far. The doors separated just enough to reveal a man, scraggly grey hair and beard, like a mirror of myself, but wearing glasses and a blue lab coat. With the chains still locking the doors together, preventing them from opening any farther, he held something out to me, through the gap.

A hypodermic syringe.

Beside him, others stood. Four men and a woman. Also in lab coats. The woman looked at me with a deep sort of anger, one I didn't understand. Then one of the men pointed a gun at me, and Hank jumped up. As he reached for his own weapon, the man spoke.

"Stop! Stop now, or this is done. We can close the doors, and you'll never get what you came for." Hank froze.

I stepped up to the doors, just inches from the man on the other side. "Let me guess," I said, starting to roll up one sleeve. "Blood sample?"

He nodded.

In just a couple of minutes, it was done. He left me with a swab of cotton to hold on the tiny puncture wound.

The man looked the three of us over as he stood there, needle pointing toward the ceiling, syringe filled with my dark blood. "Might as well get comfortable. This is going to take a while."

Then the doors shut with a loud click, and he was gone.

21

The light behind the doors came back on, as did the low hum of some sort of machinery. Hours went by. Hank and Janine both seemed nervous, wired. They paced, checked and rechecked their weapons. I slept.

In the still darkness, an untold time later, the doors opened, chains falling away with a clattering sound. I jolted awake and stood, waiting to see what would happen.

And she stepped out.

For a moment, just a moment in my spinning mind, I thought it was Rosa. I swiped at my eyes, rubbing away sleep, then a tear or two. But no, it wasn't her.

The woman, the one in the lab coat who'd first looked at me with such reproach, walked out between the open doors. She stepped in front of me, and without a word did something no one expected.

She hugged me.

* * *

She'd known Rosa. She'd actually known Rosa. They worked together at NIH headquarters before Rosa pushed for her transfer to Capitol Hill.

The woman's name was Phebe Silvos. She'd worked with Rosa for three years in the very same building where we were standing, and she knew Rosa was a good and honest person. She'd heard about Rosa and me on the hill overlooking DC, about Rosa's message and her death, and simply didn't believe any of it. Someone was making up stories of a cure that didn't exist, abusing the name of Rosa, her friend who was missing and who, she'd assumed, had been dead for many months before this all happened.

And now here I was, the other half of that tale, showing up just outside her door. In a rush, Phebe told me how they took my blood and ran tests on it. She said something about analyzing its reaction with preserved zombie blood, and rattled off a bunch of terms and processes that spun even my head. Her laboratory and my experience as a general practitioner were many miles apart.

Phebe let go of me and sobbed, turning back to her colleagues. "You know we need to go," was all she said to them.

One of the men, the one who'd held the pistol on me, and still held it by his side, pointed downward, replied. "No," he said. "No, we don't. They'd *kill* us, if they knew we even thought about it." For a moment, the other men wavered, but not Phebe.

"I don't care," she said. "I'm going."

"I don't understand." I couldn't think of anything else to say.

"The *director*," Phebe said. "He wants a cure, but for himself, for his people, not for everyone else. He won't say so, but we know it. Ever since the story about Rosa, and the revolution, things have been bad. Very, *very* bad. The director pushes us. He says if Rosa could figure it out, why can't we? He left us here, but his people always come back. They'll be back to check on us. *And soon.*" She looked down at her watch, then at us with eyes of desperation.

"Who's the director?" I asked.

"Director McDaniels, the head of NIH. He's really an Army guy, a colonel or something. Not a scientist at all. The military swept in and kicked out all the old guard a long time ago. Right after the outbreak." Phebe shook her head. "He's not a nice guy. We don't want to be here when his people come back."

Janine chimed in. "But we didn't come here just for *you*. What about your machines and your lab?"

"That can't be helped now," Phebe said. "There are other labs. But this one isn't safe." She looked like a fox in a leg trap, wild with the need to get away. "Look, I know my stuff. It'll be hard, especially getting another lab setup, but I can do it. Wait — you have power, right?" I nodded, and she let out a huge sigh of relief. "Then take me with you. Let me try."

The man who had taken my blood suddenly spoke up. "I'll go, too," he said. The other men in lab coats looked shocked.

"But —" one of them cried.

"The director —" another added.

"The director is an evil man, and I've had enough of him," the man said, taking off his glasses and wiping them on the hem of his lab coat. He turned his attention back to us. He'd heard my story, and must have believed it. "This Oasis of yours in Maryland. Annapolis? How long will it take us to get there?"

Hank interrupted. "Hold on. Our people back in DC. We need to get them first."

I shot him a look. *Not now.* "What's your name?" I asked the man with the glasses.

"Joseph," he replied.

"Come on, then, Joseph," I said. "Let's go." Turning to the other men, I asked, "Are any of you coming with us?" They stood frozen as if in ice.

In the end, Joseph and Phebe were joined by two of the other men, Sanjit and Kenshin. The four of them gathered only the supplies they could carry, a few personal items, a few things from the lab. Two other men stayed behind. Phebe teared up as we started to leave. "Will you be safe?" she said them. "What'll you tell McDaniels?" They didn't reply, but just watched us leave.

* * *

There was no way we could make the reverse journey across the divide right away. It was after nightfall as we left the lab building, and

I wasn't the only one unwilling to make the attempt in the dark. The first order of business was to get clear, somewhere we wouldn't be found by either McDaniels' men or whatever random zombies were about. NIH's walls encircled a lot of land, a lot of other buildings. Joseph suggested an abandoned maintenance building on the southeast corner of the campus, and we hastened to get there.

Overnight, as we slept propped against the walls of a grimy room in a grimy building, I heard tiny sobs from the two newcomers. I had no idea what they were leaving behind; they had no idea what was lying ahead.

* * *

In the morning, Hank and Janine faced an unenviable task: get a group of seven people, four of whom had no experience outside the walls, across the divide. Hank shook with nervous energy. Janine looked determined, but her occasional sideways glances at Hank told me she was concerned.

For me, I had a feeling, deep in my gut, that this was the end of the journey. Between the lingering pain of my many injuries, my age, the losses I'd suffered — I just didn't think I could take much more. I was hopeful that I'd found the people we needed. Somehow, the rest would have to take care of itself. Like a wave crashing ashore, I felt I'd gone as far as I could, and now it was time to retreat back to the sea.

Phebe didn't know me, but she was perceptive. She studied me with a strange, careful eye. "Are you all right?" she asked as we prepared to leave.

"Yeah, yeah," I said, waving away her concern. But I wasn't all right. My arm, shoulder, and chest throbbed with old wounds. But more than that, my heart was heavy. "Hank," I said, getting his attention. "When we get back to HQ, the hospital, I want to leave for Annapolis as soon as possible. The same day, if we can. It's time to leave the city behind once and for all." I could tell Hank wasn't sure where this request was coming from. "And besides," I added, lowering my chin, "I have a debt to pay." Visions of Oliver, backing away from the open doorway, filled my mind. *What did Oliver tell them? Celia must think I'm dead. If she's not dead herself.*

I knew there was very little holding Hank in DC. It wasn't his city, not originally. And he wanted something better, for his people, for himself. For Janine.

Hank had heard my entire story. Everyone in our small group had. I didn't bother leaving out Oliver's treachery when I told my tale to the scientists. Now, after a few moments of reflection, Hank seemed to understand that it was about more than the cure. He clapped a hand on my shoulder. "If Oliver hadn't done what he did, I'd probably never have seen you again, or had this chance to help find a cure. So in a weird way, I should thank him." I shuddered at the thought. Hank went on. "But that doesn't excuse him. What he did was unforgiveable. I want to help you repay that debt, any way I can."

So we set off.

* * *

One thing was sure, I was careful. I'd be damned if I was going to fall into that water again.

The four scientists did their best to follow Hank and Janine's lead. In fact, they even helped me, providing a steady hand here and there as we crossed the river. While we saw zombies, they were farther off, and didn't chase us. And Phebe and her colleagues were so new to the outside world that we didn't need to remind them to keep a healthy dose of fear in their hearts. With them, fear might have been all they had.

By the end of the day, we were back inside the more familiar part of the walled city. As we approached the hospital, it felt almost like a letdown. We had escaped the domain of Director McDaniels, crossed the divide, and found our way back to safe haven. And not much happened. I almost wished something had. I felt like there were very bad things waiting out there for Phebe and the others, and I wanted them to be ready. But I kept quiet. A day of peace was worth savoring.

We didn't get within 200 yards of the building before the feeling of calm satisfaction was whisked away.

"Janine, Hank, it's urgent!" It was James, in his faded fatigues, running up to us. They didn't say a word in response. They just ran.

* * *

We'd only left the morning before, but something had gone terribly wrong while we were gone. At some point, a kid — a boy of maybe 10, no parents, taken in by the group — had been bitten, infected, while he was outside the hospital. For whatever reason, he played it off. Maybe foolishness, maybe ignorance, maybe desperation. But he kept it quiet. He hid it. And then, he turned.

He slept in a room with other kids, all orphans of the disease. And during the night we were away, he bit three of them before he could be restrained. The entire group was in a panic, tempers flaring all around.

It wasn't until I walked in trailed by the four scientists in their lab coats that the arguments fell quiet. A woman who spent most of her time caring for the orphans grabbed at my shirt as I brushed past her. "*Do you have it?*" she pleaded. I stammered, noncommittal, and she turned to Phebe, pawing her like a desperate animal. "*Do you?*"

Phebe looked at her, equal parts revulsion and pity, trying to pull away. "It doesn't work that way," she said. "I — *We* have a lot of work to do. It's going to take a lot of time. I'm sorry."

"We don't have a lot of time!" the woman said. They're just kids!" She wailed, but two other women came up and hugged her, consoled her. Reluctantly, she let herself be led away.

We put down the first kid that same day. Within four days' time, we had to put down the other three infected kids, too. After that, it was hard to find anyone who wanted to stay in DC. By the seventh morning, our entire group was standing at the front doors of the old hospital, ready to leave.

22

We gathered in the street before daybreak, hundreds of people. Less than a dozen wanted to stay behind. Then, as they saw the others pack up to leave, they broke down and joined us. No one wanted to be left alone. Or miss out on the cure.

Hank had sent scouts to every other huddled group of people living nearby. No one else chose to join us, even after hearing our story. I can't say I was surprised. Would I believe it if I hadn't lived it?

The light of day was just starting to creep into the eastern sky, a peach-tinted glow. There had been some rain during the night, but it had moved on to the north, and the day was dawning a little warmer than those before it. A thin bank of fog clung to the ground in all directions, not enough to blind us, but lending a mysterious air to the day. Like it was all a dream. Except for the sounds of straps being cinched or the occasional cough, it was quiet. The group was too nervous for idle chatter.

Phebe, Joseph, Sanjit, and Kenshin — who went by Ken — were pressed into the middle of the pack. I didn't come out and say it, but I tried to make sure they had a place of relative safety, deep in the center. We had fought so hard, done so much to find them, we needed them safe.

Hank and Janine filtered through the crowd, ensuring that everyone was set, all the supplies were packed and ready, all the children were supervised, weapons were loaded.

We hadn't even set off before we saw them, the goddamned infected.

At first, they looked more like aimless feral animals, frittering around in the distance, scavenging for any small morsel. I don't think any of them actually saw us. Maybe they heard something. Maybe *felt* something. They were so far away that we couldn't hear a sound. They were just ghostly apparitions, dimly moving in the fog.

A general sense of unease went through the large group. Hank had a decision to make: move or stay. More than one person was eyeing the hospital, considering a quick return to home and safety.

Hank spoke in a loud whisper. "Not everyone can hear me, and we need to be quiet. Once I'm done talking, pass this along to the people behind you, but keep your voices low." He looked around to be sure he had everyone's attention, at least those close enough to hear. Then he started up again with a new vibrancy. "*We are leaving.* We have food and water. We have guns and other weapons, and we have plenty of strong hands to protect us as we walk. We have a plan. This journey is *never* going to be easy. And there's never going to be a day without those... *things* —" Hank waved a hand toward the zombies in the distance. "— unless we *make* that day. So we're leaving, now. To get to The Oasis and try to remake the future!"

It was a lot of bravado, but it did the trick. Slowly, people nodded and turned their backs on the hospital. To Janine, Hank said, "Are we all set on the plan?" She nodded, but he continued, for himself as much as for anyone else, it seemed. "You and the A group up front, in the lead. The rest of the scout groups, B through G, on the flanks, and me with Z group in the back." Each group consisted of four scouts   those people who were most familiar with staying safe in unsafe places. The people used to handling weapons. Janine plus four in the front, three groups of four on each side, and Hank plus four in the back. Thirty-four people guarding more than 300, on a journey that would take us until well past nightfall, if we were lucky enough to make it in one day.

"I remember," Janine said. "We're all set."

"All right. Good luck." And Hank turned and started off toward the back of the group.

Janine grabbed his hand and spun him back around, pulling him close and planting a passionate kiss on his lips. It was the only time I ever saw them publicly display affection. The first... and last.

* * *

Three-hundred souls, plus or minus, with dozens of zombies following behind. We made a macabre parade. Humans huddled together, shuffling feet, pulling carts, a loose circle of defenders around us. And slowly, with an eerie steadiness, zombies trailed after us, drawn by the muted sounds of our passing.

It was like they felt the end was coming, too. Like maybe their options were running low, and they had to do something to try to survive. Without a collective intelligence, it was just animal instinct. But still, they followed. Maybe we could have just waited them out, let them die. But we had a lot to lose, too. If they got to us, it wouldn't matter if they were healthy or in their death throes. We would die, and our last chance would die with us. We worked to stay as far ahead of them as we could.

Janine set the pace as fast as the group could manage, and guided us around any obvious areas of trouble. Hank kept close watch on the rear. On occasion, a zombie would pop up suddenly, near one side or the other, and be put down quickly and quietly by a heavy blow from one of the flanking scouts, usually wielding the hammer weapon I'd first seen Hank use. Some of our people uttered little gasps at these attacks, a few of which were dangerously close to our scientists. *Our scientists.* I realized I'd begun to think of them that way, and of the entire group as *our people.* Maybe even *my people.* I wasn't sure what to make of the idea.

Slowly walking east and out of the city, our huddled mass was shadowed by dozens of zombies. Two oddly symmetrical groups. Us, slogging along, looking for safety, and the infected, nearly blind but following their instincts.

I stayed near the rearguard, close to Hank. Janine was far enough ahead that we couldn't see her except for the rare moments when she was positioned uphill from us. Then she'd crest the hill and disappear again. If I happened to catch Hank's eye, he seemed concerned, watchful of Janine, like he knew something bad was about to happen.

It was only about an hour until we reached the eastern wall. The barricade that for so long had kept the city safe now threatened to become a bottleneck. With a horde of zombies so close behind, we couldn't afford to slow down, but there was no clear way through.

Luckily, Hank had planned for this, too.

Janine's A group trotted ahead as soon as the wall was in sight. In a short while, they gave the *all clear* sign. A few minutes after that, they gave a new sign: *This way.* In a dark space under a bridge, part of the wall had fallen away, and that was where we made our escape from the city. Scout groups B and E went through the gap in the wall first, taking up positions to guard people as they came through. They were followed by Janine's team, who again moved to the front, waiting for the rest of the group.

Slowly, the masses narrowed themselves to nearly single-file and pushed through the opening. In the back, our progress dropped to almost zero, and the throng of zombies that had been shadowing us came closer. A sort of electricity began to build in the air. It was clear something was going to happen, and I could see Hank readying himself, so he could handle it with a clear head.

He ordered two of the flanking groups, D and G, to attach themselves to the rearguard, where they formed a curved line, protecting the group. I saw the scientists from NIH pressing forward, trying to gain the gap and get out. Phebe paused, just for a second, and nodded to me as she ducked through the wall. I stayed back, knowing I couldn't really help Hank, but not wanting to abandon him either.

Trying to spare the group, particularly the slower families and children toward the back, Hank took the fight to the zombies. He waved his hands, urging the scouts forward, and they advanced.

Plowing into the masses of zombies, the scouts used blunt objects and long knives to kill them one after another. Initially, it seemed like easy work. But after a time, the frenzy began. Every new zombie that entered the fray was furious and slathering, a mini whirlwind of chaos. Hank's team was smart and effective, but not superhuman. Little by little, they were driven back, toward me, toward the group.

By then, the middle section of the group had passed through the gap and was gone. But more than a hundred people still remained inside the walls, pushing to get free.

From the side streets, new signs of motion. More zombies, coming to investigate the sounds of violence, bolstering the attacking group. Hank was sweating profusely, and his team was wide-eyed and heaving. The smell of dead zombies overwhelmed every breath, like animal carcasses in a slaughterhouse, reeking and spouting gore. Some of the scouts flinched at the blood; they must have figured it was a sure path to infection. Suddenly Hank took a step toward an attacking zombie, slipped in a puddle of slick blood, and fell to the broken pavement. With an oomph, the air rushed out of his lungs, and the zombie prepared to leap at him.

Without conscious thought, I fired.

I hadn't even realized my pistol was in my hand, yet the zombie fell dead. Hank jumped up, avoiding the spray of blood, gave me a dire look, a nod of thanks.

Then he was springing toward me, pulling out his hammer-like tool. At the last moment, he slid to my left, swung his arm in a harsh downward blow. I just had time to flinch and look sideways as his weapon brained an infected dog that was inches from tearing into my leg.

Then Hank was gone, back into the battle.

God, a *dog*. And a brown one, at that. I blinked, and behind my eyes saw fresh red blood splattered on dry yellow corn, Celia on the ground, blood flowing. Addy dead, but not before she'd been lost to the fury of the disease. My heart sank as I opened my eyes again, not sure which was worse: my memories or my reality. Among the approaching mass of human zombies were other forms: dogs. Many more infected dogs. I don't know why, but all of my conviction drained out of me.

It was lost. Hopeless. An impossible task.

Everything was *lost*.

We were the final hope for a cure, and now we'd come to our end.

There was no way these few scouts could prevail. It was only a matter of time, as the last third of our group pushed frantically toward the gap, trying to get through.

People were shrieking, trying to stop the others behind them from pressing too hard, smothering them. I backed up toward the last of the group as Hank's scouts pulled inward. They formed a tight semicircle, firing weapons, slashing with blunt tools.

Just yards away, a growing wall of zombies surged closer. For another moment, they walked in their slow, frittering way, seeking a distinct target. Former humans, former dogs, and now even infected rats and raccoons moved together in an angry, buzzing cloud, nipping at any close target. They tore at each other even as they looked for us. Their bites didn't seem to mean anything to each other, because their leprosy had robbed them of feeling. Instead, they gave the horde a jarring gait. As a group, they had an odd slowness to their approach, like they were building up to something.

Then, finally, they were close enough to truly see us. In an instant, slow pursuit became manic attack. They jumped.

And we knew we couldn't withstand the assault. We were dead.

Suddenly a sound like 50 cannons exploded in my ears, and the zombies fell, many of them at once. Infected humans, spraying gore. Infected dogs, tumbling onto the pavement, their death throes awful to behold. Infected rats and raccoons, practically vaporized out of existence.

I looked around at Hank and his team, saw they were dumbfounded.

Then, as the zombies fell away, we saw them.

People. Regular living humans, like us, joining the fight from our right flank, wiping out the phalanx of zombies.

Through the zombie horde, we could see them, but barely. Men with guns, arranged like a military assault, but wearing the makeshift, patched clothing that told us they were like us: just another pocket of refugees in the city.

"It's Duke's men!" The call came from somewhere to my right, a voice I didn't recognize. People were helping us? Joining us? Maybe they believed our story after all.

I looked again at Hank, slack-jawed, dead-eyed, splatters of blood and dirt on his face and clothes. He looked so much like a zombie himself, filthy and staring. It gave me pause. *Wait. How will they tell us from the zombies?*

I screamed at the people nearest me. "Wave your hands! Up high!" I raised my hands above my head, shook them wildly. People looked at me, confused. But soon, Hank understood and followed suit, and so did the others. We yelled, we waved. And the approaching onslaught dimmed but didn't disappear. Our saviors began to understand who we were — and what we weren't — and they were adjusting their aim.

But it wasn't fast enough.

Something flashed past me to the left, and I whipped my head to follow it, only to see one of the flanking scouts fall dead to the ground. A young man in his twenties. A stray bullet took away everything he'd ever be, or say, or do. I waved my hands, ever more hysterically, yelling, "Stop! We're human! We're *not infected*!"

Just to my right, I heard a wet sound and something like popping bubbles. With knowing dread, I turned to look, saw Hank as he drew a hand up to his neck, then pulled it away. It was covered in blood, which very quickly soaked his clothing, turning everything a dark purplish red.

Hank fell at my feet, the right side of his neck torn out by a passing bullet, his eyes staring up at me in shock and terror. I dropped to my knees, grabbed him, pressed a hand to the wound, trying to stop the flow of blood. I looked into his eyes. This friend who had saved me on more than one occasion. "No," was all I could say. "No." There wasn't enough tissue left for me to work with. There was nothing I could do.

He tried to talk, but no words came, only more bubbling, more gurgling. Horrible sounds. Sounds that, as a doctor, I knew were beyond repair.

Around us, I had the sense that others had approached, made a circle. Many of them held their breath. With only a quick, desperate glance, I saw new faces. The men who had come to our rescue. And who now stood around me in shock at what they had done. Some bowed their heads. Others closed their eyes. Everyone seemed to know they were watching something awful. In just a few minutes, with too much of his blood seeping into the ground, Hank faded from consciousness.

Oh God, I thought. *No.* I knew it was too late. In only a few minutes more, Hank would be gone. *Thank you for all you've done, my friend. I'm sorry it's your time.* I held his hand as it spasmed uncontrollably.

With a wet rasping sound, Hank took his final breath. And I noticed a pair of feet skid to a stop in front of me.

How? Why? Those were my only thoughts at first. *Why are you here? You don't need to see this. How could you have known to come?*

Janine fell with a wail that tore my heart. She grasped at Hank, tearing him from my grip, causing the last of his blood to spill from his neck. His heart had nothing left to give. She held him, rocking like a mother with child, as Hank left this Earth.

23

With the bulk of the zombie horde destroyed, we pushed the rest of our group through the gap. We'd made it outside DC. To me, this was a welcome liberation, a third time leaving a place that I never wanted to see again. But for almost everyone else in our group, I knew this was a fearful trek into the unknown.

Almost unbelievably, Hank and the young scout — I didn't even know his name — were the only two casualties.

Hank. Damn it. I repeated those last few moments, wondering if there was something I could have done.

Janine walked like a ghost. I'd been next to her as she watched Hank die. Yet that paled in comparison to watching her walk away from his body as we prepared for our final exodus. She left him lying in the middle of the road, hands folded across his chest. A peaceful repose to last eternity. Once Janine turned her head to walk east again, she didn't look back. Her eyes were empty. Her feet moved her along, and she became a painful echo of me in the days and weeks after Rosa died. Janine walked the same way I had, not all that long ago. I knew her soul, knew that she herself didn't understand how she kept going, knew that her mind couldn't even consider the question, knew that she would walk all day and feel no bodily pain. Knew that nothing would cut through the anguish that filled her heart.

The group moved on, with Janine simply occupying a random place in the middle, the people on either side of her guiding her gently along. In her state, there was no point even asking if she'd rejoin the vanguard. The new people, those who'd saved us and accidentally killed Hank, bolstered our surrounding guards, many of them walking with a visibly heavy feeling of guilt. There were about 40 of them, all men, pretty heavily armed, with lot of pistols and ammo. I met their leader, the one named Duke, graying, bearded. He took over the rearguard. But there was a need in the group for some sort of guide to take Janine's place.

That fell to me.

Although the route was simple — back along Route 50 east, straight toward Annapolis — we had to navigate the abandoned cars and dead bodies and cracked pavement that had made long-distance travel since the outbreak so risky. With the others' help, I did my best to steer around anything that looked dangerous and continue forward. But I kept scanning behind, as far back behind our group as I could see, any chance I got.

Most of the zombies following us had been killed in the fray, but not all.

In time, their numbers grew again.

24

With the new people, we were nearly 400 strong. They added significantly to our protective outer ring, but we kept drawing unwanted attention. We were too big of a group to go unnoticed.

I looked back each time I heard some little shout of surprise or the sounds of a scuffle. From time to time, zombies came at us from the sides as we passed. But mostly they just fell in with the ever-growing collection of infected humans, rats, raccoons, and dogs that trailed behind us. They were a good distance off now, but our path was simple to follow — the wide highway. Empty and wrecked vehicles helped shield us from their poor vision, but also slowed our progress. Our inadvertent noise, and maybe just our heat, drew the zombies along. They *sensed* us.

Hours wore on, and miles dropped behind us. I estimated we'd left at around five in the morning. With our size and slow, plodding gait, I thought we'd be lucky to get to The Oasis much before midnight.

In the afternoon, as we walked, I started to think about our biggest problem. *How were we going to get rid of the zombies before we reached Annapolis?* We couldn't just bring them back with us.

I knew our scouts each had at least one pistol and as much ammo as they could carry. They also had their blunt instruments, hammers, axes. One scout, Terrence, from Z group, mentioned to me he had two flare guns and several flares. I considered what to do with that information, but didn't have any great ideas.

I left a scout to lead the way briefly as I faded to the back and talked to Duke. He spoke in a gruff voice, a low bass with a thick, gravelly rasp. From the way his men looked at him, it was clear he led them as more of a father figure than a military general. I immediately liked that about him. He told me that his men had been keeping tabs on our group at the hospital for months. When our scouts had asked them to join us, they were understandably skeptical. But then, when he got the report that we were all headed east, he knew we were leaving, probably for good. He knew about the radio broadcasts, the stories and rumors of a new Oasis. He figured there must be some truth to it if we all were going, and brought his small army to see what was happening. That's when they'd found us and joined the fight.

Duke was a good leader, better by far than me. He'd even had the sense to run two pairs of scouts up ahead on the highway, to look out for approaching trouble or at least identify the best path forward. The scouts alternated coming back at regular intervals to report whatever information they had.

"Duke," I said in a tired voice "We've got to get rid of those things." I nodded behind us at the zombies. "Sooner rather than later."

Duke considered this. He pulled out a package of cigarettes. Tobacco and paper with a synthetic filter, old-school Camels, from before the infection. I couldn't imagine how stale they must have been, but if that was his pleasure, so be it. Now I knew where his rasp came from. He lit a cigarette with a match from a small pack. In that moment, two things occurred to me. First, how smoking had been so common in the old days, even though it was clearly bad for you. Obviously, that was from my past life as a doctor, intruding on my present. Then, from a more current perspective, I thought of how much of an extravagance this was, wasting matches for one man's personal pleasure. I shook off both thoughts as irrelevant to our current situation.

Duke exhaled a plume of blue-gray smoke. "Light. Noise," he said. "That's pretty much it."

"That's pretty much what?" I asked.

"Pretty much all they respond to," he said, puffing little clouds into the crisp spring air.

Of course, I thought. *I knew that.*

I stepped away from him, considering our options. As we gained the top of a small hill, I looked back, seeing ever more zombies staggering after our tired group. We walked on, lost in thought.

Celia, you're like a daughter to me. I love you, and good luck, I thought. I hope you can see through Oliver, at least better than I did.

Celia. And even Janine. They were my hope. A tired smile spread across my face as I walked east, focusing on one idea.

Not much farther.

25

The group was beyond exhausted, our pace slowing miserably. Behind a white wall of clouds, the sun went down, and night came. Thankfully, the moon was nearly full, and cast a bright but muted glow behind the clouds. It was the only light as we walked on and on. Nondescript places passed and faded behind us. I knew we were close to Annapolis.

I was tired. So tired. My many aches, which had started as dull throbs during the day, had grown into deep, unyielding pains. My arm. Shoulder. Leg. Chest. The pieced-together shell of my mortal coil throbbed. I was simply spent. And worse than the physical toll of the journey, Janine's plight brought to mind Rosa, Harvey and The Oasis, even Addy. The dog who hadn't deserved her fate. Still, I was the leader, or one of them. I had to keep going. I twirled the tattered bracelet I wore, barely held together by threads, my only physical connection to Rosa.

The gap between our group and the horde behind us was becoming dangerously narrow. If we couldn't gain some ground, by increasing our speed or delaying the zombies, we'd soon be in the middle of another deadly battle. Duke instinctively saw this and sent some of his men toward the back. He thought a fight was inevitable. I didn't quite agree.

I knew there was another option.

I conferred with Duke, explained my plan, and he nodded, grimly. He sent word through his men, making preparations. They hardly knew me, they had no reason to argue.

But Janine.

I thought she was too far gone to pay attention to what was happening. I thought word could be sent around without breaking her frozen facade. I was wrong.

She snapped to life, like an alarm clock had brought her sleeping body back to consciousness. She rushed right over to me. "What're you doing?" she asked, wild with sudden energy. I looked at her eyes and saw they were bloodshot and raw. She was frayed, like cloth where the seams were pulling apart with age. Or wear.

"I'll do it," she said, and we both stopped walking, even knowing how precious each footstep was, keeping us ahead of the horde. Others slowed around us.

"No, Janine."

"Yes. I have to."

"No," I said again. But what argument did I have? If I invoked Hank's memory, she'd never relent. And while she'd known, Rosa, the pain that was currently overwhelming her wouldn't allow that sort of connection to the past.

In the end, I didn't say anything. Our eyes locked, hands intertwined, and we looked at each other, two souls 40 years different in age. But inside our gaze, there was *understanding*. I believe she knew then that we'd experienced the same thing, and that I had to do this one thing or I'd never find peace. As her tears began to flow, she nodded. But she couldn't let go of my hands, and instead she pulled me toward her, hugging me. Her body shook as she sobbed, and I tried to console her, but a clarity came over me at the same time, and I gently nudged her to start walking again.

* * *

In the full of dark, a pair of Duke's scouts returned again. *We've got to be close*, I thought. Duke talked with the men, then walked over to me as they ran off again. "We've got a bit of a problem," he said.

Just ahead of us was the Severn River bridge. The small arch that had goaded us to turn south and find this new Oasis in the first place. We'd come so far. From the bridge, we'd soon be able to see the three radio towers of our waiting home.

But...

The scouts, mostly looking for zombies to kill or avoid, hadn't expected to find *humans*. In fact, they'd run smack into another group of scouts, moving in the opposite direction, toward us. Scouts from The Oasis. After a moment of contact, they scrambled back to us as the other scouts retreated the way they'd come.

A short time later, a second pair of Duke's scouts made their return trip. They told us about a blockade being erected on the bridge. *Damn it*, I thought. *It has to be Oliver.*

An internal rage flared. I hoped beyond hope that Celia hadn't been swayed by Oliver. There had been two factions at The Oasis when I left, north and south. I wondered which one was in power now.

Before we'd set out from DC, I'd seen someone shoving a bullhorn into a backpack. I asked around, found out where it was, and sent for it. Once I had that in my hand, I pressed hard, urging everyone through the final distance to the bridge.

* * *

"*Oliver!*" I shouted through the bullhorn. "Let us pass!"

I hadn't known for sure that the blockade was Oliver's doing, or even if he'd made it back to The Oasis. But my fears were confirmed when a squat shadow stood up, balancing on the uneven crest of the barricade. Surprisingly, the coward had come himself, and he shouted a reply. "No! We don't have the resources to support you. You've got to find some other place. My men are prepared to shoot if they need to." In the dull moonlight, I couldn't see anything except dark shapes moving on the bridge.

We didn't have time for this game. The zombies behind us would be upon us soon.

"We have the right people now — scientists who can take my blood and make a cure for everyone," I said. "You've got to let us through." I took a long pause, drawing breath. "There are zombies right behind us. If you don't let us in, they won't only be the end of us. They'll be the end of you and everyone at The Oasis." I could hear muted words of concern passing among the men on the bridge with Oliver. I'm sure I knew most of them. Oliver was a cancer, and they had been infected by him. But that didn't make them bad themselves. "Will you really stand by and watch your only hope for a cure destroyed in front of your very eyes?" More murmurs, louder.

I looked back, over the heads of our group. A dark, indistinct mass was heading toward us.

The infected were too close now. I had to decide.

There was no answer from Oliver. I dropped back, grabbed a bag of supplies that Duke had gathered for me. It was very light. Would it be enough? Janine came over, asking again, with her eyes. I shook my head, and she began to cry. She gave me another long hug that threatened to crush my resolve. Just when I thought I'd drop my head to her shoulder and weep, she pulled away, and in a moment I was sure of myself again. I had to go. We exchanged nods, and I stepped away.

I jogged to the back of the group, where the scouts were directing people toward the others up front. Now that we couldn't go any farther, we were bunching up on the western side of the bridge. I reached into my bag, pulled out the orange plastic form of a flare gun, and popped in a flare. The zombies were close enough that I could hear their ragged march, see individual shapes emerging from the night.

I called out to the group. "Everyone stay down and stay quiet!" My shouting drew the keen attention of the zombies. Their pace quickened. It was time.

I swiveled to my right, aimed the flare gun at a bank of trees just beside the highway, and fired.

The flare blazed hot, a tiny sun of bright red, illuminating the night. Just before it hit the trees, I heard a commotion from the bridge. I almost turned to see what was happening, but then the world exploded as the flare hit a tree and bounced down into the overgrowth. It hissed and burned in the long grass, and the nearest zombies devolved into frenzy, rushing toward it. The flare didn't last long, but it was enough to ignite some of the grass. Zombies dove toward the heat and light, at first frantic to reach the source, then, when they started to burn, frantic to get away. But the other zombies piling up behind them made their escape impossible.

We watched as a pocket of zombies — human, dog, rat, raccoon — collapsed into the fire and were consumed, flailing in terror and pain.

But it wasn't enough.

The zombies that were too far away to be compelled into the blaze continued to walk toward us.

All of my options had been exhausted. With a heavy sigh, I lifted the bag, ran toward the fire.

Behind me, I heard Janine gasp.

Nearing the blaze, I ran through a break in the tall barrier wall that skirted the highway, and dove into the woods. A few zombies followed, but not the bulk of the group.

I pulled out the bullhorn. "Hey! Hey! Here!" I screamed. "*Come to me! Come on, you bastards!*" I made senseless sounds, just to keep up the noise, just to get their attention.

Slowly, the mob turned.

As I backed into the trees, away from every living human I knew, I fired a second flare, off to my right. Another bouncing, blazing comet in the dark night. The two fiery red beacons, along with my wordless ranting on the bullhorn, continued to turn the zombies toward me. The ones in front were chasing me directly. Those behind simply mimicked the ones they followed.

For a moment, I stared.

One man. A dark copse of trees and who knew what beyond. A hundred infected creatures, maybe more. For a second, my heart sank with hopelessness. Then something happened.

I reached the very bottom of despair, with nowhere farther to fall.

And my heart turned to stone.

Through the bullhorn, I shouted, "Come and get me, you sons of bitches!" I laughed, made whooping calls, turned and pushed into the trees. I fired a third flare, making a trio of growing blazes. Zombies walked into them and were burned. But others kept after me.

I staggered and fell, nearly tumbling down a small hill. The moon offered only the slightest visibility amid the trees, and the three fires behind me only deepened the crazily shifting shadows as I ran.

I felt an intense ache, deep, deep inside.

An ache not directly connected to any of my injuries, but an ache in my soul. A weariness of *being*.

It made me even more angry.

Spinning around, I saw two infected dogs closing on me, and I popped in another flare, fired. The red flame zipped along the closest dog's knobby backbone and set its fur alight. The dog howled, and with a mindless fury, the other dog dove at him, tearing into him before sensing the flames that quickly spread to his own body.

I had two flares left.

I continued down the incline, and my foot splashed into water. Immediately, I stopped and turned my head.

In the pale moonlight I could see that I'd exited the tree line and reached the edge of the river. I had to either change course, swim, or be overtaken by the diseased creatures chasing after me. The water was still frigid, with summer a month or more away. I decided to change course.

And a beacon called to me.

A white beast, almost glowing in the light of the moon, in stark contrast to the black waters and shadowed woods around it.

A sailboat.

I raced along the curve of the shore, toward a small dock that jutted into the river. Behind me, shouts and frenzy followed, but I didn't want the zombies to give up on me. I fired another flare into the woods, lighting another glowing blaze. And again I shouted wordless insults into the bullhorn. *Just follow me, you bastards. For the love of God, follow me.*

In droves, they did. I saw so many shapes rushing out of the woods, through the manic red flames and dancing shadows, toward me. Large and small, they came toward the lights and the blaring sound. I found a button on the bullhorn that set off a shrieking alarm, and held it down. It drove them even more mad.

I stumbled through the irregular scrub of the shoreline, over to the dock. What I planned to do once I reached the boat, I had no idea. But it was a goal, any sort of goal.

Behind me, snaps and growls. Several zombies pitched into the muddy water and couldn't get out. They flailed and raged as the waters took them. The others followed my sound, my high, piercing beacon.

I felt the accumulated anger of their numbers, and I threw it back at them. *I hate you all, forever.* It wasn't a rational thought, but I was beyond rational thought. The disease had taken everything from me, my former life, my job, my love, my friends, my health. And now, there was nothing standing between me and the infected. I jumped onto the dock.

With a *flap flap flap* I pounded along the warped planks, eyeing the boat, hoping it would offer some shelter. I stepped over the railing, the frayed and useless cable, and onto the deck. Carefully maneuvering toward the cockpit, I ducked in and out of the vertical wires that held the mast tense and upright. I spared a glance back to see several dozen zombies spilling onto the dock. *Shit*, I thought. *Shit, there's no time at all.*

I fumbled for the wooden slats that barred entry to the cabin, saw a tiny padlock securing them shut. I dropped the bullhorn, still blaring its alarm, onto the floor of the cockpit.

Without thinking, I slammed the hard plastic flare gun into the small metal lock, and the lock burst open. My hand caught on the clasp and the skin tore, blood speckling the boat's white frame.

A tall, ropy zombie leaped onto the boat, landing right next to me, but I'd already loaded the last flare. As he moved to strike me, I fired, and red flames erupted in his gut. He screamed a hideous scream, burning alive. I dove for the hatch.

And I felt it tear away. Time froze as that multi-colored bracelet she had made for me fell. Rosa's bracelet. A worthless trinket, invaluable. It dropped toward the edge of the boat. Before I could move, it slipped off the side of the boat and into the waiting waters below.

There was no time left, but I spared a moment anyway. A moment to remember. To weep. To steel myself. And to be reborn.

My rage became infinite.

With pure fury, I pushed back the hatch and started to pull out the first of the wooden slats, but another zombie fell into the cockpit, drawn to me and to the infected man still burning behind me. I took two instinctive steps up toward the open hatch, ducking to miss the boom. It was irrational, but rational thought had left me.

I dropped inside.

* * *

Pain hit me everywhere, as I collided with the steep wooden stairs, tumbled, and fell into the cabin. My head hit the side of a bench and I ended up on my back, stunned, staring up through the open hatch at the uncaring night sky above.

I heard a thud.

Then another, and another. Steps. Snarls and snaps. The zombie I'd hit with the flare kept blazing in the rear of the cockpit. Others jumped or fell into the boat and immediately went to him, drawn by the flames and the harsh sound of the bullhorn. They were burned as they approached. It kept repeating. Zombies fell into the flames, roared their pain. More thuds on the deck, more frantic steps, more shrieks.

And...

The boat...

Was it dipping lower in the water? How many zombies had jumped on board?

I was still on my back, looking up at the sky, and for a moment the clouds parted and a single star shone down on me.

Damn you, I thought. *Damn you.*

The single star mocked me. Aloof, distant, uncaring. Nothing that I'd ever done, ever loved, ever wanted, mattered to that star, not one bit.

I had nothing left but rage.

The bracelet, my last real connection to her, was gone.

I struggled to my feet, just as one of the infected bastards — his slashed and pitted face framed by long, stringy hair — popped into view, peering blindly down through the hatch. I started, but then my anger grew even greater. I reached up and grabbed the hatch. And as the zombie extended its spindly arms down toward me, I slammed the hatch home, breaking bones.

Even with its diminished ability to feel, the thing let out a horrible cry. I relented long enough to let it pull back its broken limbs. Then I closed the hatch completely.

26

On deck, sound and fury reigned. The deafening bullhorn, the burning zombie, the zombie shrieking with broken arms, and countless others drawn to the noise and light. The boat was definitely dipping lower in the water.

More thuds and snarls. More zombies on the boat. And splashes, and the frantic sounds of survival. Zombies were drowning. *How many had I killed? How many were left?*

I stumbled through the dark cabin, toward the south-facing portholes. I needed to see what was happening.

Outside, in the dull glow of moonlight obscured by clouds, I saw a throng of infected on the dock, just feet away, pressing against the boat. As I watched, some leaped over onto the deck, some fell into the dark waters, and some stayed put, raging on the pier. Behind them, past the dock, I saw it. The bridge.

Up on top were the forms of several people, some sort of standoff.

Could it be? That short, stubby figure… Oliver? And another person, taller, thinner. I wanted to believe it was Celia. In an instant, my heart realized how much I'd missed her.

The short one was being cowed, pushed back, losing position. The taller one was taking control. I wished I could hear what was being said, understand what was happening.

Then, a mass of movement. Dozens of people, hundreds, rushing across the bridge. From my right, heading to my left, toward the east. Toward The Oasis.

It had to be Celia. She'd wrested control from Oliver. The bridge was finally clear, and the people from DC were getting through. They let out a huge cheer.

A very, very *loud* cheer.

No.

Don't.

Closer to me, I saw the first reactions. Zombies turned their heads. Away from the mayhem on the boat, and back toward the bridge.

No…

I pressed one palm against the porthole's glass, willing them to stop.

The horde, though diminished from losing so many members to fire and water, was still formidable.

And suddenly, incomprehensibly, they were turning away from me.

* * *

For what seemed like eternity, I sat in the cabin, on the raised seat, looking through the porthole. Watching them leave. To attack my friends again. And I knew what the zombies would find. At the back of the group were the slow ones: the women with children, the elderly, the infirm. Involuntarily, I let a moan escape, a sound of remorse.

What more can I do?

I slammed a fist sideways into the leg of the chart table, then immediately regretted it. My hand throbbed, seemingly in time with all my other injuries. The table leg cracked and buckled, and the table's top slid partly open.

I closed my eyes.

This is the end…

This is the end…

My eyes popped back open.

The end? Of what? Of the world? Hardly. It will endure. Of humanity? Probably not. People still lived in random pockets here and there. Of The Oasis and the cure? That was it. That was what I couldn't bear. Rosa had led me to this path, and I couldn't let it go. I couldn't let her go before every ounce of my strength was gone, too.

I slammed my other fist into the table, to hell with the pain.

My mind went back to the one thing that I could never erase from my vision: Rosa's death. Her head snapping back, over and over again. I shook my head, squinted my eyes.

I don't want this!

I screamed at the heavens. I screamed it, again and again, spittle flying.

I don't want this!

My heart felt like it would burst from anger, rage, fear, loneliness, longing, hate. Love.

And there, in the open crack of the chart desktop, was an answer.

A tinge of orange plastic.

27

I've made up my mind.

I hope they have enough, with Celia and Janine and all the researchers. But there's nothing more I can do.

Except save them. Give them a chance to write their part of this horrible tale. I'll pull every one of these damned infected bastards toward *me* and away from *them*.

I'm going to go out.

I've gathered the new orange flare gun from the chart table. There were even six flares. I popped in the first, and have the others in my pocket. Maybe they'll all work, or maybe not.

Maybe I'll make it 10 steps. Or maybe not.

But I'm going to do it and I'm going to keep on firing.

Until I can't do it anymore.

For Celia and the others, and the researchers of the new Oasis. God, I hope you can do it. *Please.*

For Harvey, Hank, and Janine of the old Oasis. May your legacy lead to the cure.

For Rosa.

For Rosa.

Without you, the world would never have even had a chance. Nor would I.

I love you.

Maybe I'll see you soon.

I'm going out to raise hell among the damned now.

EPILOGUE

If you're reading this, you need to know.

He saved them. Those hundreds of people on the bridge. Every one. He gave himself up for them, the people he barely knew.

I found these pages four months ago, in the boat he hid in, still tied to the dock. I don't really know how to write this, but I feel I need to add something. To fill in something at the end. To put something down for whoever comes next. Because you need to know. If he hadn't done what he did, they probably all would have died.

And if we're the last, or the seed for whatever is next, he made it happen. He took the zombies away. He gave himself up.

We saw him, at the last, overwhelmed by the horde. He was my friend and I will always miss him. Without him, I would have been dead a long, long time ago.

He was a doctor, in the truest sense. He healed people. I mean, in the end, he might have even healed the world. His blood is in us all now. Through me.

They got it to work, the researchers from NIH. It was hard as hell, and took a very long time. But they built a new lab, got equipment. And they used my blood and Janine's blood to find the cure. To replicate it.

We've been able to cure almost every person who has come to us. A few people get sick and die, and that hits us all hard, since we're trying to save them. But for the most part, they all live.

At last count, there are more than two thousand of us. We've annexed the peninsulas on either side of the new Oasis. We have teams cleaning up the nearest parts of Annapolis, and there are many among us who plan to relocate there soon.

We've taken down the fences. We're free again. There are still zombies — humans, dogs, rats, raccoons… we even found infected cats and mice — but since we're now cured, we deal with them differently. We know they're lost, and that they have to be put down.

But the total fear is gone. They can hurt us, they can kill us if we aren't careful. But they can't *infect* us. And one day, we hope, we will outlast them.

Our children can live free. Our people can sleep soundly. The zombies live on, for now. But they can't win.

As I write this, it's been 12 months since they began distributing the cure. The first year of freedom has passed, the first year of freedom in too long.

Every day I think of the blood in my veins, the blood that saved me and so many others. His blood. I know his whole story now, from these pages. I know that most people would have given up.

The word goes out and the people come in, every day now. *Look for the three towers. Come to us for the cure. Come to The Oasis.*

And even though he isn't here, it's *his* Oasis. His legacy, in honor of Rosa, and a gift to us all.

We are all his children.

— Celia Frederick
The Free City of Oasis, Maryland
Year 1

THE END

Thank you so much for reading my book! Here's a little bit about me, Keith Soares. I live in Alexandria, Virginia, with my wife and two daughters. By day, my wife and I run a web, mobile and app development studio, which means that writing is my second job. Creativity has always been a huge focus for me, whether making music, coding video games, drawing or writing. *The Oasis of Filth* is my first published novel.

Visit my website at **http://keithsoares.com** for information on other books and upcoming projects. While you're there, I hope you consider joining my mailing list where I can keep you updated on future books.

www.ingramcontent.com/pod-product-compliance
Lightning Source LLC
Chambersburg PA
CBHW020623020726
47494CB00001B/26